THE ISLES
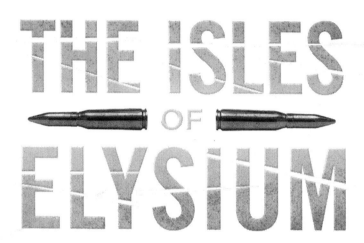
OF
ELYSIUM

BOOK 6 IN THE BABYLON SERIES

SAM SISAVATH

Published by Road to Babylon Media LLC
www.roadtobabylon.com

Edited by Jennifer Jensen and Wendy Chan

ISBN-13: 978-0692426470
ISBN-10: 0692426477

THE COMPLETED PURGE OF BABYLON SERIES

The Purge of Babylon: A Novel of Survival

The Gates of Byzantium

The Stones of Angkor

The Walls of Lemuria Collection (Keo Prequel)

The Fires of Atlantis

The Ashes of Pompeii

The Isles of Elysium

The Spears of Laconia

The Horns of Avalon

The Bones of Valhalla

Mason's War (A Purge of Babylon Story)

ALSO BY SAM SISAVATH

The Allie Krycek Vigilante Series

Hunter/Prey

Saint/Sinner

Finders/Keepers

The Red Sky Conspiracy Series

Most Wanted

The Devil You Know

For everyone who kept the faith.

ABOUT THE ISLES OF ELYSIUM

Every journey has an ending.

He's survived the Purge and battled overwhelming odds, but now Keo is back on the road and more determined than ever to fulfill a promise made nearly half a year ago.

What he didn't expect—or want—was to end up in another bloody conflict.

With the help of some old friends and some dangerous new ones, Keo must figure out a way to keep everyone he cares for alive. In a world where creatures maintain unquestioned dominion over the night and opportunists lord over the day, that's easier said than done.

Keo is not the devil-may-care mercenary he once was, but he's never backed down from a fight before, and he's not going to start now.

A year after The Purge, mankind is still an endangered species, but the Isles may finally offer the path to victory...

BOOK ONE

WELCOME TO TEXAS

ONE

I should have stayed on the Trident.

That thought rushed through Keo's head as he watched water from Galveston Bay pool around his boots. The only thing standing between him and the bottom of the Gulf of Mexico at the moment was the fiberglass hull of the boat that had been his home for the last three days and two nights.

And the morning had started off so well, too.

He was halfway through a bag of roast beef MRE, and Santa Marie Island—the place he had been chasing for half a year—was finally within sight. There were times when he didn't think he'd ever actually make it here. After all the days and nights, weeks and months, and the pile of trouble that he'd had to overcome, there it was.

Pollard, Song Island, and ghouls.

Lots of ghouls.

A hell of a lot of ghouls.

But there it was, at last, and he was so close he could almost feel the sharp edges of the rocks that haloed the ridgeline of the island. The rooftops of houses poked out from one side to the other, and there was a raised hill in the center of the place with a couple of residences on top of it. One of those homes would have made a perfect sniper's perch.

I bet Danny and Gaby could hold off an army from up there.

He had approached the island from the east and could just make out the marina with the naked eye. It extended out from near the bottom of the oval-shaped landmass and was a welcoming sight, even if he couldn't spot a single boat among the slips. Not that he expected to find any. If previous experience was any indication, boats were few and far between these days. Or, at least, ones that weren't already being used by ghoul collaborators, guys he'd rather avoid whenever possible.

Santa Marie Island was coveted real estate, and according to Rachel, he was looking at an island that was eight kilometers long and one and a half wide. The size made it easy to spot from a distance once he slipped into Galveston Bay. There it was, sticking out of the ocean like a fabled land, with the Texas coastline (*Everything's bigger in Texas*) surrounding it in the background.

He was a few minutes away from finally reaching land, finding Gillian, and finally (*finally!*) running in slow motion up the beach and into her arms like in the movies. Keo should have felt dumb running that kind of scenario through his head, but what the hell, he was feeling a little giddy at that moment.

That was when the guy came out of nowhere and started shooting at him.

Keo assumed it was a guy, anyway. The shooter was positioned on the ridge to the left of the marina. The man was a decent shot and the round *plopped!* into the water just a few feet from Keo's starboard.

For about four seconds after the shot, Keo had a rare moment of indecision.

Maybe it was the fact that he had finally (*finally!*) reached

Santa Marie Island after months of traveling that slowed his reaction time, or maybe he just hadn't expected the first person he would see after three days on the ocean would try to kill him. Considering the past year, he really shouldn't have been that surprised. Who *wasn't* shooting at him these days?

He was back to his old self just as the second loud *crack!* rang out and was followed by a bullet punching into the floor of his twenty-two-footer just a couple of feet from the nose of his boots.

Water instantly began to spring inside, pooling around his feet.

Oh, hell.

The third shot nearly took his head off. It was so close that Keo heard the *zip!* as the large-caliber round slashed through the air a few inches from his right ear. He finally did what he should have done when he heard the first shot and dropped to his stomach, bracing with his hands against the now-wet floor of the boat.

He reached to his right and grabbed the steering end of the trolling motor, jerking it left until the boat started to turn. The good news was due to the motor's low power, he had only traveled another twenty meters toward the island after the first shot. The bad news was that it was taking longer to turn than he would have liked, and meanwhile the guy had a perfect (and closer) bead on him.

Crack! Crack! Crack!

Three more shots, about three seconds apart. That meant the guy was using a bolt-action rifle. It took at least one second to eject the spent shell casing, another second to punch in a new round, then a third second to take aim and squeeze the trigger. Three seconds was impressive, but it also meant the guy wasn't taking his time. He was shooting too fast, either because he was an amateur and was rushing it, or he was really good.

Keo leaned toward the former when a fourth bullet sailed harmlessly over his head and a fifth punched into the starboard because Keo was forced to present that side of the boat as he completed the U-turn. The last round missed by a mile.

Then the boat had finished its turn, and Keo kept it pointed away from the island. He waited for more shots—he was still well within range of a bolt-action with a good scope— but none came. The shooter had apparently decided to save his ammo. Or maybe the idea was just to scare Keo away. He wasn't exactly scared (Okay, maybe just a little), but he had definitely gotten the hint: He wasn't welcome on Santa Marie Island.

He turned his attention to the Gulf of Mexico making its way into his boat. The craft had continued to take in water while he was scrambling to keep his head attached to his shoulders, and the shiny half-empty bag of MRE he had been eating a moment ago was now floating in front of him.

Damn. I should have stayed on the Trident...

He didn't stop completely until he had put another 200 meters between him and the shooter and felt safe enough to cut off the trolling motor and pick himself up from the wet floor. Keo plugged up the bullet holes with wooden plugs from an emergency kit, then spent the next twenty minutes collecting and tossing the water back into Galveston Bay using a ceramic mug with "The World's Greatest Boat Captain" written on the side. The mug was a good-bye gift from Lara before he left her and the *Trident* behind. There was still water in the boat when he finally stopped to rest, but at least he wasn't sinking anymore.

After the short rest, Keo walked up to the bow and looked back at the island with a pair of binoculars. He could just make out the lone figure standing at the same part of the ridge as before, watching him back with his own binoculars. If the man expected him to just turn around and leave, he was very disappointed right now, because Keo wasn't going anywhere.

Gillian was on that island. Or she was supposed to be. Either way, he wasn't leaving, not after all the trouble he'd gone through to get here.

Keo was still too far away to make out the face or any distinguishing features on his nemesis. At first he thought it might have been Mark shooting at him, but he dismissed that idea because Mark couldn't hit the broad side of a barn, much less a moving boat. Of course, it didn't take a well-trained sniper to hit a slow-moving target like his twenty-two-footer, especially if that rifle was equipped with a really good scope.

For a few minutes, neither one of them moved. Keo kept expecting the man's reinforcements to show up, but they never did. Was it possible he was being thwarted by a single individual?

After a while, the shooter disappeared from the ridgeline, and about a minute later he reappeared at the marina before walking all the way out to the end of one of the docks.

Five minutes after that, with nothing except the birds in the air, the fishes breaking the surface, and the calm waves of the Gulf *sloshing* against his hull to break the monotony of silence, Keo concluded that the man had no help coming. Instead of relief, that realization made him just a little bit depressed, because if there wasn't anyone else on the entire island to lend a hand...

What was that Lara had said to him, once upon a time?

"You honestly think your girlfriend actually made it to Santa Marie Island? That she's wearing a bikini and waiting on the beach every morning, waiting for you to finally show up?"

Maybe, maybe not. But he had to find out for sure one way or another. After all these months, he had to be absolutely certain. And there was really only one way to do that, and it was staring back at him.

Crack! as the guy fired again and the round sailed harmlessly over his head.

He went down on one knee and waited for the man to try again, but the shooter didn't. Instead, the guy lowered his rifle and just looked back at him.

Keo thought about returning fire with the M4 but decided he didn't want to waste a couple of bullets on some dick-measuring contest. He had a full magazine and three spares in his tactical pack, with the rest of his ammo geared for the MP5SD, his primary weapon. The German gun had served him well in the last twelve months, and Keo was the kind of guy who appreciated that kind of unquestionable loyalty.

He sat down on one of the high-raised seats in front of the steering console, opened a bottle of water, and took a sip. The November weather was a tricky beast; last night's temperatures had dropped to around thirty degrees, only to climb back up to fifty at sunrise. It had since settled at around sixty, though with the cool breeze he could almost believe it was fifty-five.

What to do, what to do?

There were only two directions open to him: Go forward, or go back.

He didn't fancy the latter. He had come this far and braved too many obstacles to turn back now. The very idea of back-tracking made him want to vomit.

So it was a no-brainer. He had to go forward.

But how?

A lone shooter was a dream scenario. It had been almost an hour since the first shot, and he was still just staring at one man with a rifle. No reinforcements. No help.

...and no Gillian on the island.

Maybe.

Have to find out. One way or another, have to find out for sure.

Keo stood up and waved his hands to get the shooter's attention. The man went rigid and peered at him with his binoculars. With the man watching, Keo unslung his MP5SD and laid it on the seat behind him.

"Can you hear me?" he shouted, folding his hands into a funnel over his mouth to project his voice across the water.

He listened and heard a reply, but he was too far away to understand the words. It could have been a *Yes,* or possibly a *No,* or maybe even a *Come any closer and I'm going to shoot your balls off.*

Keo sighed. He had done some pretty dumb things in his life, and many of them since the world went kaput, but he had to know. *He had to know.*

He walked back to the trolling motor, gripped the tiller, and switched it on. The low whine started gradually before increasing in volume. He directed the boat forward, back toward land, all the while watching the man closely. He waited for signs of an aggressive move that would likely be followed by a gunshot. Or two, or three.

He had gone twenty meters when he shut off the engine again.

Closer now, he stood up and shouted, "Can you hear me?"

The sun was in his eyes, which made it difficult to see how the man was reacting. But at least he could make out the rifle easily enough. If that barrel started moving, he would know he was in trouble.

Ten seconds ticked by in absolute silence, then twenty...

"Yeah!" the guy finally shouted back, his voice bouncing against the water's surface until it reached Keo as barely a soft whisper. "What do you want?"

"For you not to shoot me!"

He couldn't be sure, but the guy might have laughed. "What else?"

"I need to get on that island!"

"You and what army?"

"No army, just me!"

A brief pause. Then: "Why?"

"I'm looking for someone!"

"Who isn't?"

Smartass, Keo thought, but shouted, "I'm coming in, so don't shoot!"

The guy didn't answer, but he also hadn't raised his rifle into a firing position, either. That was a good sign. A really good sign. Now all Keo needed to do was grease the wheels a bit. How? Maybe offer something he had that the guy needed.

And what would that be?

Weapons? Probably not. Santa Marie Island was a part of Texas, and there was a good bet you could find plenty of guns in all the houses that dotted the ridgeline. Even out here, you weren't going to convince a Texan to part with his Second Amendment rights.

So what, then? Maybe something more valuable than bullets these days. Which would be?

Ah.

"I have supplies!" Keo shouted.

"You got supplies?" the guy asked. Keo might have barely heard his voice over the distance, but he swore it sounded almost hopeful.

You willing to risk your life on that, pal?

"Yeah!" he shouted back. "I got supplies! Let me dock, and I'll split it with you!"

Another long pause, but this time only ten seconds went by.

Then, "Put your weapons down and come in slowly, hands where I can see you the entire time! You make one wrong move, and I'm gonna plug ya!"

'Plug ya'?

Keo grinned to himself before shouting back, "Deal!"

This is such a bad idea, he thought as he unclasped his gun belt and let it drop to the still-wet floor.

Bad idea or not, he had to get on that damn island. He had to make sure, one way or another, because he was faced with one absolute certainty at the moment: He couldn't keep doing this forever. Hell, there had been a few times when he had almost convinced himself to stay on the *Trident* with Lara and the others. Carrie had done everything she could to make him stay. She'd said all the right words, made all the right overtures, and if he wasn't the complete idiot that he was surely being at the moment, he would have stuck around.

But no, he had to be here, standing on a boat in the middle of the ocean voluntarily letting his holstered sidearm, along with the ammo pouches, *thump* to his feet.

Keo made sure his actions were "loud" enough that the guy watching him the entire time with binoculars could see everything. Finally, Keo switched on the trolling motor again and guided the twenty-two-footer forward one more time, all the while telling himself that this was stupid, that it was possibly the dumbest thing he had ever done, which was saying something given the last few months.

But he had to know.

One way or another, he had to know for sure...

The "man" wasn't a man at all. He was a teenager. Barely seventeen, maybe just a few months past his sixteenth birthday. Keo made a mental note to ask him later when he was certain the kid wasn't going to shoot him, which at the moment wasn't a given.

The teenager was lanky and wore mud-caked boots, jeans, and a stained cream cotton sweatshirt that looked like he had put it on a few days ago and hadn't gotten around to taking off since.

He wasn't exactly the picture of a survivalist, and from the looks of it he had acted as his own barber very recently. The fact that this *kid* almost blew his head off made Keo just a little bit queasy.

Okay, a lot queasy.

His almost-killer might have been young and skinny and looked as if he was starving, but he was also holding a cherry-red bolt-action rifle, and at this range—less than fifty meters—he wouldn't have had any trouble putting a nice large-caliber round through the boat and Keo at the same time. So Keo eased his vessel toward the marina and did everything humanly possible not to look or act threatening.

Speed wasn't an issue, because trolling motors were not made to go fast anyway, which also meant if he had to turn around now...well, he'd have better luck jumping into the ocean instead. They didn't call him half-dolphin for nothing, after all.

Up close, the docks looked much bigger than it had from afar, especially without a single vessel tied in place. He guessed at least two or three dozen numbered (and very empty looking) slips, some bigger than others. That made sense since there weren't a lot of other ways on or off the sea-locked landmass except by boat that he could see. Maybe there was a small airstrip somewhere he hadn't been able to spot, but he thought it unlikely given the uneven nature of Santa Marie Island.

Once he finally slid past the day markers, "No Wake" signs, and other warnings that surrounded the island, he was sure the boy wasn't going to shoot him. The teenager continued to hold the rifle at the ready in front of him anyway, forefinger in the trigger guard for a quick lift-and-shoot motion, if necessary.

Smart kid.

"You got a name?" Keo shouted, before realizing he was close enough now that he could have asked in a normal voice.

"Gene," the kid said. "You?"

"Keo."

The kid gave him a look before saying, "What kind of name is Keo?"

"Chuck was taken."

Gene gave him a confused look. "Hunh?"

"Just a joke."

"Oh. You Chinese or something?"

"Or something."

Another confused look.

At the ten-meter mark, Keo said, "You're not going to shoot me, are you, Gene?"

"If I was gonna shoot you, I would have done it already, don't you think?"

"Good point. Just wanted to make sure, that's all."

"Sure's sure."

Keo didn't know what that meant, but he decided not to ask. He said instead, "You alone, Gene?"

"No."

For some reason, Keo didn't believe him.

Gene held up his rifle. "I got my friend Deuce here with me."

Keo grinned and angled the boat toward the dock before switching off the motor and letting his forward momentum take him into one of the slips.

"What now?" he asked.

"I dunno," Gene said. "I guess we tie up your ride and you come up." He shrugged. "Work for you?"

Keo nodded. "Works for me."

"All right, then."

He tossed his line over and Gene tied the boat in place.

Up close, Gene had bags under his eyes. He clearly hadn't been sleeping well and hadn't for some time now. He was wearing fingerless wool gloves and the sun glinted off large-caliber bullets around his waist, housed in their own individual loops. The getup made him look like a bandit out of a Western, the rifle almost bigger than both his arms put together. The scope on top was massive, which explained how he had managed to put holes into Keo's boat from such a long distance. Even an amateur could have managed that. If the teenager had just been a little better, Keo would be fish food by now.

Thank God for amateurs.

He climbed onto the dock while Gene gave the boat a cursory look before asking, "You said you have supplies?"

"MREs, bottled water, and beef jerky."

"What kind of water?"

"Filtered."

"Where'd you get those?"

"From a hotel."

"No shit?"

"Nope."

Keo looked around at the rocky ridgeline of Santa Marie Island, taking in the still houses to the left and right of him. He didn't know what he expected, maybe more...life. Instead, it was like looking at a vivid painting rather than a real place that people actually used to live in.

"So how long have you and Deuce been here?" he asked.

"For a while now," Gene said. "Who was it you were looking for?"

"A woman named Gillian."

Gene shook his head. "Never heard of her."

"You didn't even think about it."

"Don't have to. Never heard of her."

"Well, shit."

Gene shrugged. "Sorry, man."

Keo sighed.

Yeah, you and me both, pal.

TWO

"Where is everyone?" Keo asked.

"What you see? That's it," Gene said between mouthfuls of cheesy lasagna. Or what was supposed to be lasagna, anyway. The kid didn't seem to notice the difference though.

They walked up the road from the marina, passing houses with overgrown lawns and stalled vehicles along the curb and driveways. Santa Marie Island looked frozen in time, a picture of what once was. He didn't have any trouble imagining that things were exactly like this a year ago. He kept expecting to see a housewife in a flower-print dress and apron calling her husband, who would likely be busy mowing the lawn, in for dinner. Or a dog barking. Or kids on bicycles swerving up and down the sidewalk, trying not to hit him.

But there was none of that.

Instead, there was just the quiet, the overwhelming smell of abandonment. He wondered how the people on the island had learned about The Purge and how they had reacted. There were very few barricades over the windows, which told him they hadn't been prepared when the end came.

The streets were curved, rarely staying in a straight line for very long, and there was a noticeable incline almost as soon as they began walking away from the marina at the southern tip. Santa Marie Island was big enough for more than one subdivision, including the expensive luxury houses along the ridgeline. The ones inland to his right looked like cheaper options. Though even "cheap," he imagined, was probably still pricey, given the locale.

Location, location, location, as the saying went.

"Ferry," Gene was saying, looking at him. The kid must have been reading his mind. "There's another marina on the other side. It's twice the size, and there's a big ramp just for the ferry."

"They got here by ferry?"

"I think so."

"I don't see it anywhere. The ferry."

"It's gone. Someone took it. Or sunk it."

"Not in these waters. A sunken ferry would stick out like the proverbial sore thumb. Unless they towed it out into deeper waters and then did the deed, which doesn't make sense. Why go through all the trouble?"

"I never thought of that."

Keo looked back at him. "Where do you stay at night, Gene?"

"I move around. You can't spend more than one night at the same place."

"Why not?"

"They know."

"They?"

"Yeah. *They.*"

"They're still here?" Keo asked as his hand instinctively reached for the MP5SD hanging off him by its sling.

"Won't do any good," Gene said. "I've put a .308 round right into one's head, blew its brains out, and nothing. It just kept coming."

"Are you using silver bullets?"

"Silver bullets?" He stopped eating momentarily to stare at Keo.

"They work."

"The fuck you say," Gene said.

Keo smiled. "Anything silver works. Something about the metal interacting with their bloodstream. You have to get it inside them, though. So shooting's the easiest way—the safest way by far —but stabbing them with something silver works just as well."

"What are they, allergic to silver or something?"

"Beats the hell out of me. I just know it works."

He pulled out a spare magazine from his pouch and handed it to Gene. The kid thumbed out a round and held it up. It was midday, and the warm sunlight glinted off the smooth silver tip. Gene eyeballed the bullet with intense fascination, pieces of lasagna clinging to his chin, though he was blissfully unaware of it.

The kid finally slipped the bullet back into the magazine and handed it to Keo. "I've seen some silverware in a lot of the kitchens. Maybe I can use them as weapons."

"Real silver?" Keo asked.

"What do you mean?"

"Silver is expensive, Gene. People don't just keep them in the drawer and use them as everyday utensils."

"Oh. I guess that makes sense."

"Although I do know about a couple of guys who stumbled across a pair of silver crosses inside an abandoned apartment. They ended up using them as knives."

"They must be the luckiest guys alive."

Keo thought about Danny and that knife of his. "They were."

"'Were'?"

"That's the problem with luck. Sooner or later, you run out of it."

"Did they? The guys you're talking about. Did they run out of luck?"

"One of them did."

Gene didn't say anything for a moment. Then, finally, "That sucks."

"Yeah."

"Anyway, how can you tell real silver from the fake kind? You know, in case I run across a pair of silver knives or something."

"There are a couple of ways. Silver makes a distinctive ring when you tap them against one another; it also melts ice faster."

"Seriously?"

"Which part?'

"Both."

"Yeah."

"How do you know all of this?"

"Someone once paid me entirely in silver."

"For what?"

"Some of this, some of that, and a little of whatever."

"I don't know what that means."

"Don't worry about it." Then, "How long have you been here by yourself?"

The teenager shrugged, but he didn't answer right away. He went back to eating what was left of the lasagna, though at this point Keo wasn't sure if there was very much still in the bag by the sound of Gene's spork scraping the bottom.

"A while," Gene finally said.

"Why are you still here?"

"Because it's safe. Well, mostly."

"How do you avoid the ghouls night after night?"

"Ghouls?"

"That's what these people I met called them. Ghouls."

"Cool name," Gene said. "But no. I mean, yeah, them too, but I don't really have to worry about them too much. I've gotten good at staying away from the houses where they're hiding. There are signs, if you know what to look for. But I'm really talking about guys like you."

"Guys like me?"

"People on boats."

"Is that why you shot at me?"

Gene gave him an almost embarrassed grin. "Sorry about that, by the way."

"No harm, no foul. Unless you count my boat. So you've had trouble before."

"Yeah, you can say that." He tossed the empty MRE bag into a trashcan that was already brimming with garbage. The bag bounced off some cans of beans and landed on the sidewalk behind them. "I wasn't always alone."

"Besides you and Deuce?"

Another grin. "Yeah, besides me and Deuce."

"What happened to your friends?"

"Soldiers came and took them," Gene said.

"You've been here before," Keo said.

"Yeah, I like it," Gene said. "I can see the whole island from up here."

"Is that how you spotted me?"

"Nah, I was just walking around when you showed up. I do that every morning. Go around the island, taking note of anything that might have changed during the night. It's how I keep track of their movements."

"The ghouls."

"Uh huh."

They were inside one of the two-story houses on the hillside in the middle of the island. From the second-floor windows, Keo could see the entirety of Santa Marie Island's five-mile stretch. The house faced west with a great view of the Texas coastline, along with a clear line of sight to the large marina in the center. He had to use a window at the back of the master bedroom in order to see the east marina where he had docked his twenty-two-footer. The boat looked incredibly lonely out there all by itself.

There were empty cans of nonperishables on the first and second floors, and more signs that Gene had made use of the house in the recent past. The teenager told Keo that he didn't worry about leaving evidence of his presence around since he never stayed at the same place two nights in a row anyway. In the bathroom of the master bedroom, Keo was surprised to find weapons—assault rifles, handguns, and boxes of ammo—housed inside the tub.

"I didn't know where to put them," Gene said when Keo asked about the guns. "I found most of them around the island after we showed up. Maybe some of them belonged to your friends."

"Why the bolt-action and not one of the assault rifles?" Keo asked.

"I learned to shoot with Deuce, so I guess I'm comfortable with it. What kind of gun is that?" he asked, nodding at the MP5SD.

"Submachine gun."

"It doesn't look like it can shoot far."

"It can't. It's a close-quarters weapon."

"Are you good with it?"

"Depends on who you ask. You never told me how long have you've been here, Gene."

Gene was sitting on the floor behind him, going through the supply bag, while Keo looked out at the Texas coastline in the distance. Cool air from the open windows vented out the second floor, making it easier to be around Gene, who stank. It had obviously been a while since the teenager showered, and it hadn't occurred to him to just take a swim in Galveston Bay every morning. Keo himself had done exactly that on the way over here.

"You mean, did I ever come across your friends?" Gene asked.

"Yeah."

"Three months ago. But I definitely never met anyone named Gillian, or who looked like her."

Three months ago? Keo crunched the numbers in his head.

The last time he had seen Gillian, Jordan, and the others was almost six months ago. That would have given them more than enough time to reach their destination before Gene. A three-month window. Possibly two, if they were somehow delayed. After all, it had taken him almost six months to finally get here, so who was to say it hadn't taken them just as long? If, that is, they had made it at all.

More ifs and maybes. He didn't have a single clue what had happened to them. All this time, and he was probably chasing a ghost.

Well, shit.

Gene opened one of the water bottles and drank it. When he was done, he let out a whistle. "Man, this is good stuff. I ran out of bottled water months ago, and I've been drinking rain all this time, but this... Wow."

"It's better cold," Keo said absently.

"Everything's better cold, except the weather."

Keo smiled. The kid really did have a way with words. "You said the soldiers took your friends?"

Gene nodded. "We ran across them a couple of weeks after we arrived. They cruised up to the western marina, and like idiots we went out there to greet them. They caught the others, but I managed to escape. They come back here every now and then to look for me, or to see if they can catch other two-legged fish."

"That's why you shot at me."

"Normally they come from the west, but they've been known to try to sneak up on me from the east."

"Why don't you just avoid them entirely?"

"What do you mean?"

"If you shoot at them, won't they know you're on the island?"

Gene shrugged. "They already know I'm here. But knowing and finding me isn't the same thing. I know every house on this rock, all the good places to hide. They always look for me, but at the end of the day, they always get bored and leave."

"How often do they come looking?"

Gene thought about it. "About once a week since I've been here. The last time they came was about five days ago, so you know, they're due. They have bases all across Galveston Island. I'm surprised they didn't hear you coming through the channel."

"I was using a trolling motor. Ran out of gas about eight kilometers out."

"Kilometers?"

"About five miles."

"Oh. Anyway, that probably explains it. Otherwise they might have intercepted you before you ever reached Santa Marie."

"They do that a lot?" he asked, thinking about Gillian and Jordan coming on Mark's boat. Was that what had happened to them? Did they get intercepted?

"That's all they do," Gene said. "People are always showing up here. Like you. Like us. Maybe like your friends."

Keo stared out the window at the coastline in the distance. The land, or what little of it he could see, was brown and gray under the sun. What were the chances Gillian had made it inland? Maybe they had decided to bypass the island entirely?

"When was the last time you left this place?" he asked Gene.

"Not since I arrived. Why would I?"

"For one, you're running out of food."

"Not really."

"No?"

"There's a big ocean out there. Once I run out of nonperishables, I figure I could always learn to fish."

"You mean you don't know how to fish?"

Gene gave him a noncommittal shrug. "I'm a fast learner. And I've been hoarding books about doing all sorts of things."

"Is one of them fishing?"

"Fishing, hunting, shooting, all kinds of things."

Keo glanced at Gene's rifle leaning against the wall nearby. Deuce looked well-used, its stock noticeably chipped.

"So what now?" Gene asked. "You came here looking for your girlfriend, but she's not here. She probably never even made it. So what're you gonna do?"

He sighed.

Good question, kid.

Keo spent the next few hours walking around the island. For a place that stretched eight kilometers long, Santa Marie was a lot smaller than it looked from the water, with one main road that encircled the place. It was well designed to accommodate a small and privileged population, and he could see why it was so attractive. It was isolated, but just a boat ride away from the mainland, and perfect for those who could afford its limited space.

As he walked out in the open, Keo could feel their eyes on him. They could see him, but he couldn't return the favor. For every house that looked empty, there was one or two that showed clear signs of occupation, either by the pulled curtains or the furniture stacked on the other side of the windows to stave off the bright sun.

Come out, come out, wherever you are...

If Gene's theory was correct and the creatures had arrived by ferry that first night and never left, then the islanders were still here, somewhere, either hiding in their old bedrooms or basements, or wherever they could find a dark, damp place. That led Keo to wondering how long these things could survive without fresh blood. Or did they even need fresh blood at all?

The things he didn't know about them could fill a book...or a dozen.

Keo had completed a full circle around the island when he saw a figure moving on the roof of one of the homes in front of him. He unslung the MP5SD and slipped behind a power pole, realizing too late that it was much too small to hide his entire frame.

He peered out and watched the figure, silhouetted against the sun, picking something up from the roof. It was a man—he could tell that much by the shape and shoulders—and as he straightened up—

It was just Gene, and he was cradling a couple of plastic two-liter Coke bottles in his arms.

The teenager spotted him and shaded his eyes, then shouted down, "Hey, what are you doing?"

Almost putting a bullet in you, that's what, Keo thought as he came out from behind the pole.

"I scared ya?" Gene said, not even bothering to hide his amusement.

"What are you doing up there?" Keo shouted up. He stood outside the house, which had two garden gnomes that had been completely overtaken by the weeds, giving them the impression of children lost in a forest.

Gene held up one of the bottles. "Just retrieving this," he said. Then, "Give me a sec," and disappeared off the roof.

Keo put the submachine gun away and looked around the

street. He would never get used to the quiet, the nothingness staring back at him. He had no idea how the kid had survived by himself for so long. Keo would probably have gone insane after a month. Oh, who was he kidding? He probably wouldn't have survived the first few weeks.

Gene came out from behind the house, cradling the two bottles in his arms. One was half-full, the other even less than that. "Forgot to get these after the rain last week."

"Are they clean enough to drink?"

"Only if you don't subscribe to the theory that rain is just the gods taking a leak, then I don't see why not."

Keo chuckled. "You've been here by yourself way too long, Gene."

"Yeah, you're probably right."

They walked up the street, back toward the house on the hill.

Keo glanced briefly back at the house Gene was standing on the rooftop of a few moments ago. "No ghouls?"

"Not the last time I checked, but I didn't go inside."

"Scared?"

"No point. I took whatever I could from the place last week."

"So how'd you get to the roof?"

"Ladder in the back. You wouldn't believe what you can find in people's backyards if you look hard and long enough." He walked in silence for a moment before adding, "They usually stay away from the smaller houses. There's a whole nest of them in that red one near the west marina. The thing is, they don't really move around that much. My mom had a word for it, but I can't remember."

"Lazy?"

"Nah. Something with an *L*, though."

Keo looked at the Coke bottles in the teenager's arms. "How many of those do you have sitting around?"

"Dozens. I told you, I could live here for the rest of my life on just the fish alone. I mean, I don't want to, but if I had to, I could."

"What about your friends?"

"What about them?"

"Have you tried looking for them?"

Gene shook his head. "I wouldn't know where to start." He paused, then glanced at Keo. "What about you? You decided what you're gonna do next yet?"

Keo sighed.

"I take it that's a no," Gene said.

"Maybe tomorrow—" Keo started to say, when he stopped and looked backward toward the east side of the island.

"What?" Gene said.

Keo shushed him, then unslung his MP5SD.

The very familiar whine of boat motors in the distance, closing in fast...

THREE

He had heard motors—more than one, he was sure of it—but as it turned out, there was just one craft; it just happened to have two motors in the back powering it. It was coming from the east, which meant it was probably cruising around the Gulf of Mexico when it decided to swing over to check out Santa Marie Island. Just his luck, it was heading straight for the marina, where his boat was tied up.

It was some kind of offshore fishing boat, bigger than his twenty-two-footer by a mile, and a hell of a sight better looking, too. What he wouldn't have given to have had something that comfortable during his three days on the ocean. He might have stretched it out to a week, just to prolong the solitude.

The boat coming toward him now had a sleek deep V hull design and shiny navy blue colors on the outside, with an all white interior. Probably twenty-eight or twenty-nine feet long with a three-meter beam. He couldn't see the man behind the steering console in the middle because of the enclosed T-top that hid him, but he didn't have any trouble picking out the two soldiers on the bow. One was crouched and peering through binoculars at the marina, while the other stood watch with a rifle in a sling.

He couldn't make out any details across the distance, but it wasn't hard to spot their uniforms. Soldiers. Except these guys were wearing dark black and not the brown and gray camo of the ones he was used to seeing back in Louisiana.

"What're they doing back so soon?" Gene said next to him.

The teenager was whispering, even though he didn't have to. They were flat on their stomachs along the ridgeline, about fifty meters from the marina to their right, and surrounded by plenty of rocky formations to hide them from even binoculars. The vessel was still more than 500 meters away but closing in fast, thanks to its dual motors.

"The same ones that took your friends?" Keo asked, just to be sure.

"Yeah, that's them." Gene lowered his binoculars. "Maybe they heard my gunshots…"

"See what happens when you shoot at strangers?"

Gene snorted. "Whatever. If you hadn't shown up, I wouldn't have fired."

"And you wouldn't have had that delicious lasagna MRE."

"That's true." Gene reached for his rifle lying nearby.

"What are you doing?" Keo asked.

"I'm going to shoot them."

"Not yet."

"Why not?"

"Let them get closer. You're not going to hit something moving that fast anyway. You could barely hit me, and I was crawling toward you."

"Good point."

"Let them come up," Keo said, thinking, *And I'll figure it out as we go.*

It didn't take long for the saltwater boat to reach the marina. The pilot deftly glided the vessel into the slip behind Keo's twenty-two-footer, while one of the soldiers up front hopped onto the dock and pulled security. He watched the man go into a crouch and aim his rifle up and down, then side to side. Meanwhile, the second man tossed the line over, then followed it and tied the boat into place. They had clearly done this many times before, so he wasn't dealing with complete amateurs.

"You think it was your boat or my shooting?" Gene asked.

"Does it matter?"

"Just curious." Gene had slid his rifle up next to him and was clutching it. "You sure we shouldn't—"

"Yes," Keo said. "Besides, I need to find out what they know."

"How're you gonna to do that?"

"I need to take at least one of them alive."

The motors cut off, and blessed silence once again swept across the island. All three of the soldiers were on the dock now, and one of them jumped onto the tied twenty-two-footer. He searched through the compartments under the console, then spent a few seconds peeking into the livewells.

"I can take them," Gene said.

"No."

"But—"

"*No,*" Keo said, probably a bit louder than he needed to that time.

It had the desired effect, though, and Gene sighed as if Keo had given him a spanking. The kid unclutched his rifle and laid his chin against the ground and pouted.

The soldiers were moving up the dock, the *clomp-clomp-clomp* of their heavy boots against the wooden structure echoing all the way up here. To his absolute non-surprise, they were all well-armed, wearing gun belts and sidearms, and the sun reflected off the barrels of their assault rifles. Either M4s or AR-

15s, though given how every soldier he had met in Louisiana seemed to have been armed with the US military-adopted M4s, he was leaning toward the former.

"Okay," Keo said. When Gene lifted his head expectantly, he asked, "You see the fat one?"

The kid peered through his binoculars. "Which one?"

"The one in the back."

"That's the fat one?"

"Yes."

"He doesn't look that fat."

"Okay, the biggest one in the back, then."

"What about him?"

"He's yours. When I make my move, you take him out. Got it?"

"What about the other two?"

"Don't worry about them. I'm going to kill the second one and keep the third one alive for questioning."

"Can you do that?" Gene gave him an earnest look. "I mean, you can do that?"

"Yes," Keo nodded. "I can do that."

"Okay. So when should I shoot?"

"After I make my move."

"And what's that? Your move?"

"When one of them goes down."

"Oh, okay."

"Get ready," Keo said, then began sliding backward, away from the ridgeline.

Gene watched him go, looking so much younger than he had earlier this morning. Keo had thought he was seventeen, but he was probably closer to sixteen. Which made the fact that Gene had managed to survive these months on Santa Marie Island all by himself something of a miracle.

"Don't sweat it; you can make the shot," Keo said.

He didn't so much as have faith in Gene's shooting ability than he did in the high-powered scope mounted on top of Deuce. They were, from what he could tell, less than a hundred meters from the marina. Even someone as distance shooting-challenged as Keo could have made the shot all day long with the equipment and position.

"I can make the shot," Gene repeated, likely more for his own benefit than Keo's.

When he was far enough away that he was sure the angle kept him from being spotted from below, Keo picked himself up from the ground. He brushed off dirt and pebbles clinging to his clothes, then turned and, bent over at the waist, moved quietly down the sidewalk.

Like most marinas, this one was slightly angled with the entrance at the top and the docks at the bottom, with the parking lot spread out in the middle. The only potential hiding spot Keo had seen when he first walked through the place earlier was a natural defilade made of rocky formations and a wall of dirt that flanked the entrance. It wasn't very much at all, but at least it would keep him invisible from anyone approaching on the other side.

Keo slid against the wall of dirt now, and out of pure habit checked the weight of the MP5SD to make sure he had a full magazine in place. The submachine gun was equipped with its own suppressor, which made it longer and less mobile than its smaller cousin, the MP5K. The weapon was heavily chipped and dented, and Keo was resigned to the fact that sooner or later he would have to look for a replacement. Like everything these days, even the German gun would eventually fall apart.

It was too bad Gene didn't have two-way radios, otherwise Keo wouldn't have needed to risk peeking around the wall of rock to glimpse the docks and the three soldiers walking up it at the moment. They were taking their time, which was probably a byproduct of being in control of the surrounding area and, most likely, having everything go their way for a long time. Even if they knew Gene was on the island, they were used to him hiding from them.

As he had guessed, they were carrying M4s. New models, from the looks of it, and nearly identical to the one he had left behind in Gene's two-story house on the hill. Of course, he'd gotten that carbine from Song Island, and the Rangers had converted it to full-auto. Would these bozos have done the same thing to their weapons? He guessed he'd find out pretty soon.

There was fifty to sixty meters of open space, including the parking lot, from where he was and the end of the docks, plus a generous amount of trucks, many with boat trailers, left behind to block his view of the soldiers, and vice versa. The windows of the vehicles were coated with the elements, and not a single one looked even remotely usable. Gene had told him he'd found keys to some of them, but after trying a half dozen or so, he'd given up trying to find one that still worked.

Given the range of the MP5SD, there was no way he was going to hit them from this distance, even if he could shoot around the cars. No, he'd have to let them come closer and make use of the submachine gun's close-quarters ability. Of course, that would mean Gene would have to wait just a little bit longer to—

Crack! as a single rifle shot smashed the silence.

Or not.

He stuck his head out into the open a second and watched the soldiers scrambling around on the docks. The two up front, anyway, while the third had fallen and was grabbing onto his left thigh, where he had been shot.

Gene had missed—sort of.

The two able soldiers returned fire on Gene's position

along the ridgeline to the right of them, the *pop-pop-pop* of their assault rifles rolling back and forth across Santa Marie Island.

Ah. Three-round bursts, and not full-auto.

He should have felt better about that, but of course two people letting loose with a string of three-round shots were still two people too many when lead was involved.

Gene hadn't fired a second shot, probably because he was trying not to get his head blown off at the moment. That was awfully smart of him, but Keo didn't have that luxury. Well, he did. He could stay right where he was, and either the soldiers would come closer or they would turn tail and—

Shit, he thought when he saw the soldiers turning and heading back toward their boat. One of them had grabbed the wounded (not really "fat") man and was half-dragging and half-carrying him, while the third continued raining fire on the ridgeline where they'd last spotted Gene.

Keep your head down, kid.

That was exactly what he should have done, too. There was no point in pursuing the soldiers. Hell, he'd have to get a lot closer just to shoot them with his weapon.

Yup. The smart thing here was to hang back. He could always wait for another group to show up. Gene said they came around regularly, didn't he? Once a week?

Just hang back and wait. There was no point in doing something stupid now, when the men down there didn't even know he existed. He could gather intelligence about the operation around here some other way. Maybe even find out if they had Gillian somewhere, if he was really, really lucky.

Right. Because he had been really lucky these last few months.

Keo sighed and slipped out from behind cover and jogged across the parking lot.

He used the parked vehicles as cover, darting from one to the other, but always moving east toward the docks.

While he was going as fast as he could, the soldiers had bogged down halfway back to their boat. The wounded man had proven too hurt to keep moving and was sitting down while the second one tried to dress his wounds, blood spurting on the deck around them. The third soldier was pulling security, pointing his rifle at the ridgeline and still searching for something to shoot. Gene was being very smart, though, and not giving the man anything.

Keo was halfway to the docks, willing the guard to keep his eyes focused on the ridgeline, when the man decided to look down and saw Keo just as he slid behind a blue Chevy truck. The man didn't waste any time and opened fire.

Ping-ping-ping! as bullets pelted the other side of the vehicle.

"Hurry up!" someone shouted between shots. The shooter. "Let's go, let's go!"

The gunfire was continuous, bullets smashing into the truck, some going astray and chipping the pavement around him. Finally, after about ten seconds of nonstop shooting, there was a brief respite.

Keo peeked out from behind the bumper at the soldier as the man was backing up, reloading as he went. His friends had stood up and were continuing to hobble back to their boat.

Should have parked closer, dummies.

Crack! as a bullet punched into the wooden dock floor in front of the third soldier.

Gene, back in play.

But before Gene could correct his errant second shot, the soldier turned toward another part of the ridgeline and opened up with a new magazine.

Keo took the opportunity to slip out from behind the Chevy and race across the parking lot. He picked up speed as he went, taking the remaining meters in a matter of seconds and reaching the docks just as the soldier turned back toward him.

He let loose with a burst and didn't release the trigger until the man fell sideways and off the dock, *splashing* into the water below.

The other two were almost at their boat. They were shouldering each other, alternating between hobbling and running, when they turned around just as their comrade disappeared into the water behind them. They hadn't heard Keo's gunshots because the MP5SD barely made any noise when it fired, except for the cyclical whirring of its parts. Compared to the crash of the M4 and Gene's rifle, Keo might as well be spitting. So the remaining soldiers weren't reacting to Keo's gunshots, but rather the loud *splash* of their friend falling into the water.

Keo was running full speed up the dock now, stepping on the trail of blood one of the soldiers had left in his wake as he was dragged off. He switched the submachine gun's fire to semiautomatic as the second soldier dropped his friend and tried to unsling his rifle.

Keo shot the second soldier once in the thigh, then as the man screamed and grabbed for his leg, shot him again in the chest. Unlike his friend, this one only crumpled to the deck, where he lay still and didn't move.

The not-really-fat soldier looked shocked to see the body fall next to him. Then he snapped out of it and glanced over at Keo before scrambling to unsling his rifle.

"Don't make me kill you!" Keo shouted.

The wounded man looked conflicted, and Keo was sure he might finish going for his M4 after all—there was at least a fifty-fifty chance—but the man was apparently smarter than he looked. Either that, or he wanted to live more. He pulled his hands away from the rifle and placed them over his thigh to stanch the bleeding instead.

Blood was squirting out through the man's fingers when Keo finally reached him. He grabbed the wounded man's rifle and tossed it up the dock, then kicked the dead soldier's rifle into the water. Once he secured the remaining soldier's handgun—a nice-looking Smith & Wesson .32 semiautomatic—Keo took a step back to catch his breath.

"Keo!" Gene, waving with both hands (and Deuce) at him from the ridgeline.

Keo waved back. "All clear!"

He looked back at his captive. Like the soldiers Keo had encountered recently, this one had a name tag over his right breast pocket. It read: "J. Miller." Unlike the ones in Louisiana, Miller and his fellow Texans had a patch of the Lone Star State over one shoulder.

"We gotta stop meeting like this," Keo said.

"Huh?" Miller said, blinking the sweat and sun out of his eyes.

"Me, you guys, and marinas."

Miller continued to blink at him, unsure how to respond. He finally said, "I don't know you, man."

"No? Hunh. I must be thinking about some other douchebags in uniforms, then." He looked down at the blood oozing out between Miller's fingers. "Hurts?"

"What do you think?"

"Looks like it hurts."

"That's because it does."

"You need a doctor?"

"I got medical supplies in the boat."

"Oh, do you now? That's convenient."

Miller didn't say anything.

Keo glanced at the dead soldier nearby. His name tag read: "Matthew." Keo hadn't caught the third soldier's name before he did his swan dive into Galveston Bay. Not that it mattered. Fish food didn't need names.

"So," Keo said, looking back at Miller. "I have a few questions. You mind answering them for me?"

"I got a choice?" Miller asked.

Keo grinned. "Of course you do. It's a free country, isn't it? Well, it used to be, anyway."

FOUR

J. Miller, as it turned out, was a former paramedic, and when Keo tossed him a first-aid kit he had retrieved from the soldiers' boat, the man quickly took out what he needed, cut off a large chunk of his pant leg, and treated his own wound. He worked without making a sound, though every now and then his breathing accelerated slightly.

They were in the parking lot, with Miller leaning against a white Bronco and the sun beating down mercilessly on both of them. Keo gave Miller space to keep himself from bleeding to death while Gene had retreated back to the ridgeline overlooking the western marina in case more soldiers tried sneaking up on them.

When Miller was finished, Keo handed him a refilled bottle of water, also from the soldiers' boat. The vessel was packed with supplies, including spare magazines with 5.56 rounds but no 9mm, which was what Keo would have preferred. He'd only used up half of the bullets in his MP5SD and he still had two full spares, but a man with extra ammo (especially the right kind) was a rich one these days.

Miller, his hands covered with his own blood, swiped them on his one good pant leg before taking the water and gulping it down in one long swig. He was in his early thirties, with a somewhat pudgy face and already stripes of gray among his dark hair. He eyed Keo suspiciously over the bottle as he drank.

"Careful there, don't wanna drown yourself," Keo said. "How's the leg? Any broken bones?"

Miller slowed down but kept drinking. "It went clean through."

"Lucky you."

"Yeah, lucky me," Miller said, clenching his teeth.

"J. Miller," Keo read. "That's a first."

"What's that?" Miller said, lowering the bottle. He sighed with relief.

"The initial on your tag."

"There was another Miller in my outfit, so I had to add a J."

"What's it stand for?"

"Jack."

"Ah. So should I call you Jack or Miller?"

"I don't give a shit," Miller said, and handed the bottle of water back.

Keo put it away. "Fair enough."

"Who the fuck are you, anyway?"

"I'm just a guy with a gun. Those two back there your friends?"

"Yeah, I guess."

"You guess?"

He shrugged. "I've only known them for a few months. It's not like we had dinner at each other's houses or anything."

"You guys have houses out here?"

"Rooms might have been more appropriate. So what's the deal with you and the kid?"

"I guess he lives here. I just showed up earlier this morning."

"Your boat..."

"Uh huh."

"What are you, Japanese or something?"

"Or something," Keo said. "You did pretty good there with the leg."

"I could still use some real medical attention, I'm not gonna lie."

"And where would you find something like that?"

"T18 has a full medical staff."

"T18?"

"Where I'm based."

"What's the *T* stand for?"

Miller gave him an *Are you kidding me with that question?* look. Then he said, "Texas."

"I guess that makes sense."

"Where you from, anyway?"

"San Diego. But I'm assuming you meant recently. In which case, that would be Louisiana."

"I've never been to Louisiana," Miller said almost wistfully.

"Not too late. It's just next door. I hear the traffic's pretty light these days."

"Can't. Got a job to do."

"I can appreciate that. But speaking of going places, how far is T18?"

Miller clammed up. Apparently he realized (too late) that he shouldn't have said anything in the first place.

"Look," Keo said, "here's the deal. I need information, and you have it. I'd prefer if you told me what I needed to know without all that messy bloodshed. Er, well, more bloodshed. I mean, you're already hurt, but you can still walk. Mostly. Just tell me what I need to know and we're cool. You go your way, and I go mine. Tell me that's not the best deal you're gonna get all day."

Miller gave him that long look again, as if he could read Keo's face.

Good luck with that, pal.

"Well?" Keo said. "What's it going to be?"

"You know where League City is?" Miller asked.

"For the sake of avoiding further pointless questions, let's just pretend I've never stepped foot in the great state of Texas in my entire life."

"It's about thirty miles from here. Up the I-45. It used to be a town called Wilmont."

"How big is T18?"

"Pretty big."

"Okay, let's put it another way. How many people are in T18 right now?"

Miller thought about it for a moment, then, "Around 4,000."

Keo whistled. "That's a lot of people."

"It's probably the smallest town in Texas. There's one outside of Dallas that has almost 10,000."

Keo wished he could say he was surprised. From everything he had heard, there were a hell of a lot more towns out there he would never know about, all of them filled with survivors. He used to think the creatures had either killed everyone or turned them into ghouls, but he couldn't have been more wrong. There had been a plan in effect from the very first day of The Purge, and he was only now starting to fully grasp the scope of it. He had never been especially good at out-of-the-box long-term thinking, but Keo had to admit, what the creatures had done and what they were currently doing out there was beyond impressive.

"Good to know," Keo said, hoping his face didn't betray his thoughts. "So, let's pretend you and your friends caught survivors running around out here. Say, like my little buddy Gene. Where would you take him?"

"Our orders are to take everyone we find to T18."

"How many did you take in the last, say, six months?"

"Me personally? None. I just joined Matthew and Bo out here two weeks ago. Before that, I had guard duty back in town."

"So this is a promotion?"

"It beats looking at the same patch of dirt every day."

"Thirty miles is a pretty long drive to take people back and forth."

"Not if there's nothing between here and League City."

"Nothing?"

"I mean, there are small towns, but no one lives out here if they can help it. It's not exactly fertile ground."

"What about T18?"

"It's the exception. It's connected to Trinity Bay by a river, and there are large undeveloped lands in the area."

"Wildlife?"

"Yeah, sure. Some of them are just starting to come back now that the crawlers aren't feeding on them anymore." Miller paused, then added, "You're looking for someone."

Keo nodded. "I am."

"You think they're in T18?"

"Don't know. I guess the only way to find out is to go there and look."

Miller smiled at him.

"That's funny to you?" Keo asked.

"If you go to T18, you won't come out alive."

"Really."

"Really," Miller nodded.

"I thought these towns were paradise. Peace and quiet. Sanctuary from the night. All that good stuff. You telling me all of that's a big fat lie?"

"They're supposed to be, but T18's different. It's...problematic."

"How so?"

"It's at war. If you go there, you better choose sides."

"So tell me who the good guys are."

"That's the problem. There's no such thing. There's just the bad guys and the badder guys."

Sounds familiar, Keo thought, and asked, "And which ones are you and your buddies?"

"The bad guys," Miller said. "The badder guys? Trust me, when you meet them you're going to wish you were on our side."

"You believe him?" Gene asked.

"I don't know," Keo said. "Maybe. Or he might just be a very good liar."

"You can't tell?"

"I'm not a human polygraph, Gene."

"What's that?"

"What's what?"

"Polygraph."

"A lie detector."

"Oh."

Gene glanced back at Miller, leaning against the same Bronco with zip ties around his ankles and wrists. They had found bundles of the stuff inside the compartments of the soldiers' boat. No doubt they came in handy whenever Miller and his crew ran across stragglers such as Gene's friends. Or, possibly, Gillian and the others a few months earlier. Though, according to Miller, he was new to the gig, which meant Keo had shot the wrong men.

"I don't know how you can trust him," Gene said.

"I can't. But as long as I have a gun and he doesn't, I don't have to."

He had said it louder than necessary, even though they

weren't so far from him that Miller couldn't already hear everything they were saying anyway.

"You can come with me," Keo said.

The teenager looked surprised. "Me? What would I do out there?"

"Try to find your friends."

"I don't even know if they're still alive."

"When the soldiers took them, were they still alive?"

"Yeah."

"Then they're still alive now."

"How do you know that?"

"The towns Miller was telling me about? They don't kill you. It's not a prison. Not really, anyway. I mean, yes, it is in a sense, but it's not a death camp by any means. Think of it more like a federal pen for white collar criminals, with only minimal possibilities of shower rapes."

Gene gave him that patented confused look.

"Point is," Keo continued, "if they did take your friends to T18 or one of the other Ts, that means they're still alive and probably fine as long as they play by the rules."

"How do you know all this?"

"The question is, how is it that you don't? Weekend warriors like Miller have been setting these towns up for months now. First the camps—"

Gene's eyes lit up at that.

"You know about the camps," Keo said.

The kid nodded. From his expression, he knew a lot about the camps. He might have even been in one of them once upon a time, and for a moment Keo thought about asking Gene to pull up his sleeves to show him his arms, but decided against it. Being victimized by those creatures was traumatic enough; he didn't feel the need to force Gene to relive it, too.

"They're gone," Keo continued. "The camps. From what I've

been told, they started moving people over to these resettlement towns months ago." He glanced back at Miller. "Right?"

Miller nodded. "Right."

Gene was staring at Miller intently. Keo wasn't sure what he saw in the kid's eyes—maybe anger, a little bit of fear, but definitely a lot of dislike.

"Kid," Keo said, directing Gene's eyes back to him. "It's your choice. I'm not going to force you to do anything you don't want to. If you stay, you can keep half the supplies like we agreed, and I'll give you half of the soldiers', too."

"What about him?" Gene asked.

"He's coming with me."

"What if he comes back with more men?"

"He won't. Whatever happens, I promise you won't see him again."

Gene nodded reluctantly, then said, "So when are you leaving?"

Keo glanced at his watch: 3:14 p.m.

The afternoon had crept up on him, leaving him just three hours before sunset. He thought about all those houses behind him along the streets and the things that may or may not be hiding inside, watching them at this very moment.

Keo looked back at the docks, at his boat in the slip next to the soldiers' bigger vessel. He had spent the last few days in the Gulf of Mexico sleeping under the stars on his way here. It had been some of the best night's sleep of his life because he didn't have to worry about anything crawling up and over the gunwales. He would have no trouble doing that for one more night.

But that was back when he was out there in the middle of the ocean all by himself, and not this close to the Texas coastline. Even if he took Miller's boat, a gunfight out in the open water would not end well for him, especially if they had more than one gun onboard, which they certainly would. If his experiences with the soldiers in Louisiana had taught him anything, it was that where you found one patrol, you usually found more.

"Tomorrow morning," Keo said, turning back to Gene. "Until then, show me how to survive the island at night."

Instead of staying at the two-story white house on the hill, Gene led him and a hobbling Miller further up the street. Keo had given Miller a paddle from his boat to use as a crutch, and the former paramedic turned human collaborator seemed to be moving surprisingly well for someone with a hole in one of his thighs. He only clenched his teeth every now and then and had decided to smartly keep any complaints to himself.

The fact that Miller seemed to be taking captivity so well made Keo doubt everything the man had told him. Guys who were that calm while facing the wrong end of a gun were dangerous enough to come up with clever lies, like a town with two warring parties. But Keo kept his suspicions to himself. He would find out one way or another if Miller was telling fibs in the morning. Right now, there was the night to worry about.

One problem at a time.

The house Gene took them to was another two-story, this one squeezed between two much smaller residences. It sat along the north end of the island, with a quaint backyard overlooking the bay. A mailbox with the name "Tanner" greeted them as they walked up the driveway.

"You've been here before?" Keo asked Gene.

The teenager nodded. "Couple of times." He pointed at the exposed windows and the living room on the other side. "That's how you know if they've been inside the houses."

"The curtains..."

"Yeah. If they're inside, they'll pull the curtains or something, like furniture, to block out the sun. The tricky part is tricking them while not letting them know you're tricking them."

"Tricky," Keo said.

"Heh," Gene grinned. "I see what you did there."

Keo smiled back at him.

Gene walked on forward, then opened the door—it wasn't locked—and leaned inside and seemed to sniff the air for a moment. Satisfied, he glanced back at Keo. "Smells good."

"Smells good?" Keo said.

"Yeah, they have a smell. Like shit mixed with garbage. It always lingers when they've been inside a house."

"Sounds good to me," Keo said. Then, nudging Miller in the back with the barrel of his MP5SD, "In you go. You're our guinea pig for the day."

Miller grunted before taking his first tentative step inside, the paddle under his armpit *clack-clacking* against the tiled floor.

There were no signs of a struggle, and the place was spotless except for old, faded stains here and there. Dried blood, from the night the creatures invaded Santa Marie Island, probably. What must it have been like as the creatures took the population one by one, multiplying as they went? The only way off the island would be through the marinas, but how many had made it? How many even knew to flee before it was too late?

Keo closed the door behind him. "Should I lock the door?"

"No," Gene said.

"What about the windows?"

"No, everything has to be the way they were when we found them. They're smarter than you think. If they see something wrong with a house, something that wasn't there the night before, they'll know someone's inside. A locked front door, a closed curtain, even the slightest things. We have to trick them without letting them know they're being tricked, remember?"

Smart dead things? Now where'd he heard that before?

Right. It was something Lara said, about how the creatures were dead but not stupid. A motto her boyfriend had come up with that had kept them all alive. For a while, anyway. As far as Keo knew, it hadn't helped the ex-Ranger in the end.

Gene led them up a flight of stairs, their footsteps against the carpeted steps the only noise in the entire house.

"How do you know they didn't sneak in through the back door since the last time you were here?" Keo asked as he and Miller followed the teenager up.

"I can tell just by looking at the floor," Gene said. "Or the walls. Things moved, broken furniture, glass, that kind of thing. And like I said, they smell. Once they're inside a house, the stink doesn't go away for weeks even after they've moved on. Can you smell it?"

"No."

That wasn't entirely true. He did smell something. Abandonment. But that was normal these days. You couldn't stick your head into a building, a vehicle, or anything with enclosed spaces and not get a whiff. It was everywhere.

"No smell means they're not inside," Gene was saying.

The second floor was wide open, with curtainless windows exposing the calm waters of Galveston Bay on the other side.

"You sure we're going to be safe up here?" Keo asked.

"I've stayed here before," Gene said. "The last time was almost three weeks ago. They've never come close to sniffing me."

"First time for everything."

"Trust me, we'll be fine."

Famous last words, kid.

Miller, moving in front of him, must have had the same thought, because he gave Keo a quick look.

"What?" Keo said.

"I didn't say anything," Miller said.

"Uh huh." Then, "I have a question for you."

"What?"

"How do they know to avoid you?"

"Avoid me?"

"Yeah. How do they know not to have you for dinner?"

Miller seemed to actually think about it for a moment. "I don't know. They just do."

"That's it? You're not even curious?"

"It works. I don't care why or how, just that it does."

"I bet that's what the Nazi sympathizers said during World War II."

"There's a difference between me and them."

"Oh yeah?"

"I'm still alive."

"For now."

Miller snorted. "Have you looked around you?"

"What about it?"

"There's no winning here, sport. We're down for the count. The faster you accept it, the easier it'll be."

"Are you trying to recruit me?"

Miller grinned back at him. "You interested?"

Keo chuckled. "I'll let you know in the morning."

Gene pushed his way into the master bedroom at the end of the second-floor hallway. It was appropriately huge, with satin sheets crumpled on the floor. The king-size bed looked to be in good condition, though clouds of dust flitted off the sheets and across the streams of fading sunlight coming in through an open window.

The teenager led them past the bed, a massive dresser, and LCD TV, and toward a pair of doors in the back. Keo already knew what was on the other side even before Gene pulled them open. It was a bathroom, big enough to fit a couple of families and their pet. More sunlight poured in through a window behind a large bathtub and reflected off the long mirror opposite from it.

"Here?" Keo said.

"Doors are solid wood, super tough," Gene said. He knocked on one of the mahogany slabs for effect, producing dull *thudding* sounds. "They're going to need a battering ram to get through them. Push comes to shove, we can always escape through the window."

"The window?" Keo said doubtfully.

"I've tested it out. You can climb onto the roof from it."

"You're shitting me."

"Why, you scared of heights?"

"No, but that doesn't mean I want to go around climbing people's roofs, Gene."

The kid smiled mischievously before walking over and opening the cabinet underneath the sink. He took out a backpack and put it on the counter, then unzipped it and pulled out a bottle of water that he tossed to Keo. It was warm, and Keo brushed aside a generous layer of gathered dust.

"I have go-bags in all the safe zones around the island," Gene said. "Lots of water, but I'm running out of food." He also pulled out a Glock handgun. "You need another one?"

"I'm good," Keo said. Then to Miller, "What about you? You need a gun?"

Miller gave him a look that said he wasn't entirely certain if Keo was kidding. "Yes."

"Too bad. Have a seat instead."

Miller grunted, then hobbled over to the toilet in the back. It was separated from the shower stall by a three-inch wall, and the wounded soldier sat down gratefully on the porcelain lid.

Keo stared at the man for a moment. He had expected Miller to at least try to escape once during the trek from the marina over to the house, but he had remained perfectly obliging. In fact, it seemed as if he hadn't given the possibility of escape a single thought.

"How long before your friends show up looking for you?" he asked Miller.

"My friends?" Miller said. Either the guy was surprised by the question, or he really was a very good liar.

"When you don't return to T18. What happens then?"

Miller shrugged. "Hell if I know. "

"Are you telling me no one's going to care if you don't report back in?"

"Report back? Man, you're way overestimating us. We're not nearly that organized. I wish we were. It'd make a lot of things easier."

"I don't believe you."

"Believe what you want. No skin off my nose."

Keo eyed him closely, but if Miller had a tell, he disguised it well.

He looked over at Gene instead. "I've seen them climb before. The ghouls. You sure we shouldn't cover up the window?"

"There are no handholds out there," Gene said. "We'll be fine. I told you. I've been here before, and they've never come close to checking the place out." Gene pulled back the sleeve of his sweatshirt and glanced down at a black sports watch. "Two more hours until nightfall." Then he gave Keo a crooked, almost nervous grin. "Should be fun, right?"

"Yeah, sure, kid," Keo said. "But just to be safe—" he opened his tactical pack and took out a spare Glock and handed it to Gene "—here's something you can use. Magazine's loaded with silver bullets."

"Thanks." Gene took it and turned it over in his hands. "You remember all those guns from the other house?"

"Uh huh."

"You think some of them had silver bullets?"

"You didn't check?"

"It never occurred to me to."

"We'll go through them tomorrow morning and find out. Maybe we'll get lucky. Until then, let's just try to survive tonight first." He glanced over at Miller. "What about you?"

Miller looked over. "What about me?"

"You have something to add? Maybe a secret handshake that'll keep the crawlers at bay?"

"Nah," Miller said. He leaned back against the toilet and closed his eyes. "Looks like you and the kid got it all figured out."

Keo could be wrong, but he swore Miller almost smiled that time.

FIVE

Once upon a time, he was trapped inside an attic listening to the creatures as they *tap-tap-tapped* below him. This time he was inside a second-floor bathroom. The more things changed, the more they stayed the same, apparently.

Gene had heard the sudden movements—like *scratching*—from outside the house too, and his entire body stiffened. Keo could just make out the teenager's dirty sweatshirt in the semi-darkness. He sat inside the bathtub with his back against the wall, the only window inches to the left of his head. The kid's eyes kept darting between Keo and the window and Miller, sitting against the glass shower stall to Keo's right. A large swath of moonlight illuminated half of the room in a strangely serene baby-blue tint.

Keo tightened his grip on the MP5SD resting in his lap. He felt better knowing the bullets were silver, but that might not do him a lot of good if there were a lot of them out there right now. Sooner or later, he would use up his spare magazines, and then what? He remembered seeing Danny carrying a silver knife around with him. Smart. Guns ran out of bullets, but knives didn't.

I need to get me one of those. Maybe a sword.

"Hey," Keo whispered across the room at Gene. When the kid glanced over, "How many of them are out there?"

Gene didn't look like he understood the question. Or maybe he couldn't hear him.

Keo raised his voice a bit (but not too much). "The island. How many ghouls are on the island? How many houses? Ballpark figure."

"Fifty or so, I think," Gene said.

Fifty or so. Assuming at least two people to a house and four maximum would give him one hundred at least, and two hundred at the most. Probably somewhere in the middle to account for the loners, the retirees, and the divorcées. Somewhere around 150. Maybe a little bit more, maybe a little less. And that wasn't counting however many bloodsuckers had invaded the island during The Purge.

That was a hell of a lot more targets than he had bullets for.

Outnumbered again. So what else was new?

He looked over at the doors. Solid wood. Tough. He wouldn't have been able to physically hammer them down with his body. He'd need a sledgehammer at least. So Gene had chosen wisely by bringing them here. Would 150 (or so) ghouls be able to batter their way through in a single night?

Maybe. Maybe not.

He turned back to the window. His instincts were to barricade it or at least cover it up with something, but Gene had said he'd found it that way. And the kid had been surviving on the island by himself for months now, which meant he knew what he was doing. Keo hoped, anyway.

"How many?" Gene whispered.

"Hmm?" Keo said.

"How many are out there, you think?"

"One-fifty, give or take a few dozen here and there. Could be less. Could be more. I'm just spitballing numbers."

"Sounds about right," Gene said. He had Deuce between his legs, the barrel pointed up at the ceiling.

Keo glanced at Miller in the corner. The man's eyes were closed, as if he was trying to sleep, but Keo could tell by the rise and fall of his chest that the soldier was still wide awake.

"What do you think?" Keo asked him.

Miller opened his eyes. "About what?"

"How many do you think are out there?"

"I don't know. One-fifty sounds about right."

"What are the chances they'll leave you alone if you go outside in that uniform?"

"I don't know." Miller looked suddenly very uncertain. "There were always others with me when I'm out at night, and we were always on missions."

"What kind of missions?"

"Finding stragglers. People hiding out in the hills or the cities. Bringing them back to the towns."

"And here I thought everyone went there voluntarily."

He shrugged. "What can I say? There are a lot of stubborn people out there. You should know a thing or two about that."

"You saying I'm stubborn?"

"Maybe I'm wrong. It's been known to happen."

"Why don't you just leave them alone?" Gene said. There was an edge to the kid's voice, and Keo saw him flexing his fingers around Deuce.

"It's not my call," Miller said, and smartly didn't meet Gene's accusing eyes when he said it. "I just follow orders, sport."

"So you've been out there at night in those uniforms, and nothing happened?" Keo asked.

"Uh huh," Miller nodded.

"Interesting."

"How so?"

Keo shrugged. "Just wondering if that uniform will fit me."

Miller's eyes widened a bit, and he opened his mouth to say something when—

Crash!

He froze. And so did Gene and Keo.

Broken glass from downstairs. The living room windows; Keo was sure of it. The island was so still, the silence so complete, that the noise might as well be cannons going off right under them.

"Oh, shit," Gene whispered. "I don't understand. We didn't leave any clues down there. They should have just run past the house like all the other times."

Maybe they can smell us.

He didn't know if they could or not, but what else could it be? They had left the front of the house exactly the way they had found it this afternoon. They had even left the bathroom window curtainless for fear of messing with the status quo.

So how the hell did they know?

"Give me a gun," Miller said. He was fidgeting in his corner. "I need a gun."

"What's the matter?" Keo asked. "You don't think that uniform's going to save you?"

"I think I don't wanna find out."

"Well, tough nuts."

"Come on, man."

"Let me think about it," Keo said. Then, a second later, "I've thought about it. The answer's still no."

Keo gave the window another quick glance before scrambling to his feet and darting across the pool of moonlight and onto the other side. Gene anxiously watched him slide against the thick double doors and press his hands and ear against the smooth and slightly cool mahogany finish.

He willed his heartbeat to slow down, then held his breath and listened.

Footsteps.

The familiar *tap-tap-tap* of bare feet against carpeted flooring.

At first they were distant, like faded echoes, but they quickly grew in volume. A lot of them.

Too many, racing up the steps to the second floor.

Growing louder, and louder—

Keo staggered away from the door as...

...silence.

He waited for the inevitable. The familiar pounding of flesh against wood. He had heard it before—too many times to count.

But there wasn't any this time.

What the hell?

Behind and to the right of him, Gene had stood up inside the tub, his rifle gripped tightly in front of him. Miller was a statue in the corner, his eyes glued on Keo. They were both waiting for the relentless assaults against the door, too.

So where was it?

Keo pushed his ear back against the smooth, wooden surface. He listened for the telltale signs, the *tap-tap-tap* of bare feet moving around outside, but he could only hear...

Silence.

He'd heard them earlier, hadn't he? Of course he had, because Gene and Miller had heard them, too. They had broken through the living room windows and raced up the steps and converged on the second floor.

So where were they now? Had they searched the main bedroom and finding no one, just decided to...leave? Without even bothering with the two doors on the other side of the room?

Yeah, right.

"Well?" Gene whispered behind him. "What's out there?"

The kid looked rooted in the tub, and the sight of him clutching Deuce made Keo smile for some reason. He turned back to the door and leaned against it for the third time, listening to the overwhelming silence outside.

Finally, Keo shook his head.

"I told you," Gene said, and although he did his best to sound confident, he couldn't hide the slight trembling in his voice. "They'll check the houses, but if they don't see anything out of the ordinary, they'll move on."

"Are you sure there's no other way inside?"

The teenager shook his head. "I checked. It's just those doors and this window."

Keo didn't tell him about the last time he had been in a building that was supposedly secured. That time, the ghouls had found a way in through the—

"Vents," he said.

"What?" Gene said.

"AC vents."

He hurried away from the door and began scanning the ceiling, looking for grates designed to blast air into the room in the summer and heat in the winter.

There, just above the mirror over the long sink counter with the two faucets for him and her. Except it was small. Too small. Barely one-by-one-foot. Even the scrawniest ghoul was going to have difficulty crawling through that thing.

"What about the vents?" Gene asked from the bathtub.

"Nothing," Keo said. "False alarm."

But he didn't completely breathe easier. They were still in a house and on an island teeming with ghouls. There were at least a hundred of the monsters outside right now, scouring the homes and buildings and parked vehicles for signs that someone stupid enough (*like me*) had arrived on Santa Marie Island and decided not to leave before sunset.

Dammit. He should have taken the twenty-two-footer back out and slept on the ocean like he had the last few nights. He should have risked the chances of running into one of Miller's friends. At least out there he'd be able to hear trouble coming from miles away. And if push came to shove, he could have always gone into the water. He'd done it before.

Shoulda, woulda, coulda, pal.

"This is wrong," Miller said.

Keo looked over at him. "Now you have something to say?"

"This is wrong," Miller repeated.

"What is?" Gene asked.

"They've never been this quiet before," Miller said. He was breathing hard for some reason.

"Never?" Keo said.

"Not when they know people are nearby. People that aren't us. In uniforms. And they goddamn *know* you're in here."

"You don't know that," Gene said. "They've always passed the house over. Tonight's no different."

Keo thought the teenager was trying to convince himself more than he was Miller.

"They know," Miller said with absolute certainty. "Trust me, they know. I've been around enough of them that I can tell when they know. And they fucking *know*."

Keo and Gene exchanged a quick look.

"Then why—" Gene started to ask, but he didn't get to finish before the *crack!* of a gunshot broke the island's quiet and the window next to him shattered.

Gene ducked down, dropping Deuce and throwing his arms over his head.

Keo dived to the floor as a bullet slammed into the ceiling above him. He landed hard on the dirty and shoeprint-caked slate tiles, but even through the rain of glass shards falling into the tub around Gene, he heard the echoing *ploompt!* from outside.

Grenade launcher. That was a grenade launcher!

He expected an explosion, waited to be screaming in agony as fire and shrapnel ripped through him, but instead he looked up and saw a cylindrical canister appearing out of the night like a bulbous bullet, but slower and shinier. It slipped through the broken window and rainbowed from one end of the room to the other before bouncing off the counter behind him. The loud *hissing* filled the air even before the object had settled, telling him that he was wrong—it wasn't a grenade, but a gas canister.

Keo grabbed his shirt and pulled it up and over his mouth and nostrils. His eyes stung immediately even before the smoke managed to engulf his side of the bathroom. When he had first seen the room he thought it was big, but now as he teared up and his lungs burned, he wished it was much bigger.

The sounds of Gene and Miller coughing up a storm in the room around him invaded his senses. Gene might actually have been crying, or that might have been Miller. Maybe both. Or all three of them, for all he knew.

He was trying to maintain his grip on the MP5SD when he heard the loud pounding of footsteps. Not ghouls this time, because these were heavier and showing all the subtlety of a stampeding herd of elephants. He wasn't sure how long it had been—ten seconds? Ten minutes?—since he could barely keep his eyes open, and every time he took a breath it felt like someone was stabbing his chest with a spear, or a dozen.

The door. Someone was knocking on the door.

No, not knocking.

Banging.

It would take the ghouls hours, maybe days, to finally break through, he remembered thinking. The creatures weren't known for their strength, and he had felt relatively safe inside the confines of the bathroom. They would need something like a sledgehammer, or maybe a car to get the job done.

Boom-boom-boom!

It sounded as if they had found one of those two things right now, because the entire room seemed to be trembling each time they smashed into the doors on the other side.

He had made it across the bathroom, alternating between breathing and trying to look past the gathering smoke. It was difficult enough trying to maintain his vision through the waterfall of tears and the sensation of someone dropping barrels of ground peppers into his eyes, but every step made him want to give up and fall down and scream until the pain went away.

Boom-boom-boom!

He spun around until he was facing the doors—or, at least, where he thought the doors were—and waited. He didn't have to actually see to know where they were—he just had to follow the crushing sounds of blow after blow landing against the mahogany wood somewhere on the other side of the blanket of smoke.

The MP5SD was slippery against his hands, and someone was screaming to his right. Keo ignored everything and focused on what was in front of him, which at this point was smoke and...more smoke.

Soon, the tear gas would be sucked out through the broken window, but soon wasn't fast enough. Not nearly fast enough.

Boom-boom-boom!

His vision started to blur. Or maybe that was all the tears flooding them. God, he hadn't cried this much since...well, he'd never cried this much in his life. Of course, no one had ever locked him inside a bathroom with an exploding gas canister before, either, so it wasn't like he had any experience here.

There was a final *boom!* before the very distinctive sound of wood splintering came from across the room.

There goes a door. Maybe both.

He sought out the window and saw a figure next to it curled up inside the large bathtub. Gene, trying desperately to make himself small and be spared the tendrils of crushing smoke gathering around him like tentacles. It wasn't going to work. Poor Gene was alternating between crying and trying not to cough his lungs out.

The window!

What was that Gene had said earlier?

"Push comes to shove, we can always escape through the window."

He hadn't greeted that comment with much enthusiasm, and Keo still didn't have a lot of it as he stumbled in that direction, but he had very little choice at the moment. Unfortunately for him, while his mind had declared that this was the correct path, his legs had somehow turned to Jell-O while he wasn't looking, and he had to grab at the nearest wall to keep from falling down.

And his lungs. Jesus, his lungs were on fire.

He pushed off the wall—or was it a counter?—and braved the endless curls of smoke, using the window as a beacon of hope. If he could get to it, if he could climb out, and he could somehow crawl up to the rooftop...

Out there, he would be able to breathe again, to see, to not feel like every inch of his body was on fire.

He didn't know how far he had actually gotten before something blindsided him and Keo went sailing across the room. He must have slammed into another wall and gone down in a pile. Not that he felt it. Any of it. He just knew it was happening. At that moment, the only thing he was intensely aware of was screaming pain from his insides as it threatened to turn all of him into a pool of liquid.

Keo was on his back and looking up as the thing that had assaulted him rose up from the floor. It was a minotaur, blackened and monstrous, and it peered back at him with glassy oblong eyes.

No, it wasn't a beast from Greek mythology after all. It was just an asshole in a gas mask.

Pain exploded across Keo's face as something struck him and his head snapped backward and slammed into the slate tiles. It hurt, but the blow wasn't nearly as intense as the inferno raging inside his body, threatening to burst through his eyeballs.

Then, mercifully, there was just darkness.

SIX

Keo's lungs were still burning, but at least he could breathe again without fearing that his entire chest cavity was going to cave in with every breath. Motor control was (gradually) coming back, along with feeling in his legs and arms, though he was pretty sure his eyes were the color of mandarin oranges. If Keo weren't already covered in scars, he would have been hesitant to look at a shiny reflective surface at the moment.

Instead, he concentrated on his surroundings.

They were inside the living room of the same two-story house where he, Gene, and Miller had retreated for the night. The windows were broken, the jagged shards still sticking out of the frames covered in coagulated black blood. It looked less like plasma and more like mud: thick and still oozing.

Two men in black uniforms similar to the one Miller wore sat on the floor in opposing corners, M4 rifles lying across their laps and gas masks dangling from their hips. One was already snoring, the other getting there. A third man leaned against a wall looking out the window while spooning gobs of mashed potatoes into his mouth from a bag of MRE. Keo recognized the distinctive bulky

THE ISLES OF ELYSIUM   65

six-shot cylinder and short barrel of the M32 grenade launcher—
the weapon that had sent the tear gas sailing into the bathroom—
slung behind the man's back.

If Keo had any ideas about taking that launcher and giving
the soldier a taste of his own medicine, he quickly gave it up
when he looked down at the zip ties around his wrists and ankles.
They were the same color and brand as the ones he had used on
Miller earlier. He wondered if they found a warehouse full of this
stuff or something.

"*Finding stragglers,*" Miller had said about his mission.
"*People hiding out in the hills or the cities. Bringing them back to
the towns.*"

Keo bet those zip ties came in real handy for that. Maybe
Gillian and Jordan and the others had been hauled into T18 in
similar conditions. At the moment—and as crazy as it might
sound—that was his best-case scenario of ever finding them again.

He looked around the room again. There were plenty of signs
that the ghouls had trampled their way through the carpeting
earlier, so where were they now? The windows were wide open
and it was still obviously night outside, so what was stopping
them—

A flicker of movement, as one—no, two—*five*—emaciated
forms scampered past the windows on the house's front lawn.
More of them, on the sidewalks and streets beyond, like moving
shadows come alive.

Keo tensed, and so did the soldier leaning in front of him.
The man actually stopped eating his MRE for a while. A few
seconds, anyway, before he went back to business as usual. But
for a while there, the man hadn't been so sure.

So you're still scared of them too, huh?

Good to know, good to know...

The first five were only the beginning. There were more, flitting
across what little moonlight was visible beyond the broken

windows. If they knew he was inside the house without anything to stand in their way, they didn't show it. They appeared oblivious to him and the portable LED lamp resting on a dresser that hadn't been there when Keo walked through the place this afternoon. That was just enough light for him to see Gene lying unconscious on the floor, his back against one of the sofas in front of the windows.

Footsteps, before a pair of calm male voices appeared behind and to the right of him, coming from the kitchen.

"...back by morning," one man was saying. "I expected better from you."

"Give me a break; I almost died," a second voice said. This one sounded familiar, but it took Keo a few seconds to put a name to it, which told him he was still a little out of it from the blows he took upstairs.

J. Miller.

"Bo and Matthew weren't so lucky," Miller was saying.

Miller appeared in the living room with a second man. They looked almost identical in their black uniforms, except the second man was just a little taller and was in his early forties. Keo found out why they looked so much alike when he saw the second man's name tag: "S. Miller."

"There was another Miller in my outfit," Miller had said to him back at the marina yesterday. Of course, Miller had failed to add that the other Miller was, likely from the resemblance, his big brother.

So what else did J. Miller lie about?

"Look who's up," younger Miller said. For a guy moving on crutches made from a pair of sofa cushions duct-taped to paddles, Miller still looked his cheery self despite red eyes from the tear gas. He looked as if he had washed most of it out, a luxury Keo wished he had at the moment.

"How's the leg?" Keo asked.

"It's been better, but can't complain, considering." He jerked a thumb at the other man. "This is Steve. You might have noticed the resemblance. Yes, he's the other Miller I was referring to earlier."

"Ah, thanks for the clarification."

"He the one who shot you?" the older Miller asked.

"That's the other one." Jack nodded at Gene's sleeping form. "Shot me with that big .308. Christ, it hurt."

"You'll live."

"Not the point."

Steve ignored his brother and walked over to Keo, crouching in front of him. Besides being older than Jack, he was a little more haggard, his face lined and weathered from experience. He had the kind of calm, inquiring brown eyes that could be intimidating when focused entirely on you, the way he had them zeroed in on Keo now.

"Like what you see?" Keo asked.

Steve smiled. "What happened to your face?"

"Which part?"

Steve traced an imaginary line along the side of his own face, starting from the temple and finishing up at the jawline.

"Rollercoaster accident," Keo said.

"I've heard those can be dangerous."

"You have no idea."

"His name's Keo," Jack said.

"Keo?" Steve repeated. "What kind of name is that?"

"Mike was taken," Keo said.

Steve chuckled. "Is that right?"

"Yup. I was heartbroken, too. Really wanted to call myself Mike."

"Life's full of disappointments."

"Tell me about it."

"Anyway, I hear you're a dangerous man, Keo. Took out two of my guys on the docks like it was nothing."

"I wouldn't say it was nothing. It was definitely something."

"A real badass, huh?"

"I do all right with the ladies."

"What did you use to do before all of this?"

"You mean before I found this quaint little island?"

Smack! as Steve's open palm struck Keo across the cheek.

He wasn't prepared for it, which as it turned out was a good thing, because he was too stunned to actually feel the pain. Steve had a pair of meaty hands on him, which made sense since the man looked like a solid 220 pounds of muscle. It was hard to stay blubbery at the end of the world.

"Was it something I said?" Keo asked, trying to shake the blow off.

"What did you use to do?" Steve asked again.

"This and that."

"Probably ex-military," Jack said. He was leaning against a nearby wall, clearly enjoying the show.

"Nah, but close," Steve said. "I can smell ex-military guys, and he's not one of them. It's all right. You don't have to tell me now." Steve stood up and looked at Jack. "Get some shut-eye and rest your leg. We're heading back at sunup."

Jack nodded and found himself a spot on the same sofa that Gene was lying against and lay down.

"The creatures," Keo said.

Steve, who had settled on the floor across from him, said, "What about them?"

"They're going to stay out there the entire night?"

"You scared?"

"Fuck yes."

Steve grinned. "Don't worry your pretty little head off. They'll stay away."

"How does it work? How do they know to leave you alone?"

"You ever heard the phrase need-to-know?"

"No one ever told me."

Steve snorted. "They're not coming in as long as we're in here."

"You sure about that?" Keo asked, watching as three more of the creatures darted across the windows. Just seeing them out there, with nothing to protect him if they stopped and turned around on a whim, made his skin crawl.

"You better hope so," Steve said. He laid his M4 across his lap, then looked up at the soldier with the M32. "This is Horace. He's running around on five cans of warm Red Bull and enough caffeine to keep a herd of longhorns going. Try anything, and he has my permission to put you out of your misery."

Horace winked at Keo. He was a big man with an Army buzz cut. "Don't you worry. I'll take good care of you, spud."

"I feel so special," Keo said.

"The only reason you're still alive is because you didn't shoot my little brother," Steve said. "That, and you treated him like a human being after he was wounded. Otherwise I'd have fed you to those things outside."

"I guess it still pays to be a good guy these days."

"I paid you back by letting you keep breathing, but I don't owe you shit after that. Keep that in mind."

Oh, I'm keeping it in mind, all right, Keo thought while trying to ignore the tingling radiating from his cheek.

Keo opened his eyes to large doses of sunlight in his face and Steve sitting next to Gene on the sofa across the room. They looked like they were talking and had been for some time. Steve's soldiers were already outside the house, moving around on the lawn. The one with the M32, Horace, was on the sidewalk beyond.

"You did the right thing," Steve was saying to Gene. "You'll find out when we get there that all this running around was a waste of time."

"And I can leave anytime?" Gene asked.

"Absolutely, but you won't want to once you see what's there."

Gene nodded, though he didn't look as if he quite believed Steve, but was too smart to say so if he did have any doubts.

"Morning," Jack said, coming out of the kitchen with an open can of SPAM. He was shoveling large chunks of it into his mouth and talking at the same time. "You said you wanted to visit T18. This is your lucky day, sport, because that's exactly where you're going. Excited?"

"I can barely contain myself," Keo said.

Jack chuckled.

"Let's get going," Steve said. He stood up before fixing Keo with a hard stare. "One wrong move, and you're a dead man. Do we understand each other?"

"Crystal."

"Good man." He turned around and called through the broken windows, "Donovan, Taylor. Come get our guest of honor." Then to Gene, "Come on, son. Time to go home."

Gene nodded mutely, the kid who had fought off the soldiers these last few months seemingly MIA after last night. Keo couldn't really blame him. He'd been in his share of scrapes, but getting gassed in a bathroom, well, that was something he didn't want to go through again if he could help it.

Donovan and Taylor came back inside and pulled Keo up from the floor. He paid very close attention to Donovan, who had his MP5SD and pack slung over his back.

"Go for it, you know you want to," Taylor said, grinning knowingly at him.

Keo smiled back, but thought, *Damn.*

Donovan pulled out an all-black tactical knife from a sheath strapped low to one of his thighs and sliced the zip ties around Keo's ankle, but left the one around his wrists. Then Taylor gave him a (not so) friendly shove in the back as they led him outside.

If the sun was ridiculously bright before, it was practically blinding as he walked down the driveway. The crisp morning air flooded his lungs, and for a moment Keo almost believed there was nothing wrong with the world. He took a moment to stare at the impressive sight of birds flocking in formation above him. That ended when Taylor gave him another shove in the back, this time with the cold barrel of his rifle.

Steve turned in the street and led the way toward the eastern marina. Horace had taken point, while Jack limped on his two crutches behind him. They were moving slowly, probably for Jack's sake. Keo let the cool air cleanse the remains of last night's gas from his face and eyes. What he wouldn't give for a bottle of water to wash away the rest.

He was very aware of Donovan and Taylor moving step-for-step behind him. They were keeping their distance—Donovan further back than Taylor. He thought about making a run for it every time the narrow spaces between houses popped up to the left and right of him, but whenever he calculated the distance with the time he'd need to make it to safety, the results always came out against him surviving.

"You stopped at Galveston Island on your way over here?" Steve, walking in front of him, asked.

"I was thinking about going back for a visit," Keo said. "Nice?"

"Oh, yeah. Tons of things to see and do. The seawall in particular. Now that's engineering."

"You from around here?"

"Pearland. You know where that is?"

"Nope."

"Up I-45. Close enough that I spent most of my free weekends down here. I've always wanted an oceanside house."

"So what's stopping you now? Pick one. Or fifty."

"You know that old saying, 'I don't want to join a club that will have me'? Now that there's no one around to keep me from taking any house I want, it doesn't quite have the same cachet. Know what I mean?"

"You a man who worries about cachet, Steve?"

"Who doesn't?"

"I could care less."

"No?"

"Nope. Give me a gun, a boat, and I'll be out of your hair."

Steve turned around but continued backpedaling down the street. He smiled at Keo. "And if I don't?"

"I'll probably end up killing you."

"Just like that?"

"Just like that."

He chuckled, though it sounded just a little bit too forced. "One of these days, you're going to tell me what you used to do for a living. Until then—" he spun back around, "—I'll have to be satisfied with knowing I can put a bullet in your head any time I feel like it."

They took all three boats with them, including Keo's twenty-two-footer. Personally, with the bigger and more powerful vessels the soldiers had arrived in, Keo would have dumped his, but Steve had other plans. Like the one Jack had come in yesterday, Steve's was an equal-size offshore model with two engines in the back.

Steve had, he told Keo, approached Santa Marie Island last night using trolling motors to escape detection. Just that alone made him much smarter than all the other "soldiers" Keo had met the last few months, including the poor bastards that had assaulted Song Island.

Once they put him inside Steve's boat, Donovan zip tied his ankles back up and placed him on a bench up front alongside Gene.

"You okay?" Keo asked the kid.

Gene gave him a nervous smile. "Yeah, you?"

"My eyes still sting a little."

"Mine, too."

"Can we get some water?" Keo asked Steve, standing behind them at the console.

"No," Steve said. "Consider it punishment for shooting my little brother in the leg. Now shut up and enjoy the ride."

Taylor piloted Keo's twenty-two-footer, while Jack and Horace followed behind them on the second offshore vessel.

They cruised along Galveston Bay for a while before Keo spotted civilization in the distance and what looked like a fairground to the left of a channel. Carnival rides, including a Ferris wheel and a large red round structure, jutted out from behind a long boardwalk next to the bay. He imagined the place teeming with tourists on the weekends, a far cry from the ghost town it had become.

There was always something sad about seeing a once-thriving city abandoned, left to tilt against the wind and the elements. How long would these rides stay up? Maybe another year. Maybe a decade. That would probably depend on their construction, he guessed. That red thing, whatever the hell it was, looked like it could last a few more decades before tumbling back down to earth.

If there was once thriving life to the left of the channel, there wasn't much on the right side. He glimpsed warehouses, businesses, and overgrown fields of grass spread across undeveloped land. The juxtaposition of the two areas was stunning, and Keo found himself drawn back to the structures along the boardwalk to his left. Abandoned or not, at least there was a lot to look at over there.

They cruised through the channel, passing silent buildings and sun-bleached parking lots still filled with vehicles. It wasn't until they went underneath a highway that stretched across the channel that they finally saw a shipyard. It covered a huge chunk of the water and was spread out to both sides. The multitude of open slips told him hundreds of boats had once called this place home. Where were all those boats now? At the bottom of the bay, probably. Maybe the vessel he was riding in now was one of the lucky few survivors.

After the shipyard, it became a series of turns and empty houses and buildings and more (though much smaller) docks with empty slips. Keo lost track of how many times they eased around a bend, and each time he thought they might have reached their destination, they kept going. The path was wide enough that Donovan felt at ease keeping their boat moving at a reasonable speed. At this point, the soldiers had probably traversed this same area so many times it would have been second nature to them by now. To Keo, one stretch of water and empty parking lots and the wooded areas that surrounded them looked like the dozen others they had passed in the last hour. He stopped trying to make sense of his scenery after a while.

One thing was certain: They were getting further inland.

Donovan didn't slow down until they had slipped under a large highway that ran west to east. Signs told him it was Interstate 45, with Galveston back east and Houston, along with the rest of Texas, to the west. Once they went under the I-45, the river began narrowing and thick patches of woods sprouted up to both sides of them.

Keo knew they were getting close to their destination when he started seeing men in black uniforms moving among the trees to their right. Sentries. They were all very well-armed, and a few of them waved to the boats. Donovan and Steve waved back.

Soon, the soldiers gave way to civilians along the riverbanks. Like the soldiers, they were concentrated only on the right side. A dozen or so women were washing clothes against the rocks while half-naked kids jumped into the water, which had to be cold given the falling temperature. Keo was reminded of documentaries about frontier times, before washing machines and dryers were invented.

The people waved excitedly at them as they passed by. He had to look long and hard before he could conclude that they either wanted to be here, or they were really good actors.

"What are they doing?" Gene asked, straining to see the women—and they were almost all women, except for the children —off the boat's starboard.

"Washing clothes," Keo said.

"I've never seen that before."

"That's how people used to wash clothes before washing machines."

"No, not that," Gene said. "Her."

He was pointing at a young woman standing further up on the bank holding a laundry basket and talking to a couple of older women as they scrubbed clothes against some boulders. She had a noticeable belly, but it wasn't because she was fat.

She was pregnant.

Now that he had seen one, it was easier to spot others. Two more women who also looked pregnant, though not nearly as far along as the first one.

He thought about Carrie and Lorelei; the girls had fled one of the collaborator towns and had ended up at Song Island with him.

"*It's not the sex,*" Carrie had told him. "*It's what happens afterward. With the babies. You understand, right? Why we couldn't stay? Why we ran?*"

Because the babies didn't belong to the women who would give birth to them; they would belong to the ghouls, to continuing the cycle of humans supplying blood to the creatures for years, decades, and generations to come. That was the foundation of an "agreement," the why and how towns like T18 existed in the first place, because the people here—the women washing clothes by hand, the children swimming in the river—had come voluntarily. They had agreed. Sanctuary and safety, in exchange for human slavery.

Keo wasn't entirely sure what he was feeling. He had heard the stories and believed them, but to actually see it in person was an entirely different universe. Part of him didn't blame them for choosing this path, but the other part, the one that had kept him alive this last year, felt a bit sick to his stomach.

He glanced back at Steve, standing next to Donovan behind the center console. "Why am I here?" he asked, shouting over the roar of the double motors to be heard.

Steve didn't answer, and for a moment Keo thought the man hadn't heard him. He seemed preoccupied with waving back to a couple of kids that were chasing after the boat along the banks, as if Steve were some kind of returning hero.

"Why am I here?" Keo asked again, shouting louder this time.

"You'll find out," Steve shouted back.

"I'd like to know now."

"I bet you would, but you'll find out when I decide you can find out. And not a moment sooner."

"They look so happy," Gene said next to him. He looked

mesmerized by the sight of the women and children. "Are they really that happy? Is this real?"

"I don't know," Keo said.

"They look so happy," Gene said again.

Don't be fooled, Keo was going to tell the kid, when he caught a glimpse of a figure among the civilians on the riverbanks.

A woman, and something about her seized his attention. It helped that she was standing up just as their boat passed, and she was clearly taller than the other women around her, which made her stick out even further.

Keo shot up from the bench, wobbly on his feet because of his zip-tied ankles, and looked back at her until they locked eyes over the river.

She was moving up the riverbanks, trying to keep up with them, but there were just too many people in her way, and a few seconds later she disappeared behind some tall trees.

After all this time, all these months and uncertainty, there she was, still as breathtakingly beautiful as the day he sent her away on Mark's boat, hoping to save her life.

Gillian.

SEVEN

They had taken over a small city called Wilmont and turned it into T18. The place was separated into two parts, with a residential district and a commercial area connected by a wide steel bridge further up the river. As far as Keo could tell, the left side of Wilmont was abandoned, with the civilians (and Steve's men) congregating entirely on the right side.

And among those civilians was Gillian.

She had seen him too, he was certain of it. They might have locked eyes for just a brief second or two, but the way she had looked back at him, following the path of the boat, he could tell she recognized him.

Gillian.

The fact that she was still alive, after all the ifs and maybes of the last six months, was the best news he could have hoped for, especially after the disaster that was Santa Marie Island. The problem was, he was still in zip ties and being boated away from her.

That left Keo to focus instead on his new surroundings.

The marina where they docked was tiny compared to the

shipyard they had passed earlier, but it had a full complement of boats, anywhere from thirty to forty of them (*So that's where all the boats went*), occupying almost all of the available slips. Heavily armed soldiers stood watch, with two stick figures moving along a walkway that ringed the top of a rocket-shaped water tower in the near distance.

They were led up the dock, with Taylor and Donovan (still carrying the MP5SD and Keo's pack, with all the silver bullets) up front. Keo watched Steve stop momentarily at a stainless steel metal box resting on a long pole just inside the parking lot, in front of the docks, and opened it. He took out the boat keys and hung them inside, then closed it—there was no lock, just a latch— and continued on.

Keo made a mental note of the box's location and, more importantly, its contents.

He saw mostly men standing guard along the length of the marina, and the last time he had seen this many near a shoreline, he was lobbing grenade rounds at them. When Keo saw men on horseback moving back and forth along the banks nearby, he nearly did a spit-take.

"What's the matter, you don't like horses?" Steve asked.

"I like horses just fine," Keo said. "It's the guys on top of them that bother me."

"Welcome to the new world order. You hear that?"

Keo listened for a moment. "What am I supposed to be hearing?"

"Nature. That's the whole point of this, you know. We're going back to our roots. That's what they want."

Keo didn't have to ask who "they" were. Different people might have different names for them—ghouls, nightcrawlers, bloodsuckers, creatures, even monsters—but they were always the same. *They.* That was all you really needed to say.

"You ever wondered why they want it like this?" Keo asked. "Taking us back to the Stone Age?"

"I know exactly why, and I'm good with it."

"It must be nice to care so little about your fellow human beings."

Steve chuckled. "Don't make me slap you again, Keo."

"We wouldn't want that now, would we? Especially me."

"That's a good boy."

They walked through a wide-open (and very empty) parking lot that took up a huge chunk of the marina and toward a pair of buildings to the right side of the grounds. Men milled around inside one of them, visible through open doors and windows. A large warehouse that looked like it could hold a handful of boats at one time squatted to one side of the buildings. Keo wondered what was inside. It probably wasn't boats...

"Expecting trouble?" Keo asked, looking around him at the armed men.

"You never know when you'll run into someone with a fancy German submachine gun," Steve said.

Keo grunted. "It's not that fancy."

"What's the matter, an American gun like the M4 isn't good enough for you?"

"I didn't know you were so patriotic, Steve."

"Rah rah, and all that jazz."

They were heading toward one of the two buildings next to the warehouse. Someone had spray painted "Marina 1" and "Marina 2" on the walls.

"Your boys look a little on edge," Keo said.

"Nothing we can't handle," Steve said. They stopped in front of the buildings and Steve nodded at Taylor and Jack. "Take the kid to Processing." And to Donovan and Horace, "The two of you with me."

Steve pulled open the door and stepped inside Marina 1.

Behind Keo, Taylor was leading Gene away while Jack waved one of the soldiers on horseback over. Gene looked over at Keo, and if he expected to see fear in the teenager's eyes, he would have been disappointed. Gene looked almost happy, as if he had come home.

"See you around, Gene," Keo said.

"Yeah, see you around, Keo," Gene said.

Jack had traded places with the horseman and had tossed his crutches to Taylor. "Save them for me, just in case." He looked over at Keo. "Don't worry about the kid. Look at him. Once he sees what T18 has to offer, he's never going to want to leave. They never do."

Jack turned the horse around and galloped off, while Taylor led Gene after him.

"Come on," Donovan said, and poked Keo in the back with the M4 again.

Keo followed Steve into Marina 1.

It was an office suite, with a big desk where a secretary would have sat and a row of empty cheap plastic chairs along the walls for the guests. A dead plant draped over the side of a faded brown pot and magazines were strewn along a chipped table. Keo walked across dirty, heavily mud-caked tiled flooring and into a back hallway that Steve had disappeared into earlier.

They walked all the way to the end before Donovan said, "Inside," and gave him another shove in the back with the same barrel.

He stepped inside, expecting Donovan to follow, but the man instead turned around and headed back to the waiting area.

Steve had already made himself comfortable inside a nice big office. The place looked heavily lived in, with a blanket and pillows on a pullout sofa along one wall and empty plastic bottles of water littering the corners.

The older man was pulling up the lone window, letting the

cool breeze from the river rush inside. He looked comfortable, like a king in his (shabby) throne room. "Have a seat, Keo."

Keo sat down on a surprisingly comfortable chair in front of a desk, its laminated surface covered with a large and heavily annotated map of the area that finally allowed him to see T18/Wilmont in relation to the rest of the Gulf Coast. They were on the outskirts of League City, on the other side of the I-45 highway. A long river, like the slithering body of a snake, stretched from T18 all the way to Galveston Bay.

Steve walked back over. "I saw that."

"What's that?"

"You looking at the map." He smirked. "You think you've committed enough important details to memory?"

Keo smiled. "You give me too much credit. My memory is shit. I was just trying to figure out where I was."

"Ah," Steve said, though he clearly didn't believe a single word Keo had said.

The man sat down on an executive chair and opened one of the drawers and produced a half-full bottle of Jack Daniels, then grabbed two shot glasses from another drawer. Keo watched him expertly pour the Tennessee whiskey into both glasses before sliding one across the desk.

"To your health," Steve said, and downed his.

Keo hissed as his went down. Even as he was tilting the glass to his lips with his still zip-tied hands, he briefly considered using it to bash Steve's head in and grab his weapons, including the M4 Steve had leaned against the wall behind him.

"It's been a while, huh?" Steve said with a grin, watching him closely. *Too* closely. It was going to be tough to catch Steve off-balance.

"I'm more of a brandy man."

"I can see that. A world traveler like you."

"How you figure?"

"Oh, come on. You're not from around here, we both know that. You couldn't find Pearland on a map if I put a gun to your head."

"What is that, a city made of pears?"

"Cute." He poured himself another glass and offered Keo another one too, but Keo waved him off. "You should learn to appreciate American whiskey. There's nothing like it, especially now. Soon, there won't be Americans anymore. No Europeans or Asians or blacks and whites and Mexicans, either. They'll just be humans and nonhumans."

"Oh, I don't know about that. I think they'll always be Asians and blacks and whites to some people."

"Neanderthals," Steve said, and emptied his second glass with a flick of his wrist.

"I didn't know you were such a progressive fella, Steve."

A chuckle. Keo couldn't tell if that was the whiskey talking or if Steve really was an easygoing guy. Of course, that easygoing guy had given him a nice slap last night for absolutely no reason. Okay, so there was a reason, but it was far from justified.

"I'm pragmatic," Steve said. "It's just us and them now. The faster the human race accepts our new position on the totem pole, the easier it'll be for us as a species to move forward. We're obviously the second-class citizens at the moment. All of us. That's fine, someone has to be. But there are classes within classes. People who embrace that get to keep on keeping on."

Keo looked out the window as two armed men in black uniforms walked the riverbanks behind Steve. "You need that many guns to keep on keeping on, Steve?"

"Can't be helped. We have a bit of a problem, you see." Steve leaned slightly across the table. "You wanna hear about it?"

"Do I have a choice?"

Steve shrugged.

"Gee, Steve, what kind of problem do you have?" Keo asked,

with all the enthusiasm of a man being forced to recite a line at gunpoint.

Steve smiled. "I like you."

"I don't blame you. I'm a likable guy."

"Was that before or after this?" he asked, tracing the left side of his face with his finger.

"Scars give a man personality. You should try it."

"I'll stick to looking handsome." He leaned back in his chair. "So, this problem of mine. You see, everyone here's gotten with the program, but not everyone out there has. I still have people running around causing trouble."

"Like me?"

"Nah, you're just a straggler."

"And that's a good thing?"

"I put people who haven't gotten with the reality of our situation into two categories: The ones that don't know any better, and the ones that are determined to make things miserable for everyone else. You belong in the former category."

"Yay for me."

"Then, of course, there are the ones in the latter category. They're the reasons my men have to guard the marina and the bridge and the surrounding areas every second of daylight. Obviously we don't have to worry about the nights."

"Obviously."

Steve offered to pour him another glass, but Keo turned it down again. "So that's my dilemma," Steve said, pouring himself a third shot. "I have people I need to take care of—the ones here, who depend on me and my men—but there are troublemakers out there making it difficult. That's where you come in."

"I didn't know this was a job interview."

"It is. Consider it your last job interview."

"How so?"

"If you don't pass, I shoot you."

Keo smirked. "I guess I better pass, then."

"I would think so."

"So what's the job?"

"Jack told me what you did on that island. That was impressive."

"I had help."

"The kid?"

"Yeah."

"The kid shot Jack from the ridge when no one knew he was up there. I saw that scope on his rifle. A half-blind coal miner could have made that shot. And he actually missed. He was aiming for Jack's chest. You, on the other hand, went at two of my guys straight on with nothing but that German gun. That takes a lot of guts. And skill."

"You don't care that I killed two of yours?"

"I care, but I can respect that you did what you had to do. Besides, plenty more where they came from."

"Classes within classes, right?"

Steve nodded while eyeing Keo over the rim of his glass. "That's right. And right now, I need a man like you, Keo."

"To do what?"

"To do what you do."

"You'll have to be a little more specific. I do a lot of things. Some of them even involve whipped cream."

"Unfortunately I'm all out of whipped cream, but I do have Gillian."

Keo smiled back, doing his very best not to betray his thoughts. He remembered waking up on Santa Marie Island to find Gene and Steve talking. They had been for some time, too. Now he knew what the topic of conversation had been.

"You don't look surprised," Steve said. "I guess you saw us talking this morning. Don't blame him; he's just a kid. What is he, seventeen?"

"I thought he was sixteen."

"Either/or. Doesn't matter, I guess. These days, you have to grow up fast or you don't grow up at all."

Steve finished his third glass and put it down softly. The man's hand, Keo saw, was steady. *Too* steady, even after three shots.

"Back to you and Gillian," Steve said.

"What about me and Gillian?"

"That was her, wasn't it? On the riverbanks while we were coming up? Come on, don't deny it. The way you stood up and stared." He put a hand to his chest and grinned. "It was so romantic."

Keo remained as stone-faced as possible but internally cursed himself for giving it away on the boat. He should have known someone like Steve would have noticed.

He had to be careful around Steve. Very, very careful.

"The kid described her to me, and it was a no-brainer to put two and two together," Steve continued. "I still remember the day she showed up. Hard to forget someone like that. Tall, black hair, and green eyes? Not a lot of those around these days. We caught her on a boat just off Galveston."

"Just her?"

"There were others, but to hear the boys tell it, they tried to fight back and, well, bad things happen when you fight back. She survived, though, and we brought her here. That was...hmm..." He was either really thinking about it or was doing a good job of selling it. "Five months ago? Maybe six? Processing has all the information, if you're curious."

"Maybe I can ask her myself."

"Maybe." The man was watching him closely, reading every flicker of emotion on his face. "She's gorgeous. I can see why you spent all this time trying to find her. I would, too."

Keo leaned forward and pushed his glass back toward Steve, who smiled and refilled it.

"So what's the job?" Keo asked.

"Right to the point? Fine. I need you to do something for me. Do this one thing, and you can either stay here with Gillian or take her and run off to...wherever. I personally don't think there's anything better out there, but hey, it's still a free country."

"Is it?"

Steve gave him a noncommittal shrug. Keo picked up the refilled shot glass and sipped the whiskey. It went down easier the second time.

"What's the job?" he asked again.

"I need you to kill someone for me," Steve said.

Keo smiled.

The more things changed, the more they stayed the same. Even at the end of the world, there were still people who wanted him to take away other people's lives for their own purposes. Except this time Gillian was the payment.

Hell, he'd done worse for less.

"Who's the target?" Keo asked.

"What do you need?" Steve asked.

"My guns," Keo said.

"And?"

"That's it."

"That's it?"

"I'm a very simple guy. Have gun, will assassinate."

Steve chuckled. "So I was right about you. You were born for this. Even before the world went to shit."

"Some people can play the piano, I can do this. So who's the target?"

"His name's Tobias. He's the reason I have men on the bridge and at the marina, and sentries all around town. He's a real pain in my ass."

"He's alone?"

"No. He has some men with him."

"How many is 'some'?"

"Maybe as few as a couple, and maybe as many as a dozen."

"A dozen is manageable."

"Is that right?"

"I've gone up against worse odds."

"Well, shit, you really are a bad man, aren't you?" Steve laughed. "Glad you're on my side."

For now, asshole.

"One thing," Keo said.

"What's that?"

"I want to see Gillian first."

Steve shook his head. "Can't do that."

"Why not?"

"You may have agreed to the job, but you haven't earned my trust yet, Keo. You're not going anywhere past this marina until I know I can absolutely trust you not to screw me over."

"So tie me at the hip to Donovan."

"You'll probably kill Donovan if he ever got that close to you."

Keo smiled. He had to admit, Steve had a good point. Given how many times Donovan had unnecessarily prodded him with the barrel of his rifle, Keo would have liked nothing more than to get him just a little bit closer and return the favor.

"At least let me talk to her," Keo said.

"You already saw her on the riverbanks. She's fine. Better than fine."

"I see her in person, or no deal."

Steve pulled out his sidearm—an impossibly smooth and polished Colt 1911 series semiautomatic—and laid it on the desk with a heavy *thunk!*, then glared across at Keo. "I have a better idea. You keep pushing me on this and I put a bullet in her leg. She doesn't need two legs to wash clothes. What do you think?"

Keo stared back at him.

Steve didn't move, didn't look away, and didn't flinch.

Fuck.

"Yeah, okay," Keo said. "So where do I find your friend Tobias?"

Steve picked the gun up and slid it back into its holster. He didn't laugh or grin like an idiot, and his face remained perfectly unmoved. Keo had absolutely no doubt the man would have shot Gillian just to spite him, which further convinced him that the only way he was going to survive T18 was over Steve's dead body.

I can live with that.

"Jack will brief you on everything we know about him," Steve said before glancing at his watch. "You have seven hours and thirty minutes to find Tobias, put a bullet in his head, and get back here before sundown."

"What if I don't make it back before nightfall?"

"Then I guess you better find a nice and safe place to hide until morning."

EIGHT

"You're really good at that," Keo said. "You raised on a farm or something?"

Jack chuckled from his horse's saddle. "Conroe, Texas. We had more fish than horses out there. I guess I've had a lot of practice."

"You boys been here long?"

"Long enough to be one of the original guys that had to clean up the houses for all the new arrivals. Let me tell you, that's grunt work I'd rather not do again."

"Who gets the houses?"

"The worthy ones."

"Like you?"

"Like I said: The worthy ones. That can be you too, if you play your cards right."

"You mean if I can find Tobias, kill him, manage to get away, and return to the town still breathing."

"I thought all of that was implied."

"Hard to tell with you, Jack, on account of your propensity for lying."

"A guy's gotta do what a guy's gotta do."

I'll keep that in mind for next time, dickhead.

"You can do this," Jack was saying. He sounded almost encouraging, for a dickhead. "Steve says he's pretty sure you used to do something like this back in the day."

"What did Steve use to do...back in the day?"

"He was a cop. A detective. A pretty good one, too. Smart. Why do you think he's running the show around here?"

"I thought it was because of his charming personality."

"It ain't that charming."

For a guy with one bad leg, Jack was easygoing, being a dickhead notwithstanding. Then again, he was riding on a horse while Keo had to walk next to him up the length of the bridge that connected T18 and the rest of what used to be the city of Wilmont. It was midday and would have been peaceful if not for the loud, echoing *clop-clop-clop* of horseshoes against the steel floor.

A pair of soldiers with binoculars keeping a constant watch on both sides of the river barely paid them any attention as they walked past. There were four soldiers on the bridge, including two manning a guard station on the right lane, leaving just the left open for back and forth travel. The setup was really just two large desks stacked with sandbags underneath a camo canopy that provided plenty of shade. What Keo really paid attention to was the M60 machine gun perched between the two men.

Four men on a bridge were not nearly enough to keep T18 from invasion, but that probably wasn't the point. The men were just a buffer, with more soldiers manning a swinging metal gate behind them. The figures he had seen earlier moving around the ringed walkway of the water tower were still there, further down the river. Now that was a hell of a perch, and likely one he'd have to evade or take out first if he ever expected to escape the town.

"Have they ever tried to attack the bridge?" Keo asked.

"They're too smart for that," Jack said. "Why do you think they've been giving us so much trouble? If they were stupid, Steve would have snuffed them out a long time ago."

Keo looked up at Jack. The younger Miller was eyeing the other side of the bridge as if he expected the mysterious Tobias to be lying in wait for him. The full extent of Jack's "briefing" had involved pointing out the last spot they had skirmished with Tobias's group and what the man looked like. Tall, blond, blue eyes, and formidable. He might as well be describing Captain America.

"You respect him," Keo said. "Tobias."

"You have to respect the enemy in order to effectively fight him."

"One of Steve's sayings?"

Jack grinned but didn't deny or confirm.

They stopped next to the guard station in the middle of the bridge. The steel structure extended about fifty meters from side to side and about fifteen meters above the water. Keo couldn't see much of anything on the other end except a two-lane country road flanked by walls of trees. The city's main commercial district was supposed to be beyond that. As with the right side, the left half of what used to be Wilmont was surrounded by thick woods.

And somewhere out there was Tobias.

"This is where you get off," Jack said. He picked up the duffel bag lying across his saddle and handed it down to Keo. "Do us both a favor and don't open it until you're on the other side. You know, in case the boys here get itchy fingers. It's been a while since they've shot anything, so you don't wanna tempt them."

"Heaven forbid," Keo said, and slung the bag over his shoulder. It was heavy, which was a good sign.

He glanced at his watch: 12:15 p.m. Just over six hours until nightfall.

"You sure you don't want something with more firepower for

the job?" Jack asked. "Not too late. I can ask one of these boys to let you borrow their M4."

"It's not the size of the gun, Jack; it's the finger behind the trigger."

"Is that what you tell the ladies?"

"I do just fine with the ladies."

"I bet. I've met Gillian, by the way. I can see why you'd be willing to take this job just to get back to her. She's something."

"Yes, she is."

"You've tapped that before, right?"

Keo didn't answer.

"Of course you have," Jack smiled. "Why else would you be running around out here doing Steve's bidding. Must have been some—"

"Watch yourself."

Jack chuckled. "Fair enough." Then, "Well, good luck, sport, because you're going to need it. Tobias is a hard man to find and a harder man to kill. But after seeing what you did back at Santa Marie, I'm sure you're more than up for the job."

"Tell me something," Keo said, looking up at Jack.

"What's on your mind?"

"You always knew your brother was going to come looking for you, didn't you? That's why you never tried to escape yesterday."

"We're brothers. That's what we do; look out for one another." He picked up the reins and was about to turn the horse around when he paused, adding, "Oh, one piece of advice. When you get Tobias in your crosshairs, don't hesitate. You're probably only going to get one shot at him."

Jack galloped off, the *clop-clop-clop* of horseshoes against the steel bridge like gunshots.

Keo started walking. He didn't bother looking back because he could feel the men behind the sandbags manning the M60 watching him closely. The thought of being on the wrong side of that monster when it unleashed its full fury made him shiver slightly.

About three kilometers from the bridge, Keo came upon the first sign of civilization—a shopping center with sun-baked concrete floors and gray buildings that had been stripped of most of their signs. A slight wind moved through broken storefront windows without resistance, and overgrown grass swayed against the edges of the expansive and mostly spacious parking lot.

The sight of the abandoned stores and the few dirt-covered cars around him was like stepping through a portal in time, a reminder that he was living through the end of civilization as he knew it. He couldn't even summon the curiosity to search the buildings for hints to Tobias's whereabouts. It was all incredibly depressing, and Keo quickened his steps to get through the lot as fast as possible. Besides, there was little chance Tobias would leave clues this close to T18.

All things considered, this was one of his better days. He'd found Gillian, and that alone made up for everything else. It felt as if someone had lifted a 500-pound safe off his chest. He was optimistic for the first time in a long time, and it made leaving Carrie behind on the *Trident* easier to stomach.

He was almost giddy as he flattened his finger against the trigger guard of the MP5SD hanging from a sling in front of him. Having the submachine gun back was another major plus, and Jack had even been nice enough to return his pack intact, including the spare magazines and his gun belt with the silver bullet-loaded Glock. From the way the younger Miller had simply handed the bag full of weapons over, Keo guessed his captors hadn't bothered to pay very close attention to his supplies. Either that, or finding guys loaded with silver rounds wasn't anything new to them, which Keo doubted.

The only thing he was missing was food and water. Apparently they expected him to find his own rations out here. Or maybe that was just another incentive to hurry up, finish the job, and return to T18.

Not that he needed more incentive, with Gillian back there...

He was grinning to himself like an idiot when something small but fast—incredibly fast—hit the parking lot about two feet in front of him and chipped concrete flicked at his face like little bees.

Sniper! Shit!

Keo darted out of the open and slid against an old Chevy minivan with peeling white paint that, thank God, was just a few feet away. He was trying to come to grips with the absence of a gunshot as he pressed against the dirty vehicle when the back windshield to the left side of his head exploded. Except this time he heard the subsonic round as it shattered the glass and punched its way into the floor of the car behind him.

He dropped into a crouch and hurried toward the front, waiting for a third shot that didn't come. He reached the driver-side door, ignored it, and rounded the front bumper until he was leaning against the dirty grill of the Chevy.

He waited again for more follow-up shots, but nothing was exploding around him, so he assumed the guy didn't have a clear shot. That meant his position in front of the minivan was good, which in turn translated to the shooter being somewhere behind him.

Keo recalled the layout of the area in his head.

There was an Archers Sports and Outdoors next to what looked like a pizza place featuring some guy in a toga, and a dozen or so other businesses that he hadn't paid very much attention to. One of them might have been an insurance place and the other was—

The Archers. It had to be the Archers.

Whoever it was, he was using a rifle with a suppressor, because Keo hadn't even heard either one of the two gunshots. That was hard to do with a rifle. Even the best suppressors left some kind of noise, especially against the nearly silent backdrop of a dead world. Firing from a high angle, which any sniper worth his salt would be doing, would increase the possibility of noise. And yet he hadn't heard a single peep when the first bullet nearly took his head off.

He was pretty sure the shooter was on top of the Archers directly behind him, about one hundred meters across the parking lot. There was nothing but a lot of open ground between him and the store. Oh sure, there were a few cars sprinkled here and there, like the minivan that had saved his life, but not nearly enough of them for one hundred meters' worth of safety.

Still, he had to be sure.

Keo stood up quickly, turning around and looking through the dirt-speckled front windshield of the Chevy and out the exposed rear area and across the parking lot at the Archers—

The man saw him almost at the same time Keo spotted him, perched along the edge of the sports store. Sunlight glinted off the long barrel of the rifle as it twitched, and Keo dropped back down as the round pierced the windshield and *zipped!* a few inches over his head.

Too close!

Okay, so now he knew exactly where the guy was. On top of the Archers, just as he had guessed.

So how was he going to use that information?

He had no idea. It wasn't like he could counterattack, even if he desperately wanted to. Keo had never been the kind of person to take being shot at lying down. But one hundred meters was probably ninety meters too many, and as pissed off as he was at the moment, he wanted to stay alive even more—especially now that he had found Gillian.

The shooter clearly had a good scope on top of his rifle. Or maybe not. He did miss the first shot, didn't he? Then again, he'd only missed by two feet...

Maybe, maybe not.

Keo sat on the concrete pavement, which was curiously both hot and cold against his butt. He didn't really have much of a choice at the moment. He could run or fight, and fighting seemed like a lost cause. Besides, he had other fish to fry. One named Tobias, to be very specific.

Yes, the sniper had him pinned behind the minivan, but it was difficult shooting a moving target from across an entire parking lot. The guy would have to be pretty good, and he had already proven that he wasn't, even if that last shot had come dangerously close.

He knew one thing for sure: He definitely couldn't stay here forever. Even if the shooter didn't have reinforcements—though the chances of him being out here alone were pretty slim, especially this close to T18—Keo was working against the clock. He had less than six hours to find and kill Tobias and return to town. Failing that...

Failure is not an option.

Unless you fail.

He smirked to himself, then glanced down at his watch.

Did he say six hours? It was more like five.

Time flies when people are shooting at you.

There wasn't very much to the right and left of him, and behind him were the stores. His only choice was forward, back toward the same long stretch of road that had brought him here from the bridge in the first place. On the other side were a couple of large warehouses, hard to miss given their size, their front yards like jungles. There was nothing behind them but woods.

Thick woods. He could easily get lost in there. If he made it across alive, that was. But his best option at the moment was to lengthen the distance between him and the shooter. The problem with that was, the warehouses were at least another hundred meters away. That was a hell of a long distance to run, even if the guy had proven not to be a world-class marksman.

The things I do for you, Gillian.

He sighed and rose from the ground.

Keo counted to five, but on *three* decided to play a trick on himself and pushed off the grill of the Chevy and ran forward as fast as he could. His pack thumped against his back as he began zig-zagging, hoping to make getting a bead on him more difficult.

It seemed to work when the first two shots went wide—one landing to his right, the other to his left.

At the twenty-meter mark, Keo decided to run straight for a while before breaking off and going right for another fifteen. Each time he changed directions, the shooter had a hard time keeping up, and three more shots missed him by wide margins. Keo started noticing that each round was falling further behind him, which meant the guy was having difficulty adjusting.

The sniper finally stopped shooting—or at least the ground stopped exploding around him—when Keo successfully crossed the road and entered the overgrown lawn of the closest warehouse. He passed a sign with a guy holding a welder's torch, but he was moving too fast to read the company name.

The large twin doors into the building had been pried open long ago, leaving a gaping hole for Keo to easily slip through without the need to break his stride. A good thing, because as soon as he darted out of the open there was a loud *pang!* as a bullet ricocheted off the metal wall behind him.

A little late there, aren't you, pal?

The interior was steel walls and roof and solid concrete floors. Heavy machinery lined the cavernous room, which actually looked much bigger inside, and the ground was sticky with year-old oil spills and God knew what else. Every step he took produced a *squeaking* sound that echoed (too loudly) off the walls. The air was musky and smelled of chemicals, more oil, and a lot of grease. He couldn't find any evidence as to what the warehouse had been used for once upon a time, and as he hurried through it toward the back, he guessed it didn't really matter.

It was just another old relic of the past, like Santa Marie Island, like the boardwalk and fairground at the channel and the strip mall with the sniper behind him. No one was going to come in here anymore except guys like him looking for shelter, and soon nature would reclaim this area. He'd be surprised if he could even still see the warehouse in ten, maybe twenty years. Unlike back at the shopping center, there were no concrete parking lots to keep the woods at bay on this side of the street.

It took a while given the size of the building, but finally he reached the other end and made a beeline toward a steel back door. The lever was covered in black gunk that might have been oil or grease or a combination of the two—or possibly something else entirely. He was reaching for it when there was a *crack!* and a round *ping!* off the metal surface, ricocheting into an assembly line machine behind and to the right of him.

Keo spun and fired back without aiming, or really knowing what he was shooting at. He was also darting left when more than one rifle opened up in return.

The sound of unsuppressed gunfire inside the warehouse was deafening, and they were quickly joined by the multiple *pings!* of bullets bouncing off walls and machinery around him, every single one of them seemingly trying to track him down.

Out of the frying pan and into the bonfire.

Daebak.

NINE

They stopped shooting only after he had made it behind cover. Through the fading echoes of ricocheting bullets, Keo picked up the loud *squeaking* of shoes from the front of the warehouse. That told him there was definitely more than one shooter, but he had already figured that part out when they unloaded on him.

It couldn't have been the sniper. There was no way that guy could have gotten down from the Archers and crossed the parking lot so fast. Which left him with what? Maybe those reinforcements he was sure the man must have had waiting in the wings, finally arriving. A sniper left behind to watch the road and lie in wait for Steve's people would be armed with a two-way radio so he could relay information about enemy movements.

He'd waited too long, giving the shooter the time to call in his friends. It had to be Tobias's people. Of course, Jack hadn't said anything about an ambush at the first hint of civilization, but then again, that was Jack. Lying Jack. Or, in this case, information-hiding Jack.

Dickhead Jack.

"Spread out!" someone shouted.

A male voice. Deep. Keo wondered what the chances were that he was hearing Steve's best friend Tobias giving orders.

Right. Like your luck's that good, pal.

Hard metal poked into his back. Part of some kind of manufacturing equipment. He'd never spent a day of his life inside a warehouse working an assembly line, so the shape pressing into him was just another mystery he didn't have any interest in exploring. It was cold and heavy and easily stopped bullets, and that was all he really cared about.

"Hey!" the same voice shouted. "You still alive back there?"

The man was still near the very front of the warehouse, which was of course part of an elaborate trick to divert his attention. The man's "friends," the ones ordered to spread out earlier, were moving slowly in his direction right now. Keo could hear their shoes *squeaking* against the grease and oil and God-knew-what-else covered floors as they did their best to move silently.

Not quite silent enough, boys.

Keo leaned out the right side of the bulky object behind him and saw two men moving steadily up in his direction, almost hugging the wall. They were half-crouched, half-walking, and were still a good forty meters away when he spotted them. They were both wearing sneakers and civilian clothes, and he swore one of them had on a Houston Rockets cap, though they were in a dark patch of the warehouse and he didn't get a clear look at them.

When they saw him peeking out, their reaction was priceless. It was like looking at two deer caught in a car's headlights.

That lasted for about half a second before one of them snapped off a shot while the other darted behind something shiny for cover. The round *pinged!* off whatever it was Keo was leaning out from behind, forcing him back behind cover. He stuck his MP5SD out and squeezed off a short burst up the warehouse, heard the satisfying *ping! ping!* as his rounds bounced off something solid.

Hopefully that would send them scurrying back. Or, at least, halt their advance.

"Make this easy on yourself!" the same man shouted, his words booming off the steel walls and high ceiling. Despite the distance between them, the ensuing echo meant Keo didn't have to strain to hear him. "There's no way out of here! I got people on the other side of that door, too. You're trapped!"

Keo sighed. And here he had been hoping to eventually make a run for the back door and slip out into the woods the first chance he got. Then again, people tended to lie a lot these days. Jack was proof of that. So what was to keep this other guy—

The lever on the back door moved up and down, but it was locked and whoever was on the other side gave up on opening it a few seconds later.

Or not.

"Come on now!" the man shouted. "You gotta know you're trapped. Don't prolong the inevitable!"

"What do you want?" Keo shouted back.

He figured he didn't have anything to lose. Maybe, if he was lucky (*Yeah, right*) one of them was Tobias. If so, that would make his job a lot easier. Well, maybe not easier, easier. But definitely cut down on all that time he was going to have to spend looking for his target, something he thought might take a while. Like a day or two...or a week.

"*He's out there, somewhere,*" was all Jack had been able to tell him about Tobias's whereabouts.

Yeah, thanks for that, Jack, you lying piece of shit.

"I want you to come out!" the man shouted.

He sounded much closer than before, but Keo was trying to keep tabs on the *squeaking* shoes instead of concentrating on the voice. That was a diversion, and had been from the very beginning. The shoes, on the other hand, didn't lie, and they were definitely getting closer. They were also coming along the walls to both the right and left of him, but of course he could hear the ones to his right much clearer because of proximity. His spray-and-pray earlier might have forced them behind cover, but it hadn't lasted.

How long did he have? Not long enough.

Running out of time again. So what else is new?

"And then what?" Keo shouted back.

"We can talk!" the man said.

"You wanna talk?"

"Yes!"

"So why'd you start shooting?"

"That was a mistake!"

"No shit! The sniper out there, he one of yours?"

"Maybe!"

Keo grinned. "I'm not from Texas, but is everyone in this state a fucking liar?"

The man actually chuckled that time.

Keo listened past it for the familiar *squeaking* of footsteps, but failed to find one. That was disturbing, because there was no reason for them to stop their advance. They had him cornered like a rat inside the warehouse.

And time was running out. Sooner or later, it'd be dark. That was the other problem. The always-over-his-shoulder problem.

Sooner or later, it was always going to be dark.

"Depends on who you talk to!" the man was shouting back.

"What do you want?" Keo shouted.

"You already asked that!"

"Try telling the truth this time!"

"God's honest truth! We just want to ask you some questions!"

"Oh yeah? Is that all?"

"Yup!"

He leaned out the side of the machine, ready to fire, but there wasn't anyone in the open. He pulled back, then looked across the warehouse to the other side. Nobody there, either. Maybe they really were going to wait him out. Hell, that's what he would have done, too.

"What's got you so curious, my friend?" he shouted.

"You came from T18, didn't you?" the man asked.

The voice didn't sound any closer than before, which was another hint they might be content to wait him out instead of the more risky approach of bum-rushing him. So maybe they really were curious about him. Could he really stake his life on that, though?

"I get the feeling you already know the answer to that one!" Keo said. "Let me guess: You have lookouts?"

"Maybe!" the man said. "What are you doing out here by yourself, my friend?"

"So we're friends now?"

"Why not?"

"Friends don't shoot at friends!"

The man laughed. "Come on, how many times I gotta apologize for that?"

"How about one more time?"

"All right! Sorry about trying to kill you! Now, what are you doing out here all by yourself, buddy?"

"That's better! And the answer is, I was sightseeing!"

"Oh yeah?"

"Yup! Figured, what the hell? Maybe I could pick up some flowers for the old lady, too!"

"She waiting for you in T18?"

"That's right! You don't wanna stop me from coming back home with flowers, do you?"

"As a matter of fact, yes!"

THE ISLES OF ELYSIUM   105

"Well, shit, that's darn rude of you!"

The man laughed again.

Keo flicked the fire selector on the MP5SD to full-auto and took a breath.

The *squeaking* noises had picked back up again from his right. He could hear it coming from his left, too. They were getting closer, but not rushing it. They didn't have to, and they knew it.

Dammit. If it wasn't for shitty luck...

He'd found Gillian again, after so long of not being sure if she was even still alive. But there she was, on the riverbank, looking back at him. Beautiful. He couldn't see the green of her eyes over the distance, but he imagined them sparkling at the sight of him. Hopefully he didn't still look like he had just been tear gassed the night before. He wondered how he was going to explain all the other scars to her. The one along the left side of his face, in particular, was going to be a doozy.

"Remember those assholes from the cabin? Well, they had a leader, and he was determined to slice my face open."

Yeah, that should work.

He sighed again and slid up the length of the cold machine behind him and counted down to five. But this time, he would go the full five. No more surprising himself by going at three. Nossirree Bob—

Pop-pop-pop!

Automatic rifle fire, and it wasn't coming from inside the warehouse, either.

What the hell?

More than one firing at the same time, too, he was sure of it.

Pop-pop-pop! Pop-pop-pop!

A dozen. Maybe even more than that. There was a full-fledged gun battle going on outside the warehouse at this very moment.

Then, suddenly, the *brap-brap-brap!* of a machine gun raining death, the loud roar of the weapon drowning out everything else.

Jesus fucking Christ.

That was the M60. Which meant...

"It's a trap!" the same voice that had been trying to cajole him out of hiding shouted. "Everyone get the fuck out of here! It's a trap!"

The man hadn't finished screaming "trap" when the shriek of bullets punching through the warehouse's metal walls flooded the cavernous room. The *ping-ping-ping!* of bullets ricocheting off machinery around him, followed by screaming, then the very clear squawking of handheld radios blasting away with panicked voices.

Keo blocked out all the sounds—hard to do, with the M60 drowning the air in an unending tide—and focused on the back door in front of him. What were the chances there were still people on the other side? Now, with the hellacious gunfire pummeling everything in its path out in front of the warehouse? Would the ones out back rush to assist or flee? Or stand their ground? That would depend on how well-trained these guys were.

Whatever was out back—if anything—it was definitely better than being stuck in here among the flying bullets and the shrieks of people dying behind him.

"Ambush!" someone else was shouting. "It's an ambush!"

Screw it.

Keo didn't bother counting. He pushed off his hiding spot and ran forward and fired at the door. It took half of his magazine to demolish the door lever. That was way too many bullets, but it couldn't be helped because he had to make sure—

He kicked the door and it swung wide open, harsh sunlight blinding him momentarily.

Keo waited for gunfire as he exposed himself, but either the men who had tracked him into the warehouse were already dead or too busy fighting for their lives against the machine gun at the front, or they weren't paying him any attention.

He lunged out, thankful to be outside and breathing fresh air again. Hell, to be breathing at all. He was surrounded by grass that went up almost to his waist, and Keo began swimming through it and toward the wall of trees on the other end. He wasted a half second to consider taking a peek at the battle out front but decided he'd rather not be anywhere close to whoever was letting loose with the machine gun, or the poor saps on the wrong end of it.

The *brap-brap-brap* seemed unending, crushing everything else that might have made a sound, including the returning *pop-pop-pop* of assault rifle fire.

Give it up, boys, he wanted to tell them. *That's an M60. You're not going to win against that monster.*

Keo slipped into the woods, immediately feeling the drastic change in temperature as the high canopies blocked out most of the sun. That, more than anything, alarmed him, but he kept moving because the opposite direction was untenable at the moment.

Even safe beyond the tree lines, he could still hear the barrage of gunfire from behind him, until suddenly...it just stopped.

The M60 had gone quiet.

Maybe he was wrong after all. Maybe Tobias's men had managed to knock down the gunner—

Then it was back, louder and more ferocious than before, if that was even possible.

Or not.

It had to be Steve's people attacking. Maybe even the same guys back on the bridge, or they could have had more than one machine gun. It wouldn't surprise him, given the armaments the soldiers he'd met in Louisiana had been lugging around. The ones at Beaufont Lake had been armed with an M240, a more modern squad automatic weapon than the M60, but just as dangerous in the right hands. They also had what seemed like an unlimited number of military-grade M4s and the ammo to endlessly feed them.

The shooting continued nonstop behind him, but it had lessened in volume the further he waded into the woods. Keo might have felt sorry for the poor saps back at the warehouse if they hadn't been trying to kill him.

Sucks to be you, boys.

He kept moving, not really sure where he was going, just knowing that he didn't want to be anywhere close to the gun battle when the winners started spreading out and looking for survivors. Even if that was Steve's people back there, the fact that they had laid down a hellacious amount of lead meant they weren't very concerned about his safety. For all he knew, Steve might have sent him out here for the express purpose of drawing Tobias out.

Shit. Had Steve just dangled him out there as bait? So he could then charge in with his men and waste Tobias's people? *If* those were Tobias's men back there. For all Keo knew, they could have been more of the "stragglers" that annoyed Steve and just happened to have picked on the wrong victim.

There was no denying that those other shooters had shown up pretty fast, right about the time Keo found himself besieged inside the warehouse. So they were around the area, waiting for a sign, because they likely hadn't heard the sniper shooting earlier. Keo hadn't heard the gunshots, and he was the one being shot at. Anyone at the bridge, or the wooded area around it (or wherever the hell Steve's men had been hiding) wouldn't have heard a whimper. But those gunshots in the warehouse, on the other hand...

He stopped in his tracks.

The shooting behind him had ceased entirely, leaving a quiet lull that, even more than the sound of the M60 firing away, gave him goose bumps.

It was over, and Keo didn't have to think very hard about who had won.

What now? Carry on or go back to T18?

Did he even have much of a choice? Whatever Steve's game, walking back after that carnage was probably not going to end very favorably for him. No. The smart move here was to keep going, then decide what to do later when he had more intel.

He pushed on, even though he didn't have a clue where he was going and there wasn't anything resembling a trail for him to latch onto. It didn't take long for him to get flashbacks to another time and another place when he had spent way too many days inside a wooded area much like this one. Back then, he was being chased by a madman with a small army.

The more things changed...

He was thinking about Pollard, about Norris and Allie, when he stepped on a twig and it *snapped!* under one of his boots.

Keo paused and looked down just a split second before the wire sprung out from the ground, scattering dried leaves that had been camouflaging it, and slipped around his right leg. The razor-thin steel line dug into his ankle as it tightened and he was shot into the air like a rocket. The sky above him flipped until he was staring at the ground and Keo found himself hanging upside down from a tree.

He'd stepped right into a snare trap!

He scrambled for the MP5SD, but it was on the ground below him. He still had the Glock, and Keo was reaching for it when something hard and metallic pressed into the back of his neck, the rifle barrel cold against his exposed skin.

"Draw it, and you're a dead man," a voice said behind him.

Keo took his hand away from the Glock.

The figure scrambled around him in a wide circle, giving him plenty of space in case Keo had any ideas about grabbing for his weapon. He was a short man (or maybe he was actually tall, since it was a little difficult to tell proper height while hanging upside down) wearing green and brown hunting clothes, boots, and green and black camo paint on his face. Brown eyes peered out at Keo.

"This must be a Texas thing," Keo said.

"Shut up," the man said. He took out a radio with one hand and keyed it. "I got him. The guy from the warehouse."

"Bring him in," a woman answered through the radio. "He's got a lot to answer for."

"Maybe I should just shoot him."

The man was holding a large rifle with one hand. Like his face, the weapon was covered in a camo pattern. He cocked his head slightly to one side, one eye focused on Keo from behind his rifle's scope despite the short distance. At this range, the bullet would probably take off half of Keo's head. If one didn't do the job, and given the magazine under the weapon, the man would easily be able to try again with a second trigger pull.

"Whoa, whoa," Keo said. "Let's talk this over."

"Shut the fuck up," the man said.

"No, bring him in," the woman said through the radio. "Tobias's orders."

The man hesitated.

"Did you hear me?" the woman asked.

"Whatever you say," the man said, and put the radio away. He took a step back before slinging his rifle and producing a knife from a sheath along his hip. "This must be your lucky day, Chinaman."

Not quite, but hey, the day's still young.

Because Keo had heard it clearly. The woman on the radio had definitely said the name "Tobias."

Keo didn't need to look at his watch swinging underneath him to know what time it was. Despite the thick canopies on the other side of his boots, there was still at least five hours of sunlight left.

Five hours to kill Tobias and return to T18.

He'd done more with less time. `

TEN

His captor was in his late twenties and maybe just a year or two younger than Keo himself. He learned this useless fact while they were moving through the woods when the man wiped the camo off his face with a rag that he then stuffed into his back pocket. The wiring that had snared Keo was now binding his hands in front of him, the thin piece of steel digging into his wrists, just deep enough to hurt but not draw blood.

Keo walked up front, moving slowly because he had no idea where he was going and a part of him was afraid of stepping into another trap. From the looks of the man keeping a decent distance behind him, rifle no doubt pointed right at Keo's back, he had been out here for some time setting up plenty of snares. The damn thing had been strong enough to hold him suspended, so either the man was looking for big game or he was hunting humans. The only other option was that he was hoping to catch something that used to be human, but that didn't really make much sense in the daylight.

They were definitely moving deeper into the woods because the canopies were getting thicker and the temperature was

THE ISLES OF ELYSIUM   113

continuing to fall around him. Keo kept sneaking a look at the darker parts of his surroundings, the places where shadows lingered, and imagined black eyes watching him back. He might have shivered and hoped his captor didn't notice.

"What're they for?" Keo asked.

"What?" the man said. He moved quietly, almost like a cat. No wonder Keo had never known he was hiding nearby.

"The snare. What was it for?"

There was no response, just the *crunch-crunch* of shoes over brittle grass. Keo couldn't see the man's face, so he didn't know if he didn't want to answer or if he just didn't feel like talking.

"Humans?" Keo said anyway. "Or things that used to be humans? Is that it? You trying to snag yourself a ghoul?"

"Ghoul?" the man said.

"The creatures."

"You call them ghouls, too?"

'Too'? Keo thought. *Curiouser and curiouser.*

"So do you, apparently," he said.

There was no response that time.

"Where are we going?" Keo asked.

"You'll know when we get there."

"What if I walk right into a hole and fall down or something?"

"I guess you better watch your step, then."

Keo smiled. "I'm Keo, by the way."

"Good for you."

"You got a name?"

"Yes."

"Wanna share?"

"Nope."

"Don't be that way. I have to call you something."

Silence.

Keo sighed. "This is how misunderstandings get started, you know."

"There's no misunderstanding," the man said. "You set us up."

"I didn't set anyone up. You ambushed *me*. The sniper—"

"Bullshit." Then, "Turn left here."

Keo turned left, though there were still no trails, old footsteps, or anything that would indicate this was a well-traveled route. So what exactly was his captor using to tell directions? Or maybe the guy was making it up as he went. That seemed unlikely, though.

"He's out there with his men," Jack had told him.

"Where exactly?" he had asked.

"If we knew, you think we'd need you to go out there to find him for us?" Jack had laughed. *"They're all over those woods on the other side of the river. We could never pin them down. I wouldn't be surprised if they had some hillbilly survivalists among them."*

Hillbilly survivalists. Like the one behind him right now? His no-name captor didn't really sound like someone who had spent most of his life in the wilderness. Or the hills. Or wherever the hell Texas hillbillies came from. Not that Keo would know the difference anyway. He didn't meet many hillbillies growing up in San Diego and had managed to avoid them in the years since. Though, he had crossed paths with a few in the French countryside that might fit the description—

Focus.

Keo figured he had until they reached wherever they were going to get out of this jam. If he met Tobias with his hands bound and weaponless, he was likely as good as dead. The man walking behind him had made it pretty clear they thought he was responsible for the ambush at the warehouse. Even the woman on the radio had indicated the same thing.

"Bring him in. He's got a lot to answer for," she had said.

As if he were the one who had tried to pick off some poor sap with a sniper rifle and not the other way around. As if he had run into the warehouse so Steve's men could then corral his pursuers and blast away with an M60. Of course, he had a feeling they weren't going to believe him when he tried to sell that story. Never mind that it was the God's honest truth.

Just his luck. The first time he had truth on his side, and it wasn't going to do him a lick of good.

"What's he like?" Keo asked.

He didn't expect an answer, but his captor said, "Who?"

I guess he feels like talking after all.

"Tobias," Keo said.

"You'll find out soon enough."

"Give me a hint."

"Keep walking."

"One more question..."

"Shut up."

"You a hillbilly?"

"What?" the man said. Keo grinned at the insulted tone. "What did you just call me, Chinaman?"

"Hillbilly. I was told there were Texas hillbillies all over these woods. I was just wondering if you were one of them."

"Fuck you."

"Whoa whoa, let's keep it civil, okay? I'm not saying there's anything wrong with being a hillbilly. Even a Texas one. No judgments here, pal."

"Man, I'm getting real sick of the sound of your voice."

His captor had picked up his pace. Keo knew that from the slight increase in the sound of the man's footsteps. He was getting closer...

"It was a genuine question," Keo said.

"Shut your mouth."

"Is Tobias a hillbilly, too?"

"I said, shut up."

He sounded much closer that time. *Much* closer.

"Can I ask you a question?" Keo said.

"No."

"Is it true that hillbillies inbreed?"

Keo was waiting for it, and when it finally came—the cold touch of the rifle's barrel starting to poke him viciously in the back of the neck—he dropped down, spun around, and swept his right leg from front to back in a wide arc. His captor went down and squeezed the trigger at the same time. The gunshot exploded, scattering birds in the vicinity, the *buzz!* of the bullet passing over Keo's head.

The man landed on his butt with an *oomph!*, but somehow still managed to cling onto the rifle. Keo lunged forward and drove his knee into the man's face, slamming the back of his head into the ground. The gun fired again, the second shot *buzzing* past Keo's right shoulder this time and shattering a tree branch behind him.

Before the man could pull the trigger a third time, Keo leaped on top of him, driving both knees into his chest. His captor let out a surprised grunt as Keo captured the rifle's barrel with his bound palms and wrenched it free. He tossed it, then lifted himself slightly before dropping back down with his entire weight. Another loud grunt, the man's eyes flaring, his lips twisting in intense concentration—

The knife. A big monstrous thing with a gleaming metal blade like something out of the Jim Bowie collection was coming out of the man's sheath along his hip.

Aw, crap.

Keo dove to the other side—away from the knife—and slipped his arms over the man's head until he had the steel wire binding his wrists positioned in front of his captor's neck. Keo shoved the heels of his boots into the ground and pulled back even as the man whaled desperately at his arms with one balled fist while trying to swipe blindly at his head with the knife.

Keo didn't let go and didn't relinquish pressure on his victim. He held on through the convulsions, the kicking and punching and slashing against empty air. He only lessened his stranglehold when the body in front of him finally relaxed, the knife hand dropped to the ground, and the man stopped struggling.

He sighed and finally pulled his arms up and rolled away and lay on the damp ground for a moment to catch his breath. Clear white skies poked through massive tree branches above him, so he still had plenty of time.

He finally sat back up and rolled over and reached for his captor's neck, feeling for a pulse. Weak, but present. He hadn't been trying to kill the guy, just cut off his oxygen; but that was a fine line to tread and it was difficult to show finesse with his hands bound.

But the guy was still alive, and that was all that mattered. Keo had a feeling he was going to need a guide to find Tobias.

Find the girl. Kill some guys. Live happily ever after.

If all went well, he'd only have to kill one guy. God knew he'd had to do a hell of a lot worse and for much less.

———

"What's your name?" Keo asked.

The man blinked at him, the long red stripe across his neck like a glow-in-the-dark scar against the black and green of his shirt collar. His nose was broken at the bridge, and Keo had stuffed some pieces of wadded cloth he'd cut off the man's shirt using the Jim Bowie knife into his nostrils to stop the bleeding.

"Look, I need to call you something, right?" Keo said.

The man seemed to think about it for a moment. Finally, he said, "Wyatt."

"See, there you go. Now we're friends." Keo smiled. "Well, close enough. So, where do I find Tobias, Wyatt?"

Wyatt didn't answer. He sat on the ground with his back against the tree, the same strand of steel wire that had been biting into Keo's wrists earlier now binding his hands in his lap. Keo had taken back his MP5SD, Glock, and pack, and tossed Wyatt's rifle into a nearby brush and taken the man's Smith & Wesson semiautomatic.

Keo glanced at his watch: 2:56 p.m.

"Tobias?" Wyatt said. "You mean you *want* to find Tobias?"

"Uh huh."

"Why?"

"I have a message for him."

"A message?"

He could see Wyatt trying to read him and not doing a very subtle job of it.

"Yeah, a message," Keo said. "Like one of those singing telegrams. That's me. Except I'm not a very good singer. But I can hum pretty good."

That elicited a confused look.

"Joke," Keo said.

"Oh."

"So where's Tobias?"

"I don't know."

"You don't know?"

Wyatt shook his head.

"You do realize that you were taking me to him a moment ago, right?" Keo said.

"I don't know what you're talking about."

"No?"

"No."

Keo sighed and slung his submachine gun and drew the Glock. He pointed it at Wyatt's kneecap and squinted behind the sight.

"Hey, what are you doing?" Wyatt said, suddenly alarmed.

"I'm going to shoot you in the kneecap."

"Why the hell you gonna do that?"

Keo looked up at him. "To get you to tell me where Tobias is. Duh. I know it's going to hurt, but trust me, I've had experience with this. I once shot a guy in the kneecap while we were both on a boat. He was perfectly happy to assist me after that."

"Hey hey, come on now."

"Hold still. It won't hurt. Okay, that's a lie. It's definitely going to hurt a lot."

"Don't, okay?"

Keo pulled back a second time. "Why not?"

"I..." Wyatt's eyes darted behind Keo, as if he expected someone to come out of the woods at any moment and rescue him. When no one did, he said, "I'll take you to him. Just...don't shoot me in the leg."

"I was going to shoot you in the kneecap."

"Yeah, don't shoot me there, either."

Keo stood up and holstered the Glock. "See? Now we're almost best friends."

Wyatt sighed and stood up, using the tree behind him for support.

"How far away are we?" Keo asked, even though he thought he already knew the answer. Wyatt had fired two shots, and no one had showed up in the last ten minutes. That meant the camp wasn't close by.

"Not far," Wyatt said. "Maybe another hour by foot."

"You guys have vehicles?"

"Yeah."

"I didn't hear any earlier."

"We're pretty deep in the woods. We'll have to start circling back toward the road."

Keo nodded. "So you do know where you're going."

"Yeah."

"Lead the way, then. Just keep in mind that I'm not against cutting short our burgeoning friendship, Wyatt."

Wyatt grunted and started off, moving in the same path they had been going earlier. Keo noticed the man's head turning slightly left and right. Wyatt probably thought he was being slick, that Keo wouldn't catch the movements. He was, of course, looking for his weapons, the same ones Keo had tossed earlier. Keo decided not to tell him that he was looking in the wrong direction.

"What does he look like?" Keo asked. "Tobias."

"He's a guy," Wyatt said.

"Really? And here I thought he was a bear."

Wyatt snorted. "What do you want with him, anyway?"

"I'm going to ask him to friend me."

"Friend you?"

"You know, like on Facebook."

"You have Facebook?"

Keo smiled. "Joke, Wyatt. Just a joke."

"Oh," Wyatt said, and Keo thought he sounded just a little too sad when he said it.

They walked through the woods for another ten minutes, then fifteen, and though Wyatt insisted they were moving back to the road, Keo couldn't tell if he was lying or not. After a while, Keo was sure Wyatt was leading him to a dead end, that maybe the guy never knew where he was going in the first place and was just hoping to stave off getting shot for as long as possible.

After about an hour of pointlessly stumbling around one identical section of woods after another, Keo was about to stop Wyatt and use the bullet-in-the-kneecap as incentive when he saw sunlight filtering in through a wall of trees in front of them.

He grabbed Wyatt by the shirt collar and jerked him back roughly, then deposited him to the ground. "Stay, boy."

Keo stepped forward with the MP5SD at the ready and looked out.

They'd slowly been angling back toward civilization after all, and he was now looking out at a strip mall with a Valero gas station and a row of businesses on the other side of a two-lane road. Sunlight glinted off the barrel of a rifle just barely visible on the rooftop of a Wilmont Mutual Insurance office building. The shooter's head poked up briefly before disappearing again behind a cut-out picture of the Statue of Liberty.

Keo scanned the rest of the buildings and saw a second, then a third man, the two stationed at opposite ends of the connecting rooftops. They were watching the streets and surrounding area with an alertness that told Keo they were waiting for an impending attack. The rest of the strip mall looked deceptively empty, but Keo didn't buy it.

Behind him, Wyatt was picking himself up from the ground when Keo grabbed him by the shirt collar and walked his former captor back to the tree line.

"Your friends?" he asked.

Wyatt nodded.

"Why here?" Keo asked. "Why are they still hanging around so close to the ambush site?"

"Maybe that's what we want."

"Come again?"

"Tobias isn't stupid."

"Go on..."

"Maybe he wants the people from T18 to try to hit him again."

"You're saying this is a trap? Tit for tat, is that it?"

Wyatt shrugged.

"How many men do you have left?" Keo asked, looking back out at the sentry perched behind Lady Liberty as the man raised his head briefly to glance down the street before ducking back down.

"I don't know," Wyatt said.

"You don't know?"

"I don't know how many made it back from the ambush. I was inside the woods, remember? That's my job. Scout the area for signs of movement coming and going from the town and report back. I wasn't even supposed to be involved until the shooting started. Then you just ran right at me."

Keo still couldn't spot any movements behind any of the storefront windows, but that didn't mean the buildings were empty. If this was a trap, an attempt to lure Steve's people into a payback ambush, the shooters would be hiding and waiting to strike.

Clever dogs.

"Is Tobias in there?" he asked.

"I guess," Wyatt said.

"You guess?"

"They told me to bring you here, so I guess he's in there, somewhere."

"Makes sense," Keo nodded.

"So what happens now?"

"Give me a second."

"I mean, to me." Wyatt sighed. "Tobias won't be happy that I led you right to him."

"He told you to take me to him, didn't he? Why wouldn't he be happy that you did exactly as ordered?"

That seemed to confuse Wyatt temporarily. "I guess…"

"Besides," Keo said, "I just want to talk to the guy. Sit down and have a chat. Maybe over some warm beers—"

Snap!

Keo spun around—a difficult feat, since he was still half-crouched—in time to see two figures emerging from behind a thick brush. They were both huge men, their faces painted in camo like Wyatt earlier (*More of Tobias's scouts,* Keo thought). More importantly, they were both armed and by the look on their faces, they were equally surprised to see him.

"Fuck!" one of them shouted, even as he lifted his rifle—an M4 with a red dot scope on top.

Keo was wondering how the hell had they gotten so close without him hearing them until now even as he jerked Wyatt in front of him. Wyatt gasped and tensed up as he realized what was happening. Keo abandoned the MP5SD—it was too long, making it too cumbersome for what he had in mind—and drew his Glock and jammed the barrel under Wyatt's chin at an angle.

"What the fuck is this?" the same man shouted. Then he added, as if he couldn't quite believe it, "Wyatt?"

"Don't shoot!" Wyatt shouted. "Don't fucking shoot!"

"Yeah, listen to him," Keo said.

"Fuck!" the second man shouted, pointing his bolt-action rifle at Keo. Or trying to, with Wyatt in the way.

Keo smiled. The constant barrage of profanity was amusing to him for some reason. He just hoped the sight of him hiding behind Wyatt, his Glock against the man's chin, was enough to keep them from squeezing their triggers. Either the M4 or the bolt-action could do some serious damage at this distance. Which was to say, if someone fired, he was a dead man. Really, really dead.

The two scouts shuffled their feet, not sure whether to move forward, back, or side to side; or just stand there and keep their weapons pointed at him. Keo was just glad no one had fired a shot yet even though he realized all the screaming might have already drawn attention from the strip mall behind him.

He threw a quick look back, out past the trees and into the streets, and sure enough there was movement at one of the buildings. The Wilmont Mutual Insurance office doors were opening and people were pouring out. Armed people.

Goddammit, I hate it when I'm right.

He looked back at the two men in front of him. Like Wyatt, they were wearing hunting clothes, and one of them had blood splatters along his pant legs and shirtsleeve. The blood looked fresh, too.

"Come on," Keo said to Wyatt, pulling him slightly to the right.

Both men quickly followed, their rifles never leaving him.

"Where the fuck you going?" one of them shouted. Keo didn't know why he was still shouting.

He had a good point, though. Where the fuck *was* he going? Not front. Not side to side. And certainly not back—

Dammit. There was nowhere to go but back.

He tightened his left hand around Wyatt's neck, then began dragging the other man backward. He felt the warmth of the sun splash against his back almost as soon as he stepped outside the woods and into the overgrown grass jungle.

The sound of heavy footsteps overwhelmed everything else, and Keo spun around briefly, Wyatt still in front of him, to face at least six men running in his direction with rifles swinging in front of them. They were just about to cross the parking lot when they saw him, slid to a stop, and took aim.

Great. Now instead of two guys with rifles, he was staring at six.

Six? It was more like nine, because the three guards on the rooftops were now training their rifles on him, too. That prompted Keo to press his body even tighter against Wyatt's. Thank God Wyatt was around six foot, which was just an inch shorter than Keo.

"Don't shoot!" Wyatt was shouting. "Don't anyone shoot, for Christ's sake!"

There you go, Wyatt. Keep at it, pal.

The fresh sounds of footsteps behind him forced Keo to drag Wyatt south along the shoulder of the road. The two scouts burst out of the tree line to the left of him a second later. Now he had men with guns at two directions—front and from the right.

They kept pace with him as he pulled Wyatt southward, and they stopped when he stopped. That lasted for a few seconds until a couple of them got smart and ran further down the street before crossing over to outflank him.

He stopped, now with men on all three sides and just the woods behind him.

The woods. He could probably get lost in there. He could always come back later and find Tobias. Steve didn't say anything about killing Tobias today. There was no timetable, there was just the job.

Yeah, that could work.

Of course, he was assuming the pissed-off looking men with guns—half of them haggard, their civilian clothes splashed with blood—would let him just back up into the trees without a fight. That was a pretty big if right there, but what the hell, it wasn't like he had much of a choice at the moment.

"Get ready," Keo said.

"What?" Wyatt said.

"Get ready to move."

"Christ, you're going to get us killed!"

"Shut up and get ready—"

"Don't shoot!" someone shouted. It was a woman. He

thought she sounded like the one that had talked to Wyatt over the radio earlier. "No one goddamn shoots!"

She pushed a couple of men out of her way and jogged across the street toward him. He watched her closely from behind Wyatt's head, doing his best to expose as little of himself as possible to the shooters. He just hoped the riflemen on the rooftops were as bad a shot as the one that had tried to take him out earlier.

"Jesus Christ," the woman said. "It really is you. I was pretty sure you were dead."

Keo blinked once, twice.

The sun was in his eyes, but there was no mistaking who the woman was. She'd cut her hair short and the boots made her look taller—and she had been pretty tall to begin with—but it was definitely her.

Of all the people that had escaped on Mark's boat, she would have been the one he'd put money on surviving. Besides, Gillian had made it, so why not her, too? Despite what Steve had told him about her and Mark dying when his men first encountered them, a part of him never really believed it.

"Well, shit," Keo said.

She stopped a few feet away and seemed to sigh with a mixture of frustration and annoyance. "What kind of name is Keo, anyway?"

He smiled. "Donnie was taken."

She smiled back, then held out her hand toward him. "Give me the gun, Keo, before someone loses their shit and we all end up dead."

"Can I trust you?"

"I don't think you have much of a choice right now, do you?"

Good point, he thought, and took the gun away from Wyatt's chin and held it out to her. "So what now?"

"Now you meet Tobias," Jordan said.

BOOK TWO

THE TIES THAT BIND

ELEVEN

"I can't believe you're still alive," Jordan said.

"You said that already," Keo said.

"What happened to your face?"

"Long story."

"I bet. We spent days and weeks wondering what had happened to you and Norris, not knowing if you were dead or alive or captured...or worse."

"Just days and weeks? What about months?"

"We eventually had other things to worry about."

"Santa Marie Island."

She frowned. "They were waiting for us when we got there."

"The soldiers."

"Yeah."

"What happened, Jordan?"

"She's alive. You know that, right?"

He nodded. "I saw her back at T18."

Jordan didn't respond right away and instead continued leading him through the strip mall while men with guns watched him like a hawk. Despite taking his weapons and pack, the others were still nervous, and he saw fingers in trigger guards. He didn't blame their skittishness; he had, after all, just shown up in the aftermath of what he now knew was a bloody fight with Steve's men. These guys were beat up, hurt, and licking their wounds. You had to be extra careful around men who were on edge, especially when assault rifles were present.

"How is she?" Jordan finally asked.

"You don't know?"

"It's been a while since I've seen her."

"What happened?"

"We'll talk about it later."

"I might not have a later."

"You'll be fine. Just...be truthful."

"Tobias?"

"Yeah."

Well, you wanted to find him, pal.

Mission accomplished.

She led him into the insurance building and across (*fresh*) blood-covered carpeting while the others returned to wherever they had been hiding before he showed up. He followed Jordan into a back hallway that was just a little bit too dark for his liking.

"You're waiting for them," Keo said. "The soldiers. You're trying to lure them up the road and into an ambush."

She gave him a quick, sharp look.

"Wyatt gave it away," he said.

She nodded, relaxing. "We have men planted along the roads. If they'd followed us like we had hoped, we would have had hit them back. We've done it before."

"But they didn't bite this time."

"No..."

"Still, pretty gutsy move."

"Yeah, well, it takes guts to run around out here. But you probably know a little bit about that."

"Just a little bit, yeah."

Jordan opened the last door into a small office. There were two people already inside, and one of them—a woman, even though Keo only saw her from the back—was busy wrapping fresh gauze around the thigh of a man with short blond hair. The man's pant leg had been cut away, and a pool of fresh blood was gathering on the floor under him. Like the men outside, he looked haggard and on edge.

The man looked up when they entered. "This him?"

Jordan nodded. "Keo, this is Tobias."

Tobias eyed him. Jack wasn't far off when he described the man—the steely blue eyes, square jaw, and the six-three frame. Early forties, though he could have passed for a man five years younger with a shave and a decent haircut.

The woman working on Tobias was in her fifties and Hispanic, and the gun belt around her narrow waist looked awkwardly strapped on. She swiped at some gray hair and gathered up the bloody rags and bandages and tossed them into a nearby trash bin that hadn't been emptied in over a year.

"I'll get Denver to make you a crutch," the woman said.

"Thanks, Pita," Tobias said.

"Try not to break the stitches, if you can help it."

"That's the trick, isn't it?"

"Yes, well, do your best," she said, and left the room, leaving the door open behind her.

Tobias picked up a black jacket and slipped it on before hopping off the desk and making his way to a chair in a corner. He sat down and drew his sidearm—a dull black revolver—and placed it in his lap before looking across at Keo again.

"What kind of name is Keo, anyway?" he asked.

"Matt was taken," Keo said.

"What?"

"It's...just something he says," Jordan said, shaking her head. "He thinks it's funny."

"You guys know each other," Tobias said to her. It wasn't a question.

She nodded. "We met a while back."

"He set us up."

"He says he didn't."

"Let's hear him say that."

"I didn't set you up," Keo said.

Tobias didn't take his eyes off Keo. "Convince me."

"Convince you of what? Your guys tried to kill me. Why don't you convince me why I shouldn't be pissed off right now?"

Tobias narrowed his eyes, and Keo almost smiled. Almost. He bet they didn't expect that response from him. It was a risky approach, but at the moment he didn't think he had very much to lose.

What was that old saying? Ah, right. *"The best defense is a good offense."*

"What were you doing out there?" Tobias asked.

"It's a free country," Keo said.

"Not anymore."

"I was never very good at following rules."

"He's not wrong," Jordan said. "Ron shot at him first, then Mack and the others chased him into the warehouse. I know him. He wouldn't set us up like that."

"Maybe..."

"I can vouch for him. Keo and I have been through a lot together."

"Are you willing to bet your life on it?"

"Yes," she said without hesitation.

Keo couldn't help but glance over at her. She stood calmly next to him, facing Tobias. He remembered the first time they had met—in a cabin in the woods, pointing guns at each other.

Things got better after that initial encounter, but even so, Jordan was the last person he expected to find out here, giving her word to the man he was supposed to kill.

"People change, Jordan," Tobias said. There might have been a little warning in his voice. He pushed back up to his feet with a grimace, then holstered the gun. "He's going to have to answer a lot more questions. Like what he was doing in T18 in the first place. But all that can wait until we get back to base. Until then, he's your responsibility."

She nodded.

Tobias pushed past Keo and Jordan and hobbled out the door.

Jordan looked after him for a moment, then over at Keo.

"Thanks—" he started to say.

"Shove it," she said. "He's got a point. We know you came from T18, so you better have a damn good reason." He opened his mouth to answer, but she cut him off again. "I said *shove it.* You have a couple of hours to come up with a better answer than whatever you were about to say, because I can't protect you forever."

"I was just going to ask about what happened to Mark and the others," Keo said.

That was a lie, but he needed her back on his side, and the best way to do that was to remind her of their mutual experiences...and friends.

"A lot," she said quietly.

"What happened?" Keo asked when they were back outside in the strip mall parking lot watching Tobias and his men pack up their gear to move.

Keo counted four wounded men being helped out of the buildings, including two that had to be carried outside. They had hidden Jeeps and trucks in the back of the lot and were now carefully loading their wounded onto them, with Pita standing by giving instructions.

"We made it to Santa Marie Island about two weeks after we left you at the cabin," Jordan said. "But they were waiting for us. They were already on the island. Of course, we didn't know that. They shot Mark and brought us to T18."

"I saw Gillian, but I didn't see Rachel and her daughter."

"How long were you there?"

"A few hours."

"Why?"

He shrugged, and she gave him a suspicious look.

"Whatever, Keo," she said. "You're going to have to tell Tobias everything later anyway. I just hope you come up with a better story than that."

I'm working on it, he thought, but said, "What about Rachel?"

"She didn't make it," Jordan said.

"Christine...?"

Jordan shook her head. "When the soldiers first showed up, things got messy. Mark and I fought back and..."

She stopped and didn't say anything for a while.

"We can talk about it later when you're ready," he said.

"They're gone. That's what happened. They're gone. Only Gillian and me made it off that island alive."

He thought about the little girl, Christine, and her mother Rachel, and all those months in the cabin with him and Norris and Gillian. The mother and daughter were easy to like, even though he had done his best to keep his distance. A part of him always doubted they would all make it to Santa Marie Island, but to finally get there, only to lose everything...

He looked over at Jordan. She was staring at the men, but he knew she wasn't really seeing them. It was easy enough to guess where her thoughts were at the moment. Back at Santa Marie Island, back to that day...

Keo felt suddenly very guilty about making her relive it.

"Is this everyone?" he asked, hoping to draw her back.

Tobias had hobbled into the Jeep's front passenger seat while two of the wounded were being loaded into the back. Pita climbed in after them, along with two other men. The others were piling into the truck, a beat-up gray Honda Ridgeline.

"No," Jordan said. She looked down the road. "The others will follow us later, when we're sure T18 isn't going to press their attack."

They watched the two vehicles turn into the road and pick up speed as they went.

"So we're walking?" Keo asked.

"The only thing more precious than lives these days is gas." Jordan waved to the three men who were still standing guard on the rooftops of the strip mall and shouted, "Let's go!"

Keo followed her across the street and back to the tree lines. He felt naked without his weapons, and that feeling got worse when they stepped into the darkened woods. Despite wearing a long-sleeve shirt and pants, he shivered anyway.

What he wouldn't give for a gun, or two. And silver bullets, of course. Always silver bullets.

Tobias's men followed them inside, then immediately began spreading out without having to be told. Everyone seemed to know what they were doing, including Wyatt, who gave Keo a hard stare before vanishing behind one of the many identical trees around them.

There were, he counted, five other people inside the woods with him and Jordan at the moment. Five people meant five potential sources of weapons. He'd prefer his MP5SD and the silver ammo, but he was good at making do. He had been looking for the man who had taken his things, but the guy had either left with Tobias or was somewhere else in the woods at the moment.

"Don't even think about it," Jordan said beside him.

"Think about what?"

"You know damn well what." She flashed him a warning stare with her brown eyes.

He smiled innocently back at her. "I'm just following you, Jordan. That's all I'm thinking about at the moment."

"Uh huh."

"You don't believe me?"

"No."

"I'm hurt."

"And I'm a virgin."

"You mean you're not?"

She rolled her eyes. "This isn't a date, Keo."

"Too bad."

The last time he saw Jordan she was a shooter in training, but she had clearly progressed past that stage. As he watched her walking with a gun belt and her beat-up M4 held at the ready in front of her, he had no doubts she had been putting all those lessons at the cabin to good use since they separated almost six months ago.

"Where'd you get all the M4s?" he asked.

"T18 supplies them. But don't tell them that."

"Mum's the word. How long has this been going on? You guys and T18."

"Before there was even a T18. You know about the camps?"

"I've heard of them."

"T18 was just a camp when we first showed up. It wasn't that bad in the beginning, despite how they brought us here. I mean, I wanted to kill every last one of them for what happened back at Santa Marie Island, but it wasn't like we had a lot of choices, or chances."

"You and Gillian."

"Yeah."

"She stayed and you left. Why?"

"You'll have to ask her."

"I'm asking you."

"And I'm telling you, you'll have to ask her."

"Was it the whole pregnancy thing? Is that why you left?"

"That was a big part of it. The 'donating'—" she used air quotes "—blood part, I might have been able to live with. It made me physically sick each time they forced us to go into those tents and give blood, but the idea of conceiving and then raising a child for that cycle to continue? That made me want to throw up."

"I saw a lot of people back there. They seemed okay with it."

"Yeah, well, I'm not a lot of people, Keo."

He looked over at her again. She was still the tall athletic girl he had almost killed back in Louisiana, and the same college student who had kept Mark and Jill alive for months after The Purge. Her hair was shorter, but somehow the new cut complemented the shape of her face more.

"What?" she said, narrowing her eyes back at him.

"Nothing."

"So stop staring like a perv."

"Sorry."

"So, have you come up with a better story yet? Because, make no mistake about it, Tobias would have killed you back there if I hadn't stopped him."

"And I appreciate that."

"That's not the point. You need to make him believe you weren't a part of the ambush. Can you do that?"

"*I didn't know about the ambush because I came here to kill Tobias,*" he thought about saying, but of course, didn't. He said instead, "It's the truth."

"I don't think Tobias is going to like your truth very much.

And out here, what he says goes."

"Even with you?"

"Even with me."

"You guys involved?"

"What?"

"Are you guys—"

"I heard you the first time." She paused, then, "Why would you ask me that?"

"I don't know. Back in the office, the way you guys were talking..." He shrugged. "The two of you seemed to have a very copacetic relationship."

"Just because we see eye-to-eye doesn't mean we're screwing, too."

"Why not?"

"Why not?" she repeated, as if she didn't understand the question.

"The guy's Captain America. Who doesn't want to jump Captain America's bones?"

She actually smiled. "I was always more of a Punisher fan myself."

"Punisher? I didn't know you rolled that way."

"What way?"

"Sex and punishment?"

"Oh, God," she groaned. "I meant the Punisher. The comic book character?"

"I don't read comic books."

"He had a couple of movies. Three, I think."

"I don't watch a lot of movies, either."

"What exactly did you use to do with all your free time, Keo?"

"Troll bars for women."

She sighed. "Why did I even ask?"

He smiled. "So, that's a no on the sex and punishment?"

They had been walking for half an hour, and it didn't seem as if they were any closer to reaching their destination. Keo spent most of that time keeping tabs on Tobias's people, but they moved like ghosts, coming and going around him. He had no trouble at all understanding why Steve had such a hard time pinning them down. These people had made themselves comfortable out here, with guys like Wyatt and the two scouts he had encountered earlier probably giving the soldiers fits around T18.

The only person who was close enough for him to even consider taking her weapons was Jordan. Maybe it was the soft gooey part of him that had developed in the last year despite his best efforts, but the idea of hurting her for her guns didn't sit well with him.

You've gone soft, pal. Real soft.

"I'm sorry about Mark," he said after they had been walking in silence for a while.

"Yeah, me too," Jordan said.

She was slightly in front, the handle of her holstered Glock staring invitingly back at him. It was tempting. So, so tempting.

He thought about Gillian. He could do it for her if he had to. Finding Gillian again after all these months was a minor miracle, and all he had to do to be permanently reunited with her was kill Tobias and return to T18. But to do that, he needed guns, such as the one staring back at him right now...

"What happened to you?" Jordan asked, looking over her shoulder at him. "After the cabin, we were pretty resigned to you and Norris being dead. Even Gillian. She kept waiting for you to find us, you know. After Santa Marie Island, and even when we were at T18. I would catch her staring off at nothing for long stretches until it occurred to me she was looking for you. Waiting for you to show up to rescue her."

"Norris and I ran into trouble."

"What kind of trouble?"

"The kind that kept me away for almost six months."

He told her about Pollard. About Joe. About running for his life in the woods of Louisiana and not knowing where the hell he was going, until he finally ran out of room. He skipped the part about Allie but told her Norris had found some survivors to stay with and that he was probably still safe right now, living out his remaining years.

Then he told her about Song Island. About Lara. And about the soldiers.

"Jesus, how many of them are out there?" she asked.

"My understanding is that they're everywhere. Every state. Maybe every country. Who knows?"

She was speechless for a moment. After a while, she shook her head. "I guess it makes sense. Everyone we knew in the camp was either from Texas or Louisiana, so we didn't get any information about what was happening in the rest of the country. Talk about a myopic view of the world, huh?"

"The big picture is overrated."

"Yeah, maybe."

They walked on for another few minutes in silence before Keo said, "Are we almost there yet?"

"What are you, ten?"

"It's going to get dark soon, Jordan."

"We're almost there. The base is temporary because we never stay at one place for too long. Sooner or later, they find us."

"The soldiers?"

"No."

She's talking about ghouls.

He thought about his guns again, about the silver ammo inside them...

"What are you carrying?" he asked.

"About five pounds lighter since the last time you saw me," she said, grinning back at him. "I like to think I'm at my perfect fighting weight."

He chuckled. "You got funnier."

"You think?"

"Uh huh."

"I try."

"What about silver?" he asked. "Do you guys know about silver?"

She stopped and turned around, then stared at him curiously for a moment. "Do you?"

"About silver?"

"Yeah."

"I know a lot about it."

"What do you know?"

"The people I told you about, on Song Island? They're the ones who sent out those broadcasts about the silver."

"No shit? We picked up their broadcast over a month ago. We didn't believe it at first, but we tested it out and now we're believers."

She pulled out a spare magazine from her pouches and tossed it to him. Keo thumbed off a round and held it up to what little light managed to pierce the canopies, easily making out the silver tip.

"Silver bullets," Keo said.

"The problem is finding enough silver lying around out there." She took the magazine back. "I just have the one for the Glock. Everyone has just one, too. Everything else is loaded with regular ammo. We put them in at night and never before. They're more valuable than gold these days."

He kept his mouth shut about the silver loaded in his weapons that one of her people was carrying around out there. Chances were the man hadn't inspected his belongings very closely, so he could still retrieve them later. Hopefully. The last thing he needed was to "share" the valuable bullets with strangers he was planning to double cross as soon as he got Tobias in his crosshairs.

"What else do you know?" Jordan asked. "Do the other things the islanders mentioned actually work? Bodies of water? Ultraviolet lights?"

"The bodies of water, yeah."

"How?"

"I have no idea. I just know it works."

"You saw it?"

"I saw it."

"What happened?"

They turn to stone and drown, he thought about telling her, but it sounded crazy even in his own head.

"It works," he said instead. "I don't know how. Just like I don't know how shooting or cutting them with silver works. It just does."

She nodded. "Where's a scientist when you need one, huh? An explanation would be nice."

Keo glanced at his watch again. 3:14 p.m.

"Clock's ticking," he said.

"Relax, we're close. This isn't our first rodeo, you know. We have this entire area mapped out. We know where everything is."

"And yet T18 still managed to ambush you."

Her entire body flinched, and Keo instantly regretted saying it.

"Sorry," he said. "Were some of them your friends?"

"A lot of them were my friends."

"I'm sorry, Jordan."

She sighed. "Whatever."

"I mean it."

She nodded but began walking faster in front of him. He had

to pick up his pace to catch up.

"Have you come up with a better story yet?" Jordan asked after a while.

"I'll just tell him the truth," Keo said. Then, "Can I ask you a question?"

"Can I stop you?"

"Probably not."

"Then go ahead."

"What are you still doing here? You, Tobias, and the others. Why are you guys spending your days making life miserable for T18?"

She didn't answer right away.

"Jordan?"

"These guys helped me escape," she said finally. "I'm paying them back."

"That doesn't explain why they don't just pack up and leave. Why is Tobias keeping the others here?"

"Almost all of them still have friends and family in town. They won't leave until they get everyone out."

He recalled seeing the soldiers along the riverbanks, at the marina, and riding around on horseback. It wasn't just their numbers or their weaponry that Tobias's people were going up against, but the enemy also had the night, not to mention the creatures inside them, at their side. Steve and his brother had all the advantages. *All* of it.

Keo had seen lost causes before, but this was ridiculously unfair.

"Jordan," he said.

"What?"

"How many did you lose back there?"

"Seven."

"How many do you have left?"

"Not enough," she said quietly. "Not nearly enough."

TWELVE

The temporary base Jordan took him to was a YMCA building, about half a kilometer from the long and empty stretch of I-45 in the distance. It was part of a business center, but had its own separate area. Two empty swimming pools greeted them as they stepped out of the woods and trudged through thick, overgrown grass that covered the backyard.

Keo followed Jordan while the rest of Tobias's people emerged out of the tree lines around them. Wyatt was among them, along with the two familiar scouts. They were greeted by sentries along the rooftops of the YMCA. One of them waved, and Jordan returned it.

Keo checked his watch again. 4:41 p.m.

"How long have you guys been here?" he asked.

"Two days," Jordan said. "Counting today. Can't afford to stay in one place for too long. Like I said before, it's not the soldiers we have to worry about. They usually don't wander out this far unless they come with everything they have. You saw all the boats they have back there? They can afford to stick to the river, use it to go back and forth from the Gulf. This far from T18, it's just the crawlers we have to stay one step ahead of."

"It must be tough, fighting a two-front war."

"It's not easy, no."

The YMCA building was only one-story, but it was spread out with multiple wings. There was a shooter on three of the rooftops, possibly even the same men that had been at the strip mall earlier.

"I usually try to steer clear of big buildings," Keo said.

"So do we," Jordan said. "They like using them for nests. But this one's secure, for now."

They skirted around the bigger of the two swimming pools and entered the main building through a metal back door guarded by a man with an M4.

Jordan nodded at him. "Hey, Tim."

"Welcome back," Tim said. "I heard things went sideways out there."

"Yeah, they did."

"Who's he?" the guard asked, looking at Keo.

"Keo."

"What kind—"

"Don't," Jordan said.

Keo smiled and followed her into a back hallway. It was surprisingly bright inside, thanks to a series of high ceiling windows flooding the room with sunlight. He could hear activity on the other end even before they stepped out into a large cafeteria where Tobias's men were gathered.

Pita was there, moving through the wounded men that had traveled here earlier by vehicle. Three of them were unconscious while a fourth drank from a bottle of water as Pita undressed his bloody bandages and grabbed a fresh roll from a teenage girl who was acting as her helper.

He counted about two dozen men in all, including Wyatt and

the others that had arrived with them. The three or four men who hadn't had to brave Steve's ambush were easy to tell apart from the rest—they were the ones without blood on their clothes. Besides Pita and the girl, there were only two other women in the place. Like the men, they wore gun belts, but unlike Jordan, they didn't look very dangerous at all.

Keo looked around but couldn't find Tobias anywhere. Maybe he was in a back room, trying to come up with a plan to regroup after the shellacking they had taken. No one went toe-to-toe with an M60 and came out unscathed.

"Is this it?" Keo asked.

"There was a lot more this morning," Jordan said quietly. She grabbed a man with a thick red beard as he was walking past them. "Where's Tobias?"

"Back office with Reese," the man said.

"Thanks," Jordan said. Then to Keo, "Come on."

He kept pace with her through the cafeteria, which looked abandoned despite the company of men and women moving around it at the moment. The cavernous feel, he guessed, was because the room was designed for a large army of hungry teens and not the two dozen or so people eating MREs or talking quietly among themselves. They all looked beaten and whipped, and he wondered how long Tobias was going to be able to keep this fight up after today.

"Where'd you get all the MREs?" he asked.

"Same place we get most of our weapons. T18."

"You have an inside man."

"We have inside *men*. One of them supplies us with as much nonperishables as he can get his hands on."

"Where does he get them?"

"T18 has a storage warehouse filled when the Millers raided the surrounding areas. One of them sold mail-order civilian versions of Army MREs. Prepper food. That's what we've been living on for the last month or so. Before that, we were surviving off the land."

"Hunting?"

"Hunting, fishing, whatever it took. It's a big river. They can't guard every inch of it twenty-four hours a day."

"They seem to go back and forth along it just fine in those boats."

"That's because we don't attack the riverbanks if we can help it."

"Why not?"

"Didn't see you them?"

He was going to ask who, but he remembered the women and children along the banks washing laundry and swimming.

"Civilians," he said.

"Yeah. We're trying to save them, not get them killed. So we do our best to keep the fighting contained to just us and the soldiers. It's not always ideal, but no one said this would be easy."

Keo wanted to tell her that he had seen a little bit of what Steve had at T18, and that "this" wasn't just *not* going to be easy, it was going to be downright impossible. But that would have antagonized her, and right now he needed at least one ally at his side.

Even so, Keo kept close enough to Jordan that he was within easy lunging distance of the Glock in her hip holster. If she noticed or was uncomfortable with his closeness, she didn't say anything. He was thinking about how he was going to kill Tobias and somehow keep both him and Jordan alive when she opened a door marked "Director."

He hadn't taken more than a couple of steps inside when he saw a flash of movement out of the corner of his right eye. Keo turned, started lifting his hands to ward off an attack, but the man was faster and pain exploded across Keo's face as the butt of a rifle smashed into his forehead.

The blow would have done more damage if he hadn't seen it coming just in the nick of time and turned slightly. The result was more of a glancing blow, but it was enough to stun and stagger him.

He glimpsed a buzz cut as the man followed, pressing his attack, even as Jordan shouted, "What the fuck, Reese?"

The man ignored her and swung his weapon at Keo's face again, but Keo managed to dodge the oncoming strike this time. The wooden stock flashed across his face for a split second before Keo grabbed the barrel with one hand, pulled his attacker off balance, then slammed his cocked elbow into the back of the man's neck.

He heard a satisfying, pained grunt.

Keo followed his attacker-turned-victim, hoping to finish this as soon as possible (and that rifle, he could definitely use that rifle), when something rammed into the small of his back. He might have screamed; he couldn't be entirely certain. But he definitely felt the boot stepping on the back of his left knee and dropping to the floor.

He glanced back over his shoulder just in time to see Tobias, all six-three of him hovering with an M4 clutched in both raised hands. Tobias didn't look happy or sad, he just looked like a man doing a job.

It was the last thing Keo saw before the collapsible stock of the carbine hit him in the face and he dropped like a sack of meat.

"Jesus, your face looks like shit," Jordan said. She was whispering and looked concerned as she dabbed his face with a wet...something. "That throbbing pain? That's your forehead. It was bleeding so much even Pita thought you were going to bleed out. Lucky for you, it stopped."

Yeah. Lucky. That's me.

He grimaced and fought the urge to reach up to touch his forehead, where the strong odor of antibiotic ointment was coming from. Someone had been very generous with it. He guessed too much was better than not enough when you were dealing with possible infection.

His entire face hurt. At least both Tobias and Reese had aimed straight for the noggin and spared his nose. Having it broken once was enough, especially now that it had all but healed. Well, mostly, anyway.

He was lying on a cold, hard floor and staring up at a patch of moonlight spilling in through a high ceiling window. Something soft, probably cotton, was rolled up underneath his head, allowing him to turn it with minimal effort and take in his new surroundings.

He and Jordan were inside some kind of classroom, and they weren't alone. One of the women he had seen in the cafeteria was sitting against the opposite wall next to one of the wounded men; her eyes were closed and she was stroking his forehead while he snored. Pita and her teen assistant leaned against each other in another corner; they were both asleep. Unused school desks were scattered around them, some lying on their sides.

Nightfall.

There was barely any noise inside the room except for their breathing and the light snoring around them, as if everyone just knew not to be too noisy. Maybe a survival instinct kicking in unconsciously after a year of living in a post-Purge world.

What was that Lara liked to say? *"Adapt or perish."*

These people had clearly adapted. You didn't survive this long without understanding the rules. Making a sound in the middle of the night (*What time is it?*) was one of those things to be avoided at all costs.

It was impossibly quiet outside. Even the birds were afraid to make any noise. He was relieved to discover that the window in the back of the room was closed tight. He and Jordan, along with everyone in the room, were sitting along the sides, with Pita and the girl underneath the window. Even if one of the ghouls had crawled up there, they wouldn't be able to see them.

Hopefully.

Next to him, Jordan put down the balled T-shirt she had been using on his face and leaned tiredly back against the wall. It wasn't just the day's events pressing down on her—the ambush, the losing friends—but his arrival probably hadn't contributed to her peace of mind. What should have been a happy reunion for both of them had instead kicked off a bloody and challenging day for her.

Mom always did say my timing sucks.

"You okay?" he asked.

She gave him a wry look. "You're the one with the big cut on your forehead. Did you always look this ugly?"

"Kick a man while he's down, why doncha."

"Sorry."

"You look tired."

"I am tired." She sighed and looked at the window. "They're out there, you know."

"I know…"

She glanced back at him. "So, are you ever going to tell me what happened to your face? I mean, before this afternoon. That scar looks pretty nasty."

"The guy I told you about?"

"Pollard?"

"Yeah. He tried to carve my face with a knife."

"Damn."

"That was after he stabbed me."

"Jesus, Keo."

"No, just Keo."

She tried to stop it, but the smile came through anyway. He returned it, because he couldn't help it, either. Jordan had always been a pretty girl, even with the short hair that made her look less "girly" than he remembered. The dirt on her face that she hadn't bothered to clean since the road, the worry lines on her forehead, and the dry skin—none of those things took away from her.

He must have been staring, because she wrinkled her nose at him and said, "What?"

"Hmm?"

"You're staring. Again."

"Sorry."

"It's okay, but at least buy me dinner first, for God's sake."

He chuckled, and they went back to looking at the room and the window. He expected to see them out there at any moment crawling around like spiders, but there was just the bright moonlight. Instead of being relieved, it just made him paranoid. After so many peaceful nights on the *Trident*, being back on land left him overly anxious.

"You didn't know Tobias was going to do that?" he asked.

She shook her head. "I didn't." She sighed, then, "He's going to kill you tomorrow."

"He said that?"

"Not in so many words, but I've been around him long enough to know what he's thinking. He doesn't trust you, and he's already lost too much today. We all have. He's not going to risk it."

"Why didn't he put me out of my misery after he knocked me out?"

"Because I wouldn't let him. He wanted to, but I made it pretty goddamn clear that if he didn't at least give you a chance to explain, then I was done, too. I've been loyal to him, and Tobias is a man who values loyalty."

"So I have until morning."

She nodded.

"What time is it?" he asked.

"Around ten. You've been unconscious for half the day." She looked down at him and narrowed her eyes. "Why are you here, Keo? I can't help you if you won't tell me the truth."

"The guy in charge of T18 gave me a job. I wasn't exactly in a position to say no."

"Steve?"

"Yeah."

"What was the job?"

"He wanted me to kill Tobias."

Jordan didn't say anything, and he couldn't be sure if that was surprise or disappointment on her face. Maybe a lot of both.

"I'm doing this for Gillian," he said.

"What's she got to do with it?"

"In return for taking out Tobias, I get Gillian."

"'Get' her?"

"He wouldn't let me see her, or even talk to her, until I do this for him."

"Does she know you're here?"

"She was at the riverbanks when Miller was bringing me in. She definitely saw me." *I hope,* he thought about adding, but decided he wanted to believe it, too, so he didn't.

"And she looked okay?" Jordan asked.

"From what I saw, yes."

She nodded. "We need to get you out of here." She glanced across the room at the door. "There's a guard outside. He has orders to shoot you if you try to escape. That's why no one in here has a weapon, including me."

It hadn't occurred to him that Jordan was unarmed, but he saw it now. Her holster was empty, and she didn't have the M4 he'd seen her carrying all day. Even her sheath was missing its knife.

"Tobias wouldn't let me stay with you if I didn't give up my guns," she said.

"I thought he trusted you."

"Not after I've been vouching for you all day." She pursed her lips. "We had a pretty loud, knock-down, drag-out screaming match after he...love-tapped you."

"What did he say?"

"It doesn't matter what he said." Her face hardened, turning serious. "He'll give you a chance to explain yourself tomorrow, but the truth is, it won't matter. He's already decided to kill you."

Keo believed her, even if she was talking about a guy who looked like Captain America.

"Keo," Jordan said, her brown eyes still focused on his bruised face. "You need to get out of here before morning, or you're going to die."

"I can't go out there."

"You have to. In the morning—"

"I'll talk to him," Keo said.

"There's no point. I told you, he's already made up his mind."

"Then I'll just have to make him change it."

"How?"

He smiled and hoped it was at least partially convincing. "I got a plan. Trust me."

She frowned.

He guessed he wasn't all that convincing after all.

THIRTEEN

The one that tried to take his head off yesterday, Reese, was a stout man with a bad goatee. He entered the classroom with another man around eight in the morning to collect Keo. Pita and the girl had woken up before Keo opened his eyes, leaving just him, Jordan, and the couple across from the room.

"Rise and shine," Reese said. Then, in what sounded like an Australian accent, "It's judgment day."

"That's an Australian accent, you idiot," Jordan said.

"Huh?"

"Arnold Schwarzenegger, who plays the Terminator in *T2: Judgment Day,* is Austrian."

"Whatever, close enough," Reese said, annoyed. "Now get your asses up."

Keo hadn't gotten very much sleep last night, most of it spent trying to figure out how he was going to survive the following morning. Jordan had dozed off around midnight and woken up a few minutes before Reese showed up. Morning sun blazed in through the high window and washed over half of the room, making it easy to notice that both Reese and the other man, who

kept a safe distance just in case Keo tried anything, were very
well armed and alert. He wondered if they had coffee in the
cafeteria.

"Where's Tobias?" Keo asked, rubbing his eyes.

"He's waiting outside," Reese said.

"I need to talk to him."

"Oh, you're going to get the chance to talk to him, all right.
Get up." Reese put his hand on the butt of his holstered sidearm
for effect. "Time to pay the piper."

Not nearly ominous enough, pal.

Keo stood up, surprised he wasn't more wobbly on his feet.
Being knocked unconscious had, ironically, done him a lot of
good and Keo felt refreshed, as if he had been sleeping for days.
Jordan had more trouble, the day's events showing on her face as
she tried to fight through the muscle aches and sores.

He gave her a hand. "When was the last time you had a full
night's sleep?"

"Can't remember," she said, and gave him a brief smile.

He returned it.

"I must look like you did last night," she said, running her
hands over her face, her palms coming away dirty. "Ugh."

"You look fine. Better than fine."

She smirked. "You're full of crap, but thanks anyway."

"Let's go," Reese said before turning and leaving the room.

Keo and Jordan followed him out into the hallway. Reese
walked in front while the second man trailed behind them, still
keeping a safe distance. Keo heard voices and activity even before
he stepped back into the cafeteria.

The rest of Tobias's people were packing up their things,
everyone moving with purpose. There was an efficiency to the
way supplies were being bundled up, despite the fact that they
were now working with fewer men. These people had been doing
this for a while now, and even still clearly dazed and shell-

shocked by yesterday, it didn't stop them from doing their jobs. Tobias had trained them well.

The man himself stood over a table, looking down at a map. He was talking to a couple of men when he glanced over. Unlike last time, Keo didn't see Captain America in those eyes—instead, he saw his would-be executioner.

Damn, this better work.

"You come up with a story yet?" Jordan asked, keeping her voice just low enough that only he could hear.

"Yes," Keo said.

"You better, because I'm not going to be able to get you out of this."

"Any advice?"

"Just pretend Tobias is one of those women you pick up in bars. If you can get him to drop his pants, you're home free."

Keo grinned.

By the time they reached him, Tobias had folded the map and slipped it into his back pocket. He nodded at Reese, then said to Keo, "Let's talk outside."

He led them to the same back hallway that Keo and Jordan had come through yesterday, limping noticeably on his wounded leg. There was another guard at the back door, and Tobias pushed the door open for them. They stepped out into the thick backyard jungle, the bright and warm sun hitting them in the face.

Keo breathed in the cool, crisp morning air. He hadn't realized how thick and musky the interior of the YMCA was until now. Out here, he could almost believe he had a decent chance of surviving the next few minutes.

"Jordan," Tobias said. He had stopped and turned around. "Step aside."

Jordan didn't move. "No."

"He has a lot to pay for."

"He didn't know Miller was using him to draw us out."

"Bullshit," Reese said. He stood slightly to the right of Tobias, his hand still resting on the butt of his holstered sidearm, finger tapping anxiously against the walnut grip.

Keo heard the sentries moving around on the rooftop above and behind him and wondered if they were paying attention to what was about to happen down here.

"Ron shot at Keo first," Jordan said. "Then he called the others in to finish the job. Ron did what you put him up there to do, Tobias."

"I didn't know anything about an ambush," Keo said.

"But you came from T18," Tobias said. His voice was calm and measured. Compared to Reese, who had a tendency to raise his voice, Tobias could have passed for the Dalai Lama...with an assault rifle.

"Yes, I did."

"What were you doing there?"

"The same reason everyone else ended up at T18. I was captured at Santa Marie Island."

Tobias's eyes moved to Jordan.

"Like I already told you, we know each other from Louisiana," Jordan said. "My friends and I came to Santa Marie first, and Keo was supposed to follow. It just took him longer than expected."

"Got held up," Keo said. "Better late than never, right?"

"But you left T18 with your weapons," Tobias said. "That's not possible unless you've also put on a black uniform."

"You see a uniform on me?"

"You don't need to wear one to be one."

"Like a spy," Reese said.

"I'm not a spy," Keo said. "I'm not very good at sneaking around. I prefer the frontal approach."

"The fact remains," Tobias said, "you left T18 with your weapons. That says everything."

"That's because Miller gave me a job."

"Steve?"

"Yeah. Steve Miller."

Tobias narrowed his eyes. "What kind of job?"

"Find you, and kill you."

Reese reflexively gripped his weapon but stopped short of pulling it out.

Jordan, meanwhile, had tensed up beside Keo; apparently she hadn't expected him to use this tack.

For his part, Tobias hadn't reacted. Either the man had ice water in his veins, or he wasn't surprised by Keo's admission.

Cool as a cucumber, this guy.

"Steve sent you here to kill me," Tobias finally said.

"I had to find you first," Keo said. "That's what I was doing when your sniper took a shot at me. What happened after that was out of my hands. I didn't know Miller was planning an ambush using me as bait. It's not my fault you converged on one lone target so close to T18. That's a leadership problem."

Tobias grunted. There was a heaviness in his face that Keo recognized. He had seen that look in the eyes of commanders who actually cared if he survived a job or not. Those types of men were far and few, but he could always tell them apart from the ones who didn't give a damn if they lived or died.

"And what do you get in return?" Tobias asked.

"I get to live happily ever after."

Tobias looked to Jordan, who nodded. "My friend Gillian," she said. "The one that came with me to the camp. She and Keo are involved."

"A woman," Tobias said. Then he chuckled. "It's always a woman, isn't it?"

"It's the truth," Keo said.

"I believe you. The question is, what do I do with you?"

"That's the easy part."

"How so?"

Christ, I hope this works, Keo thought, and said, "Miller expects me to kill you and return to T18. But he didn't say anything about bringing back your head on a pike. You understand what I'm saying?"

"Steve never asked you to bring back proof."

"Right. It didn't occur to me until now why that was. It's because he didn't think I was going to survive yesterday's action. They pointed me up the road and waited for your guys to swoop in and try to kill me. It was win-win for him. I either kill some of your men, or your men get me, then his men get yours. I'm guessing he had people in the woods nearby, waiting for me to walk past like a sucker. I doubt he expected you to send that many to finish me off. That was stupid, by the way. Why the hell did you send so many to kill one man?"

Tobias shook his head, looking very frustrated. "There were only five men backing up Ron, and they weren't supposed to engage you. I had to send reinforcements when Steve attacked."

"What did they use, technicals?"

Tobias nodded solemnly. "And ground forces. It looked like he threw everything he had at us. It was overwhelming. We're lucky we only lost seven men. It could have been much worse. All-of-us-dead-level worst."

"The point is, Miller doesn't expect me to come back. So when I do, and with proof that I killed you, he'll want to see it."

"Proof?"

"I need to convince him I got the job done."

"What kind of proof?"

"You tell me. You've been fighting him for how long now? What would it take for Miller to believe I killed you?"

Tobias seemed to think about it before he said, "And then what?"

"Then I kill the fucker," Keo said. "That sound good to you?"

"That's your big plan?" Jordan said. "Convince him to let you double cross Miller?"

"He's thinking about it," Keo said.

"Yeah, but..."

"Jordan, it's not like I had a lot of options. It's either this or let them execute me. I really don't want to be executed. I kinda like living."

They were back in the classroom, except this time they were alone, with a guard outside the door. Everyone was gathering their things into the vehicles parked up front, leaving Keo and Jordan to wait for Tobias's decision. He would know in a few minutes if he was going to live or die.

If he were a betting man, Keo would guess fifty-fifty.

Jordan leaned her head back against the wall next to him and threw her arms around her bent knees.

"Relax," Keo said. "Whatever happens, you'll be fine."

"Is that what you think this is? That I'm just worried about my own hide?"

"Aren't you?"

She sighed. "You're clueless."

"I don't understand..."

"Never mind, Keo."

He looked at her for a moment, not sure where any of this was going. He had never been particularly good at reading women, but—

"They were friends, you know," she said.

"Who?"

"Miller and Tobias."

"I figured that one out myself."

"How?"

"He kept referring to Miller as 'Steve.'"

"Yeah. They were friends for a long time after everything happened. They were in the camp together. Then one day, they were running things."

"How did that happen?"

"I don't know for sure. Tobias never told me, but I've heard rumors that they—the creatures—choose leaders. I don't know how, and frankly it gives me goose bumps to think about communicating with those things."

"The blue-eyed ones."

"You've heard of them?" she asked, looking over.

He nodded. "The people I knew at Song Island have experience with them. A lot of experience. The ones with blue eyes are like the overseers—the commanders. They can talk, too."

She stared disbelievingly at him.

Keo shrugged. "That's what I heard."

She shivered. "Great, now I'm going to have nightmares. As if the black-eyed ones weren't bad enough."

"About Tobias and Miller..."

"They were in charge of T18 back when it was still just Wilmont. Ran the whole place for a while. It was just after the transition to a full-fledged town that they had a falling out and Tobias left, taking some of the men with him."

"Reese?"

"Uh huh. He was one of them."

"Why did Tobias leave?"

"It was that whole agreement with the ghouls. Tobias was always uneasy about the daily bloodletting, but I think it was the pregnancies that did it. I know that's what happened to me. 'Donating' wasn't so bad, but seeing those pregnant girls and knowing what would happen to their babies, to the human race in a year or a decade from now..." She shivered again. "I couldn't take it. Tobias couldn't, either. Since then, he's been trying to help as many people escape from T18 as possible."

"How's that working out?"

"Not great." She leaned her chin against her knees. "We haven't managed to get any of the pregnant ones out. It's mostly been the men, with a few women in between, like Pita. She was one of the nurses in the camp. She left with the girl that's always hanging around her, Shelley. Pita didn't want her to become like the others, so we managed to help them escape. They're valuable, you know. Anyone with medical skills, especially the doctors. There are only a few of them in each town, but I hear they're constantly training nurses. Pita was doing a lot of that when she was there."

"How does it work? Escaping the town. You said before that you have inside help."

"Tobias talked a few people into staying."

"That must have taken some convincing."

"Well, he does look like Steve Rogers."

"Who?"

"Steve Rogers. Captain America's civilian alter ego?"

"Ah. So if Tobias is *Capitan* America, who's Reese? Robin?"

"Bucky. Robin is Batman's sidekick. Bucky is Captain America's."

He narrowed his eyes at her. "Are you making this up?"

She smiled. "No. I guess you really didn't use to read comic books."

"Too busy chasing girls."

"Of course," she said, and rolled her eyes at him.

"How does a jock like you know so much about comic books?"

"My brother had stacks of them. Sometimes I would partake."

"Ah."

"Anyway, without the inside guys, we probably wouldn't even have what little success we've managed so far, never mind the M4s and MREs."

"Where do they get those, anyway? The weapons?"

"I don't know, but they have crates of military-grade stuff in town. Grenades, handguns, you name it." She paused for a moment before continuing. "What do you think?"

"About what?"

"The town they're building. T18."

"I never got past the marina. Miller gave me the job as soon as I arrived."

"And he never let you see Gillian?"

He shook his head.

"And yet you took the job anyway," Jordan said.

"I wouldn't have if I hadn't already seen with my own eyes that she was alive."

"Did you really think he was going to keep his side of the bargain?"

"What can I say? I have too much faith in people."

Jordan chuckled. "Since when?"

"People change, Jordan."

She looked over at him and stared for some time before finally nodding. "You really have changed, haven't you?"

"Here," Tobias said, tossing him something huge and sparkling. "That'll convince Steve you killed me."

Keo looked down at a big, gaudy, diamond-encrusted ring that no man with any semblance of taste would be caught dead wearing. Which probably explained why Tobias didn't have it on him but had been keeping it somewhere else. It was bigger than Keo's thumb and featured the state of Texas in the center, with the words "State Champ" on top.

"It's the only thing of value I have from the old world," Tobias said. "Steve would know I wouldn't give it up to anyone unless I was dead. It should get you back into T18 in one piece. What happens after that is up to you."

"You don't want me to kill Miller?" Keo asked.

"I don't care one way or another. Steve is just a mouthpiece for the creatures. They'd just replace him with someone else if he was gone. My goal was never to kill Steve or his people; it was always just to save the townspeople." He sighed, looking at the ring in Keo's palm. "I don't know why I held onto it. Maybe it was just a reminder of what used to be. If you're still alive when we meet again, you can give it back to me."

There was a line of vehicles filled with people and supplies waiting in the parking lot of the YMCA. Reese was in one of the cars and Wyatt was perched in the back of a truck. The street behind them was empty, and he could see the raised structure of I-45 in the distance. It looked gray and never-ending, but also strangely inviting.

"So this is it?" Jordan asked. "You're giving up?"

Tobias gave her a pursed smile. "Not by a long shot, Jordan. But for now—right now—it's time to take a break." He glanced back at his people. "They're tired. I'm tired, too. My number one job was always to make sure they stay alive. That means giving them time to get healthy. After that, we'll reevaluate."

"What about the people back in T18? They're going to wonder why you've stopped communicating with them."

"They're smart, and they'll get by until we make contact again."

Jordan shook her head. She wasn't convinced.

"You're not coming with us, are you?" Tobias asked her.

"No."

"About yesterday..."

"It's not yesterday," Jordan said. "Keo's going to need my help to get back to T18 and save Gillian."

That caught Keo by surprise, and he looked over at her.

She avoided his stare and focused on Tobias instead. "She's my friend, too. I owe it to her."

"All right," Tobias nodded. "It's not like I could ever make you do anything you didn't want to, anyway."

He waved to Reese, who, along with another man, grabbed some weapons and packs out of one of the trucks and jogged over to them. Reese didn't look happy when he handed them over—including the MP5SD and Keo's pack—but Keo couldn't care less. He was too busy clasping the belt back on and beaming as he checked the magazine inside the submachine gun.

Tobias was looking at Keo closely.

"What's on your mind?" Keo said.

"The Steve I used to know was a good man. We wanted to do what was right for people, but somewhere along the way he went astray. The Steve that sent you out there as bait is the one you're facing now. If you get the chance, pull the trigger. Not for me or for my people, but for your own sake."

"I've never had much trouble pulling the trigger when it needs to be pulled."

"I don't doubt that at all. He sent you out there for a reason. Steve, for all his faults—and God knows he has many—was always a very good judge of character. He always knew how to manipulate people, how to make them do things that would benefit him."

"I don't think that was a compliment. To him or to me."

"Maybe not," Tobias said. "But I'm guessing it's pretty accurate."

Keo shrugged.

Tobias turned to Jordan. "I'm taking everyone to the backup location. You remember where that is?"

Jordan nodded. "I remember."

"When you get tired of this guy, come find us."

"No promises."

"No promises," he repeated.

Tobias turned around and whirled his hand in the air, and the vehicles fired up. The sudden loud blast of machines scattered birds in nearby trees, and more than a few creatures in the over-grown yards around them, on both sides of the streets, scampered away. Keo wondered how long it would take Steve's people to track them down to this location by just the noise alone.

Reese pulled up in the truck and Tobias hobbled into the front passenger seat before leaning back out and nodding at the two of them. "Good hunting."

Then they were gone, the caravan turning into the street and heading toward the interstate. Keo and Jordan watched them go, bright sun shimmering against the roofs of their vehicles, the smell of exhaust filling his nostrils for the first time in a long time.

"Well, that was easy," Keo said. "I was expecting more screaming and gunplay."

"There's a reason we followed him for this long," Jordan said. "Tobias is a good man."

Keo held up the gaudy ring. "He's got bad taste in jewelry though."

"We better get going. That much noise is going to attract attention, even this far from T18. Just like we have scouts around the woods, Miller does, too."

Keo put the ring away and looked at her. "What are you still doing here, Jordan?"

"Gillian's my friend, too," she said, walking off, "and I'm tired of losing friends. That includes you, Keo."

FOURTEEN

"You don't have to do this," Keo said for the third time since they left the YMCA behind and began the trek back to T18. That was almost an hour ago.

"Shut up," she said.

"I'm serious. I can do this on my own. I have the ring of power. Its gaudiness will be more than enough to strike down the bad guys."

She smirked. "You don't even know if it's going to work."

"Tobias seemed to think it will."

"It's been months since he talked to Miller. People can change a lot these days. You, of all people, should know that."

They walked in silence for another few minutes, passing parts of the woods that he didn't recognize from yesterday. Jordan was leading the way because she was more familiar with the area, and according to her, just as it didn't pay to stay in the same place for too long, it wasn't smart to travel the same path more than once if they could help it. She knew better, so he deferred to her experience.

"So what's the plan?" Jordan asked. "You're just going to

walk up and hand the ring to Miller and ask him to pretty please give you Gillian?"

"You act like that's a bad plan."

"It's a stupid plan. He didn't expect you to survive yesterday. He practically dangled you so we'd expose ourselves."

Jordan had a point, but Keo knew men like Miller. They were cunning and dangerous, but also vain. When presented with the opportunity to take a prize like Tobias's state championship ring and lose nothing in return, would Miller really turn it down? Keo didn't think so. Which was good, because he was going to put his life on the line for that belief.

Solid plan, pal. You just forgot the part where everything turns to shitburgers and you get killed.

"About Gillian," Keo said. "You never told me what happened."

"What do you mean?"

"T18. You left and she didn't. You never told me why."

"We talked about it more times than I could count, and I thought she was going to leave with me." She looked momentarily lost in thought, maybe reliving all those conversations with Gillian. "But when the time came, I left and she stayed behind."

"What happened?"

"I don't know. You'll have to ask her when you see her again."

"And she hasn't tried to leave since?"

Jordan shook her head. "I sent her messages using one of our inside guys, but she never answered. The only thing left would have been to get our guy to approach her, and I didn't want to risk exposing him like that in case—"

She didn't finish.

"In case of what?" Keo asked. When she still didn't say anything, "Jordan."

"You'll have to ask her when you see her again," was all she would say.

"Jordan..."

"She was different in the weeks leading up to the escape. To this day I don't know what happened, but when the time came, I was the only one who left. Only she can say why."

He thought about pressing the issue, but one look at her and he knew he wasn't going to get far. If anything, it would probably piss her off.

So he asked instead, "How long have you been running around out there with Tobias's gang?"

"Three months. It feels like three years. Time has a way of slipping by out here."

They walked on, moving as quickly as they could without making too much noise. Keo caught a couple of squirrels sitting on a branch nearby watching them pass, and he grinned. He had a long and glorious history with squirrels.

"So, these people on Song Island," Jordan said after a while. "They sound like good people."

"Sure, if you don't mind all the crazy shit they do."

"Hunh."

He gave her a curious look. "Meaning?"

She had walked on in front of him, but he pictured her smiling to herself when she said, "You calling someone else crazy. That's a good one."

He grunted. "You haven't met these people. They're all nuts."

"I'd still like to meet them one of these days. Especially Lara."

"Maybe you will."

"You think he found them by now? Her boyfriend Will?"

"He'd have to be alive first to do that."

"You don't think he is?"

"We were out there for a month and never heard a peep from him. If he was still alive, he would have already made contact." He shrugged. "But what do I know. From what everyone keeps telling me, he's too stubborn to die, so anything's possible, I guess."

"That'd be nice, wouldn't it?"

"What's that?"

"People finding each other out here. Like you and Gillian."

"Happily ever after?"

"Maybe just a happily for now—"

Clop-clop-clop!

Jordan froze and started lifting her rifle, but Keo grabbed her by the arm and pulled her down to the ground first. They ended up behind a thick bush on their stomachs, faces pressed into the soft earth just as two men on horseback galloped past them.

Soldiers in black uniforms, M4s thumping against their backs.

They were heading off in the same direction Keo and Jordan had just come from: toward the YMCA building. It had to have been the cars firing up at the same time. Tobias's people had made a hell of a ruckus, but they could afford to, because they were abandoning the base.

He was hoping one of the soldiers might be Jack Miller, who would have made for an even better bargaining chip than Tobias's ring. But that turned out not to be the case. Even though he only saw the two men from the back as they were riding away, one was too thin and the other was too tall to be Jack.

Next to him, Jordan had eased her carbine forward and was gripping it perhaps just a little too tightly. He could tell she wanted to fight.

He shook his head and they exchanged a brief look, then waited for the *clop-clop-clop* to slowly fade into the background.

When they couldn't hear the soldiers anymore, they picked themselves up and brushed the dirt off their clothes.

"They're heading for the YMCA," Jordan said.

"If we move farther back into the woods, away from the road, can you still find T18?"

"I've been walking and running and fighting around here for months now. I could find T18 with a blindfold on."

"So that's a yes?"

"Yes, smartass."

They continued on, but also moved deeper into the woods. It wasn't a guarantee they wouldn't run into more soldiers, but Keo didn't feel like taking any chances now. He'd already taken too many unnecessary risks on his way here, and having found Gillian, he wanted to play it as safe as possible.

"Kill Steve. Save Gillian. Live happily ever after."

His head had started bothering him as soon as they left the YMCA behind, and it only continued to get worse during the long walk back to T18. The quick spurt of adrenaline from the near-miss with the mounted soldiers hadn't helped, either.

"You okay?" Jordan asked when she saw the way he was touching his head.

"A little dizzy," he said, stopping momentarily and leaning against a tree. "I guess I'm still not over getting my head bashed in by your friends."

She looked at him worriedly for a moment. "You need to rest. Get off your feet." She glanced around them, then bit her lips for a moment. Finally, she said, "Come on. I know a place around here."

They headed off again, Jordan taking him deeper into the woods.

"So everyone's gone?" Keo asked when they had been walking for a few minutes.

"Gone?"

"Tobias's people."

"Except for the ones still in town, yeah."

"How many inside agents do you have?"

"Two that I know of for sure, more that only Tobias knows about. They're risking a lot to help us, and he doesn't want to unnecessarily endanger them. The more people know, the greater their chances of being discovered."

"So except for the undercovers in T18 and you, that's it. Tobias has officially thrown up the white flag."

"You heard him. He said he was just going to rest, to let the others heal up."

"And you believe that?"

She sighed. "I don't know."

"Sorry."

"What are you sorry about?"

"You followed Tobias because you believed in him. It's never an easy thing when your leader decides he's had enough, and *vamos*."

"I guess."

"And you've never slept with him?"

She threw him an annoyed look.

Keo raised his hands in surrender. "I was just double checking."

"When you feel like triple checking, just keep in mind that I know where we're going and you don't," she said, moving ahead of him.

He smiled and followed her.

They were now moving through a part of the woods that made him a little uneasy. The canopies were getting thicker, which meant the sun was having a harder time finding its way through. As a result, the air had grown chillier and Keo instinctively clutched the MP5SD in front of him.

"You know where you're going?" he asked after a while.

"The woods might look endless, but it's not. There's a cabin not far from here that we've used before."

"Is that a good idea? If you know about it, what are the chances that the soldiers do, too?"

"We'll have to risk it. You need to rest for a while. That light-headedness you're feeling is a result of the blows you took. You might have even gotten a concussion, and it's just now showing up."

Keo felt his forehead again. The cut had started to scab over, but it was going to be a while before it healed. The good news was that it would definitely heal, unlike the scar along the left side of his face. Pollard's farewell gift wasn't going anywhere anytime soon, if ever.

Thanks again for that, Pollard, you sonofabitch. I'm glad both you and your son are dead.

"Okay," Jordan said as she finally slowed down before stopping completely.

She held her rifle at the ready as she peered through two trees at an old cabin sitting in a rough circular clearing that would be, in a few years, swallowed back up by the woods. Two dirt-encrusted windows flanked a door and a chimney jutted out on one side of the roof. The building looked just big enough to have a couple of bedrooms in the back.

The bright spot was that the clearing was wide open to the skies, and a thick pool of sunlight shone down on the cabin. It was a far cry from the last few minutes, when it seemed like they were walking deeper and deeper into the lightless bowels of the woods.

Jordan crouched at the edge and listened, and Keo joined her. He had to put his hand down against the ground because the sudden movement nearly made him keel over.

"You okay?" she whispered.

He nodded. "Yeah."

"You sure?"

"Yes, Mom."

She pursed her lips.

"Anything?" he asked.

She shook her head. "Looks clear. You ready?"

She got up and jogged into the clearing and slid against the wall next to one of the windows before he could respond. Keo sighed. He would have liked to sit and listen for another thirty minutes, maybe an hour. Not just to be sure they were the only people around, but because he could have used the rest. But that was just wishful thinking now, and he hurried over to join her outside the cabin.

The window next to them revealed a dust-covered floor, along with a kitchen lit up with sunlight through the windows above the sinks and a barren fireplace on the other side. There was no furniture to speak of, and the only thing staring back at them were the heads of two deer mounted on the far wall next to a darkened hallway that was just a bit *too* dark for his liking. The passageway led into the back of the house.

"Anything?" he whispered.

She shook her head. "You?"

"Maybe this isn't such a good idea. I can rest in the woods," he said, even as another throbbing pain rushed through him. He gritted his teeth and hoped she didn't notice.

It must have shown on his face anyway, because she looked more determined when she said, "No cover. If they find us out here, we'll have nowhere to run. In here, at least we have a chance."

He started to argue, but she had already moved toward the door, and Keo had no choice but to follow.

The handle was a simple lever, and she pressed it and pushed the door inside and stepped in a half-second later. Keo had to admit, she had developed a pretty nice rhythm since the last time they saw each other back at Earl's cabin. Being out here with

Tobias's people, fighting Steve and the town, had definitely increased her battle movements. Now all she needed was a little more patience, a notion that Keo thought was funny since he'd never really been known to have a whole lot of that himself.

Dust brushed against his face as he stepped inside the cabin. The living room smelled slightly stale, but he blamed that on the lack of ventilation thanks to all the closed windows. The back hallway was partially submerged in shadows, but he didn't detect movement or see obsidian eyes staring back at him.

Jordan had slung her rifle and opened up her pack. She pulled out a bottle of water and an old Tylenol bottle and handed it to him. "Sit down, drink, and rest for a while."

"You came prepared," Keo said. He turned the bottle over and noticed the expiration date.

"Don't worry, that's just a suggestion," she said. "Probably. Anyway, the town's not far from here. Maybe another hour, so we can afford to stay awhile or until you're ready to move again."

"It's just a small headache."

She peered at his face—or specifically, his scabbing forehead. "He really laid you out good. I thought you were going to bleed to death in that office last night."

"That bad?"

"But you look okay now. Still ugly as hell, but better."

"Gee, thanks."

"I mean, compared to the first time I saw you."

She walked to the kitchen and laid her pack and rifle on the island counter, then began flipping through the top pantries and pulling drawers along the counter. Dust erupted every time she opened something, then again when she closed them.

Keo shook out two of the pills and washed them down with water. He walked over to one of the windows, and staying as far away from the grime-smeared windowsill and glass panes as possible, looked out at the clearing and the woods beyond. He couldn't help but remember all those months at Earl's cabin at the start of The Purge.

Gillian was there. So was Norris, and Rachel and her daughter, and the girl, Lotte. Jordan and her friends didn't show up until later. Then there was that whole mess with Levy, and the garage...

But most of all, he remembered the good times. The days and nights and weeks and months when they didn't have anything to worry about, when it seemed like they could hide from whatever was going on in the world around them. At the time, he had no idea what the ghouls were doing, and thinking back, he didn't care. He would have been happy to live however many months or years he had left at the cabin with Gillian and Jordan and the others.

What was that old saying? *"Ignorance is bliss."*

What he wouldn't give for a little bit of ignorance right now.

"Did you take the pills?" Jordan called from the kitchen.

"Yes."

"Take a few more later. They won't make you drowsy."

He did feel better, though it wasn't really the pills but mostly the resting, the not moving his feet every other second. The throbbing remained, but it wasn't nearly as unbearable as it had been a few minutes ago when they were out there in the woods.

He finished off the water, then putting the bottle away (you never knew when an empty bottle would come in handy), called back to Jordan, "Find anything?"

"Not a thing."

"Did you expect to find something?"

"Maybe."

"You said no one's been here awhile. Why wouldn't Miller put someone out here? Use it as a station or something."

"He did, once. Not just here, but other locations around the area. The strip malls, the warehouses...until we convinced him it

was a bad idea. Nowadays, he sticks to the other side of the river."
Then, "I've been meaning to ask you. What did you do back
there to make Miller think you could kill Tobias for him?"

"I'm not convinced he thought I could. Chances were, he was
hoping I could take out a few of your people. Best-case scenario,
maybe make your men reveal themselves."

"That's probably true. You do make pretty good bait, Keo."

He grunted. "Stop trying to butter me up."

"Don't take it too personally—" There was a loud *thump!*
followed by a clattering sound, then Jordan's voice, screaming,
"*Keo!*"

He turned back to the kitchen, but she wasn't there. Her rifle
and pack were still on the counter, but there were no signs—

Jordan was on the floor on her stomach behind the counter,
both hands clawing at the wooden floorboards.

"*Keo!*" she shouted again.

He unslung the MP5SD and ran to the kitchen. He was
halfway there when Jordan managed to spin around onto her
back and lifted her head, looking at something on the other side
of the counter. Her Glock was lying across the kitchen where she
had sent it clattering when she fell.

He changed directions at the last second, and instead of
running to the right side of the counter, he went left where
Jordan's feet were. When he finally made the turn and saw it,
Keo might have actually frozen for a full second.

The bottom half of the creature's body was hidden inside the
cabinet under the sink, where it had apparently been hiding
when Jordan stumbled across it. It had lunged out through the
open door and had gotten a hold of her legs and was trying to pull
her toward it—pull her *out of the sunlight* and into the shadows
that fell over its part of the counter. She was kicking at it, but it
had two solid grips on one of her legs and wouldn't let go.

It must have heard him coming, because its head snapped in

his direction and twin lifeless black eyes settled on him. He lifted the submachine gun and pointed at it, and the creature actually *sneered* at him.

"Don't shoot me, Keo!" Jordan shouted.

Keo almost laughed.

Gee, thanks for that suggestion, Jordan. Real helpful there.

He fired three times into the cabinet, splintering the door and sending rounds inside rather than trying to hit any specific part of the ghoul's body. He didn't know how many times he hit it, but once was enough and its head flopped to the floor even while its body continued to jerk up and down with Jordan's struggling motions.

She finally realized it had stopped trying to pull her into the darkness under the sink and stopped kicking. Jordan stared at it, gasping for breath, before finally regaining enough control to reach forward and pry its bony fingers off her leg. Then she scrambled backward and up to her feet. She picked up her Glock and stumbled away from the kitchen, then looked over at him.

"What?" he said.

"There's more of them in there," she said, almost gasping out the words.

"Where?"

"The lower cabinets."

"Which ones?"

"*All of them.*"

"How do you know?"

"I heard them when I was on the floor. And I can smell them. Can't you?"

Keo took a quick, involuntary step away from the cabinets. "You sure?"

"You can't smell them?"

He sniffed the air. There was that smell again, the same one he had detected when he first entered. But it seemed to have gotten stronger...

"Yeah," he said.

"What should we do?"

"What do you mean?"

"Do we just...leave? What if someone else comes in here and stumbles across them later?"

Keo aimed and fired a shot into one of the closed cabinet doors.

He heard something scurrying behind the cheap wood paneling for a moment before settling into silence again. He had to remind himself that they were just bags of bones, and if losing a head or a limb didn't bother them, squeezing into the small spaces of the cabinets probably didn't register at all.

"Screw this," Keo said. "We can't save everyone. We can barely save our friends."

He took another couple of steps back and picked up her M4 and handed it to her. Jordan grabbed her pack and slung it back on.

"Let's go," he said. "I'll rest later, when I'm dead." That drew a quick, almost pained look from her. "Too soon?"

She gave him a half-smile, but it was easy to see she hadn't completely recovered from being grabbed by the ghoul and almost dragged into its hiding place. Keo knew from experience that even though the creatures looked like emaciated little children, they were goddamn resilient. It probably helped that they didn't care about self-preservation when they locked onto a prey.

He was still backing up when a flicker of movement drew his attention.

He spun toward the hallway in the back and the smell hit him. It was bearable earlier, but that had all changed. The stench was suffocating now, because there were so many of them out in the open and squeezed into the hallway at once.

Jesus Christ, where did they come from?

It had to be the back rooms. They had been inside (Sleeping? Resting? What exactly did ghouls do in the daytime?) until now.

They crowded into the hallway, so many that Keo didn't know where the shadows began and their numbers ended. Black eyes peered out of the darkness at him, but it was the growing overwhelming smell of rot and decay that got to him. They would have come out if not for the swaths of sunlight splashing across the living room, an invisible barrier they couldn't cross even though he could tell they wanted to with every fiber of their being.

"Oh God," Jordan breathed beside him.

She drew her Glock, the one with the silver magazine, and pointed it at them, but Keo grabbed her arm before she could fire.

"There's too many of them," he said. "One or ten dead won't make any difference. But we have limited ammo. Especially the right kind."

She nodded, and they backpedaled toward the door together, side by side.

"You sure you're okay?" he asked.

She shook her head and shivered slightly.

He knew how she felt, and didn't feel better himself until he opened the door and stepped outside. The warmth of the sun against his back was like a mother's embrace, and fresh air filled his lungs once again.

He forgot about his throbbing headache and turned around and followed her back into the woods without a word.

FIFTEEN

After the near-miss with the riders, then the surprise at the cabin, they took the rest of the way back to T18 slowly while listening for sounds of more soldiers and other things that might be hiding in the darker parts of the woods around them. And there was a lot of it, further increasing Keo's paranoia.

Gradually, he noticed that the air had become chillier, and when he glanced up at the sky, it had darkened since the last time. He had to look at his watch to make sure it wasn't even noon yet.

"You feel it?" he asked.

"What?" Jordan said.

"The air."

She paused for a moment. "I think it's going to rain."

"Does it rain a lot out here?"

"This far inland? It's only rained twice since I've been here."

"Maybe you guys are due."

"I guess. How's your head?"

"I took two more pills."

"That's not what I asked."

"The pills are kicking in, but I'll feel better when we finally reach T18."

Finally, around midday, he heard the familiar rush of water and they approached the tree line slowly before going into a crouch and looked out.

Like yesterday, there were people on the opposite riverbanks, maybe even the same ones. Women were washing clothes while children jumped into and frolicked in the river. A few soldiers stood around in the back, some chatting with the civilians. The sound of laughter and inane chatter was completely incongruent with the world as Keo knew it, and had been surviving in, for the last year.

He stared at them in silence for a moment. These people were at home and at peace with their choice. He could tell that just from the way they talked and moved around. His first instinct was to pity them, but maybe they were the smart ones. They had accepted and embraced the reality of the world, and from the looks of it, they were happy. People like him and Jordan, on the other hand, were living hand to mouth, getting by on what they could scavenge, and always looking over their shoulders.

Who was he to pity them? They would probably pity *him*, and he would have a pretty hard time convincing them it should be the other way around.

Jordan hadn't said a word since they looked out across the river. He wondered if she was rethinking the last few months of her life. She had been trying to rescue these people, but they probably had no idea and might not have been all that grateful if she had succeeded.

"Jordan," he said softly.

She looked over.

"You okay?"

She nodded, then got up. "Let's get going. I don't want to be caught out here when it starts raining."

She stood up and pushed through the brush. She was moving too fast, as if she was in a hurry to get away from the civilians and their carefree laughter on the other side of the river. She was already a full meter ahead of him when Keo saw something black moving against the green and brown of the trees and branches in front of her. Jordan had her head slightly down and didn't see it. He would have screamed at her if he could, but there was no time and he was afraid someone else might hear him anyway.

Jordan finally looked up and froze at the sight of the man stepping out through two large trees. He was wearing a black uniform and he mirrored her response, halting completely at the sight of her. They stared at one another for just a second, though he imagined it must have seemed longer to the both of them. Time had a habit of stretching endlessly when you were staring death in the face.

"Hey, wait up," a voice said behind the man.

That seemed to spur the man into action, and he reached for his sidearm because his M4 was slung uselessly behind his back.

Jordan, on the other hand, hadn't moved at all.

Keo fired past Jordan, the *pfft!* of his gunshot sounding much too loud to his own ears even though he knew for a fact it was little more than a coughing noise. The soldier had a name stenciled across his name tag, but Keo didn't get the chance to read it before the man fell to the ground on his stomach and face—

Revealing a second figure coming out through the same trees behind him.

Jordan was still stuck in time, and by now Keo had already caught up to her. He almost pulled the trigger again at the sight of the second black-uniformed body but somehow stopped himself. It wasn't the fact that the second one was barely out of his teens. Age didn't enter into Keo's calculations at all.

The teenager's eyes went straight to the dead man in front of him. For a split second Keo thought he would turn around and run for it, but instead the kid scrambled to unsling his rifle.

Jordan finally snapped out of her stupor and began fumbling with her carbine, but she was having as much difficulty getting a handle on it as the soldier seemed to be. Keo didn't let either one of them get to their weapons first before he fired a second shot, his bullet sailing over the soldier's head and hitting the tree behind him on purpose. Bark flew into the back of his head, and the kid ducked as if missiles were coming at him.

That gave Keo another extra second or two, enough time to grab Jordan's arm. He said, "Don't," and kept going.

The soldier had gotten back up. He was already gasping for breath, and when he saw Keo coming right at him, it only made him scramble faster for his weapon. But he was having so much difficulty Keo wondered if his rifle was covered in oil.

The teenager had finally gotten a firm enough grip to raise the M4 when Keo reached him and slammed the stock of his submachine gun into his neck. He gagged, the rifle forgotten, and reached up as Keo shoved the MP5SD's suppressor into his cheek, putting a finger to his lips. "Shhh."

Jordan hurried over, skirting around the dead man on the ground. She was hyperventilating but slowly getting control. "Jesus, where did they come from?"

The soldier was looking at Keo, his face turning slightly blue. Keo grabbed him by the back of his shirt collar and sat him down on the ground, his back against a tree, before disarming him. The teenager didn't fight, probably because he was too busy trembling.

"When was the last time you shaved?" Keo asked. When he got a confused look back, he said, "Never mind, just thinking out loud."

He crouched in front of his captive and waited for him to

gather himself. Like all the other soldiers he'd met, this one had a name tag with letters stenciled across it: "Eric."

"In and out, slow breaths," Keo said. When Eric had turned less blue, "There you go. Better?"

Eric nodded. He opened his mouth to say something, but Keo shook his head and Eric stopped short.

"Just listen," Keo said. He produced Tobias's ring from his pocket and held it up, then turned it around, making sure Eric got a good look and had enough time to read the inscription at the top. "See it?"

Eric stared at the gaudy piece of jewelry as if his life depended on it.

"Got it memorized?" Keo asked.

The teenager looked unsure.

"Good enough," Keo said. He stood up. "I want you to go back to Steve and tell him what you saw. Tell him Keo wants to give it to him. He's to meet me at the bridge in an hour. Got all that?"

Eric nodded.

"Get up." The teenager stood up and Keo patted him on the shoulder, then pointed him across the river. "Off you go."

The soldier looked at him, then at Jordan, maybe wondering if this was a trick. It didn't take him long to decide to risk it anyway, and soon he was running off. They could hear him *snapping* branches as he barreled his way through the woods long after he had disappeared out of view.

Keo turned back to Jordan and found her staring at the dead soldier behind them.

"You okay?" he asked.

She didn't answer, and he wasn't even sure if she had heard him.

Keo put a comforting hand on her arm. "Jordan. You okay?"

She finally looked up. "I know him."

"The kid?"

"No, him," she said, looking back down at the dead man.

"Who was he?"

"He was in the camp when we first arrived. His name's Dominic. He helped us get used to how things were. We..." She paused. "We were friends. I always thought I'd be helping him escape one of these days. The last thing I expected was to see him out here in that uniform."

The last thing he expected was to see you out here, too, Keo thought, remembering the stunned look on the dead man's face when he saw her.

Jordan had gone silent next to him. She had said they were friends, but the way she was looking down at the back of Dominic's head, with broken twigs in his hair, he guessed they were more than that.

"Sorry," he said. "I had no choice."

"I know," she said. Then, already moving off again, "Let's get out of here before your messenger boy decides to bring back more of his friends."

"So how's this brilliant plan of yours going to work?" Jordan asked. "You're going to kill him when he shows up on the bridge? Then what?"

"Killing him isn't going to get me closer to Gillian," Keo said. "That's the whole point of this, remember?"

He looked out of the tree line and toward the bridge, almost a full 200 meters in front of him. They were far enough to be invisible among the woods, but close enough to see with binoculars. It had taken them an hour to find the location, most of that time spent skirting around areas that could potentially have soldier presence.

By the time they reached a safe spot, his watch had ticked to 2:16 p.m.

He could see the two behind the guard station in the middle of the bridge easily enough. They looked alert behind the M60, as did the four soldiers walking around them. Four, instead of just the two that were there yesterday. They kept to their half of the steel structure, probably because they didn't want to get caught in front of the machine gun. Smart.

There were no signs of Steve, which was problematic. It shouldn't have taken Eric all that long to report in. Unless Steve sensed an ambush, then he wouldn't show up. It wouldn't surprise Keo if he was wary of just that, especially after what he had done to Tobias less than twenty-four hours ago.

Maybe he'd even send Jack in his place—

Or not, Keo thought as Steve himself appeared on the other end of the bridge with Jack riding on a horse next to him. The lesser Miller, perched in his saddle, made for an awfully tempting target.

Next to him, Jordan was clutching her rifle so hard he could hear the sound of her fingers tightening.

"Don't," he said. "I need him alive for now."

Jordan didn't say anything.

"Jordan..."

"I heard you the first time," she snapped. Then, in a softer voice, "So what now?"

"I'm going to go out there and give him the ring."

"And then?"

"Hopefully he'll keep his word and take me to Gillian."

"'Hopefully'? Christ, Keo. I didn't know you were that stupid."

"I think he'll keep his word."

"What makes you think that, for God's sake? He can't be trusted."

"I'm relying on what I know about men like Miller."

"What, that they're all assholes?"

"That, too."

"And if he does exactly what I think he'll do, and shoots you as soon as you hand the ring over?"

"That's what you're here for."

She didn't say anything.

"Can you hit him from this distance?" he asked.

"Are you kidding me? It's too far. I'm not that good."

That makes two of us.

"Then you'll have to get closer," he said.

"How much closer?"

"As close as you need to make the shot if I'm wrong. But you have to promise me you won't kill him if I'm still alive." He looked at her, catching her eyes and holding them. "Remember, we're here to save Gillian. After I make sure she's fine, we can all get out of here. I told you about the *Trident?*"

"The yacht?"

"Yeah."

"What about it?"

"I know how to contact them. All I'll need is a ham radio. When I get Gillian, we'll leave Texas behind. The three of us."

"Your friends on the boat will come get us?"

He nodded. "All I need to do is make contact."

She clenched her teeth for a moment, then nodded. "Okay. But what about Miller?"

"If he gets in the way, I'll kill him."

"What if Gillian doesn't want to leave, did you think of that? She didn't want to leave with me last time."

"Yes, but I have to find out for certain. I spent six months looking for her, Jordan. I can't just half-ass it now." He paused, still holding her gaze. "Agreed?"

"You're risking a lot on a hunch, Keo. Miller could order

them to shoot you down as soon as you show up and just take the ring from your cold, dead hand."

"I agree, he could do that. But I'm going on faith that he won't."

Jordan almost laughed. "Faith in *Miller?*"

"Not in him, but in men like him. He thinks of himself as a commander, and every commander collects soldiers. Certain types of soldiers. If he believes that I've killed Tobias for him, I think he'll want to keep me around."

"I don't understand..."

"Any man who accepts the kind of job I did—and can pull it off—is valuable these days, don't you think?"

She smirked. "You ever consider that maybe you're thinking way too highly of yourself?"

He chuckled. "That's entirely possible, but I don't think so."

"You willing to bet your life on that?"

"Why not? I've been doing it for the last six months, looking for you guys. What's one more day?"

She shook her head before staring intently back at him. "Just shoot him, Keo. Then we can try to save Gillian my way. Without Miller around, the town won't be nearly as dangerous. We can do this together. You don't have to go out there and risk everything on some stupid hunch."

"I'm relying on human nature."

"Whatever you want to call it, it's not worth your life."

She looked conflicted, as if she wanted to say something but couldn't put it into words. Keo wished he were better at reading women, but he didn't know what was going on behind those deep brown eyes of hers at the moment.

"If everything works out, can you find someplace to survive the night alone?" he asked.

"Big if..." But she nodded. "There are plenty of places around here to lay low. Don't worry about me."

"I can't help it. It used to be I was just worried about me, but these days, I find myself worrying about other people, too. Frankly, it's annoying."

"Welcome to the human race."

"Eh," he shrugged.

She smiled, and he thought it was a very nice smile despite the dirt on her cheeks and flecks of something green and brown in her hair.

"If this blows up in your face, there's another way out of town," she said.

"Your inside guys?"

"One of them. His name's Dave. I've never actually met him before, but Tobias seems to trust him."

"How do I make contact?"

"He works in the main cafeteria. Most of them wear name tags when they're working, so you won't have any trouble finding him. Oh, and he's a black guy."

"Okay. A black guy named Dave who works in the cafeteria."

"The *main* cafeteria."

"There's more than one?"

"Two. One for the soldiers and one for the general population. Big town, remember?"

"So what does Dave look like?"

"Didn't I just say I've never met him?" She looked annoyed, which wasn't anything new. He had that kind of effect on women lately.

"Right. So Dave the black guy who works in the cafeteria."

Keo turned back to the bridge.

Miller had reached the middle and was looking around with his hands on his hips. Jack, on the horse next to him, was saying something.

He looked back at her. "You don't have to do this. It's not too late to catch up to Tobias."

"Are you tired of me already?" she asked with a slight smile.

"It's not that—"

"I'm just messing with you, Keo."

"Ah."

She stood up. "Good luck. I hope you're right about Miller, because otherwise you're a dead man."

Tell me something I don't already know.

He watched her jog off with her rifle. When he couldn't see her anymore, he listened to the soft *crunch-crunch* of her boots against the ground. Eventually, even that faded, and he was left with just his slightly elevated breathing.

Why was he breathing so hard?

Right. Steve. The soldiers.

And that M60...

He slung the MP5SD just as Steve shouted, "Keo! You out there? You said you wanted to see me, so here I am!"

He paused for a moment at the sight of a squirrel perched on the biggest tree he'd ever seen in his life. The tree had been there before Wilmont was a glimmer in its founder's eyes, and would likely be here long after he and Steve and everyone else in T18 were gone. The squirrel was staring blankly at him.

Keo grinned back at the animal.

"Keo!" Steve shouted. "Where are you?"

He could hear the growing agitation in Steve's voice. Apparently everyone was getting annoyed with him today.

Keo decided to let the man keep waiting a little longer, just to give Jordan enough time to get to her spot.

"Keo! Get out here or I'm gone!" Steve looked down at his watch for dramatic effect. "You have one minute!"

Keo stood up.

This is such a bad idea. A really, really bad idea.

The squirrel must have agreed, because it seemed to shake its head at him before turning and trotting off along the massive branch of the tree.

"Keo!" Steve shouted. "You out there? I don't have all day!"

He sighed and took a step outside the tree line and onto the road and waited for the M60 to cut him down like the idiot he clearly was.

Any minute now...

SIXTEEN

He reached the bridge, and he was still alive, so he kept walking.

Steve watched him coming, but Jack and the other soldiers were scanning the area with binoculars. Even the two perched on the water tower to his right were focused on the bridge. One or both probably had their rifles pointed at him at this very moment, though they were too far downriver for him to be sure. He'd rather not know anyway.

He hoped Jordan had found a decent spot to shoot from if this whole thing went sideways. What the hell was he thinking anyway, putting his life in the hands of a man like Steve? The guy had sent him out there to kill his best friend. Okay, former best friend.

Of course, that wasn't entirely true. Steve had sent him out there more as bait to lure in Tobias's fighters, who he knew were hiding in the area. That was clever, and exactly the kind of thinking Keo was relying on: a man who could make that kind of tactical decision would see the value of keeping someone like him alive and working for his cause. How different was Steve from all the men Keo had worked for in his ten-plus-year career with the organization?

If the answer was a lot, then this was going to be a very short walk.

But he had made it onto the bridge, and a full minute later, he was still alive.

Definitely a good sign.

If Steve was going to kill him, he would have done it by now. Probably. Instead, the man stood perfectly still, hands on his hips, and squinted across the steel structure at Keo as he walked toward him.

Keo looked from Steve to the two behind the M60. One of the soldiers was permanently fixed behind the machine gun while the other held the ammo belt, waiting to feed it into the black metal monster. The other four guards continued moving around, looking for danger around and under them.

He walked with his hands at his sides, the MP5SD behind him. There was a good chance he could draw the Glock in his hip holster if someone started shooting, but it was unlikely he was going to hit much of anything from this distance. Especially when those two behind the sandbags started unloading.

"You look good for a dead man!" Steve shouted. "A little worse for wear, but apparently still in one piece! What happened to your face?"

"A painful birth!" Keo shouted back.

Steve said something to Jack, and they both chuckled. Then, back at Keo, "I didn't think you'd survive the ambush!"

"Yours or theirs?"

"Either/or!"

Keo was close enough to the middle of the bridge now that he didn't have to shout when he said, "You couldn't have given me a heads up about that?"

"I could have, but then you wouldn't have walked so casually into their sniper fire."

"You saw that."

"Not me, but guys I snuck into the area before you even showed up."

"You had it all planned out."

"I've been fighting Tobias for a while now. You have to understand the enemy in order to defeat him."

"Now where have I heard that before?"

Keo finally stopped a meter in front of Steve.

"Let's see it," Steve said.

Keo fished out the ring and tossed it over. Steve caught it and held the jewelry up to the light. The sun glinted off the diamonds and washed over the shape of the Lone Star State in the middle.

He took a moment to look up at the sky. Jordan was right; it did look like rain. Not quite here yet, but he guessed before the night was over T18 was going to get a lot of extra water. Maybe they could hang the clothes out and save themselves a day at the riverbanks tomorrow.

Steve had all but ignored him and seemed focused entirely on the ring. If Keo didn't know better, the older Miller looked almost...sad?

"They were friends, you know," Jordan had told him. *"They were friends for a long time after everything happened. They were in the camp together, then one day they were running things..."*

"He loved this," Steve said, then smirked. "I don't know why. It's ugly as fuck. What do you think?"

"I wouldn't be caught dead wearing it," Keo said.

"Yeah, me too." Steve pocketed the ring. "But I'll keep it anyway. In memory of him." Then he fixed Keo with a suspicious look. "How did you do it? Take out Tobias?"

"Does it matter?"

"I'd like to know."

"I shot him in the back of the head."

"How did you know about the ring?"

"I didn't, but I figured it was better than dragging his entire corpse back here. The ring was the most obvious personal possession he had on him."

He expected more of an interrogation, but Steve just nodded. "Come on, I think I still have a bottle of spirits stashed somewhere in my office." He turned to go, but then suddenly stopped and looked back at Keo. "Oh, just for your safety and mine, give Jack your weapons."

"And here I thought I'd earned some trust," Keo said.

Steve smiled. "You have. But you can never be too careful these days."

Keo unslung the submachine gun and unclasped his gun belt and handed them over to Jack. "You're looking spry."

"Feeling spry," Jack grinned back. "Won't be running around for a few more weeks, though. But hey, things will be calming down with Tobias out of the way. Looks like they turned tail and ran from what our scouts saw back at the YMCA building."

"I wouldn't know. I was out of there by first light."

He followed Steve off the bridge, but not before sneaking a look back at the woods on the other side. Jordan was there, somewhere, among all the green and brown. Of course he couldn't see her, but he could feel her watching him back.

He turned to Steve. "So where's Gillian?"

"You in a hurry?" Steve asked.

"I haven't seen her in half a year, so yeah, I'm in a little bit of a hurry. I want to make sure she's fine."

"She's fine. I saw her this morning."

"Why?"

"Why what?"

"Why were you seeing her this morning?"

Steve shrugged. "It's a small town, Keo. Don't read too much into it."

Keo didn't believe him, but he said, "How did she look?"

"Definitely worth killing a guy for." He walked on for a moment, before adding, "So, six months without any action?"

"I've seen plenty of action."

"But no sexy times."

Keo didn't confirm or deny. He said instead, "When do I get to see her?"

"After you and I have a little chat."

"About what?"

"Where we go from here," Steve said, "and whether you're more useful to me dead or alive."

Keo sneaked another look at the woods on the other side of the river, wondering if it was too late to signal Jordan to take the shot.

———————

"He was a star football player, but you probably already guessed that," Steve said.

He was pouring from the same bottle of Jack Daniels from yesterday, though there was, at most, just three to four more pours left. He pushed the shot glass across the table and Keo took it, then cringed at the burn as the whiskey went down.

"I think our schools might have even played each other's once or twice, but I can't remember," Steve continued. "Way before your time, obviously. What are you, late twenties?"

"Sounds about right," Keo said.

"You're pretty impressive for a guy that young."

"I didn't have a lot of choices."

"Hard life?"

"Hard enough."

"I can respect that. Jack and I were the product of divorced parents; we were raised mostly apart when we were younger. Barely saw each other until our parents kicked off. I can understand having to do what you have to in order to get by. That's what we're doing here."

They were back in Steve's office in Marina 1. Keo hadn't been certain he was going to make it off the bridge alive, but that turned out to be his paranoia getting the best of him. Steve seemed happy to keep him breathing, at least for the next few minutes.

"He was good," Steve was saying. It took Keo a moment to figure out that he was still talking about Tobias. "Got himself a scholarship to UT in Austin. Didn't play much there, though. As fast and big and skilled as you are, there's always one or five other guys faster, bigger, and more skilled."

Steve nursed his drink, staring at the glass as if he expected to find some kind of revelation swimming among the golden honey liquid.

"They were friends, you know," Jordan had said.

And yet, he still sent me out there to kill his friend.

"What happened between the two of you?" Keo asked.

He couldn't care less about the answer, but it was obvious Steve wanted him to ask. Keo didn't give a shit, but he knew an opening when he saw one, and anything that kept him alive long enough to see Gillian and figure a way out of here was worth enduring the regretful ruminations of a man like Steve.

"We just couldn't agree on the direction to take Wilmont," Steve said. "That's the old name, before we changed it to T18."

"Who came up with that?"

"No idea. It's just temporary, anyway. They say in another year or two, maybe we'll get a real name."

"Who is 'they'?"

Steve grinned at him over the brim of his glass. "You wouldn't believe me if I told you. You've only seen the black-eyed ones, right?"

"There are others?" Keo asked, even though he already knew the answer.

"Oh yeah," Steve said. "They can do things. Crazy things." He put the glass down with half of the whiskey still inside. "It's hard to explain. One of those things you have to see for yourself in order to believe."

"I've seen a lot in my time. I couldn't explain most of it, either."

"I bet you have. Seen a lot, I mean." Steve took out Tobias's ring and spun it on the desktop like a top. For something so gaudy, it was well-balanced and kept turning for a long time. "The kind of man who accepts a contract killing, then comes back after everything that's happened, is a dangerous one."

"Or useful."

"Is that why you killed one of my guys in the woods? To make yourself more useful? That's three you've forced me to replace now."

"They all had weapons when I took them out. They had just as good of a chance to put me down as I did them. The way I figured it, I was faster and shot straighter. You should thank me for having enough self control not to plug the kid, too, or else you'd be replacing four instead of just three."

Steve chuckled. "I should be thankful, huh?"

"Absolutely."

"You're probably right. Besides, I got ten volunteers for every soldier I lose, anyway."

"Everyone loves a winning team."

"Very true." He paused, eyeing Keo over the desk. "I know exactly why everyone is here, why they can't volunteer fast enough when we ask for names. But what I'm curious about is you. What makes you tick?"

Keo leaned back, then met and held Steve's hard gaze. "You're overthinking it. I don't give two shits about you or this town of yours. I'm a survivor. I've always been. I got through all this by telling myself there was something on the other side, waiting for me."

"And what would that be?"

"Gillian."

"What if she wants to stay?"

"Then we'll stay."

"Just like that?"

"I'm not fussy. And like I said, I've been out there for a year and it's nothing to write home about." He let a ghost of a smile cross his lips. "You look like you have a good thing going on here. My guess is, while you insist everyone do their duty with the blood stuff at night, you and your soldiers exempt yourselves. Am I right?"

"Perks of the job. One of many."

"So what's not to like? Free food, a steady job, and Gillian. Sounds pretty good to me."

"And you're not holding a grudge about what happened yesterday?"

"As long as you're not holding a grudge about me killing three of your guys."

Steve shrugged.

"So that's that," Keo said. "Am I pissed off about yesterday? Yeah, sure. But I understand why you did it. Hell, I can even respect it. It was clever, and a win-win situation for you however it ended up."

"You could have died yesterday."

"Same shit, different day. I could have died a thousand times in the last year, so there was nothing special about yesterday."

Steve chuckled before snatching up Tobias's ring and spinning it on the desktop again. He didn't say anything and just watched the jewelry go round and round in front of him.

Keo waited.

Had he been convincing enough? The Keo from one year ago wouldn't have had any problems selling Steve on what he'd just said, because it would have been the truth. But this version of him, this Keo who had voluntarily stayed on Song Island even when he didn't have to, then stayed even longer on the *Trident*, was less predictable.

Finally, Steve picked up the ring and put it away before standing up. "Come on."

"Where we going?"

"It's a surprise. You like surprises, don't you?"

"Do I have a choice?"

"No," Steve grinned back.

There was a plain white golf cart waiting for them outside Marina 1 that wasn't there when they first entered the building. It had solar panels on top and at the back and looked pretty well-used.

Steve climbed behind the steering wheel. "Hop in."

Keo walked around and slid in the front passenger seat. There were two seats in the back and more space where the golf bags were supposed to go. Dry mud caked the floors and fell off as Steve started the electric engine and maneuvered them through the marina, then toward the exit Keo had only seen but never gone past.

"How many of these do you have?" Keo asked.

"Three," Steve said. "Solar panels don't charge for shit, and it takes weeks just to get enough juice to power the batteries, so I usually end up having to switch between them."

"Sounds like a tough life."

Steve grinned. "Everyone's gotta make sacrifices for the greater good."

"I hear that. So, you wanna tell me where we're going?"

"Relax. If I wanted you dead, you'd be dead. The only reason you're still alive is because you're right. I can use a man with your particular set of skills. You're going to be my personal Bryan Mills."

"Who?"

"Liam Neeson's character in *Taken*."

"I don't watch a lot of movies."

"You're missing out. In the film, Neeson plays a badass ex-CIA agent with 'a deadly set of skills.' Some guys stole his daughter and he has to get her back. Never seen it?"

"Like I said, I'm not much of a cinephile."

"We can change that. I have stacks of Blu-rays at my house. Just the first two *Taken*, though."

"How many were there?"

"Three."

"They took his daughter in all three parts?"

"They took his wife in the second part."

"What about the third?"

"I don't remember. It was kind of a shit movie. Anyway, you like classics?"

"Sure, why not."

"One of these days you should come around and we'll have a movie night."

"You have electricity at your house?"

"Generator."

"I thought the whole point of living in this place was to go back to our roots. Off the grid."

Steve chuckled. "You believe everything you hear?"

"Apparently so."

"You'll learn, kid."

The golf cart hummed toward the entrance, where two soldiers rushed out of a booth to manually raise a large metal slab blocking their path. They drove past the gate, and Keo finally saw what was on the other side.

He wished he could have been surprised, but he had heard the stories and expected something like it. Even so, he was still stunned by the scope of what he saw as they drove up a road flanked by wide fields to both sides of them.

T18 had a thriving farming community, with acres and acres of crops spread out as far as he could see, hundreds of people of all shapes and sizes moving among them. There was only the tree lines to his right and the river to his left to stop the rows of wheat swaying in the slight breeze. They drove past more fields covered in stalks of corn, along with dozens upon dozens of rows of plants, fruits, and red and green and yellow things he didn't even know the names for.

The closest Keo had ever been to a farm was in the outskirts of Colombia a few years back, when he'd had to sleep inside a sugarcane field while waiting to kill someone. He'd grown up in San Diego, and before that on military bases around the world. As an adult, he'd spent almost all of his life in cities, working in jungles made of concrete instead of dirt. He couldn't have grown a tomato if someone put a gun to his head.

The cart was moving slow enough that Keo was able to get a good look at his surroundings, and he wondered how long they had been at this. He could only spot a few soldiers, most of them on horseback moving among the fields. They were less guards and more security, which made sense because he wasn't looking at prisoners forced to garden under a warm sun; these people wanted to be here, just like the women at the riverbanks.

"What are you growing?" he asked Steve.

"Everything," Steve said. "Wheat, corn, vegetables, fruits... When was the last time you had fresh corn?"

"I can't remember."

"Or tomatoes? Potatoes? What about fresh from-the-oven bread? This is just one of our agricultural fields. We have two more on the other side of the subdivisions."

"It's...impressive," Keo said, and realized that he actually meant it.

"This is what Tobias was trying to save them from. Now do you understand why he'd never have won? But that was something he could never understand. I tried to explain to him. I really did, but he just couldn't fathom why this is a better life than running around out there scavenging and hiding from the crawlers. That's no way to live."

"You're right. That is no way to live."

"I'm glad you agree," Steve said, and reached over and slapped Keo on the shoulder. "My brother Jack's a good second-in-command, but he's a little gimpy right now."

"You offering me a job?"

"Why, you interested?"

"I'm not opposed to it."

"That's what I wanna hear. But not just yet. You did me a favor removing Tobias, but let's wait and see how you feel tomorrow. After all, it's probably going to be the biggest decision of your life."

They drove on past the fields, which seemed to keep going and going around him. And to think this was just one of three in T18. Keo didn't even want to imagine how much bigger the other two were, or how much manpower was working them.

"*Around 4,000,*" Jack had told him when he asked about the population of T18.

Eventually they passed the fields, and Steve turned into a subdivision blocked by a tall rolling gate. It had a sign across the front that once read "Wilmont Heights" but had since been covered up with a banner now reading, "T18A1."

Like the marina entrance, this one also had a guard booth. A soldier rushed out as they approached and pushed the gate open for them. Steve drove through.

"There are five subdivisions," Steve said. "One's for military personnel only, and the rest are for everyone else."

"Jack told me you had 4,000. How do you control that many people?"

"Control?" Steve said, not even bothering to hide his amusement. "What makes you think we control them? They can leave whenever they want. But why would they? These houses are the only things standing between them and the crawlers at night. There's nothing for them out there."

Keo had gone through whole subdivisions during his trek across Louisiana, and the empty houses never failed to leave him utterly depressed. But he didn't get that same abandoned vibe now as they cruised up T18A1. The streets were sparse but clean, and he found out why when they drove past the first of what turned out to be a dozen or so workers along the sidewalks picking up garbage and stuffing them into bags. They were all civilians, and he didn't see a soldier in sight.

"What did these poor bastards do to get this job detail?" Keo asked.

"You ever heard the phrase, 'People who can, do; those that can't, teach'?" Steve asked.

"I may have run across it once or twice."

"Well, these guys can't even teach, so this is the price of staying in town. You get it now?"

"What's that?"

"This is what they'll do to stay here. That's how valuable this place is compared to what's out there, why Tobias would never have been able to 'rescue' them. Because they don't want to be rescued."

"Nothing wrong with picking up garbage for a living."

"It's not, but you don't wanna know what the poor bastards who can't even do this are doing to earn their keep."

"Does it smell?"

Steve chuckled. "Boy, does it ever. But hey, someone's gotta do the dirty work, right? That's how the world runs. Everyone's got a role to play. That includes you and me."

There were row after row of homes around them. They looked almost identical, except for a few add-ons and color schemes. What caught him by surprise were the yards; they all looked as if they had been recently mowed, though they seemed to lack the uniform clean-cut look he was used to seeing in suburban neighborhoods before The Purge. Almost all of the windows were open, even if he couldn't see any homeowners around. Keo guessed they didn't have to worry about crime these days.

The golf cart was the only vehicle in the entire place, its mechanical hum drawing curious looks from the people along the sidewalks. Keo was used to seeing cars and trucks parked along curbsides in subdivisions, but there were none of those here. As a result, the streets looked wide and inviting and nothing at all like what a real neighborhood should look like. In fact, there was nothing "real" about T18A1, or T18 for that matter.

Steve finally slowed down and turned into the driveway of a house near the back of the street. It was a two-story building, but there was nothing extraordinary about it. At least, nothing that would indicate this was where a man of Steve's position lived.

"Here we are," Steve said, putting the cart in park. "Your stop."

Keo climbed out. "Where are we?"

"Go knock on the front door and find out." Steve put the golf cart in reverse and started backing down the driveway. "I'll send someone to come get you later, but until then, I would refrain from wandering off."

Keo watched Steve back into the street, spinning the steering wheel, then tipping a nonexistent cap to him before driving off.

One of the men picking up garbage across the street stopped what he was doing and waved at Keo for some reason. He was in his fifties, with a full white beard and looked like Santa Claus, if Saint Nick had lost a good hundred or so pounds. Keo wasn't entirely sure what to do, so he waved back.

Then, he turned around and looked at the house. It had brick in the front but wood paneling along the sides and, he guessed, in the back as well. It had an attached garage like every other house up and down the street. There were no mailboxes, but there was evidence someone had attempted to grow flowers around the walking path.

Keo took that walkway now, up to the front door.

He was halfway there when the door opened and she looked out.

She had one hand on the doorknob, the slight breeze picking up her long jet-black hair. The months hadn't dulled the brilliance of her green eyes, and Keo couldn't have stopped the stupid smile spreading across his face even if he wanted to.

"Keo," she said. "You're here. You're really here."

"I promised, didn't I?" he said.

She smiled. "Yes, you did."

He was so focused on her face, on the way her hair fluttered behind her, that it took him a while before he saw the rest of her. She was clutching the doorknob with one hand—a bit too tightly, for some reason—while the other one was rubbing her stomach, which was a lot bigger than he remembered...

SEVENTEEN

"You're pregnant," he said.

"You always were a master of observation, Keo." She smiled at him, though he thought it was probably a little more forced than she had planned.

"How long?"

"Four months."

Four months.

It had been three months since Jordan escaped T18, and what had she said when he pressed her on why Gillian hadn't left with her?

"She was different in the weeks leading up to the escape. To this day I don't know what happened, but when the time came I was the only one who left. Only she can say why."

Four months...

Keo watched her pour hot water from a pot into a pair of ceramic mugs, then open a package and dipped two tea bags into them. He was in too much of a daze, and had been for the last few minutes, to recall where the hot water came from.

"Tea?" he said.

"Black tea. The green ones expired a long time ago, though the guys running the farms say we might be able to grow our own very soon."

She brought the mugs over and sat down across from him. Keo stared down at the tea, then at her.

"What?" she said. "You think I'm trying to poison you?"

He smiled. Or thought he did. "Of course not."

"It's really not that bad. I hated it in the beginning, but you learn to get used to things. Tea's a luxury these days."

He picked up the mug and sipped it. It wasn't bad, but he was never much of a teetotaler. The Gillian he remembered had never been one, either. He remembered the two of them finishing off bottles of whiskey they had found in Earl's basement. Then there was the occasional good red wine he and Norris would pick up during one of their scavenging trips.

But not tea. Never tea.

"It's better with some milk or honey," she was saying. "Or sugar. But those are rationed."

I bet Steve has plenty at his house. Maybe I can go and borrow some.

"Hey, Steve, you got some milk or honey? My pregnant girl-friend would sure like some with her black tea."

Girlfriend. Did he just refer to Gillian as his girlfriend?

Christ, maybe Tobias's love-tap had done more damage to his brain than he thought.

Keo took out the pill bottle Jordan had given him and shook out two.

"You okay?" Gillian asked.

"Headache."

"Does it have something to do with that?" She touched her own forehead.

"Lucky guess," he said, and tried to force a smile, but gave up about halfway.

He swallowed the pills and put the bottle away. Then he watched her sipping tea across from him, sunlight from the open windows splashing across them. He wished it were darker inside the living room so he wouldn't have to see her belly. The most painful part was that she was still as beautiful as he remembered; maybe even more so.

"I was wondering why they told me to come home," Gillian said. She put the mug down and placed her hands over her belly. "It's supposed to be safe for me to work until the end of my second trimester. Some of the women here are in their third, and they're still in the fields."

"Isn't that dangerous?" he asked, because he didn't know what else to say.

"You would think so, but I guess not." She pursed her lips. "I'm glad you're alive, Keo. I spent a lot of restless nights worrying about you. When I saw you yesterday on the boat, you looked so different. I'm not talking about the scars. Everyone has scars. I wasn't sure then, but seeing you again, here, I was right. You've changed."

"For the better?"

"I don't know. Maybe."

She was watching him closely and Keo found it difficult to meet her stare, so he stood up and walked around the living room to get away from it.

The walls were almost entirely barren. There were no pictures or signs of the previous owners. He guessed that was on purpose. Out with the old, in with the new...

"It's kind of plain, huh?" Gillian said, as if reading his mind. "I'm just glad I have a room with a carpet and a bed and honest to goodness pillows. They gave me the house because I'm pregnant. We all get one. Otherwise, they put you in one of the other subdivisions."

"Steve told me there were five in all."

"Steve?"

"Steve Miller. The guy who runs this place."

"You're on a first-name basis with him already?" she asked, sounding slightly amused.

"I make very good first impressions," he said, managing to smile convincingly back at her that time.

"I remember," she smiled back.

Keo found himself next to an empty bookcase. He absently ran his hand over the thick layer of dust on one of the shelves, then had to wipe it off on his pant leg.

"Aren't you going to ask me?" Gillian said behind him.

"Ask what?"

"Who the father is."

Christ, do I have to?

"I assumed he's out there working somewhere," he said.

"He's one of the doctors." She paused, maybe waiting for him to say something in reply, and when he didn't, she added, "He's a good man, Keo. I didn't...really plan it. It just kind of happened."

Keo walked across the living room and sat down on a stool next to the kitchen counter. The tabletop was spotless unlike the bookcase, and he rested his elbows on it and ran his fingers through his hair. It was dirty, and he needed a shower in the worst way.

"His name's Jay," she said behind him.

She was probably looking at him, but he didn't feel like turning around to make sure. Instead, he stared across the kitchen at his reflection in a silver refrigerator, at the scar along his left cheek that looked freakishly out of proportion for some reason. He wondered why they still had the refrigerator since there was no electricity to run it. Maybe they were using it as an extra storage container. He could have thought of better uses for it, like storing Jay's body. A good man or not, Keo bet he could fit the fucker in there just fine, even if he had to chop him up into little chunks to do it.

"Keo," she said. "Say something."

"That's why you didn't leave with Jordan," he said.

"I wanted to, until I found out I was pregnant."

Four months ago. What was he doing four months ago? He wished he could remember...

"She's alive?" Gillian asked. "Jordan?"

"Yes."

"Thank God. I've been so worried about her." She paused, then, "Did she tell you what happened to the others? Mark, Rachel, and Christine?"

He nodded.

"That didn't have to happen," she said. "They didn't have to die, but they did because we made bad choices."

Keo stood up and walked to the back door, peering out at the backyard and the thick tree line in the background.

He didn't know why he was moving around. Maybe he was hoping to find a way out of the house and away from her, from her belly. Of course, if he really wanted to do that, he could. None of the doors were locked, and the windows were all open...

There was a wooden fence out behind the house, about six feet high, separating the subdivision from the woods out back. Six feet. He could hop that easily and be in the woods before Steve even knew he was gone. Despite the presence of darkening clouds, there was still enough light out there. A few hours' worth, at least. He could find Jordan, hiding somewhere out there, and go...someplace far from here.

So what was stopping him?

"You can leave anytime?" he asked.

"Anytime," she said.

"And they won't try to stop you?"

"No."

"How do you know?" He looked back at her. "How can you be sure?"

"Keo, what do you see out there?"

"Trees."

"Right. Trees. If you want to leave, go ahead. They're not going to stop you. Why should they? That's why all this fighting is so unnecessary. People are dying out there for no reason. It's not perfect in here, but it's worse out there."

"They brought you here against your will, Gillian. They killed Mark and Rachel and her daughter in the process, remember?"

"I know that. Don't you think I know that?" She looked visibly frustrated, maybe even angry with him. "I'll never forget what happened to them. But I can't change the past, or dwell on it. I can't afford to." She put her hands over her belly again. "I have to think about the future."

And where do I fit into that future?

He knew the answer without having to ask it, without having to hear her say it. He could see it in the way she caressed her stomach, as clear as day. Gillian couldn't afford to dwell on the past, and that was exactly what he was—the past.

"Keo," she said.

He met her eyes and watched her get up and walk over to him.

"I'm really glad you're alive," she said, and he wanted desperately to believe her. "Seeing you here, safe and sound, is a miracle. I didn't think I would ever see you again, get to touch you again..."

She placed her hand against his cheek, over the ugly scar that Pollard had left behind. Her skin felt warm and welcoming, and he couldn't help himself and closed his eyes and leaned into her palm.

"Keo," she whispered, and he had never heard such a

wonderful sound coming out of another human being as his name from her lips.

When he opened his eyes, she was crying, but not making any sounds.

"Keo," she whispered again.

He kissed her.

He expected her to push him away, to tell him there was only (*fucking*) Jay now, but she didn't. Instead, she kissed him back and pressed forward until Keo felt her growing belly, filled with another man's child, rubbing against him. He should have been disgusted, even angry, but he wasn't.

He wanted her. Desperately.

Maybe it was all the months alone, with only Norris's complaining for company. Then, later, almost dying on Song Island. Though, he thought it was more than that. It was a primitive longing for her, for this woman he had been searching for, for so long now, never really sure she was even still alive.

And to finally find her again...

She began pulling away, and even though he didn't want to let her go, he had no choice, and did.

She was gasping for breath as she stepped back. "Keo..."

The way she said his name drove him crazy and he reached for her again, but she pushed him away and took another step back. She wiped at her tear-streaked cheeks and smiled at him, but he could tell it took her a lot of effort just to do that much.

"Jay's a good man," she said. "I'm sorry."

She turned and walked away, and he watched her go up the stairs until there was just the sound of her footsteps.

Then, seconds later, a door opening and closing softly.

"Shit," Keo said to the empty room.

Five houses.

Then ten.

They all looked the same. Mostly. One was two stories, one was one story, then he found another two story. One had three stories, and a woman in one of the bedroom windows watched him walk by along the sidewalk. She looked young, maybe in her late teens, and she was combing her hair. He didn't see a belly, but there was a good chance she had one.

...*just like Gillian.*

The people who had been cleaning the streets when he first showed up were now gone. Maybe they had moved on to the next subdivision, or maybe the work was done. He didn't think so, though. A place this large, with this many streets and homes, had to have plenty of trash even without the trappings of what civilization once had to offer.

The sky above him had also gotten noticeably darker since the last time he was outside. Rain was definitely coming. And soon.

He had been walking for an hour and was still no closer to the front gate. He didn't recognize any of the streets, mostly because they all looked identical. Had he taken a wrong turn somewhere? Or had he been walking in a straight line this entire time and missed a turn? Did Steve even make a turn—

Honk!

A car horn, so small that he thought it might have come from a toy, blared behind him.

Keo turned around as Jack drove up in a golf cart. It may or may not have been the same one in which his brother had driven Keo here a few hours ago. Keo's mind was still too clouded from his visit with Gillian, and he couldn't be sure one way or another.

The younger Miller stopped in the street next to him. "There you are. Someone said they saw a weirdo walking around the neighborhood. I thought it had to be you."

Keo grunted. "I thought I had a few more hours until you picked me up."

"Change of plans." Jack patted the seat next to him. "Climb in. Steve wants to see you now."

"What about?"

"You'll see when we get there."

"What is it about you Miller boys and surprises?"

Jack grinned. "Hey, if there weren't surprises, life would be awfully dull."

Keo climbed in and Jack drove them off.

He made a mental note of Jack's gun belt and a revolver in the holster. It was similar to Steve's setup.

Like brother...like brother.

He peeked out from under the cart's roof at the slowly darkening horizon. It wasn't just a sign of gathering precipitation, but night was also coming. A double whammy. His watch ticked to 4:56 p.m.

"What happens when it gets dark?" he asked.

"Everyone heads home at five." Jack glanced at his own watch. "So, soon. I know what you're thinking: 'But what about rush hour traffic?' Lucky you, I know how to avoid all of that."

"Yeah, lucky me."

"Oh, what's the matter, sport? The reunion didn't go as planned?"

Keo glanced over at him. "You knew."

"That she was preggers? 'Fraid so. I'm the one who got her off the fields and brought her home for ya."

"That was awfully nice of you."

"She wanted to know why, but I didn't tell her. I figured you'd like to do the honors. You can thank me later."

"I'll do that. Later."

Jack laughed. "Perk up, sport. There's plenty of women around. We did a survey last month. There are five women for every guy. Tell me you don't like those odds. The best part? They don't expect you to put a ring on it."

The younger Miller was still very amused with himself as he drove, and it was all Keo could do not to reach over and snap his neck. It was tempting. It was so tempting, but he was still walking (or riding, now) in a fog, unsure of how to proceed.

He thought about Jordan, somewhere out there, and hoped she had found shelter for the night, because darkness was coming faster than normal today.

After exiting T18A1, Jack turned left and took Keo back through the agriculture fields for a second time. Keo watched the multiple —and seemingly endless—streams of people returning home. They were talking, laughing, and looking for all the world like they belonged here, that all their life had led to this moment.

"I'll never forget what happened to them. But I can't change the past, or dwell on it. I can't afford to. I have to think about the future."

Could he really settle here? Take what guys like Steve gave him and be happy with it? Maybe find a woman and have a kid. Or two kids. So what if his children were destined to become another cog in the ghoul machine? So what if the entire human race had been reduced to chattel? *So what* if all those months of fighting and killing and almost dying more times than he could count to get here, to reunite with Gillian, had all been for nothing?

So fucking what.

"Forget her," Jack was saying. "Plenty of fish in the ocean. That ugly mug notwithstanding, you can do pretty good here, sport. I mean, look at me. I got a woman at home. She's giving birth to twins in five months. Life's good."

"They leave you guys alone?" Keo asked. "The monsters?"

"We call them crawlers."

"Why crawlers?"

"It's...nicer. Plus, Steve's orders. Don't want to start calling the bosses monsters, right? Think about the meetings. How awkward would those be?"

"Hunh."

"But yeah, they stay out of the town at night. Don't ask why. One of the mysteries of the universe. It's easier if you don't think too much about it. Better for your sanity, especially at night."

They finally reached the marina, and this time the gate was down and two of the four soldiers guarding the booth hurried out of the small building to raise it for them. Jack turned inside.

As they drove through the empty parking lot, there were noticeably fewer soldiers around than earlier in the day. He only saw two people walking back and forth on the docks, and about a half dozen more were heading toward the gate. It made sense for such a drastic drawdown of forces at night. What idiot would attack the town under the cover of darkness? For that matter, what moron would be outside, in those woods, when night fell?

Jack drove toward the office buildings, but instead of heading for Marina 1 as Keo had expected, the younger Miller turned left and parked in front of the large warehouse at the north end of the lot.

"What's going on?" Keo asked.

"Find out inside," Jack said.

They climbed out and Keo peeked up at the sky again. Just past five o'clock, but it already looked impossibly dark, thanks to the gathering clouds. He could almost taste the coming precipitation.

"Looks like it's gonna be a long and rainy night," Jack said. "We don't usually get a lot of that around here. Should be good for the crops."

"Do they come out in the rain?"

"Who?"

"Them."

Jack looked at him funny. "The crawlers? Why would they care about the rain?"

Because I've seen them turn to stone and sink in a lake. Because they're freakishly terrified of bodies of water. Maybe the rain has the same effect?

But he didn't say any of those things out loud. He had a feeling Jack didn't know—and probably didn't care, either.

He shrugged, said, "Just wondering."

"You wonder too much," Jack said. "Come on, let's see what Steve wanted to show you. I hear it's a real humdinger."

Jack hobbled the short distance to the warehouse with the help of a cane, and watching him, Keo once again went through the pros and cons of taking the man's revolver and shooting him dead right then and there.

The pro was that he would be armed again, and Jack would be dead.

The con, though, meant having to fight a lot of soldiers still inside the marina with nothing but a revolver and its six bullets. Besides the two leftovers he had seen at the docks, there were the four at the guard booth and the half dozen or so heading toward the gate.

The odds were against him at the moment.

So what else is new?

He didn't have time to do anything anyway, because the twin doors slid open as soon as they approached them, revealing two more soldiers in black uniforms standing in front of a bright LED lamp. They stepped aside for Keo and Jack.

The interior of the warehouse was massive, and shelves lined the sides. The high ceiling was reinforced with thick beams, and a dozen or so black birds watched Keo walking underneath them like curious spectators, as if they knew something he didn't.

It wasn't the shelves or the lone twenty-eight-foot yacht parked in its own slot to his right that drew Keo's attention. It was Steve. He was standing in the middle of the room, his back turned, and he was holding a knife in one hand. Blood on the blade dripped to the ground where there was already more than one fresh pool.

Steve looked over his shoulder as Keo and Jack entered the warehouse. "Hey, how'd the reunion go? Or should I take reports of you walking around the neighborhood all by your little lonesome as not a good sign?"

"Sounds about right," Keo said. "Jacky boy says you wanted to show me something."

"Come see." He turned around. "Goes to show you, you never know what you'll find unless you make the effort to look."

Steve stepped aside to reveal a figure hanging from the ceiling beams by a blue rope.

It was a woman, though it was hard to tell because her face was covered in blood and one eye was almost entirely shut, the flesh around it black and purple. She had short blonde hair and her lips were cut, her nose possibly broken, and Steve had cut ribbons into her shirt with the knife, leaving the flesh underneath dripping red with blood.

Jordan.

EIGHTEEN

The rope was a double braid nylon, the kind used to tie up boats, and it must have bit into her wrists as they kept her suspended in the air half a foot off the ground. Thick rivulets of blood dripped down the sides of her face and onto the concrete floor, where they were quickly absorbed by the larger pools already gathering under her dangling boots.

Keo willed himself to take slow and steady breaths, pushed aside his accelerated heart rate, and took stock of his situation.

Steve, behind him, was armed, and so was Jack in front of him. The two soldiers at the doors would also be a big problem. He would have to kill Steve first, because he was closest. He could do that by taking the knife and jamming it into his throat, or go for the revolver in his hip holster. There were six bullets in the gun. One to Steve's head—at this range, Keo couldn't have missed if he had blindfolds on—then the second shot would take out Jack.

The two at the doors? Depending on how alert they were, he could probably take both out before they could return fire.

Probably.

He was being overly generous of his own skills, of course. But even if Steve or Jack put up a fight that lasted longer than a few seconds, he believed enough in his abilities that he could, reasonably, kill both soldiers with minimal danger to himself and Jordan, who would be hanging helplessly from the rafters throughout all of this.

And then what?

Assuming he could kill everyone in the warehouse who needed killing, that still left...all the soldiers outside. The two on the docks, the four at the front gate, and the ones still making their way out of the marina. They would converge on the warehouse as soon as the first shots rang out. Worse, they would have him cornered inside.

Not good.

No, shooting his way out of here, while dragging a half-conscious Jordan with him, was not going to work. It wouldn't serve Jordan in any way, except possibly to get her killed minutes after rescuing her.

There had to be another way.

How?

Wait. What was that Steve had said to him when he first arrived? About how he viewed Tobias's people and those he called stragglers?

"You see, I put people who haven't gotten with the reality of our situation into two categories: The ones that don't know any better, and the ones that are determined to make things miserable for everyone else. You belong in the former category."

There it was. He didn't have to convince Steve of a lie, he only had to convince the man of something he already believed.

"...the ones that don't know any better..."

"Found her about a mile from here," Steve was saying. "She had a nice hiding spot, too, but I figured she had to be nearby after what happened with Eric in the woods."

Eric was the teenager from earlier, the one Keo had spared in order to give his message to Steve. He should have known the little bastard would mention that Keo wasn't alone, that Jordan was with him. It had never occurred to him that Steve would have someone out there looking for her after he left the bridge. Steve hadn't said a word about her, and Keo had assumed...

You ass.

"She wouldn't tell me her name," Steve said. He gestured with the knife, flicking (*Jordan's*) blood back and forth across the floor. "Wouldn't say much, really. But who else would be running around out there except your friend?"

"She's not my friend," Keo said.

Jordan blinked her one good eye, looking past Steve and at him. He couldn't be sure, but he thought he saw disappointment on her bloodied face.

"No?" Steve said. "She was with you earlier."

"Doesn't mean she's my friend."

"Then who is she?"

"Just someone who decided to come along to T18. She's tired of living hand to mouth out there with Tobias. After I killed him, she asked to come back, too, wanted to rejoin the town."

"Is that right?" Steve looked back at Jordan. "So why didn't she come in from the cold the same time as you?"

"I promised her I'd talk to you about it first. Make sure you didn't hold a grudge against any of Tobias's people. She's not the only one, you know. There are others."

"How many more?"

"A handful."

Steve smirked. "Can't say I'm surprised." Then he narrowed his eyes at Keo. "Not that I believe what you're saying."

"Why would I lie?"

"I don't know. Why would you agree to kill a man you barely

know? Why would you come back here after I used you as bait? I don't know why you do most of the things you do, Keo."

"There you go overthinking it again," Keo said, injecting just enough amusement into his voice to make it convincing. "I already told you, I'm not that complicated."

He looked past Steve and at Jordan. Her good eye was closed, and she was bleeding and hurt (badly, badly hurt), but he hoped there was nothing wrong with her hearing. If she had been listening, maybe she would understand what he was doing. Or trying to do, anyway.

"He's not wrong," Jack was saying. "You saw that girl he was doing all of this for. Preggers or not, I'd probably kill a few guys just to get some of that."

Steve grinned. "She's not bad."

"She was hotter before," Keo sighed. "But she's not going to be pregnant forever. Know what I mean?"

"I don't know what you're talking about," Jack said. "My girls are glowing."

"It's probably because of all the potatoes you're feeding them," Steve said.

Jack shrugged. "Maybe."

Steve nodded at Keo, as if to say, *"Okay, maybe I believe you,"* before turning back to Jordan. He cupped her bloodied chin and lifted her head until she could look him in the eyes.

"Look at me," Steve said. "Hey."

She opened her eye slowly.

"Is he right?" Steve asked her. "You were waiting for a signal to come in?"

Jordan didn't react.

Come on, Jordan, play along...

Finally, her head moved. It was nodding, or trying to.

"Why didn't you say that when they caught you?" Steve asked.

She struggled to answer, small incomprehensible sounds escaping her bloodied lips.

"I can't hear you," Steve said. "Louder."

"No...chance..." she managed to say.

Steve let go of her chin, then pulled a small rag out from his back pocket and cleaned his hands. He did the same to the knife before sliding it back into its sheath.

"The boys did that to her face," Steve said to Keo. "I guess they got a little carried away. Tobias's people may have suffered heavy losses yesterday, but they've been hounding us for months. I've lost more than my share, too."

"What about the knife?" Keo asked.

"That was me," Steve said with a dismissive shrug. "She wasn't being very cooperative." Then, "Where are the others? The rest of Tobias's people?"

"Somewhere out there. You found where they were last night? The YMCA near the highway?"

"Scouts did," Jack said.

"They were there when I left. I guess your guys must have spooked them. I was supposed to tell her—" he nodded at Jordan "—that everything was arranged, then she would relay the message back to the others and they'd all come in at the same time."

"The lambs are coming home," Jack smiled. "I told you they'd come running back when we finally got rid of Tobias."

"Easier said than done," Steve said. "Until today, anyway." He nodded at Jack. "Get her to Bannerman. Make sure no one sees her like this."

"I hate going there. Bannerman gives me the creeps."

"Suck it up," Steve said. Then to Keo, "Come on," before starting off.

Keo looked back at Jordan and caught her staring at him with her good eye. He gave her a barely visible nod and she blinked back once.

He turned around as Jack ordered the soldiers to bring Jordan down, and he heard her grunting with relief as she was lowered to the hard concrete floor.

Outside, the clouds above T18 had grown in size and gotten much grayer. Though they had over an hour before sundown, it was already dark enough that the LED floodlights had begun switching on along the docks.

"What's going to happen to her?" Keo asked.

"Bannerman will take care of her," Steve said. "She should be fine in a couple of days."

"Those knife cuts won't be fine in a couple of days."

"Everything heals eventually, Keo. She's lucky I believed you, otherwise I would have really gone to work."

"You mean you weren't 'really' working back there?"

"That was a warm-up. You don't wanna see me really working." He stared at Keo when he added, "Trust me on that."

"Sure. Whatever you say, Steve."

"Good." He climbed into the golf cart. "The first step to a healthy partnership is to recognize your position in the hierarchy. In T18, what I say goes. Got it?"

"Gotten."

"That's a good soldier." He grinned. "Now, let's go have dinner. I'm famished."

Steve lived in T18A3, two subdivisions over from the one where Gillian (and *Fuck-You-Jay*) lived. The housing areas were separated by the same six-foot wooden fencing he had seen in the back of Gillian's house. Nothing that would keep anyone out, but just enough to separate the different areas into their own little corners.

With the gathering clouds growing darker above him, it felt as if they were driving through nightfall. Keo had to temper his growing anxiety about still being outside, especially without his guns.

"Relax," Steve said behind the steering wheel. "They don't come into town. There's an invisible line that they don't cross. When I decide I can fully trust you, I might tell you how it all works. Until then, you'll just have to be satisfied with Rule #1."

"Which is?"

"Everything within the town is safe. Everything beyond it? Go at your own risk."

"Good to know..."

Lights hanging from repurposed power poles along the road had begun slowly turning on as they traveled from the marina back to the subdivisions. The lights had come on by themselves, and he guessed they were similar to the solar-powered lamps he'd seen on Song Island, only smaller and less efficient. They weren't quite bright enough to push back the darkness completely, but there were enough of them to navigate by.

"Where'd you find the lights?" Keo asked.

"Archers," Steve said. "From Home Depot and Lowe's, too. You name it, we've raided them. That's why there isn't very much left out there. Before he went rogue, Tobias and I knew we'd be able to use all the renewable resources from the old world, so we began stockpiling them pretty early on. No one had bothered looting them, so we had our pick. The guys in charge of the other towns did the same thing."

"You talk to them?"

"Oh, sure, I call them on the phone every other day."

"Hunh."

Steve smiled, amused with himself.

They drove past the gate into Gillian's T18A1, then T18A2, before slowing down and turning into T18A3. Armed soldiers came out of another booth to push the gate open, and one of them actually (and awkwardly) saluted Steve.

They went up a street flanked by lights that were slowly coming on by themselves. Most of the lamps were hanging from power poles that no longer had any uses, with smaller versions jutting out of front lawns. There were very few lights coming from inside the homes, but he did spot a couple of soldiers walking along the sidewalks carrying flashlights.

"Where is everyone?" Keo asked.

"Settling down for dinner at the cafeterias after a hard day's work," Steve said. "All the food is kept at a central location and well-guarded, so no one will be tempted to help themselves beyond scheduled meals. Gotta keep everyone well-fed and healthy, otherwise this place shuts down."

"And keep them healthy enough to keep giving blood, of course."

"That goes without saying."

"How often do they donate?"

"Once a day, every day. We don't take enough to make them so tired they can't work. You'll discover that we do everything in moderation. We have to, or the supplies won't last. But everyone has to do and give their fair share."

"Well, not everyone."

"Now you're getting it. Privileges, Keo. Humans may have been relegated to second-class citizens in this brave new world, but there are still classes within classes. You're one of us now. Enjoy it."

Until I put a bullet in your head, Keo thought, thinking about Jordan hanging from the rafters in the warehouse back in the marina.

"So where are we going?" he asked instead. "To the cafeteria for dinner?"

Steve chuckled. "Does the President of the United States eat at Luby's?"

———

Steve lived in a two-story house that was almost exactly in the middle of T18A3. Keo had expected something bigger and more grand as befitting the "president" of T18, but it looked like all the others—half brick up front and mostly wood paneling along the sides and in the back.

Solar-powered LED lights in the ground lit their way up the driveway and to the front door. Each light no doubt had a very sharp point on the other end, and Keo fantasized about pulling one of the stakes up and shoving it into the back of Steve's head as he followed the man up the walkway.

Steve didn't knock or need a key to open the door. He just opened it, and the aroma of fried chicken hit Keo as soon as he stepped inside.

"Yum yum yum," Steve said, smacking his lips. "Now that smells good!"

"Be ready in a few minutes!" a woman called over to them.

"That's my lady," Steve said. "She's a great cook."

"Fried chicken?" Keo said. "You have chicken?"

"We have a farm behind one of the fields. Chickens, ducks, cows... Where do you think the horses come from? A man can't live on MREs and vegetables his entire life, Keo."

"Does everyone get fried chicken?"

"Sure, once a week. Maybe once every two weeks. Portions, anyway."

Classes within classes. Right.

The woman in the kitchen was picking up pieces of drumsticks frying in a pan and putting them onto plates. She glanced over at Keo and smiled. Mid-twenties, blonde, and much prettier than someone like Steve deserved. She was wearing a flower-printed dress and an apron, and her hair was done in an old-fashioned style that made Keo wonder if he had stepped into a real-life *Leave It To Beaver* episode.

"Keo, this is Lois, my better half," Steve said. "Darling, this is Keo."

"Is that Japanese?" Lois asked.

"Korean," Keo said.

"Oh, cool."

"Keo's a half-breed, right?" Steve said.

"Honey, that's not nice!" Lois said.

"He doesn't mind. Right, Keo?"

"Right," Keo nodded, just barely suppressing a grimace.

"See?" Steve said. He went into the kitchen, slipped his arms around Lois's waist, and nuzzled her neck. "Smells good. And the food, too."

"Steve," Lois said.

They were doing that pretend-annoyed thing that husbands and wives did in front of company. Keo wanted to throw up.

"Show Keo where to clean up," Lois said. "I'll have everything ready by the time you guys are done."

"Yes, ma'am." Steve kissed her neck and grabbed her ass with both hands.

She yelped. "Steve!"

Steve laughed, and Keo couldn't decide if all of this was some theater for his benefit, or if they really were this sickeningly satisfied with their lives inside the safe zone of T18.

"Come on, you look and smell like shit," Steve said to him. "I was going to send a uniform over to Gillian's house, but I guess that can wait."

"A uniform?" Keo said.

"You might as well look the part if you're going to stay. You are going to stay, aren't you?"

Keo shrugged. He didn't want to come across as too anxious. "Maybe. There's not much out there."

"Not unless you believe the radio."

"Radio?"

"Want a laugh? Come take a listen."

Steve led him into a study that was partially lit by a pair of LED lights clamped to the windowsills. Keo saw a soldier outside across the street, smoking a cigarette, the outline of his M4 rifle jutting out from behind his back. Keo thought about all the things he could do with that weapon.

Steve walked to a dresser and turned on a battery-powered radio and fidgeted with the knobs. Keo only heard static, but Steve seemed certain there was something there and kept hunting around the dials.

"They had another message they were broadcasting before this one," Steve was saying. "It went kaput about a month ago. I assumed my compatriots did that. Anyway, one of my guys picked up this new one yesterday. It's definitely the same people." He found what he was looking for and stopped, then turned up the volume. "Here it is. Same woman, different message."

Keo already knew what he was going to hear before he heard it, because he had been there in person when they recorded the message on the bridge of the *Trident*.

"...silver. Bodies of water. And sunlight," a female voice said through the radio. "These are three things that we know for certain that can, and will, kill the creatures, these things in the darkness we call ghouls."

He almost smiled at the sound of Lara's voice but managed to stop himself at the very last second because Steve was watching him, maybe trying to gauge his reaction across the semidarkness of the room.

"For their human collaborators, the traitors in uniforms that scour the countryside in the daylight for survivors," Lara continued, "any bullet will do. If you're able, get to a place that is surrounded by bodies of water. Stock up on silver; if you know how, make silver bullets, or any silver-bladed weapons. The daylight is no longer your friend, but don't be discouraged. As long as you're breathing, as long as you are free, there is hope. We will adapt and keep going, because that's what we do. This is Lara, and I'm still fighting alongside you."

The message paused for about five seconds before it repeated itself:

"This is Lara, broadcasting to you from safe harbor. If you're hearing this, that means you're still out there, too. Remember: Silver. Bodies of water. And sunlight. These are three things that we know for certain that can, and will, kill the creatures, these things in the darkness we call ghouls..."

Steve turned down the volume until Keo could barely hear Lara's voice. "She believes it, too. Just like Tobias. She thinks you can keep fighting them. The sad part is, we've caught a couple of people listening to this propaganda bullshit. Luckily, we've managed to nip those in the bud before they got out of control. This type of thing is like a virus; if you don't stamp it out immediately, it spreads. We can't have that."

"How are you going to stop it?" Keo asked.

"Easy. I outlawed radios." Then he smiled. "Anyway, let's go wash up. The chicken smells ready."

On cue, Lois called from outside in that much-too-June-Cleaver voice, "Come and get 'em, boys!"

Lois was pretty and lively, and while she was bringing the plates of fried chicken, beans, and corncobs over, Steve leaned over to Keo and whispered, "She wants to get pregnant—you know, do her part for the town—but I won't let her. I don't know about you, but I prefer them slim and hot."

Keo smiled and nodded, but all he could think about was Gillian. She was pregnant right now with another man's baby. Four months pregnant. What was he doing four months ago? He couldn't even remember. Somewhere in the Louisiana woods, trying to survive Pollard's small army of paramilitary assholes, probably.

Steve had grabbed the biggest piece of chicken thigh on the plate and was about to wrap his mouth around it when his radio squawked, and a male voice said, "Sir? It's Grant. Come in."

Lois sighed. "Honey, why do you still have that thing turned on? It's dinnertime."

Steve ignored her, put down the chicken, and unclipped the radio from his belt. He keyed it, said, "What is it?"

"Uh, sorry to disturb you, sir, but I have some bad news," Grant said.

"Steve," Lois started to say, but she froze when Steve shot her a hard glance. She looked down at her plate of beans instead.

"Go on," Steve said into the radio.

"It's, uh, your brother, sir," Grant said. He sounded nervous.

"What about Jack?"

"He's dead, sir."

"What the *fuck* do you mean he's dead?"

Steve shot up from the table, nearly knocking it over. Lois gasped and grabbed onto a corncob as it rolled off a plate.

"The woman," Grant said, and Keo thought his voice was trembling slightly. "She's gone. Someone busted in on Doctor Bannerman's place and took her. They, uh, shot Jack while they were escaping."

Keo thought he was ready for it, but even he was surprised when Steve punched the table so hard that everything—the dishes, the chicken, and the corncobs—flew everywhere. Lois screamed and stumbled to her feet while Keo managed to grab onto a chicken leg as it bounced into the air.

"*Fuck!*" Steve screamed.

Keo didn't say anything. He took a bite out of the chicken leg. It tasted good, but then he hadn't had fried chicken in years, so Lois could have actually been an awful cook and he might not have noticed.

Besides, he needed something for his mouth to do, otherwise he might have burst out laughing uncontrollably at the sight of Steve raging in front of him.

NINETEEN

Keo still had the taste of chicken in his mouth, and maybe a small piece of meat hidden somewhere between his molars at the back, when he was driven over to T18A2, next door to Gillian's subdivision, and climbed out of the golf cart in front of a squat one-story house. There were already five soldiers standing in the driveway, with a horse grazing on the lawn nearby, oblivious to the activity.

One of the men hurried over. He was sweating even in the chilly air and with storm clouds continuing to gather above them. With thirty minutes before nightfall, it already looked pitch-dark outside, and most of the streetlights (and the few sprinkled among the lawns) had come on all around them.

"What the fuck happened?" was the first thing out of Steve's mouth.

"Someone helped her escape," the man said. Keo recognized his voice from the radio. *Grant.*

"How many?"

"Bannerman said there was just one."

"And Jack?"

"He's inside."

"What happened?"

"I don't know exactly, sir. He was inside the garage with Bannerman and the woman when it happened. They shot Roger on their way out."

Steve brushed past Grant and made a beeline for the door. The other soldiers hurried out of his path. They were all wearing gun belts and cradling M4 rifles, and Keo kept count of all the others around the area. Counting these five, there were the two standing guard at the gate and a half dozen more he had seen on his way over here.

Too many. Always too damn many.

Unlike Steve's house, the interior of Bannerman's was sparsely lit by a pair of LED lamps, one resting on the kitchen counter and another in the living room over the fireplace. It almost looked as if no one lived here, but of course the blood on the floor and a dead soldier lying facedown on the carpet said differently. Keo stepped around the blood and followed Steve to the back of the house.

Steve marched straight to a door that opened into the garage, *crunching* heavy tarp covering every inch of the concrete floor as he did so. The room had been converted into some kind of operating room, though it looked and smelled more like a butcher shop. A pair of metal tables sat in the center, flanked by steel trays with surgical instruments; one had been upended, its contents tossed liberally across the room. One of the tables was covered in blood and there were fresh, bloody footprints all over the place.

A man in his sixties, wearing white hospital scrubs, sat in a comfortable-looking armchair in the corner, cradling his arm in his lap. Someone had bundled the arm up with gauze and the man looked tired, wiping sweat from his face. The garage door was closed—and didn't look capable of opening—and there was very little ventilation, which probably accounted for the old man's perspiration.

The lack of circulating air also kept in the smell of the blood that pooled underneath Jack. The younger Miller sat awkwardly against the far wall, his head lolled to one side, eyes open, as if he had simply decided to sit down to rest and could stand up at any moment.

Steve ignored the old man and walked straight to Jack. He kicked a surgical scissor in his path and it skidded across the room. He crouched in front of his brother and held Jack's sweat-slicked face in his hands, staring at him in silence.

Keo looked over at the old man, Bannerman. "What happened?"

Bannerman picked up a bottle of water on a table next to him with his good hand and took a slow, drawn-out sip. "Some guy in a ski mask. Came in and shot Jack, then took the woman. I guess he shot someone else in the living room, too?"

"You didn't go out to check?"

"He shot me, too," Bannerman said, holding up his wounded arm as proof. "I thought it'd be more prudent to wait for help instead of running out there. I'm just a doctor."

More like a butcher.

Steve stood up and ran his fingers through his hair for a moment. Keo waited for the outburst, the profanity, but instead Steve just whirled around and walked past Keo and back into the hallway. The man hadn't spared a single glance at Bannerman, which, Keo guessed, the old man was grateful for.

Keo followed Steve through the living room, then to the front door. "What now?" he asked.

"Find her and kill her," Steve said.

Oh, that's all?

Grant hadn't gone anywhere and was waiting for them in the driveway. For a man who was barely a few years younger than

Steve, Grant looked overly small and frail and fidgeted back and forth nervously.

"There was gunfire," Steve said. "Why didn't anyone stop them?"

"No one heard gunshots," Grant said. "I think he was using a silencer or something."

"You think?"

"He must have," Grant said, trying his best to sound more confident—and failing miserably. "It wasn't until Pete stumbled across Roger's body inside the house and called it in that we even knew what had happened."

Steve didn't say anything. Instead, he squinted up at the storm clouds continuing to gather en masse above them. There was a strangely serene expression on his face, as if he hadn't just discovered his little brother was dead.

Keo glanced around him. Every soldier, even the ones across the street, seemed to know something bad had happened inside Bannerman's house, something that was going to affect all of them. Like Keo, they looked as if they were waiting for the inevitable eruption from Steve.

Any moment now...

"It's going to rain all night," Steve finally said, sounding perfectly calm. "They have two options: Make a run for it, or hide. It's too dark to go into the woods. The crawlers will be out by now, and they'd never survive for more than a few minutes in there. Anyone who has been here for a while knows that. So they'll hide." The man glanced at Keo and narrowed his eyes. "You have any ideas?"

"About what?" Keo said.

"Where they would be hiding."

"You're asking the wrong man. I didn't even know they existed until yesterday."

"They have inside help," Steve said, looking around the

streets. "I've always known that. Someone feeding them intelligence, stealing supplies for them. M4s and ammo going missing.
That's who we're looking for. Someone who knows the town,
knows where to hide. That means we have to look everywhere.
Turn this place inside out, because they're still here. I can fucking
guarantee you that."

An inside man? Right. What was that Jordan had told him?

*"If this blows up in your face, there's another way out of the
town... His name's Dave. I've never actually met him before, but
Tobias seems to trust him. He works in the main cafeteria..."*

Dave. Main cafeteria.

Maybe Dave had heard about Jordan being held at Bannerman's. People would talk. Maybe one of the soldiers who liked
eating with the civilians. Bragging, trying to impress some pretty
young girl with inside gossip.

Not that it mattered. Dave, or one of Tobias's other inside
agents, had clearly saved Jordan, though Keo still hadn't decided
if that was a good thing or not. He would have eventually come
up with a plan to rescue her himself. Heck, he might not even
have to, since Steve seemed to have bought his line about Jordan
wanting to re-assimilate back into town. The only certainty now
was that someone had acted and Jordan was out there,
somewhere.

And Steve was right. They would still be in T18 right now
because there would be no other places to go. Certainly not out
there. Not under the suffocating darkness.

"Someone who knows the town, knows where to hide."

Keo was watching Steve's face, the way he was scrunching his
eyes and sweeping the streets, as if he could see through the walls
of the homes, when something fell out of the sky and landed on
Keo's forehead. He held out his hand to catch a few more drops,
as did some of the men around him.

The rain came slowly but quickly picked up momentum.

In less than ten seconds, Keo was soaked from head to toe.

Steve, standing next to him, didn't seem to notice.

"Search every house!" he shouted, raising his voice to be heard. "They're hiding in one of these houses! No matter how long it takes, search every single building and shack and room until you find them!"

Steve left Keo in the driveway with Grant and rode off on the same horse that had been dining on the lawn when they arrived—it turned out to be Jack's—along with a dozen other mounted soldiers. Keo guessed it was faster to travel by horseback than in the slow-moving, solar-powered golf cart.

"Come on," Grant said. "I got orders to take you to Processing."

Keo climbed into the cart with Grant and they motored off, raindrops bouncing against the solar panels on top of the vehicle. The streets were already showing signs of flooding, the multiple cracks of thunder in the distance followed by lightning flashes sounding as if the gods had finally decided to punish T18 for its trespasses.

"Does it usually rain this hard?" Keo asked, shouting over the *pak-pak-pak* of raindrops cascading around them.

"Not usually!" Grant shouted back as lightning crackled again. "Hear that? This is gonna be a huge one!"

They were driving through two to three inches of water by the time they left T18A2, and Grant turned south down the road —toward Processing, wherever the hell that was. Soldiers in raincoats had begun appearing on horses and on foot around them, many wielding flashlights. They looked coordinated, some moving in groups while others spread out among the subdivi-

THE ISLES OF ELYSIUM   241

sions. Like a Western posse times ten, except these cowboys were carrying assault rifles.

"Looks like it's gonna be a long night," Grant said. "We're going to find them, though. Not a lot of places to hide around here. No one's going to harbor them, either. Sooner or later they'll run out of corners, and then we'll get them."

Keo didn't respond. Instead, he tried to imagine where Jordan and Dave (if it was Dave, and not another one of Tobias's inside men) would go. Like Steve, they would know better than to brave the woods. Even before the rainstorm it had gotten too dark, and that brought out things worse than soldiers. Would they hide out in the inside man's place? That would depend if he was single or if he shared a house with someone (or someones). Not that it mattered, because he didn't know who had taken Jordan anyway, which left him with...

Jordan. Where would Jordan go?

Keo was thinking about that as two horsemen galloped past them along the shoulder of the road, flashlights shining in his face. Compared to the Maglites they were carrying, the golf cart's own headlights were barely strong enough to illuminate the paved lanes in front of them. If not for the LEDs hanging off the poles, Grant would be driving almost in total darkness.

Thunder boomed in the distance, seemingly getting closer (and louder) with each new one. For a second Keo thought they were gunshots and was thankful he was wrong. Gunshots would mean Steve had found Jordan and her friend, but soldiers still running around searching every house and building meant the exact opposite.

They were about to pass the open gate into T18A1 when Keo tapped Grant on the shoulder. "Hey, turn left."

"What?" Grant said.

"Turn in here."

"I got orders to take you to Processing."

"You can do that later. I have to swing over and talk to a friend about something."

"Forget it."

Keo reached over and drew Grant's gun—a Glock—and pressed it roughly into the man's side. "I said, *turn in here.*"

Grant almost missed the entrance but stopped in time and turned into the subdivision. The gate was already open, which wasn't a surprise since soldiers had probably been going in and out of the place before they even arrived.

Keo spotted two people inside the guard booth, shivering against the cold. They were soaking wet and neither one felt like coming out when they saw the golf cart moving past their window. One of them did make the effort to wave Grant through. Grant started to slow down when Keo jammed the gun harder against his gut. Grant took the hint and they continued through.

Steve's people were flooding all five subdivisions at once, but that also meant they had to stretch their numbers thin. They drove past soldiers along the sidewalks knocking on doors. They seemed to be moving in groups of two, flashlights cutting through the sheets of falling rain. Every single one looked miserable and wet, and a few gave them envious stares as they cruised by under the (barely there) protection of the cart's roof. Keo just hoped he had the gun held low enough that the others couldn't see where it was pointed.

"Turn here," Keo said when they finally reached their destination.

Grant turned the cart up onto the driveway and parked out in the open. Keo took a brief second to look around him—a pair of soldiers down the street, about five houses down; two more on the opposite side further up the road. The two behind him were the problem, but they were moving slowly, the combination of the weather and the need to search every room of every house before moving on taking up most of their time. No doubt the warmth of the houses compared to the bone-soaking rain outside convinced them to make all those searches go slower, too.

He hoped, anyway.

Keo pulled off Grant's M4 rifle and shoved the Glock into his front waistband, then climbed out of the golf cart. "Get out."

Grant did and was soon hopping from foot to foot, arms folded across his chest as rain ran down his head and uniform. His teeth started chattering almost right away.

"Don't be such a girl; it's not that cold," Keo said.

He nodded toward the door and Grant moved toward it obediently, asking, "Where are we?"

"Shut up and move."

"You're not going to get away with this."

"You know what a bullet tastes like, Grant?"

Grant shook his head. "No..."

"If you don't want to find out, keep your mouth shut unless I speak to you. *Comprende?*"

The soldier swallowed and kept moving. Keo followed him, only allowing himself to shiver and his teeth to chatter when Grant wasn't looking.

Christ, it was freezing cold. And it was only going to get worse as the night dragged on. He wondered how long it was going to take the neighborhood to be completely flooded. Hopefully Steve had paid attention to the sewers so the water would have someplace to go when that did happen.

Grant was waiting at the front door, trembling underneath a pair of small solar-powered LED lights. Keo leaned across him and knocked on the slab of wood. He could only see pitch blackness through the side security windows, but soon a lamp turned on before moving across the foyer toward them.

"Not a fucking word," Keo said to Grant.

Grant nodded. Or shivered. Keo liked to think he was afraid and not just freezing.

The door opened and a man in his thirties, wearing thin-rimmed glasses, looked out at them. He was wearing slacks and a white T-shirt and used the lamp in his hand to illuminate Grant's face before moving over to Keo's.

He lingered a bit on Keo—or maybe just on the scars.

"Yes?" he finally said.

"Jay?" Keo asked.

"Yes. Do I know you?"

"No."

Keo nudged Grant in the back and the soldier stepped anxiously inside the house, glad to be out of the cold night. Jay looked conflicted, and for a moment Keo thought he might fight back, but instead he pushed his glasses up the bridge of his nose and stepped aside to let them in.

Grant sighed audibly as they were immediately embraced by the warmth of the house. It might not have air conditioning or heating anymore, but a well-insulated building still offered more than decent protection against the climate, especially one that was currently being rocked by a thunderstorm.

Keo closed the door behind them, grateful for the sudden soothing silence, with only the distant *pak-pak-pak* against the rooftop to remind him what was going on out there. "Where's Gillian?" he asked.

"She's asleep," Jay said.

"It's barely six in the evening."

"She...had a long day."

Jay was a terrible liar. What's worse, he probably knew it but couldn't do anything about it. He was either a very decent guy not used to lying, or an asshole. Keo wanted to believe it was the latter, but chances were pretty good it was probably the former.

Just my luck.

"What's this about?" Jay asked.

"Gillian!" Keo shouted.

"I told you, she's asleep," Jay started to say.

"Shut up, Jay."

The man looked as if he might argue, but like last time, decided to back down instead.

Grant, standing between them, looked back and forth, clearly picking up on the extra "something" going on between them. Or, at least, coming from Keo. Smartly, though, he kept his mouth shut.

"Gillian!" Keo shouted again.

He heard footsteps coming down the stairs before Gillian finally appeared in a nightgown, which was supposed to confirm Jay's statement that she had been sleeping. He didn't buy it. Keo didn't need to ask her, because he could see it on her face.

"Keo," she said softly, genuinely surprised to see him there.

"Grant and I were just tooling around in his cool golf cart and decided to see how you were doing," he said.

She gave him a confused look.

"Joke," he said.

"Oh."

Jay hurried over and stood next to her. "What's this about?" he asked again.

Keo locked the door behind them. "They're coming," he said, directing everything at Gillian and ignoring Jay.

"Who?" Gillian said.

"The soldiers. They're searching every house in town."

"What?" Jay said, alarmed. "Why are they doing that?"

"Stop fucking around. There's no time for that. Right, Gillian?"

She didn't answer.

"*Right?*" he said again.

She sighed. "Right."

"Where are they?"

"Upstairs."

"Gillian," Jay said.

"It's okay, Jay," she said, putting a hand on his arm. "He knows already. Keo's a smart guy."

Not that smart, or I would have been here earlier before he knocked you up, Keo thought about saying, but didn't.

Jay looked over at him, as if to say, *"Is he?"*

"Just enough to get in trouble," Keo said.

"How long do we have?" Gillian asked.

"It's probably going to take them about thirty minutes to get here. Maybe more, maybe less. How secure are they?"

Gillian thought about it. Jay, next to her, looked physically pained.

"I don't know," she said. "Not very. We didn't expect a house-to-house search."

Keo put a hand on Grant's shirt collar and dragged him forward. "I need someplace to put him."

"Jay can help with that," Gillian said.

Keo gave her a disbelieving look.

"He can keep him from running off," Gillian said. Then to Jay, "Go get your little black bag, honey."

"Why?" Jay asked.

"Trust me," she said, before looking back at Keo and adding, "And you can trust Keo. We're going to need his help to survive tonight."

TWENTY

"How did you know she'd be here?" Gillian asked as she led him up the stairs.

They were moving much slower than they really had to, not that Keo was complaining. Despite everything, being this close to her, smelling her, was still preferable to not seeing her again.

"I took a stab in the dark," he said. "She's stuck behind enemy lines at night and she can't leave the safety of the town. Where would she go? There's only one person here who she calls a friend. You. There was also her accomplice, but I took a chance that they burned their cover when they rescued her."

"That's a big chance."

"It was fifty-fifty. I'd take those odds any day of the week and twice on Wednesdays."

"Wednesdays?"

"I don't like Sundays."

She smiled, but it was gone quickly, replaced by the very determined Gillian he remembered from the days and nights of trying to survive after The Purge. "She's bad off, Keo. I almost didn't recognize her when Dave brought her here."

Ah. Dave. The cafeteria man.

"Jay almost fainted at the sight," Gillian continued.

"I thought he was a doctor."

"He is, but he's never seen someone get beaten that badly. It's really bad."

"I know. I saw her earlier."

"You saw her earlier?"

"They were torturing her at the marina."

"Jesus. Why didn't you—"

"Save her? I did. Steve would have killed her. I spun him a story and he believed me. Then Dave had to go and jump the gun. She would have been fine after a few days."

"A few weeks, maybe."

"Or a few weeks. The point is, she would have been fine. She knew what I was doing and she was playing along. Your husband's a doctor. Did he give her anything?"

Gillian sighed. "He's not my husband."

"No?"

"No."

"Boyfriend?"

"I guess."

"Maybe live-in lover."

"Give it a rest. Things are difficult enough without you popping back into my life."

"My mistake. I only spent the last six months fighting everyone in the world to get to you. Maybe I shouldn't have bothered."

She stopped on the second floor and glared at him. She dropped her voice slightly when she said, "It was hard on me, too. It still is. It's hard for everyone, okay? You, me, Jay..."

"But he's the one you're with. It can't be that hard on him."

"I..."

He put a hand on her belly. Four months, and it already

looked bigger than a medicine ball. He didn't want to imagine what she'd be like in four more months. It would be massive and impossible for him to ignore even if he wanted to. All those nights and weeks and months wondering if she was alive, imagining different scenarios about their reunion...

He felt like a two-time chump just thinking about it.

"Your hand's cold," she said.

"I've been out in the rain."

"You're going to catch a cold."

"I'll live." He looked up, seeking out her eyes. "Four months. If you'd just waited a little longer..."

She looked down at his hand, circling her belly over the nightgown. She placed her hand over his and squeezed. "I know."

"How?"

"How?" she repeated.

"You know what I mean."

She didn't answer right away.

"Gillian..."

"It just happened. It sounds stupid, I know, but it's true. I was one of his helpers and I probably saw him more than anyone in town, including Jordan. One night I was depressed and thinking about...everything. I used to do that a lot, you know. Every face I saw, I wanted it to be you. Every time someone new came through Processing, I wanted them to be you. I thought you were dead, Keo. I tried to be positive, but every day it got harder. And he was lonely, too, and I guess we just thought it would be okay if we weren't both lonely for one night."

"Jordan didn't know?"

"No. I worked in Medical and she was in Agriculture."

"Do you love him?"

The question blurted out of him. He didn't know where it came from, and he regretted asking as soon as it left his mouth.

Not because it was something he didn't want to ask, but because it was something he didn't want to know the answer to.

She didn't say anything right away, and the wide-open second floor seemed entirely too large. Although she was standing right in front of him and he could feel her belly pressing against the palm of his hand, she was more distant now than she had been in all those days and nights he thought about her, dreamed of her, and rehearsed their reunion over and over again.

Four fucking months.

"No," she said finally. "He's a good man, Keo." She looked up at him. "But I can never love him the way I love you."

"You say 'love.' Not 'loved'..."

"I know what I said."

He smiled. "Does he know that?"

"Yes."

"But he's still with you."

"He's a good man..."

"Stop saying that."

"It's the truth. Maybe one day I'll come to love him, but it's never going to be the way it was with us. Back at the cabin, all those months together after the end of the world... You can't replicate something like that." She put a warm hand against his cheek and traced the long scar. "But it has to be this way now. Because I need him to care for this baby. And I need this place to keep it safe. Do you understand?"

"But it won't be safe. Not for your baby."

"It will be." She took her hand away and wrapped both arms around her stomach. "The doctors have privileges that the others don't. My baby is going to be spared."

Classes within classes, right, Steve?

She pursed her lips. "I know it's selfish. It's not fair to all the other mothers, but Jay has a special position here. What happened to me was an accident. Or, at least, I thought it was at first. I wasn't going to keep it, you know. I was going to leave with Jordan. Then one day I felt it."

"It?"

"The baby. It kicked. After that, I couldn't go through with it. I couldn't leave to raise my baby out there. It wouldn't have survived for long. But in here, it could. I could watch it grow."

"In this town..."

"It's better than out there. Maybe if you had been here earlier, things would be different. But you weren't, so I made a choice. And I chose my baby."

She placed her head against his chest and Keo slipped his arms around her. He held her tight and never wanted to let her go, the way he had over six months ago when Pollard's soldiers attacked the cabin. He had made that choice to save her.

Joke's on you, pal.

"I'm sorry," she whispered.

"I know," he whispered back.

He kissed her hair and inhaled her scent. Just soap and water, he knew, but it was still better than anything he had smelled in months.

Then, because he couldn't take it anymore, "Let's go see Jordan."

Jordan was unconscious and lying on a bed in the guest bedroom. She was pantless and wearing an oversize button-down shirt that went all the way down to her thighs. Her face was still badly bruised, the purple and black swelling over her left eye even uglier now than when he had seen it earlier at the warehouse.

The room was dark, but there was enough LED light coming through the back window to see Jordan and her protector. He was a black man in his thirties with a shaved head, and he stood next to the window looking out at the streets—or at least what little of it he could see through the falling rain. He had a Walther P22 with an attached suppressor that he clenched tightly at his side, and the gun twitched when the door opened and Keo stepped inside with Gillian.

"Hello, Dave," Keo said.

The man grinned. "I've never heard that one before."

"What's that?"

"What?"

"What?" Keo repeated.

"'Hello, Dave,'" the man said. "From 2001."

"I don't know what that is."

"It's a science fiction movie. Stanley Kubrick? That's where the line's from."

"I don't watch a lot of movies."

Dave shook his head. "Whatever. That your golf cart down there?"

"You need a ride?"

"Hell yeah."

"This is Keo," Gillian said. "He's a friend of ours."

"'Ours'?"

"Jordan and me."

"What happened to your face?" Dave asked him.

"Shaving accident," Keo said.

"Oh yeah? I ran out of shaving cream months ago."

"I use butter."

"Butter?"

"Yes."

Dave looked like he was trying to figure out if Keo was kidding him, before finally saying, "Word of advice. You're not nearly as quiet as you thought you were being. I could hear the two of you talking through the wall."

"Sorry," Gillian said, and gave Keo an embarrassed look.

"Anyway, I'm seeing a lot of activity on the streets. Soldiers with flashlights moving through the rain. What's going on?"

"They're looking for you," Keo said. "Going house to house. Two of them are on their way here now. We have about twenty minutes to get you and Jordan to a better hiding spot."

"Shit," Dave said. "Where?"

Jay appeared behind them, squeezing through Keo and Gillian. "Excuse me," he said, and walked to the bed.

"What's he doing?" Dave asked.

"Getting her ready to move," Gillian said. "You're going with her."

"Where are we going?"

"Downstairs." When Dave still looked unconvinced, she added, "Trust me, Dave, okay?"

Dave nodded. "All right."

"Bring her down when you guys are done," Gillian said, and left them.

Keo watched her go, then looked back at Jay. The doctor was unbuttoning the oversize shirt and checking Jordan's wounds. Then he opened a black bag he had brought in with him and took out a syringe.

"What's that?" Dave asked.

"Sedatives to keep her asleep for a while," Jay said.

"She gonna be okay?"

"If you're worried about the cuts, don't be; they'll heal as long as they don't get infected. And the swelling around her eye will go down soon."

Keo looked at Dave. "You didn't exactly think this through, did you? You didn't think the soldiers would start going house to house looking for you?"

Dave shook his head. "I thought I had at least an hour to get her out of town."

"You took a big risk rescuing her from Bannerman's. Why?"

"I thought they were going to interrogate her for information."

"What kind of information?"

"I don't know. The group's whereabouts, what Tobias is planning, that sort of thing. I thought it was worth blowing my cover to make sure she got away. I was going to take her to the safe location in the woods, but the goddamn storm clouds..." He sighed, exasperated—maybe with himself, maybe with everything. "Things went to shit fast after that. If she didn't tell me to come here, we'd still be running around out there."

Keo thought about telling Dave that he was protecting a ghost, because Tobias was gone and the last time he saw the man, Keo had a feeling he might never come back. But Dave didn't know that, since people didn't walk around with cell phones and texting had ceased to become a viable communication tool these days. Where was social media when you needed them?

#UBscrewedDave.

"Tobias is going to be pissed," Dave said.

"I wouldn't worry about that," Keo said.

Dave gave him a questioning look, but Keo didn't elaborate.

Jay finally finished what he was doing and stood up, then glanced over at Keo. "Can you carry her downstairs?"

"I can do it," Dave said.

"No," Keo said. "I'll do it. She's my friend."

He carried Jordan down to the first floor, then followed Jay to the back hallway connected to the garage. They stopped at the laundry room, where Gillian was already waiting inside.

Like most homes before the end of the world, Gillian's used to get its heated water from a tank. The tall, smooth, stainless forty-gallon container rested on top of a three-foot-high shelf in the back of the laundry room inside its own closet. Gillian had discovered a few weeks after she moved in that the previous owner had holed out the shelf and had been using it to store old parts for the heating unit. She had removed everything, leaving an empty three-by-four-feet extra area.

Dave peered into the tight space before sighing. "Are you sure she'll be fine in there?"

"I gave her plenty of morphine," Jay said. "She won't feel a thing no matter how cramped it is."

"You claustrophobic?" Keo asked.

"Hell yeah," Dave said. "But I guess it's better than nothing."

Dave went back-first into the enclosed space, basically folding over into a ball to squeeze inside. He didn't stop scooting until he bumped into the back wall. Keo laid down a duvet, then lowered Jordan's unconscious body on top of it. Dave took hold of one end of the blanket and pulled it inside with him, but it took both of them to curl up Jordan's legs and head to fit. She looked so peaceful that Keo found himself staring at her for a few seconds.

"What happens if they don't buy it?" Dave asked.

"They'll buy it," Keo said. Then to Jay, "Right?"

Jay nodded. "They should. Definitely."

Keo smiled. Jay really was a terrible liar, but it looked as if Dave believed him anyway.

"Man, this is going to be a tight squeeze," Dave said. "How long do we have to stay in here?"

"As long as it takes," Keo said. "Just pretend you're a pretzel."

"Oh, great. That helps a lot, thanks."

Keo handed Dave his P22. "Just in case."

"Just in case. Right."

"Where'd you get that little beauty, anyway?"

"One of the soldiers gave it to me in return for some off-the-books rations. The guy told me it was the same gun that James Bond used in the movies."

"Bond carries a Walther PPK. This is a Walther P22."

"What, not the same?"

"Not the same."

"Shit," Dave said. Then, "I thought you don't watch a lot of movies."

"I don't, but I do read," Keo said, closing the shelf up. He straightened and wiped his hands on his wet pant legs. He was still dripping a little water from his clothes, but not nearly as much as before. "Sorry about the mess, Doc."

Jay gave him a forced smile. "It's okay. Tomorrow's cleaning day anyway."

"Cleaning day?"

"That's when Gillian and I spend an hour just cleaning the house. We do it every week. This place was a mess when we first moved in."

"Huh," Keo said. It was the only thing he could think of to say.

"Do you, uh, need something for the pain?" Jay asked.

"Pain?"

Jay was staring at the still-red gash on his forehead.

"No, thanks," Keo said. "I still get some headaches, but I've been taking these."

He took out the bottle of painkillers and Jay took a look at them.

Then the doctor nodded. "I can give you something better. Stronger."

"I'd appreciate that. They let you carry meds home?"

"I guess they trust me."

Gillian appeared at the open laundry door and looked in at Keo, then at Jay, as if sensing that something had happened between them while she wasn't there.

"Okay?" she asked.

"Good to go," Keo said.

"Fine," Jay smiled. Or tried to.

"Let's get everything ready before they show up," Gillian said. She gave the two of them another glance before leaving again.

He and Jay followed her out.

"I'll go clean the mess you guys left on the first floor," Jay said, and disappeared into the living room.

Keo looked after him, then at Gillian.

She sighed. "This has been an all-around tough day for him. First you, then Jordan...and now you again."

"He seems to be holding up fine."

"He's tougher than he looks."

"Hunh."

"You don't believe me."

"I didn't say that."

"But you're thinking it."

He shrugged.

"He is, though," Gillian said. "You'd be surprised at what he'll do if he believes in the cause. Like helping me hide Jordan and Dave. He didn't have to do that, but he did."

Keo nodded. She had a point there. Maybe he was letting pettiness get in the way of appreciating the sacrifice Jay was making. Then again, maybe he didn't care to give Jay the benefit of the doubt.

Screw you, Jay.

He followed her back up to the second floor. He wanted to say something during the walk up the flight of stairs, like last time, but couldn't think of anything that hadn't already been said or would change the outcome of the last six months.

Gillian couldn't, either, so they walked in silence instead.

They went to another room, where Grant was snoring on the

bed. His boots were on the floor and the sheets around him were still wet. Jay had injected Grant with something called synthetic opioid etorphine that had put him to sleep. According to Jay, some of the soldiers had found the opiate at an animal clinic. It took Grant a few minutes to lose consciousness, but once he did, Keo wasn't sure he could have woken the man up with a grenade.

"Jay says he should be asleep until morning," Gillian said. "So you have that long to decide what to do with him. That is, if we actually get away with tonight."

Keo chuckled.

"What's so funny?" she asked.

"Just like old times."

She gave him a wry smile. "The old times weren't that great, Keo. As I recall, we were running for our lives most of the time."

"Not always. The six months at the cabin was nice."

"Except for that. Those were okay."

"Just okay?"

"Maybe good."

"They were more than that."

She sighed. "Maybe."

"You still miss it, don't you? You still miss me."

"I told you. I'll always miss you. That's never going to change. The rest...the rest isn't possible anymore."

"I don't believe you."

"Believe whatever you want—"

He kissed her.

She let out some muffled sounds at first, and he expected her to push him away again, but instead she wrapped her arms around his neck and pulled him down harder against her mouth. Keo slid his hands along her side, skirted around her protruding belly, and squeezed her breasts. They were a lot bigger than he remembered.

Thunder crackled outside and lightning flashed across the back window, and he swore the room shook for a brief second.

"The earth moved," he grinned.

"You're so corny," she smiled.

"Hmm," he said, and kissed her again.

Harder this time, pulling her against him. He didn't even care about the baby bump anymore.

"Keo," she whispered in between the brief moments that he allowed her to breathe. "Keo. Stop it."

"No."

"Please."

"No."

"Jay's downstairs."

"Fuck Jay."

"Stop it. Please."

"No."

"God, I hate you."

"Liar."

She tried to say something else, but he wouldn't let her. She moaned incoherently against him, and he had reached one hand into her shirt to see just how big her breasts really had gotten—

Bang bang bang!

Pounding. From downstairs.

The front door.

He pulled back, annoyed and frustrated with the night, with the entire world.

"It's time," she said, gasping for breath against him. "Try not to get us killed, okay? All of us?"

"I'll do what I can," he said.

TWENTY-ONE

Jay was on the first floor, and the sound of pouring rain flooded the house as soon as he opened the door to answer the pounding. Keo was already halfway downstairs. He didn't like the idea of Jay facing the soldiers alone. The guy couldn't lie to save his life, and now he had all their lives on the line, too.

Gillian grabbed his arm and pulled him back before he reached the bottom landing. "The gun," she whispered. "Soldiers don't carry guns in their front waistband."

He nodded and switched Grant's Glock to behind his waistband, then covered it up with his shirt. He would have liked to have the M4 he had left in the guest bedroom on the second floor alongside Grant's sleeping form, but the soldiers were the only ones supposed to carry weapons.

"You're Doctor Jay, right?" a voice asked somewhere in the foyer.

"That's right," Jay answered. "What's going on?"

"We're looking for some fugitives," a third voice said.

"Oh."

Dammit, Jay, never ever play poker with your life on the line, pal.

They continued down the stairs, Gillian holding his hand the entire time and not letting go until they were almost at the bottom. Jay was leading two soldiers into the living room. They were both dripping wet and leaving large puddles in their wake, all the while shivering under cheap plastic black raincoats.

"Honey, we have company," Jay said, forcing a barely credible smile in Gillian's direction.

"Is something wrong?" Gillian asked.

The soldiers were both in their thirties, their faces and hair wet despite their hoods. Keo couldn't see their name tags because of the raincoats, but they both carried M4s over their backs and were rubbing their hands together.

Gillian went to stand next to Jay while Keo wandered over to the kitchen and sat down on a stool on the other side of the counter. The gun bulged against his back and anyone who looked closely would have spotted it, so he made sure they only saw his front the entire time he was within sight of them.

"We're looking for two fugitives," one of the soldiers said. "A black guy and a white woman. She's hurt and he's armed, and they might have come in this direction."

"We haven't seen anyone like that around here," Jay said.

Jay's voice had trembled a bit when he said it, and one of the soldiers clearly noticed. "Are you sure about that?" the man asked.

"Yeah, of course." Jay smiled. It came out, predictably, unconvincing.

Gillian must have realized how badly Jay was doing, because she sought out his hand and slipped her fingers through his. "How do you know they're in our area?" she asked the soldiers.

"They came over the fence from next door," the other soldier said. "Left a lot of blood behind, but the rainstorm washed away most of the trail so now we're going house to house."

The first soldier was peering up the second floor stairs. "Anyone up there?"

"Just one of your guys," Keo said.

The soldier looked over at him. "He got a name?"

"Grant. He was taking me to Processing in the golf cart, but then the rain hit and we decided to detour here."

"Shit, you must be someone special to be riding in that chariot," the other soldier said.

"No one special."

"Humble, too."

Keo smiled. He knew they had seen the cart outside, and he had guessed correctly that only Steve (or Jack) rode around town in those things. In a place where the haves wore uniforms, carried guns, and had horses to take them when they were too lazy to walk, the king had a slow-moving, solar-powered golf cart. It would have been an absurd concept a year ago, but then this wasn't a year ago.

"You got a name?" one of the soldiers asked him.

"Keo."

"Keo? What kind of name is that?"

"He's a friend," Gillian said before Keo could answer. "He's new in town; that's why he was being taken to Processing."

"Grant's up there?" the other soldier asked.

At this point, Keo had stopped bothering to keep them separate. Dripping wet and covered from head to toe in black raincoats, they might as well be duplicates.

"He's coming down with a cold, so we gave him one of our guest rooms to sleep it off," Gillian said. Then, turning to Jay, "Right, honey?"

"Right," Jay nodded. "I gave him something to help him sleep."

"Go check it out, Ronny," one of the soldiers said.

"You mind?" Ronny asked. Keo wondered if he was only asking that because of Jay's position.

"Go right ahead," Jay said.

Ronny walked past them and jogged up the stairs.

"What did you say your name was again?" Jay asked the other soldier.

"Owen," the man said.

"Owen. Have we met before?"

"Yeah, I had some leg pains a few weeks back. You gave me something for it, remember?"

Jay nodded. "I remember now."

"Thanks for that, by the way."

"How's the leg coming along?"

"Much better."

Keo could see Jay warming up to the moment. Maybe it was because he was in his element, talking medicine to a patient.

Even Owen looked disarmed, though his expression changed a bit when he turned his attention back to Keo. "When did you get in?"

"This afternoon," Keo said.

"Is that right? How'd you get a golf cart already? I've been here since the beginning, and they haven't even given me a horse yet."

"It's Steve's."

"Steve?" Then, as the name registered, "Oh. You call him Steve, huh?"

"He told me to."

"Must be nice," Owen smirked.

Footsteps behind them, just before Ronny came back down the stairs.

"Grant?" Owen asked.

"He's sleeping like a fucking baby," Ronny said. "Out like a light. Smacked him around and he didn't even flinch." To Jay, "What'd you give him, Doc, and where can I get some of that?"

Jay gave him an anxious smile. "He was coming down with a bad cold and I didn't want him to go back out in this weather. Doctor's orders."

"Lucky him," Owen said. "We don't have that choice."

"You checked the other rooms?" Ronny asked.

Owen shook his head. Then to Jay: "We're going to have to search the house before we can leave, Doc. That okay?"

Jay nodded. "Go right ahead."

"Just...try not to make too much of a mess," Gillian said. She was rubbing her belly, which Keo thought was a nice touch.

"We'll be gentle," Ronny said.

"Everyone stay in here until we're finished, okay?" Owen said.

They nodded as the two soldiers headed into the back hallway where the bedrooms were.

"How many rooms?" Ronny called back.

"Four," Gillian said. "Two down here, two more upstairs."

Jay and Gillian drifted over to the kitchen counter where Keo was sitting and sat down across from him. Jay laid his hands on the smooth countertop, but when he saw that they were shaking noticeably, he picked them up and hid them in his lap.

"Relax, Doc," Keo said, keeping his voice just low enough to be heard. "You're doing fine."

That was a lie. The man's face was pale, and you only needed to spend a few seconds looking into his eyes behind the wire-rimmed glasses to know Jay wasn't doing fine at all. In fact, he was doing pretty goddamn awful.

That realization made Keo reach behind his back and slide the Glock out from his waistband and put it in his lap. He kept his left hand on the counter the whole time, next to the same mug of black tea that Gillian had fixed for him this afternoon. He guessed she hadn't had time to clean it, which made him wonder what kind of conversation she'd had with Jay when the doctor came home. Clearly, she had told him everything. Or most of it, anyway.

Gillian, meanwhile, was looking across the counter at him. She was amazingly calm, and watching her sitting side by side with the nervous Jay made Keo realize just how much all those months fighting Pollard and his men had cost him.

Fucking Pollard. The man continued to haunt him even in death.

They sat staring at each other in silence for what seemed like hours, with only the constant *pak-pak-pak* of rain against the roof and the occasional crashing of thunder in the distance to break the silence. Thank God for the noises outside, otherwise Keo was sure he could actually hear Jay's heartbeat thrumming against his chest.

Gillian must have heard it, too, because she got off her stool and went to a cabinet and brought back a bottle of Pinot Noir. She pulled the cork out with little effort, grabbed three glasses from the kitchen, and expertly poured the remains into them. She slid one in front of Jay and smiled at him, and Jay anxiously picked it up and drank most of it in one tilt.

Keo picked up his and sipped once, then put it back down. He wanted to maintain all of his motor coordination if he needed to use the Glock. He prayed he didn't have to do any shooting, because even with the rain and thunder, gunshots inside a house might still travel past the walls. It would be doubly bad luck if someone were to be walking by on the sidewalk at the same moment. That wasn't even taking into consideration the potential collateral damage, which was his primary concern now as he looked across the counter at Gillian.

"Sorry, no refrigeration," Gillian said. "But we just opened it yesterday, so it's still drinkable."

"Where'd you get it?" Keo asked.

He didn't really care, of course, but talking about something as inconsequential as the origins of the wine was a simple and effective way of keeping her mind—and Jay's—off the two soldiers rummaging through their bedrooms at the moment.

"One of the doctors at Medical has a case of them," Jay said. "I'm not sure where he got it; probably from a trade with one of the soldiers."

"That happens a lot? Trading?"

"Pretty much everything other than the bare essentials is gotten through trading," Gillian said. "It's a thriving black market. I don't know if their superiors know about it, or if they just look the other way."

"What else gets traded?" Keo asked.

"Everything," Gillian said.

He was going to ask what "everything" included when Owen and Ronny came out of the back hallway.

"Sorry for the mess, Doc," Owen said. "We tried to be gentle, but we had to make sure there's no one hiding in the closets or under the beds."

"That's all right; you're just doing your jobs," Jay said. He smiled, and it actually looked semi-convincing that time.

Thank you, red wine.

"What about upstairs?" Owen said to Ronny.

"I already went through both rooms when I was up there," Ronny said. "Unless you want to wake Grant up and haul his ass into the rain with us."

"Nah, let the guy sleep it off. One of us might as well keep dry tonight." He turned back to them. "Okay, guys, we'll let you get back to sleep."

"No problem," Jay said, climbing off his stool with the almost empty wine glass in his hand. "I'll walk you guys out."

Jay followed them to the door.

Keo looked across at Gillian. She was smiling back at him, and he was trying to decide if she'd always been this gorgeous or if being pregnant had given her something extra (not that she needed it), when there was a loud *squawking* noise and they heard a muffled voice that was lost behind clothing.

The soldiers stopped in the foyer, and Owen pulled a radio out from behind his raincoat. He keyed it. "Say again?"

"Grant," a voice said through the radio. "Anyone seen Grant?"

"What about Grant?"

"Boss wants to know where the fuck he is. He's supposed to be at Processing with some new guy, but they never showed up."

Ronny had already turned around and began to unsling his rain-slicked M4. He walked back into the living room, passing Gillian, until he was standing directly across the counter from Keo. They stared at each other.

Oh so *close.*

"If anyone sees Grant or the guy he was escorting, don't let them out of your sight," the man on the radio continued. "That's an order."

"You hear that?" Owen said over at Ronny.

"Yeah—" Ronny started to say, when there was a loud *bang!* and he stumbled backward, looking more shocked than hurt.

Keo stood up from the stool and hurried around the counter as Owen dropped the radio and scrambled for his rifle.

"Jay, move!" Gillian shouted.

Jay staggered away, stunned, when Keo shot Owen twice in the chest with the Glock. The soldier crumpled to the floor, splashing blood and water in equal measures across the already wet tiles.

Ronny had fallen to his knees, his rifle clattering in front of him. He was holding onto his gut, apparently still unsure how a bullet had hit him in the stomach. Sooner or later, he would figure out that Keo had shot him through the wall under the counter. Or maybe he'd never get that far because Keo shot him again, this time in the head, and quickly picked up the rifle and checked the magazine.

A full load. Good.

Keo waited for the radio on the floor next to Owen's lifeless body to squawk, for the man on the other side to order soldiers to converge on the sound of gunshots. Instead, he just heard men talking back and forth, and the same voice repeating the message to others who were just now reporting in. There was nothing about gunshots, nothing about converging on Gillian's house.

"Report in if you find Grant or the other guy," the voice said. "Until then, everyone stick to your assignments and keep the radio clear for further updates. Over and out."

He finished unclasping Ronny's gun belt while Gillian went to Jay, who was leaning against the wall. It was the only thing keeping the doctor from keeling over as he stared at Owen's body. For a man whose livelihood was spent looking at blood, Jay gave Keo the impression he had never seen it before. Then again, maybe it was the shock of being in the middle of a violent gun battle. Either way, Gillian was whispering to him, her hands rubbing his shoulders. Jay had dropped the glass of wine sometime between when Keo shot Owen and finished off Ronny.

Once Gillian had led Jay to the stairs and sat him down, she walked back over to him. If she was scared, she didn't show it. He had to remind himself Gillian hadn't always been pregnant or playing house. Once upon a time, she had saved a group of people inside a hospital infested with ghouls.

That same woman looked at him now with steady eyes.

"What if the neighbors heard the gunshots? These walls aren't exactly soundproof."

"No, but with the rain and thunder, maybe they won't know the difference."

"That's a pretty big maybe, Keo."

"Not everyone knows what a gunshot sounds like in real life. Besides, it's not like anyone has a phone to call the cops. Or maybe they'll just ignore it, pretend they didn't hear anything. People did that even before the end of the world."

"What about the soldiers outside? I'm pretty sure they can tell the difference between gunshots and thunder."

"If they're outside and they heard anything through this monsoon, they'll be all over us in a few minutes anyway, so this conversation is irrelevant. But if we got real lucky, then it's going to take some time before they realize where these two were last seen."

"But they'll figure it out eventually. They'll ask around, and sooner or later they'll get to a house where the soldiers didn't search yet, then they'll backtrack to us."

He nodded. "Yeah. I gotta get Jordan and Dave out of here before then."

"What about Jay and me?"

Keo looked past her at Jay, still sitting at the bottom of the stairs staring at his hands. He wasn't sure what Jay was looking at because his hands looked fine and there were no traces of trembling that Keo could see from across the room.

"Keo?" Gillian said.

"I'm thinking," Keo said, and hurried across the room to the front door.

He peered out through the peephole, but he might as well be looking into an empty black ocean with the sheets of falling rain obscuring everything, including the LED lights up and down the streets. The only time he could see the sidewalk and the street beyond it was when thunder clapped and lightning lit up the subdivision for a brief second.

Gillian had followed him over. "Keo," she said, much quieter than she really had to. "What now?"

"You'll be fine," he said, trying to sound as confident as he could muster.

"How will we be fine after this?" She looked back at Owen's body, then Ronny in the living room. "This isn't fine."

"You didn't do this. I did."

"They're not going to see it that way."

"Look at him," Keo said, nodding at Jay.

The doctor was still in his own world, oblivious to them.

"What do you see?" Keo asked her.

"I don't understand..."

"He's a doctor."

"So?"

"How many doctors do you have in town?"

"Two, with four full-time nurses and a dozen trainees. Three doctors, if you count Bannerman, but no one does. Steve won't let him come near the civilians after what he's done in the past. We're lucky. I've heard from some of the soldiers that other towns have to make do with just one doctor."

"Two doctors, and Jay's one of them. That's the number you should be focusing on, because that's the number that tells me Steve's not going to do anything to him. Or to you. He can't afford to. His number one job is to keep this place running smoothly so the ghouls get their blood and the pregnancies are on schedule."

She was looking intently at him. "What's out there, Keo? When Jordan and I were trying to get to Santa Marie Island, we didn't even know places like this existed. What's happening out there that we don't know about?"

He thought about Song Island, all the stories about the towns, the soldiers, and ghouls with blue eyes. It was enough to give him goose bumps, but he didn't tell her about them. Right now, Gillian didn't need to know. Right now—and he hated to admit it —T18 was the best thing for her and the life growing inside her stomach.

"You'll be safe here," he said. "You were right not to leave with Jordan. You made the right choice."

"I know," she said. "But are you absolutely sure about your buddy Steve?"

"I know guys like him. I've been around them most of my life, even before all of this. They compartmentalize. Maybe he'll come to the conclusion that you and Jay might have something to do with it, but he'll let it go, because he knows *I* wouldn't hesitate to do this. So don't clean this mess up. Don't try to hide the bodies. In the morning, wake up Grant and let him go. Or if he's still out, go outside and get one of the soldiers. Tell them everything, that I'm responsible for the shooting. Grant will be able to corroborate most of it, including when I ordered Jay to put him out."

"You've thought all this out, huh?"

"Not even close. But I don't think it's going to really matter how good your story is. It'll be good enough for Steve to let this go, which will allow him to focus on coming after me, and especially Dave."

"Why Dave?"

"Dave killed his brother, before he came here."

"Oh."

"So you'll be fine. He has no choice but to let you and Jay off the hook."

"Assuming you're right..."

"I am," he said, thinking, *Christ, I hope I'm right.*

"*Assuming* you're right," she said anyway, "then what about you? You said he would come after you."

"Don't worry about me. Just worry about yourself." He put a hand on her belly. "And him. Or her."

"By the way it's kicking, it's probably a him."

"Either way, I know you'll be a great mother."

She tried to smile. "I'm never going to see you again, am I?"

Thunder crackled outside and lightning flashed, illuminating the lawn for a brief moment. Instead of slowing down, it sounded like the rain was increasing, as if everything up till now had just been a prelude to the real storm that was coming.

"Of course you will," Keo said. "I'll come around on the holidays to say hi. Bring gifts for the little slugger."

She tried to laugh it off before looking back at Jay. He wasn't paying attention to them; or if he was, he was hiding it well.

Gillian looked back at Keo and reached up and caressed his cheek, the one with the scar. He leaned into her palm, enjoying the warmth of her skin against his.

"Time to go," he said.

He was drenched from head to boot as soon as he stepped outside the house. By the time he had traveled the short distance from the door to the driveway where the golf cart was sitting, he was pretty sure he had gained five extra pounds just from his clothes absorbing all the rainwater.

And the cold. Jesus Christ on a stick, it was cold.

Keo didn't know if his heart was racing so hard because he was anticipating gunshots to come out of the darkness around him, or if the organ was trying to pump enough blood to the rest of his body so he wouldn't freeze to death. There was nothing out there but a murky black pool of nothing, the LED lights barely having any effect against the unrelenting elements.

There was one bright spot (*Ha ha, "bright" spot, get it?*): If he couldn't see anything, there was a good chance no one out there could see him, either. And in this weather, only the really dedicated would be out hunting Dave and Jordan. What were the chances that described a lot of Steve's "soldiers"?

If there were still people moving around in the streets, he couldn't see them. Then again, he couldn't see much of anything except the twenty or so feet in front of him at the moment. The solar-powered garden lights were little more than white dots in the darkness and he stepped off the walkway twice, his boots soaking up more water and drenching the socks inside as a result, before finding the driveway in all the nothingness.

When he finally reached the vehicle and no one had fired a shot yet, Keo breathed easier, though he still couldn't quite make his teeth stop their chattering. He was pretty sure they were snapping so fast and furious that there was a good chance he might end up biting his own tongue off by accident.

Death by chattering. Now that would be a hell of a way to go.

Fortunately, he still had his tongue when he climbed into the cart and turned the key. The raindrops landing on the solar panels above him sounded like machine-gun fire, which wasn't quite the imagery he needed at the moment.

Keo stepped on the gas pedal and spun the wheel, aiming the slow-moving vehicle toward the front door of Gillian's house. He turned around, then reversed into position, going up the slight step until half of the cart was out of the rain.

The door opened behind him and Dave came out with Jordan. He was carrying her on one side while Gillian, protruding belly and all, had the other. Keo had expected Jay and was taken aback to see the pregnant Gillian hobbling out of the door with Dave. Jordan was mummified in a thick black parka, the hood zipped up and covering almost the entire lower half of her face.

Dave carried the backpack he had brought with him, along with Owen's M4. Keo had Ronny's rifle along with his raincoat and gun belt.

"In the back!" Keo said. He had to shout to be heard over the *pak-pak-pak* of rain around them.

Keo grabbed Jordan's unconscious form from Gillian, who stood back and watched him and Dave put her into the backseat. Dave slid in next to her unresponsive body, then slipped both arms around Jordan to keep her upright.

When Dave had secured Jordan in the back with him, Keo turned to Gillian.

She stood looking back at him in the doorway, trembling arms folded across her chest for warmth. Water dripped down her long raven hair, and despite the semidarkness, he was drawn to her green eyes.

Keo glanced past her and into the house, but there was no sign of Jay, though Owen and Ronny still lay where they had fallen. He turned back to Gillian, who had put on a pink bathrobe and looked every bit like the housewife she had become. But he easily pierced through that charade and saw the woman he had survived the end of the world with, who he had been trying, all this time, to get back to.

He opened his mouth to say something, but she shook her head and shouted over the rain, "I'll see you again very soon."

He nodded. "Soon."

"Go," she said, just as thunder *boomed* in the background and lightning lit up her face for a fraction of a second.

He turned to go when she reached out and grabbed his hand. He turned back around and she was there, pressing up against him with her body and her mouth. He inhaled in her scent and tasted her lips and forgot all about the cold.

For a while, anyway—until she pulled away and smiled.

He smiled back (it came out much easier than he had expected) before letting go of her hand and turning around and climbing into the golf cart.

He removed the M4 and leaned it across the dashboard

within easy reach. He didn't look back at her but instead used the rearview mirror. She hadn't moved and stood shivering in the doorway, watching him back.

Keo stepped on the gas and the cart hummed to life and started moving, taking him, Jordan, and Dave back into the hellacious storm.

BOOK THREE

THE LAST BOAT

TWENTY-TWO

"Are you sure this is going to work?" Dave said from the backseat of the golf cart. He had to shout, or else Keo wouldn't have been able to hear him over the pouring rain.

No, but what the hell choice do we have?

"Yeah, sure," he said instead. "If there's shooting, stay low and keep Jordan safe."

"You can't drive and shoot."

"This isn't even remotely close to driving. This is sitting in a slow-moving piece of crap. Just keep her head down."

"And mine."

"Yeah, you too."

Dave smirked at him in the rearview mirror. He had every right to be concerned, because Keo himself was concerned. There was nothing about riding through a rainstorm in a slow-moving golf cart that made him feel like he was going to survive the night.

The structural husks around him—homes that were supposed to be occupied—didn't help to convince him this was going to end very well for him, Dave, and Jordan. A few lights from a window here and there managed to peek through the unending cascade of rain, but for the most part the houses might as well be abandoned.

The streets were no different. Water flooded the roads, threatening to overwhelm the cart's small tires. Keo felt like he might lose control of the steering wheel at any second, that at any moment he might hit a large puddle and end up flowing backward with the current.

This must be what it feels like to ride the Titanic *after it hit the iceberg...*

...only less fun.

It wouldn't be so bad if it wasn't so goddamn cold. He had been soaked to the bone for so long that he didn't remember the last time he wasn't shivering uncontrollably. If not for the fact he was gripping the wheel with both hands, his arms might have been shaking like a crackhead in need of a fix.

The only other sensation was the *tap-tap-tap* against the back of his seat: Dave's feet kicking, probably involuntarily. He just hoped the extra clothes swaddling Jordan, along with Dave's body heat, were enough to keep her from freezing to death. There was absolutely no guarantee she would wake up at all. Depending on how the next few minutes went, Keo might wish he were shot up with drugs, too.

He glanced up at the rearview mirror but could only see two black lumps huddled against one another, forming a single shape in the backseat. They were both wearing dark clothes, which helped to keep them somewhat invisible—

Shit.

Two figures, standing outside a house at the corner of the street to his right. He only managed to make them out because the homeowner was holding an LED lamp, and the bright light illuminated all three figures against the open door.

Keo kept both hands on the steering wheel but made a mental

note of how far the M4 rifle was from his hand as he continued driving up the street.

They must have caught the barely visible headlights of the golf cart or heard the splashing of tires against the flooded road, because they both turned their heads in his direction. He couldn't have made out their faces if he wanted to, even though they were barely twenty meters from his position. He kept the cart moving steadily forward, not that he really had any choice. The only other options were to take his foot off the gas pedal and slow down, or—

Well, that was it. He already had the pedal pushing against the floor. The damn vehicle was just *slow*.

As he passed them by, one of the soldiers turned back to talk to the civilian, but the other one continued to look after him. Keo stared forward and kept going, but as soon as he was on the other side of the intersected street, he glanced at his passenger-side mirror and saw the soldiers going into the house.

Close one.

He wondered if Dave had seen them or if he was too busy trying not to freeze to death in the back. Since Dave hadn't said anything, it was probably the latter.

They were halfway to the front gate now, and he was feeling a lot better. Not that he thought they were any closer to making it out of T18 alive, though he had settled on the odds of them exiting the subdivision at slightly under forty percent. The presence of those two soldiers had knocked those odds down some, but having passed them, he thought forty percent was probably about right.

I've had worse odds.

As the golf cart churned on, splashing an ungodly amount of water in its path, Keo upped his chances of surviving Texas at around forty-five percent.

What the hell. He was feeling a little optimistic these days.

The last time he approached the front gate of T18A1, with Grant in the driver seat, the two soldiers manning it were too busy trying not to catch a cold in the guard booth and had left the gate open.

This time, Keo wasn't so lucky.

It took all his willpower not to pick up the M4 and start shooting. He didn't do it because he had gotten lucky with Owen and Ronny inside Gillian's house, but out here there were no walls to help suppress the sound of gunshots. And he remembered the two soldiers he had passed earlier; there was no telling how many others were still walking around the subdivision, going house to house.

He was twenty meters from the heavy gate—way too heavy to ram; hell, the cart would crumble long before he could force that hulking metal barrier open—when the guards spotted him. It was likely the soft glow of his headlights, which despite not being all that bright was the only thing lit up around the area and wasn't difficult to pick out.

One of the guards hurried out of the booth, bent slightly at the waist as if that would save him from the slashing rain. The man had his M4 slung over his shoulder, which told Keo he wasn't on high alert.

Keo stopped ten meters from the gate and reached down and took out the Glock, then placed it in his lap. He kept his right hand on the gun while holding the highest point of the steering wheel with his left so the guard could see it.

The guard moved toward him, shielding his eyes with one hand against the sheets of rain that seemed to be coming at them sideways now. The wind had also picked up and the man's raincoat was pressed against one side of his body, and it looked like he was doing everything possible not to be picked up and blown into the night sky. It didn't help that he was tall and lanky.

"Open the fucking gate!" Keo shouted with all the indignation he could muster.

Behind him, Dave must have finally realized where they were and stirred. Or, at least, Keo assumed he was moving back there, because Jordan's protector gave the front seat one involuntary hard kick before going suddenly very still.

The soldier stopped at the sound of Keo's voice, and still peering from underneath one hand, shouted back, "What?"

"I said open the gate, you moron!" Keo shouted over the *pak-pak-pak* of rain. "We're freezing our asses off out here!"

The soldier hesitated. He glanced back at his partner, but the man remained hidden inside the shack with a small LED light of some sort hanging above him. With no help coming, the soldier started moving toward the golf cart again.

"Are you deaf?" Keo shouted when the man was five meters away. "You new here or something? Open the gate!"

The man was close enough now that Keo could see he was very young, his face just barely illuminated by the weak headlights.

"The golf cart," Keo wanted to shout. *"Respect the golf cart, you little prick!"*

Keo glared at the soldier like he expected something better, like he belonged and this kid was screwing up—

That might have done it.

The soldier looked back one more time before shouting, "Sorry, sir!" and rushed back up the street to the gate.

Sonofabitch. That actually worked.

Keo loosened his grip on the Glock but kept it in his lap, his chest thrumming a thousand miles per second and giving his chattering teeth a run for its money.

"Oh, fuck me," Dave whispered behind him. Loudly, too,

because Keo could hear him over the storm. "I can't believe that worked. You fucking maniac."

Keo grinned and put both hands on the steering wheel. He stepped on the pedal and the cart moved forward.

The soldier pushed the heavy black metal gate aside as Keo drove through, halfway out of there before the gate had even fully opened. The soldier looked after them as Keo turned left as soon as he was able and pointed them down the road, back toward the marina.

"This isn't going to work!" Dave shouted.

"Shut up!" he shouted back. "It'll work!"

"We're just going to drive up there and take one of the boats? And they're just going to let us?"

"Yes," Keo said, and thought, *Or die trying,* but he didn't add that part because he didn't think Dave needed to know he had adjusted their chances of surviving tonight back down to forty percent...ish.

Oh, who was he kidding? It was more like thirty-five, considering how desolate and empty the world looked at the moment. If he thought the almost invisible houses in the subdivision were unnerving, it was nothing compared to driving through the wide-open fields that were teeming with people earlier today. The crops looked as if they were being physically assaulted by the rain, most of the corn stalks pummeled to the ground while water flooded the row after row of carefully arranged soil.

The only reason the golf cart wasn't already floating instead of grinding down the road on its four small tires was because the pavement was slightly elevated, but that wasn't going to last very long. Before midnight, every street and road in T18 was going to be under water. So he wasn't terribly surprised by the lack of soldiers out here. Besides the fact that Dave and Jordan's last known trails led into the subdivisions, anyone foolish enough to hide among the fields wouldn't survive the night anyway. Drowning out there was a very real possibility.

Somewhere between the near-miss at the gate and his present location, Keo had lost track of time and didn't know how long they had been on the road. They must have been close to the marina because he glimpsed the water tower to his right, on the other side of another large field of crops. It was too dark and visibility was nonexistent, and he could just barely make out the rocket-like shape and the round top—never mind if there were any guards still braving the horrid weather up there.

He was wary about having to deal with extra guns, but maybe he was giving Steve's "soldiers" too much credit. Sure, the tower made for a great sniper's perch, but it was going to take a hell of a good shooter to hit something in this weather. If, that is, someone was still up there at the moment.

He guessed he'd find out soon enough.

Not that he had any choice, anyway. The marina was the only way out. Or, more specifically, the boats docked there. He needed one of them. The faster the vessel, the better, but he'd settle for something with enough gas to get him...where? It didn't matter. He'd figure it out once he was in the river. Until then, it was all theory anyway.

There were enough lights along the power poles to keep him from running off the road and into the overflowing ditches to both sides of him. Meanwhile, the rain had decided to bypass the cart's roof entirely and was now hitting him from the side. Keo wished he had grabbed an extra blanket for himself and hoped Jordan, back there with Dave, didn't die of hypothermia first.

He slowed down when he saw the guard shack next to the marina gate coming up. He couldn't actually see the structure, just the faded glow of two LED lamps hanging on the other side of what he assumed was a closed window.

The last time he had been driven through by Jack, there were four men with rifles manning the gate. What were the chances Steve had pulled some of them to help with the search? Because if all four had remained behind, this was going to be a very short escape attempt. Keo could see himself outgunning two—maybe even three—if he was really, *really* lucky, but four? That was asking for too much, especially tonight when he could barely feel his fingers despite the fact he had both hands clutching the steering wheel in a deathlike grip.

Keo stopped the cart completely about fifty meters from the marina entrance and looked back at Dave. The former cafeteria man was already picking up his M4 from the floor. Keo could barely make out Dave's face back there, but he could see the whites of his eyes just fine. They were wide and scared.

"How are we going to do this?" Dave asked. He was stuttering badly, except he wasn't really; he was freezing, and everything that came out of him just sounded like stuttering because his teeth were chattering so fast.

"I'm going to drive up there, kill them, then leave you behind with Jordan and the golf cart while I get us a boat," Keo said. His own voice sounded clipped, as if he had a hard time forming words. "After that, you drive over to the docks and we get out of here."

"Just like that?"

"Just like that."

"I can barely see your face and you're right in front of me. How am I going to know you've made it?"

"I'll give you a signal."

"What kind of signal?"

"Hell if I know. But you'll know it when you see it. Or hear it."

"That doesn't sound like much of a plan," Dave frowned.

"It's the best one you're going to get tonight. If we're still here by tomorrow, all three of us are dead. I know it's hard to believe, but this rainstorm is probably the best thing that could have happened to us."

"You're right; that is hard to believe." Dave shook his head. "Shit, I should have stayed at the cafeteria."

"You should have. I bet it's warmer."

"Among other things." Dave sighed. "Okay, let's get this over with. If I'm going to die, it might as well be soon. I'm not in love with the idea of freezing to death out here. Or drowning," he added, looking over the side of the cart at the inch-high rain building around them on the road.

"That's the spirit," Keo grinned.

Dave grunted back.

Keo turned around and stepped on the pedal, and the golf cart motored forward. The marina entrance looked a world away, its thick black gate the only thing keeping him from salvation at the moment.

Well, that wasn't entirely true.

Even if he got through the four guys at the gate—unless, of course, Steve had decided to double the sentry, which was entirely possible, too—there were the other soldiers inside the marina, not to mention the ones at the docks. The last time he was here, he had spotted at least a dozen men milling around Marina 1 and 2, not counting however many were at the docks. Two, the last time he had counted, but that was before Dave and Jordan made their great escape.

Then there were the snipers on the water tower. *If* they were still up there and *if* they could shoot from 200 meters in this condition.

There were a lot of ifs tonight. One wrong if, and he was a dead man.

So what else is new?

Still, he was going to have to lower his chances back to about thirty-five. That seemed about right. Not quite too optimistic, but not entirely too pessimistic, either.

He was thirty meters from the entrance when a figure emerged out of the booth with a flashlight. Rain fell in rivulets down the man's hood and bounced off the cold steel barrel of the M4 rifle in his other hand.

Keo drove all the way up to him, waiting until he was just ten meters away before he lowered his hand to his lap, picked up the Glock, and raising it back up, fired through the falling raindrops.

TWENTY-THREE

Maybe it was the rain, the frequent thunderclaps, or his inability to stop his teeth from snapping, but Keo barely heard the gunshot.

Or the second, or the third one.

It only took one round to fall the soldier walking toward him, though Keo shot him again anyway as the man was going down just to be sure.

He stopped the golf cart and turned off the engine and hopped out just as a second guard stood up inside the booth and looked out the window. The light from inside illuminated his face and the man was still turning his head when Keo shot him in the face, shattering the glass at the same time.

Keo rushed toward the guard booth.

Three shots and no return fire. Three very wet, very loud gunshots that someone had to have heard. If not the guys in the water tower, then the ones on the other side of the gate, in the marina. There was no way someone would not have heard, even in this driving rainstorm—

Thunder, twice in a row, *boomed* across the skyline behind

him. They were at least five times louder than his gunshots. Or maybe someone did hear the gunfire but just didn't care, because everything else about the night was just so much, much louder.

That's right, pal, think positive.

Keo had the Glock aimed at the broken window, waiting for a second head to pop up. He was still waiting when he finally reached the booth and kicked the door open and looked in at a lone body crumpled on the floor.

Two soldiers. That was it. Maybe he really had gotten lucky. Maybe Steve really had committed most of his forces to searching the subdivisions. Or maybe Steve just didn't realize how uncommitted his men were and most of them were hunkered down from the rain at this very moment.

He looked back toward the golf cart in time to see Dave climbing out with his rifle.

"Wait for my signal!" he shouted.

Dave nodded back. Or Keo thought he did. He might have just been shaking under the unforgiving cold.

Keo scanned the marina on the other side of the gate, which was really just a long metal pole across the wide lane. He could see the docks at the very end, and for whatever reason the pounding rain sounded much louder out here.

He expected to see men rushing in his direction, soldiers on horseback charging through the storm. Was it really possible Steve had concentrated the bulk of his forces to searching the houses? Yes, because there were a lot of houses. Five subdivisions worth. Even the military ones would be searched. That kind of canvassing required a lot of manpower.

Keo was starting to feel good about his chances again (*Fifty percent?*) as he grabbed the gate and unlatched it, then swung it out of the way. It was heavy against his wet and slightly numbed hands. When he had the gate open, he unslung the rifle and went into a slight crouch, sweeping the marina just to be sure.

There was absolutely no movement from the wide parking lot in front of him, and no sound except for the consistent *pak-pak-pak* of rain. The water was flowing down the incline floor and into the river on the other side, and at this rate it wouldn't be long before this part of T18 was submerged in water as the river overflowed.

The bulk of the marina was dark except for lights coming from his left, from one of the offices along the administrative buildings. He recognized Marina 1, where he had met with Steve twice now. He glimpsed figures on the other side of the windows milling about. Soldiers trying to stay out of the freezing rainstorm.

Keo got up and jogged through the parking lot toward the docks. He could see the boats in their slips being tossed around by the swells of the river. If not for the lines holding them in place, they would have been gone by now. Hell, he might not even need to use the motor; just untie one of those boats and let the current carry him back to the ocean—

A figure, moving at the end of one of the docks in front of him.

Keo slid to a stop and went into a crouch. There were no vehicles to hide behind, so he was stuck out in the open. At least he didn't stand out too much in the night dressed in the black raincoat. Even the M4 was black, which meant if the man didn't stare too closely—and given the distance, that was unlikely—then Keo was for all intents and purposes invisible.

The guy was walking from the end of the dock toward the middle, appearing for just a brief second in a small pool of light when Keo first saw him. Now that the man had continued on, he morphed into a moving black (and shivering) silhouette. Keo could just barely make out clouds of mist with every breath the man took and wondered if he was producing the same kind of telltale signs.

He took a moment to sweep the other docks. Were there more men walking or standing around trying not to freeze to death on those other platforms? If there were, they were doing a hell of a good job hiding themselves. Was it possible they would only leave one unlucky bastard out here while everyone else kept warm inside Marina 1?

Anything was possible, especially on a night like this. It wasn't like he was dealing with real soldiers here. These weren't men who had been whipped into shape by Boot Camp and demanding drill instructors. They were civilians playing dress up, many of them just barely worthy of the weapons they were carrying.

He suddenly felt very generous, and Keo hiked his chances of surviving the night to a whopping sixty percent.

He stood up and slung his rifle, then began walking toward the middle dock, the one where he had seen the soldier walking back and forth on. The man spotted him almost right away, but instead of going for his weapon, he stepped into a weak halo of light and rubbed his hands together and blew into them.

It was the raincoat. Of course it was the raincoat. Just like the soldier at the T18A1 gate could only see the golf cart, this one saw the raincoat and rifle and thought Keo was one of them, too. And why wouldn't he? Keo didn't just look like he belonged, he walked like it, too.

He stepped onto the dock and continued toward the sentry. Water from the surging river splashed his boots and pant legs, though by now he was already so soaked from head to toe that he hardly felt the additional wetness.

"Can you believe this fucking night?" Keo shouted.

The guy nodded back and tried to peer through the sleets of rain at him.

Good luck with that, Keo wanted to tell him.

The soldier was standing under an LED bulb and Keo

couldn't even see his face under the hood, so there was very little chance the man could see Keo with nothing at all to illuminate him. Of course, all that was going to change when he got closer. What were the chances the soldier recognized the faces of every soldier in town? It was possible. After all, Ronny had recognized Grant in Gillian's house. Or had he just gone with the name on the uniform?

"Where is everyone?" Keo shouted. "I can't see shit!"

"Nothing to see!" the soldier shouted back. "You my replacement?"

"Yeah!" Keo continued walking toward the man, letting his right hand drift casually toward the fold of his raincoat. "Go on, I got this!"

"Halle-fucking-lujah!"

The man began walking quickly toward him, still rubbing his hands desperately together. Keo calmly slipped his right hand into the folds of his coat and reached for the Glock in its holster—

"Hey," a voice said, freezing Keo in place.

Keo looked to his right at the nearby platform as a second raincoat-cloaked figure emerged out of the darkness and into another small pool of light.

"What's going on?" the second man asked. "We finally getting replacements?"

Keo finished wrapping his fingers around the Glock and pulled it out and shot the soldier in front of him in the head, then spun slightly and shot the other one in the chest—just as lightning pierced the blackened night above them, lighting all three of them up for a brief moment...then it was gone again.

The second soldier was stumbling, trying not to fall, when Keo shot him a second time in the chest, just as the thunder that had been promised a second ago finally reached them and *boomed* across the skyline.

The one in front of Keo collapsed to the dock while the

second soldier fell into the water, the moving river quickly grabbing onto his body and dragging him into its current. The speed of it surprised Keo, and he was still looking after the body when a second lightning bolt struck and—

Eyes.

An army of blackened eyes on the other side of the river, looking back at him from the banks, gleaming rain-drenched dark flesh writhing between the throng of trees.

Jesus Christ.

They weren't so much as hiding from him as they were trying to stay away from the powerful currents splashing against the riverbanks, threatening to overflow and flood the woods. There were so many of them that he couldn't have begun to count even if he had wanted to. Their numbers stretched from one side of the woods to the other, an endless multitude of moving black flesh and hollow eyes and herky-jerky movements, completely unnatural and surreal against the rain.

The river. They couldn't, didn't, or *wouldn't* cross the river.

"Relax," Steve had said. *"They don't come into town. There's an invisible line that they don't cross. When I decide I can fully trust you, I might tell you how it all works."*

An invisible line that the creatures didn't cross. Like the river. Or the tree lines. Or maybe those flimsy six-foot fences that surrounded the subdivisions.

Whatever it was (maybe all of it), the ghouls didn't cross.

He should have felt good, even safe at the sight of them wanting (*desperately*) to cross the river but holding back, but he shivered from head to toe instead.

It was only thanks to the returning darkness once the lightning disappeared that he was able to push down the overpowering need to run and hide. He couldn't see them anymore and that somehow made it better, even though he knew they were still out there watching his every movement.

He forced himself to move again, crouched, and rolled the dead soldier into the water, then walked the brief distance over to the first slip. The boat inside was a twenty-footer with a single motor in the back, thin and sleek with a T-overhead canvas. It didn't look nearly powerful enough to outrun most of the boats tied up around him, but he didn't need a fast vessel right now; he just needed one that would run. The currents would make up for any speed deficiencies.

He hurried back to the same metal box in front of the docks, the one that housed all of the keys to the boats. It was still unlocked and inside were the keys, designated by slip numbers. He found the one he needed and pocketed it and slammed the lid shut—

He didn't hear the gunshot, but he felt it *buzz* past his head just before the bullet *pinged!* against the metal box, leaving behind a large dent.

Keo spun around, quickly tracing the trajectory of the bullet back to—

The water tower.

If it wasn't for bad luck...

He would have unslung the M4 and fired back if he thought it would do any good. But it wouldn't have, because the tower was too far away and he would be essentially shooting into the darkness, because although he could just barely make out the rocket-shaped structure, he had absolutely no clue where the shooter was.

Buzz! as a second bullet passed over his head and disappeared into the parking lot behind him.

Just as he had predicted, shooting in this condition was hit and miss, and right now, thank God it was two in the miss column and none in the first. It wasn't just the distance and the suffocating darkness, it was also the wind and the cold adding to the difficulty scale.

The problem was, although the first bullet had nearly taken Keo's head off and the second had gone long, it was only a matter of time before the sniper adjusted and found just the right distance. Either that, or until he radioed—

Someone opened fire with an M4 behind him, and he turned just in time to see a figure at the front gate firing—*but not at him.* The man was shooting at the group of office buildings across the marina, the muzzle flashing, lighting up the guard booth nearby with every pull of the trigger.

Dave.

A man running out of Marina 1 stumbled and fell, his body illuminated by bright lights from inside. Other figures were moving visibly on the other side of windows, scrambling for cover as glass around them exploded from Dave's barrage.

Keo started lifting his rifle to help Dave out when another bullet slammed into the key box inches from his head—*ping!*—and ricocheted into the pavement.

He scrambled away from the box, hoping that taking himself away from the stationary object would make him a harder target to reacquire. Then again, if the guy had some kind of night-vision-capable scope, then it probably didn't matter how far Keo moved—

Buzz! as another round hit the parking lot a foot to the right of him, spraying water and concrete chunks on impact.

Keo would have gotten up and ran away if he had the time, but he didn't. Men were pouring out of the offices across the marina, and Dave had stopped firing. Either he had run out of bullets and was changing magazines, or something else had happened. Keo flicked the fire selector to burst fire and unleashed half of his rifle's magazine into the source of light across the parking lot.

He wasn't trying to hit any specific target, but simply firing at where the lights were the brightest, which at the moment was the single wide-open door that a pair of figures were rushing out of. The distance was fifty meters, and it was a little hard to miss when you were just shooting into the only source of light in, at that moment, the entire world.

His aim was true enough that both men fell out of the door and didn't get back up.

Keo spotted a tall silhouette behind one of the broken windows, looking out, and he put another burst in that direction. The man ducked his head just in time, and two others behind him scrambled for cover behind a desk.

He was waiting for more soldiers to come out of the other offices, but the windows behind those remained blackened. Which meant all the soldiers had, for whatever reason, congregated in one place. That was good for him and Dave.

That is, if Dave was even still alive.

He was standing up, looking at the gate to make sure Dave was still there, and at the same time realizing that he had stayed at the same spot for way too long when instead of a buzzing sound, there was instead a sudden sting and his right leg buckled slightly under him. Keo knew what had happened before he saw the blood pour out of the right side of his thigh and flood down the parking lot along with the rain, as if drawn irresistibly to the river.

He pushed himself back up, turned around, flicked the fire selector on his rifle to semi-auto, and squeezed off everything he had left in the magazine at the water tower. He aimed for the largest target—the barely visible tip—while knowing full well he wasn't going to hit anyone from this distance, but hoping he did just enough to distract the guy. He imagined he could hear the *ping! ping!* of his bullets bouncing off the metal tower, but of course that was impossible given the pounding rainstorm around him.

He moved left while shooting, angling back toward the docks.

Keo sent off his last round and dropped the magazine and slammed in a new one, turning around almost simultaneously as two men in the office opened fire—except not at him. Maybe they couldn't see him very well, but they certainly had no trouble seeing the golf cart as it rumbled slowly (*Christ, that thing is slow*) across the parking lot.

Keo switched his fire over to the office, again using the lights as his target finder. He stitched the two rectangle-shaped windows, forcing the two figures firing out of them to stop shooting and duck for cover.

He was still shooting when Keo heard the *buzz!* as the bullet tore through the left sleeve of his raincoat and took away a chunk of his flesh underneath. Blood poured out, but the pain wasn't nearly as bad as when he had gotten hit in the thigh. Maybe it was the cold numbing his flesh or the fact that he knew stopping to dress his injuries now meant death, but Keo managed to grit his teeth through the shoulder wound and turned around just as Dave appeared, the golf cart flying in his direction like an out-of-control lumbering beast.

"Take the first boat!" Keo shouted. "*Go go go!*"

Dave slammed on the brake and climbed out of the golf cart as Keo turned around and took a step sideways and squeezed off a round at the water tower. He took another step and fired again, and kept repeating the process until he heard Dave running past him, gasping for breath as he went.

Keo glanced back in time to see Dave make the docks and run up it toward the twenty-footer, Jordan's body a big black unmoving clump draped over his shoulder.

He glanced back at Marina 1. Lights poured out of the windows and the open door, but he couldn't detect any signs of movement. Maybe they had finally had enough and didn't think it was worth it to get their heads blown off—

Buzz! as another bullet came within an inch of Keo's right ear.

*Sonofa*bitch.

He ran after Dave and Jordan, grabbing the third and final magazine from his pouch as he did so. A hole appeared in the plank in front of him, splintering wood, as the sniper fired again. The bullet disappeared into the water below, and Keo ran past the newly created hole without wasting a precious half-second contemplating the near-miss. His entire night had been a series of near-misses. Well, that wasn't entirely true. He had two holes in him as proof of that.

Dave had already climbed into the boat and placed Jordan's body across a long bench in the back while scrambling to one of the two lines keeping the boat in place. Dave glanced up as Keo ran over. "The key!" he shouted.

"I got it!" Keo shouted back.

He reached into his raincoat pocket and fisted the key. He would have tossed it to Dave, but he didn't have any faith in either one of them making the exchange in this weather. So he ran the whole distance and leaned over and handed it to Dave instead, then ran back to unwind the bowline.

All of that took three precious seconds, enough time for the sniper to reacquire them, and there was a sharp *ping!* as a bullet drilled into the portside of the boat. Dave either didn't see or hear the impact, or he was too focused on putting the key in the ignition to do anything about being shot at. The boat's motor roared to life at about the same time Keo got the line free and tossed it into the back.

That was also when he heard the familiar *clop-clop-clop* of horse hooves and looked back and saw the elongated, shadowy forms of men on horseback coming through the marina gate. While the distance and darkness made making out their exact numbers impossible, he managed to distinguish three, maybe five forms out of the moving blob, though he had no illusions that that was all of them.

"Come on!" Dave shouted behind him.

Keo hopped into the boat just as something *buzzed!* past his head and hit the water a few meters off starboard. He pretended it was a fly instead of thinking about how close he had just come to having his brains splattered in the river.

Think positive!

He almost laughed as he landed in the back of the boat next to Jordan's swaddled form resting on the bench to his right. Dave was already reversing out of the slip, having also seen the horsemen coming in their direction, the *clop-clop-clop* of hooves somehow managing to pierce through the rain's stranglehold on sounds.

Then *boom!* and Keo cursed.

Three to five? If only he was that lucky. There had to be at least *a dozen* of them, men in wet raincoats, pulling up as they reached the end of the parking lot and began unslinging their rifles. They were almost *right in front of him*, so close that he could see mists flooding out of the nostrils of their mounts as the animals reared to a stop.

Keo opened fire into the marina, and one man fell off his horse just before the lightning vanished and darkness swallowed the world up again, the soldiers returning to their formerly indistinguishable black forms.

He pulled the trigger again and again, even as Dave spun the steering wheel and Keo had to turn around in order to keep shooting into the parking lot. He was still firing while simultaneously gritting his teeth in anticipation of return fire. The sniper had also either stopped shooting, or his shots were going wide and Keo couldn't hear it over the pouring rain and his own gunshots.

At first Keo thought the lack of return fire from the marina was because he was dropping the horsemen, but that couldn't have been it. Without any lights in the parking lot and his vision hindered badly by the rain, all he could see were indecipherable shapes moving in front of him as he waited for the inevitable.

Because he knew it was coming—a fusillade of lead that he or Dave had no hopes of surviving. They were still backing away from the docks, trying to reach a part of the river where they could use the motor and were, for all intents and purposes, sitting ducks for a good ten, twenty seconds.

"Get down!" he shouted when it finally came—the *pop-pop-pop* of automatic rifle fire that wasn't his, muzzle flashes lighting up the wide open spaces in front of him.

Except the horsemen weren't shooting at him or Dave or Jordan.

What the hell?

Maybe it had something to do with the dark shape moving between the horses, inciting the animals to let out loud furious whines and scramble about the wet concrete pavement. The thing was fast, and something—a long coat?—was fluttering around it, visible for brief half-seconds against the staccato bursts of gunfire as it moved through the throng of men and beasts.

Any hopes Keo had of seeing details were rendered impossible by the night and rain. The figure in the long coat was on the ground, then it was in the air, then it was on the ground again. It was moving so fast Keo could barely keep up with it. He didn't know when he stopped shooting, but time seemed to slow down as he stood there and watched the figure grabbing men off their horses and throwing them across the parking lot.

Something sailed through the air, and Keo instinctively ducked even though he didn't have to. A black-clad soldier, hands and feet flailing, hit the river just five feet off the starboard and was sucked under.

Then the boat's stern dipped slightly, and a motorized roar shattered the shrill wind and falling rain. Keo didn't know when

Dave had turned them around, but suddenly they were blasting downriver and leaving the docks behind.

Keo hurried to the stern and looked back toward the marina as gunshots continued to ring out and muzzle flashes lit up the parking lot again and again and again. He waited for bullets to *zip* past his head or punch into the hull of the twenty-footer, but none of those things happened. The soldiers on horseback—and some on the ground now—were firing at something among them. Something that wasn't him or Dave or Jordan. That same *something* that Keo had seen earlier, moving with a ferocity he didn't know was possible.

Slowly, the flashes began to disappear one by one until they had ceased completely. There was a brief pause before someone screamed. A shrill cry, dripping with fear instead of pain, and it burrowed its way through the cold and night and rain and into Keo's gut.

The docks were still fading fast behind him when Keo thought he saw something that shouldn't have been there, that shouldn't have been possible.

Eyes.

Blue fucking eyes.

They were looking after him, the twin orbs pulsating against the rain and darkness. He shouldn't have been able to see them through the night and distance, but there was something vibrant about them, full of life, and they drew him in like lighthouse beacons.

"Christ, you're bleeding!" Dave shouted, his voice breaking through Keo's temporary stupor.

He looked back at Dave, and by the time he turned back around, the marina had vanished into the darkness.

And with it, the eyes.

What the fuck...

It had attacked the soldiers. He knew that for a fact. It had come out of nowhere and waded into Steve's horsemen before they could open up on him and Dave. At that range, with that many guns, and with the boat in such a vulnerable position, they would have been shredded and sank in a hail of bullets.

...just happened?

He had heard the stories. From Lara and Carly, from Gaby and Danny. But he hadn't believed it. It was too much. Despite everything he had been through and seen, the idea that there was something out there more horrific than the black-eyed ghouls...

Blue eyes.

Jesus fucking Christ.

He sat down and leaned back against the starboard hull, then squinted up at Dave's silhouetted form. "You know how to drive this thing?"

"Better than you!" Dave shouted back over the roar of the motor.

Keo grinned. That was good to hear, because with the hole in his thigh and the other one in his left arm, he wasn't entirely sure he could have stood behind the steering wheel and fought against the currents and the storm at the same time.

"Hey," Keo said.

Dave looked back at him. "What?"

"Don't run aground."

"Why not?"

"You don't wanna know."

But Dave did want to know, and there was a *click* as he turned the button that powered on the spotlight at the front of the boat. They must have been everywhere, just like the last time he saw them, because it didn't take Dave very long to see them.

"Oh, fuck me," Dave said.

"Yeah," Keo said.

He closed his eyes, the *pak-pak-pak* of rainwater against his forehead, eyelids, and face fading into the background. Even the cold had ceased to matter as Keo relived the last few seconds.

Blue eyes.

He couldn't get over it. The image of it, looking after him, bounced around inside his head like a sledgehammer.

It had blue eyes...and it had saved his life.

Dae-fuck-me-bak.

TWENTY-FOUR

"You were good back there," Keo said. "Like Evel Knievel. But on a boat."

Dave chuckled. "You ever been stuck on a shrimp boat in the Gulf during hurricane season?"

"That happen a lot to you?"

"Just once. But I don't need a second time to know it's not fun. You learn a lot about what you're capable of when the wrath of God is bearing down on you."

"I'm glad I brought you along, then."

"Right, because you had a choice."

"Yeah, that too."

Dave paused, and Keo could sense him wanting to say something else.

"What is it?" Keo said.

"What the fuck happened back there?" Dave asked, looking back at him. "We were sitting ducks, and then I saw...*something*. Not just the soldiers, but something else. Did you...?"

Blue eyes, Dave. It had blue eyes, and it saved our asses.

"I don't know what I saw," Keo said. "We got out, that's all that matters."

"Yeah, I guess."

"So let's focus on staying alive."

Dave nodded and stared off the bow, though Keo didn't believe he was going to let it go because Keo himself hadn't been able to since he saw it. He had spent the last few hours trying to wrap his mind around what had happened at the marina, and it still didn't compute. If the ghouls weren't supposed to come into the towns, then what was that thing doing back there?

Better yet, why had it attacked the soldiers? Why did it save them? Or was that what it was doing in the first place? Maybe it just saw the soldiers as the easier prey and preventing them from shooting him and Dave was just a happy coincidence.

Riiight.

Keo sat in the back of the boat, his butt on the cold floor, and finished wrapping the last piece of gauze around his left arm. The round had gone through and taken a big chunk of flesh with it, but it hadn't impacted bone, which was the best thing he could have hoped for. The same with the hole in his right thigh. That didn't feel quite as bad because he was sitting down and wasn't putting a lot of pressure on it. Or, at least, that's what he told himself.

He packed up the first-aid kit Gillian had given them back at the house and returned it to Dave's pack. The bandages were constricting around his shoulder and thigh, but it was better than bleeding to death.

For the last two hours, they had been sitting on the twenty-footer as it shifted back and forth against the waves somewhere between Trinity and Galveston Bay. Even Dave wasn't quite sure where since their vision was limited by the pitch blackness and they could barely see more than a few meters around them.

Floating on the water at night again. This is starting to become a bad habit.

The rainstorm was still pouring, but thankfully not at them. They had cleared its zone almost as soon as they exited the channel along what Dave said was the Kemah Boardwalk, and as Keo had guessed when they passed it earlier, the place had once been a major tourist attraction.

Lightning continued to flash in the distance, the reports of thunder following a few seconds later. If it had seemed like they were caught in the belly of a rampaging beast before, they were now watching that same monster as it ravaged the area around T18. It had taken them nearly an hour since clearing the channel to scoop up water from the boat and deposit it back into the bay. Thank God there was a plastic jug and some small containers stuffed into the livewells.

Even so, Keo was still sitting in an inch of water as he watched and listened for sounds of an incoming pursuit. There was a definite chilly wind, but his clothing had been soaking wet since the night began so he was already used to the discomfort.

"Storm's not letting up," Dave said after a while. "That's a good sign, right? They wouldn't chase us in this weather, would they?"

"Depends..."

"On what?"

"How badly they want you dead."

Dave snorted. "What about you?"

"I didn't kill Steve's brother. I'm just an annoyance. Maybe he's pissed off at me, but blood is thicker than an annoying stranger."

"You saying that from experience?"

"Unfortunately, yes."

"I'll take your word for it." He slipped back into silence for a moment, perching at the front of the boat with his M4 gripped in his lap. He hadn't left the spot since the boat ran out of gas and left them drifting in the bay. Then, "What's the deal with you and Gillian, anyway?"

"No deal," Keo lied.

"Bullshit."

"Believe what you want."

"You two used to be a couple, right? I heard the two of you talking on the second floor, remember? I was pretty sure you guys were going to start humping like rabbits right outside my door. That would have been pretty sick, by the way."

"You have something against pregnancy sex?"

"I was talking about her doctor husband/boyfriend/whatever being on the first floor at the same time."

"I didn't know you were so sensitive, Dave."

"I'm not, but that doesn't mean I like listening to people doing it."

Keo grinned and opened one of the side pockets on the pack and took out the small, unlabeled bottle that Jay had given him. He shook out a couple of the white pills and swallowed them.

"How is she?" Dave asked. "Doc must have given her something really good to keep her knocked out through that entire mess."

Keo grunted up to his knees and moved over to Jordan, who was still lying on the bench at the stern of the boat. There was just enough moonlight for him to see her bundled form. The only part of her that was exposed to the elements was the upper half of her face so she could still breathe. The swelling around her right eye made him flinch every time he saw it, but thankfully her body wasn't shivering quite as much as when they were braving the rainstorm earlier.

It was a miracle that Dave, despite all his vast experiences, had managed to steer them around the river and out here using only the spotlight at the front of the boat as a guide. And all the while, the creatures were swarming endlessly along the river-banks to both sides of them. Keo had seen it before—when he braved a much wider channel with Lara and the others—but this time they were so close (he could *smell* them) he expected the darting, stick-thin figures to start throwing themselves through the air at them at any moment. But they hadn't, for whatever reason.

Maybe my luck really is changing, he started thinking. Then almost right away, *Yeah, right. Keep telling yourself that, pal.*

He sat back down now. "She's better than us right now. Sleeping like a baby." He picked up the M4 and checked the magazine for the fifth time in the last hour. "Anything?"

"Not a thing," Dave said. "What about you? Does it hurt?"

"Yeah, it hurts."

"A lot?"

"Yeah."

"Take some of those meds your girlfriend gave you."

Keo grunted. "I already did. I've also cleaned, disinfected, and dressed the wounds in case you were worried."

"You've done this before, huh?"

"Once or twice."

"Before or after the end of the world?"

"Both."

"Hunh," Dave said.

They continued sitting and waiting, looking back in the direction of the channel. Or, at least, where they thought it was. Frankly, it was so dark Keo wouldn't be surprised if they were looking at the wrong spot. He just had to glance around him to confirm how lifeless and lightless the world had become.

He could see the raging storm just fine from here, though,

and each time lightning flashed in the distance, he managed to glimpse some of the larger signs of abandoned civilization along the Kemah Boardwalk.

Would Steve come after them? That was a no-brainer. Steve had come all the way from T18 personally to Santa Marie Island when he found out his brother was missing. What *wouldn't* he do to avenge Jack's death?

"Dave," Keo said.

The other man looked over. "What?"

"Santa Marie Island. You know where that is?"

"It should be behind us somewhere. Why?"

"We should go there."

"What's there? Except more of those things."

"Not now, but soon. We're not going to get very far on the trolling motor alone. If Steve's not on his way here now, he will be in the morning. I'm guessing he'll bring more than just a few of his friends, and I don't think he'll be in the mood to talk things out."

"But won't they check that place too?"

"There might still be gas on the island that we can use before they get around to us. It's got two large marinas, one on each side."

"What if it's dry?"

"It's gotta be better than running around out here waiting for them to catch up to us."

"Galveston Island is bigger. There'll be more supplies still sitting around."

"More supplies, more of those things, and easier access from T18. What are the chances they'd leave that place unguarded all this time? If we have to fight our way out of this—and let's not fool ourselves, we're going to have to—I'd rather they come to us, where we have the higher ground."

Dave thought about it before finally nodding. "Makes sense, I guess."

Good, because I'm talking out of my ass here.

He wasn't very optimistic they would actually find fuel on Santa Marie Island. Steve's people would have cleaned the place out by now, and the last time he was there with Gene, the teenager had told him he hadn't run across any.

Still, for some reason that he couldn't explain, it seemed as if he was destined to end up at Santa Marie Island. And if he was going to die soon...

"Shit," Dave said, "I should have stayed at the cafeteria."

Dave got up and moved back toward the stern, where he picked up the trolling motor from the floor and attached it to the back. Keo took his place at the front, wincing as he put pressure on his right thigh.

He crouched at the bow just as a particular massive bolt of lightning flashed in the distance. For a moment, just a moment, he thought he could see the Ferris wheel along the Kemah Board-walk, but that could have just been the long, wet, and cold night playing tricks with his mind...

...just like it had back at the marina, because there was no way in hell that blue-eyed ghoul had saved his life on purpose.

Right?

Dave was right. Santa Marie Island was just behind them, and it didn't take them long to find it again. Of course, the place was over eight kilometers from end to end, and its rocky formations and the sharp angles of the houses stood out against the flat ocean landscape.

They found the island with three hours left until sunrise,

which meant they couldn't just head straight to the western marina and dock. Keo could already see silhouetted figures moving along the ridgelines, the numbers increasing the closer they got.

"Look at them," Dave whispered from the back of the boat. Keo had no trouble hearing him over the small whine of the trolling motor. "Gives me the willies every time I see them."

"You see them a lot back in town?"

"Sometimes."

They were within sight of the marina when Dave cut the motor and Keo dropped the anchor, leaving the twenty-footer to drift back and forth against the slight waves. He tightened his grip on the M4 in his lap, wishing badly for his MP5SD—and more importantly, the silver ammo inside the magazine—as he watched them pouring into the parking lot and spreading out along the fingers of the docks in waves.

"They can't swim, right?" Dave asked behind him. He was still whispering for some reason.

I think they can hear and see you just fine, Dave, Keo thought, but said, "No, they can't swim."

At least, the black-eyed ones couldn't. He had seen that himself back on Song Island, and the ones back at T18 had stayed as far away from the river as they could while still crowding the banks.

So what about the blue-eyed ones?

"They're smarter than the rest," Danny had told him during one of those days when there was nothing to do on the *Trident* but watch the endless ocean. *"If you see them, run the other way, Obi-Wan Keobi. Or shoot them in the head. That seems to work pretty well."*

Shoot them in the head? How the hell was he going to do that? Keo had seen that thing back there, the way it was moving. Danny wasn't kidding. The creature that had assaulted the horsemen was just a blur. How do you put a bullet in the head of something that could move *that fast?*

But that was a problem for another day. Right now, he focused on the black-eyed creatures along the marina. There weren't nearly enough of them to fill up the whole place, which he guessed was the good news. The bad news, unfortunately, was that there were still enough that it was difficult to make out the docks and the parking lot floor under the sea of black, writhing flesh.

"How many are on the island?" Dave asked.

"Anywhere from one to 200...or possibly more."

"Jeez Louise. And we want to go *there?*"

"There was a teenager who lived on the island for months by himself."

"I don't know about you, but I don't have any desire to stay on that rock for months."

"We won't have to. Steve will find us by morning and try to kill us first."

"Oh, okay, no worries then."

Keo smiled. "Point is, if we can't find any spare fuel, we'll either kill Steve and take one of his boats and use it to get off the island, or he'll kill us. Either way, this thing's going to be over in twenty-four hours."

"Man, if you're trying to cheer me up, you're doing a real shitty job of it."

"Just the facts."

"Yeah, whatever, Sergeant Joe Friday."

"Who?"

"Joe Friday. From *Dragnet?*"

Keo shook his head.

"You know who James Bond is, but you don't know *Dragnet* or Stanley Kubrick's 2001?"

"Should I?"

"Hell, yes. They're classics, dude."

"Ah," Keo said.

"Clueless," Dave said. Then, "Hey, she's waking up."

Keo got up and hurried to the stern. "Take the front."

Dave nodded and they swapped places.

Keo crouched next to Jordan and pulled down the zipper of her thick parka until her entire face was exposed. She had opened her eyes—or at least the one still capable of opening—and was looking back at him. Her lips were pale like the rest of her face. She was ghostlike, and she blinked up at him, overly long eyelashes flickering back and forth.

"Hey," he said.

Her good eye darted left then right before picking his face back up. Then, softly, like she had to summon all of her strength just to get the sounds out, "Did I pee myself?"

He shook his head. "No."

"Then why are my pants wet?"

"We're all wet. You don't remember the rainstorm?"

"No..."

"Lightning? Thunder? Gunfire?"

"No, no, and no. Sorry."

"Don't be. You weren't even supposed to wake up until tomorrow."

"Is that why I feel like my head's about to break open?"

"Probably."

"Good to know." Then, "You said 'we'..."

"Me, Dave, and you."

"Who's Dave?"

"Great, she doesn't even know who I am," Dave grunted from the bow. "Man, I should have stayed at the cafeteria."

"The guy who saved you," Keo said.

"Then what are you doing here?" she asked him.

"I'm the guy who saved the guy who saved you."

"Oh." She blinked once, then a second time. "I dreamt of Gillian..."

"Oh yeah?"

"She'd gotten really fat in the dream, but don't tell her I said that."

"Scout's honor," Keo smiled.

TWENTY-FIVE

Morning came and chased the ghouls back to wherever they had been hiding before nightfall. There, they would wait and wait, because inevitably their time would come again.

"Look at them," Jordan said. "That's all they do, isn't it, day after day? They come out at night and hide in the day. Then they do it all over again the next night. Do they ever starve, you think?"

"I don't know," Keo said.

"You ever think about it?"

"Not really."

"You're not the curious type, is that it?"

"I'm curious, I just don't have any answers, so I figured I should probably keep it all to myself until I do. What's that saying about opening your mouth and proving to the world you're a fool?"

"Are you calling me a fool, Keo?"

"Not at all. Maybe if we're still alive after tonight, we can talk about what these things do and don't do, and blah blah blah."

"I just realized what I missed most about you."

THE ISLES OF ELYSIUM   317

"What's that?"

"Nothing."

He chuckled. "I don't believe that."

Keo sat next to her at the bow of the twenty-footer as Dave turned on the trolling motor and guided the boat toward the marina. Now that he was approaching the island from the western side, Keo could see the large area reserved for the ferry, the ball-diamond-ball day shapes still hanging off the large metal pole next to the ramp. They were staying away from it and angling toward the docks designed for smaller crafts.

Jordan had taken off most of her swaddling, though she still kept the raincoat on. She looked better in the sunlight, and the swelling around her right eye had gone down enough that it was a good sign she'd keep improving.

"So how long before he finds us?" she asked.

The question prompted Keo to glance behind him. He expected to see Steve and his soldiers bearing down on them in a group of fast-moving boats. But there was just the brightening horizon and glimpses of sporadic and fading landmasses in the distance. In the aftermath of last night's torrential downpour, the coastline had become ghostly serene.

"We'll cross that bridge when we get to it," he said.

They didn't say anything for a while, and instead just watched the marina grow in front of them. It looked utterly inviting—wide open and empty—but of course he knew better. There were things on Santa Marie Island that would tear them to pieces if given the chance.

"Did you see Gillian?" Jordan asked.

"Yes," Keo said.

"How'd it go?"

How did it go? It went swell. She's with another guy. And she's having his baby. Couldn't have gone better.

"That well, huh?" she said when he didn't answer.

"You knew she was living with Jay all along, even before last night."

Jordan sighed. She had apparently been dreading the question.

"Jordan..."

"Yes," she said. "How'd you know?"

"You told Dave to go to her house. How would you know where she lived, or who with, unless she had already moved in with Jay before you escaped? Was the whole point of going there to get help from Jay or Gillian?"

"A little of both, I guess."

"It was a smart move. Probably saved your life. Of course, if it hadn't rained, they would have tracked you straight to her house. Dave didn't exactly do a good job of hiding your tracks."

"Hey, I did my best," Dave said behind them. "I work in the cafeteria for a reason, you know."

"You did great, Dave," Jordan said.

"Thanks. Nice to be appreciated."

Jordan looked over at Keo. "And I'm sorry. About Gillian. I didn't know how to tell you."

He nodded, surprised that he wasn't madder at her. He should have known though. All those times when he asked her about Gillian and it always seemed as if she was choosing her words carefully. Too carefully.

"I'm sorry, Keo," she said again. "I should have told you sooner. I always wanted to, but I just didn't know how. I guess I was too much of a coward."

"Water under the bridge."

She nodded, but he wasn't sure if she believed him. He wasn't sure if *he* believed himself.

"How's the eye?" he asked.

"My swelling will go down eventually, but your face isn't going to get any prettier anytime soon."

Dave chuckled behind them.

"Stop being a bitch, Jordan," Keo said. "I saved your life last night, remember?"

She smiled back. "Sorry. Thank you for saving my life."

He grunted.

With the docks almost within sight, Keo drew his Glock and handed it to her. She took it, along with the extra magazine that she slid into her raincoat pocket.

"Stay here," he said, standing up. He glanced back at Dave. "Easy does it."

"Hey, who got us through that snake of a river last night?" Dave asked.

Keo grinned. "Point taken, *el capitan*."

Keo hopped out of the boat and was on the dock before Dave even turned off the trolling motor. He moved inland, the M4 in front of him, hoping he didn't see anything behind the red dot scope so he didn't have to shoot.

It wasn't the possibility of shooting someone that worried him; it was the fact that if he had to kill at all, that meant there were others already on the island. There was no telling who might have sneaked onto Santa Marie while they waited out the night. The bad guys, as he kept reminding himself, didn't need to be afraid of the darkness.

Fortunately, no one was hiding behind one of the dozen trucks still frozen in the parking lot, or poked their head out from the ridges that flanked the marina.

He stepped off the docks and kept going. He would have moved faster if his clothes weren't still partially soaked in last night's rain and he wasn't half-running and half-limping, the pain in his thigh reasserting itself this morning. The painkillers had begun kicking in a few hours ago, and though he had been tempted to down a couple more before sunup, he had resisted.

He swept the trucks and picked up the fresh, muddy footprints along the floors. Bare footprints.

Ghouls.

The storm system that had drowned T18 last night had been moving inland from the Gulf of Mexico. It had clearly hit Santa Marie Island first before moving on, and he was looking at the rain-slicked results. It also reinforced what he had seen back in town. The ghouls weren't afraid of the rain, just the rivers, the oceans, and the lakes. Why? What was the difference? Water was water, right?

Apparently not.

He let himself breathe easier only after he had reached the marina entrance. Keo leaned out and looked left, then right, up the streets. Scanned the houses on both sides, and it was only when he couldn't detect any signs of movement that he finally lowered the M4 and let himself relax for the first time since jumping out of the boat.

He turned around and waved to Dave and Jordan, the two of them still waiting in the boat. He watched as Dave hopped out with the line and tied it into place, then helped Jordan out. They carried Dave's pack and what weapons they had brought with them and hurried up the docks. Unlike him earlier, they seemed to be moving fine, even Jordan.

Keo took a moment for himself and glanced up at the warm sun. The mid-November weather was becoming more prominent, the air getting cooler every day. For now, the sky was wide open in the aftermath of last night's storm. He imagined this was one of those days that made owning a home in a place like this worth every penny.

Santa Marie Island, whether he wanted it to or not, would make a hell of a good last stand.

It was easy to find the two-story white house where Gene had taken him that morning when he first arrived on the island. All he had to do was find the hill again—not a hard task, since it was right in the center—and then walk up to the front door.

Like Gene had done when they were last here, Keo took note of the surrounding area—the unmowed front lawn, the sidewalks, and the doors and windows. Everything was intact, and unlike at the marina, there were no muddy footprints on the driveway or nearby streets. It was as if the creatures just knew there would be no one here so there was no point in raiding the place.

Even though he was certain the house hadn't been touched since he was last here, Keo moved cautiously anyway. There was no point in taking risks now. He wanted what the house had, but he could also easily make do with what he had on hand. With that in mind, he left the door wide open, using a rock to keep it pried so a gust of wind didn't push it close, and didn't touch anything else as he made his way upstairs.

Everything was where they had left it a few days ago, including the stack of weapons in the master bedroom's bathtub. Keo picked and chose what he thought they could use (and wished he had a few more hands).

He left the house and made his way back to Dave and Jordan, who were waiting for him at the ridgeline overlooking the western marina. Dave was crouched next to a large boulder, and Jordan was peering up at the sun next to him with her good eye.

"That bad, huh?" she said as he walked back to them.

"What's that?" he said.

"I saw your reaction."

"What reaction?"

She frowned. "The good news is, I still have one good eye."

"That's definitely good news."

"The bad news..."

"There's bad news?"

"Oh, yeah."

"Which would be?"

"I don't know how to shoot with my left eye. I usually squint with my right when I'm aiming."

"Most people do."

He put the weapons down on the ground in front of her. The damned things seemed to have doubled in weight since he stepped out of the house and made the long walk back to the marina. Of course, it could just be his sore shoulder and thigh. Keo unslung his pack and pulled out boxes of bullets, stacking them next to the guns.

Jordan picked up a Colt AR-15 and turned it over. "Am I wrong, or do you expect this to go on for a while?"

He nodded. "If we're lucky, yeah."

"'If we're lucky'?" Dave said. "Your definition of luck sucks."

"Desperate times call for desperate luck," Keo said. He picked up a box of 5.56mm rounds. "Catch," he said, and tossed it.

Dave caught it with one hand. "That's a lot of bullets."

"It's really not, but it'll have to do for now. You good with the M4?"

"One's enough for me." He patted the Walther P22 in his back waistband. "I still got this."

"What happened to your fancy German gun?" Jordan asked Keo.

"Jack took it," he said.

"Miller's little brother? The one Dave—"

"Yeah."

"Oh."

Dave groaned. "I didn't even want to shoot the guy. Or the other soldier in the living room."

"So why did you?" Keo asked.

"I didn't know Jack would be inside Bannerman's garage. But there he was, and the stupid asshole went for his gun. Then the soldier comes barging in, right at me." Dave shook his head. "It got bad really fast."

"It usually does when guns are involved."

Keo picked up a Mossberg pump-action shotgun with a pistol grip and slung it, then opened a box of shells and began shoving them into the leg pockets of his cargo pants.

"You didn't happen to get me one of those, did you?" Jordan asked.

"As a matter of fact, I did." He picked up a Remington 870 from the bundle and handed it to her. "Designed for the fairer sex."

"I'm touched." Jordan clutched and unclutched the weapon. "I gotta admit, it feels pretty good."

"That's the point." He handed her another box of shells. "Use it in close quarters. The AR-15 for everything else."

He handed her a spare gun belt and she put it on, then slid the Glock he had given her earlier into the empty holster.

"How's the body?" he asked.

"Why, you wanna cop a feel?"

He smiled, and she returned it.

"Maybe later," he said. "Can you walk without pain?"

"I can't even breathe without pain." She looked down at her chest, as if she could see past the raincoat to where Steve had cut her with his knife. "They're going to scar, aren't they?"

"Yeah."

"There goes my meet cute moment with Prince Charming. Hard to make a good first impression with bodily scars."

"You'll get by."

She frowned.

"Are you sure you're okay?" he asked.

She nodded and gave him her best forced smile. "You got shot twice last night, and you're still running around. So I'll be a big girl and suck it up."

"Good. You're going to need to move around, or you're going to be a sitting duck. I'll do what I can to keep the both of you alive, but you're going to have to do your part, too."

"Relax. I know you're the badass with the past, but it's been half a year since you last trained me, and I've picked up a thing or two while I was with Tobias."

"Yeah, what she said," Dave added.

Despite all three of them having unwittingly drunk enough water last night during the rainstorm to last a lifetime, they were all parched by midday and desperate for liquid. Keo knew exactly where to find them and went looking for houses with exterior access to the rooftops. He thought it would hurt the more he moved around, but thanks to a combination of Jay's painkillers and constant motion, the pain started to ebb into the background.

It took him a half dozen homes to find the same one he had spotted Gene on top of the other day. There was a long extension ladder in the back of the house that he used to climb up to the rooftop, where he found a pair of two-liter plastic soft drink bottles duct-taped to the pole of a satellite dish. They were both almost topped off thanks to last night's rain. Keo looked around but couldn't find the caps, so he reused the duct tape to cover up the bottles and carried them down one at a time.

Dave was now on the other side of the island, keeping an eye on the eastern marina, when Keo handed him one of the bottles, then walked across the island to Jordan's position, stopping just once to take more of the painkillers, silently thanking Jay for being so damn well-stocked.

Jordan glanced over as he walked back to her. "You went shopping without me? I hope you at least got me something nice."

She was at Dave's old position overlooking the marina, the AR-15 leaning against a boulder nearby, and she had the Remington slung over one shoulder. From up here, she could see all of the marina and the Texas coastline. They were in a perfect position to spot any approaching boats, because there weren't a lot of places to hide out there.

Their twenty-footer was still tied to the dock below them, and easy enough to spot from a distance. That was the point. All he needed was to draw Steve in and they could unleash on him and his men. Of course, that was assuming Steve would be approaching from the west. If he decided to come from the east, they'd have to run over to back up Dave.

He had a fifty-fifty chance of being right, which was pretty good odds these days.

"Water?" Jordan said when she saw what he was carrying.

He handed her the bottle. "Drink up."

She pulled off the duct tape and didn't stop drinking until she was splashing water down her chin.

"Oh my God, that hit the spot," she said, handing the bottle back to him. "Rain water?"

He nodded and drank some himself. It wasn't Evian, but it wasn't salt water, so he couldn't really complain.

"Found any food?" she asked.

"Not yet."

"But you think they're around?"

"Gene, the kid I told you about, hid a lot of things around the island. He called them go-bags. Of course, finding them is another matter."

"Big island."

"Eight kilometers."

"Yup. Big island."

Keo sat down next to her, trickled some water onto a rag, and dabbed at his forehead. The cut, courtesy of Tobias's "love tap," had scabbed over, and it itched more than it hurt. He felt Jordan's eyes on him the whole time.

"You need to stop going around and pissing off people, Keo," she said. "That pretty face of yours can only take so much."

He chuckled. "Thanks."

"No offense."

"None taken."

"I mean, you're still not bad looking, but adding in that love tap from Tobias and those two bullet holes, and you've definitely seen better days."

"Stop trying to butter me up," he said, and handed the bottle back to her.

She drank again, and this time didn't stop until there was just half remaining in the container. "I'm starving," she said when she was done.

"You already said that."

"Well, just in case you forgot."

"I haven't."

She sighed and leaned back against the boulder.

"There's a bright side in all of this," he said.

"Oh yeah? Pray tell."

"Steve's coming soon, and he'll probably bring some food."

"That's the bright side?"

"I mentioned he'd probably be bringing some food with him, right?"

"I've missed your screwed up sense of humor, Keo. By which I mean, I haven't really missed it."

They sat quietly for a few minutes, listening to birds chirping as they swarmed the wide-open skies above them. Even the *sloshing* of the ocean was calming, as if last night's rainstorm had drained the sea of its power and it was only now starting to regain its strength. It was so peaceful he wanted to close his eyes and go to sleep.

He did close his eyes, but he didn't go to sleep. That wasn't going to happen for a while, no matter how tired or sore or numbed he was. Instead of lingering on what he couldn't control, Keo spent the next few minutes swapping out the bandages with fresh ones.

"Need a hand?" Jordan asked.

"Nah, I got it."

"I was just trying to be nice. I hate the sight of blood." She watched him working for a moment before asking, "So what's the deal with you and Gillian?"

He didn't answer right away, because he didn't know how, though the more he thought about it, the more simple the answer was. So much so that it pained him to finally realize it.

The deal with him and Gillian? There was no deal. That was the painful truth of it.

"She has Jay and the baby," he finally said. "I guess that's the deal."

"Sorry."

"Yeah, well, it is what it is." He finished up and shoved the supplies back into the pack. "When you were with Tobias, did you ever shoot anyone?"

"I've shot plenty of people."

"Maybe I should say, did you ever kill anyone?"

"I don't know." She shook her head. "There were a lot of skirmishes and bullets were always flying, but if you're asking me if I'm one hundred percent certain I killed someone during those moments, then no. I can't say for sure if I've ever killed anyone or not."

"What about that ambush at the strip mall? The day I showed up?"

"By the time I got there, Tobias had already sounded the

retreat. I fired a magazine into where I thought there were some soldiers, but again..."

"You can't be sure."

"I can't be sure. Sorry."

"That's nothing to be sorry about."

"Considering what's about to show up soon, I think there is. You don't know if you can count on me."

"That's not true."

"No?"

"I know I can count on you."

She looked at him seriously. "How?"

"The same way I knew I could count on you to keep Gillian and the others safe back at the cabin."

"And I did a hell of a good job with that. Gillian and I got captured, Mark's dead, and Rachel and..." She let the rest go unsaid.

"But you got them safely away from the cabin and here, just like I knew you would. What happened after that was out of your control."

"You weren't there..."

"You did the best you could."

She wasn't convinced, and turned her head and looked over at the solitary houses that lined both sides of the street instead.

"You should have been there with us, Keo," she said finally. "Things would have turned out differently if you had been."

"I know," he said quietly. "I know..."

TWENTY-SIX

"They're not coming," Keo said.

"How can you be sure?" Jordan asked.

Keo didn't have to look at his watch, thanks to the sight of the setting sun. The calm, clear skies weren't darkening just yet, but it wouldn't be long now. Maybe another hour, maybe less. In the back of his mind, he still remembered the speed with which yesterday had darkened.

"They would be here by now if they were coming," he said.

"Maybe he's dead. Steve. You said it yourself; you couldn't see anyone back at the marina, just silhouettes. One of them could have been Steve. If he's dead, would they still come after us?"

It was a fair question, and she had a point. It had been unfathomably dark back there, and he and Dave were shooting at everything that wasn't them. One of the bodies spilling out of Marina 1 could very well have been Steve.

Or was that just him trying to be overly optimistic?

"Maybe," he said.

"You didn't answer my question. Would they still come after us if Steve's dead?"

"I don't know. You've known the guy longer than I have. Would he?"

"I've seen him, and Tobias has talked about him a lot, but I never sat across a desk from him drinking shots of whiskey. You have."

Another good point. Jordan was full of good points today.

"Steve's the boss," Keo said. "He would move Heaven and Earth to find and snuff out Dave for killing Jack. Without him, the town—and the soldiers running it—might not consider us important enough to commit the manpower. I wouldn't, in their shoes. What's two or three more stragglers when they have an entire town to watch over?"

"So there's a chance no one's coming."

"There's a chance, yeah."

She cocked her head, scrutinizing him with her one good eye. In a day or two, she would probably be able to see out of the right side just fine.

"What?" he said.

"You're telling me what you think I want to hear, but you don't actually believe any of it, do you?"

He shrugged. "Maybe."

Jordan sighed. "You know what's ironic about all of this?"

"What's that?"

"This place." She looked around at the empty streets and the houses around them again. "We've been trying to get here all this time, and here we are, finally. Is it everything you thought it would be?"

"Not quite."

"Yeah..."

He glanced down at his watch. 5:11 p.m. "It'll be dark soon. We need to find a place to hole up for the night."

"And maybe find some food. Did I tell you I was starving?"

"Maybe a time or two."

"I thought I'd just remind you in case you forgot." As if on cue, her stomach growled. "See?"

He stood up. "Let's go get Dave."

"You think he's hungry, too?"

"I'm sure he is."

"Because I'm starving."

"You don't say..."

Dave heard them coming behind him and glanced up from the boulder where he was hiding, overlooking the eastern marina on the other side.

"I don't think they're coming today," he said.

"Doesn't look like it," Keo nodded.

"That's good news for us, right? Maybe they won't come tomorrow, either."

And maybe monkeys will fly out of my ass, Keo thought, but said, "Maybe. For now, let's find someplace to bunk down for the night. This island might look empty, but it's far from it."

Dave looked up at the sky, and Keo thought he might have shivered involuntarily.

"Been awhile?" Keo asked.

"What's that?" Dave said.

"Since you've been out here."

Dave tried to smile. "Something like that."

Keo thought about saying something reassuring. Not just for Dave, but for Jordan standing next to him, but with the night creeping up on them and Steve coming (*You're out there, aren't you? I know you're out there.*) sooner or later, whatever he said would have just sounded hollow.

"Let's try to stay alive tonight first, then worry about tomorrow, tomorrow," was all he could think of to say.

Choosing a place to stay the night was a no-brainer. The two-story white house on the hill in the middle, where he had found the guns, was the first and last choice he considered. From up there, he could keep an eye on the entire island, including both marinas. The house was also in a perfect spot to, even with just three people, hold off a lengthy assault.

He didn't like the idea of getting into another standoff with very few outs, but Keo had learned long ago that what he wanted and would rather do was usually not what he had to do in order to survive. Pollard, Song Island, and T18 were proof of that.

"Adapt or perish," as Lara and the folks on the *Trident* were fond of saying.

The house was flanked by a half dozen others, with a long, winding driveway that connected it to the streets. A ten-foot-tall metal fence surrounded the property, with an extensive front and backyard, and an electronic gate that they left the way Gene had found it—open. Gene might have just been a sixteen-year-old kid, but he had survived on the island by himself for months; he had done that by not attracting the ghouls' attention, which meant leaving things as he found them, including the doors, windows, and front gates.

Inside the house, they found five bedrooms, with two on the second floor, including the master. It had an attic but no basement. He found plenty of boxes (open, which probably meant Gene had gone through them already) in one half of the garage, but no car or food. Gene had once told him he had bug-out bags all around the island, but apparently the two-story house wasn't

THE ISLES OF ELYSIUM   333

one of those places. Or if it were, Keo couldn't find where the kid had hid them.

His stomach was growling when he came out of the garage and headed back to the house. He gave the street beyond the gate a last look, then peeked up at the darkening skies before slipping back inside.

Jordan was leaning against the kitchen's island counter, looking somberly at her reflection in the steel refrigerator across from her. She and Dave had gone through the cabinets, opening every door they could find in hopes of locating food that hadn't spoiled or gone bad, while he was outside. By the expression on her face, he guessed they had come up empty, too.

Piles of utensils covered the counters—spoons, forks, and butter knives. Besides food, Jordan and Dave had been looking for anything silver, but by the way the cutlery was tossed around, that search had come up just as empty.

"Any silver?" he asked anyway.

She shook her head. "Fake. They're all cheap fakes. How is it possible people who live in a house this big, that probably cost more than I'll make in a lifetime, don't have one single real piece of silver lying around?"

"Maybe that's how they got to be rich in the first place. They're frugal with their money. Why buy real, expensive silver when you can just use the cheap stuff? Most people don't know the difference, anyway."

"So that's the secret?"

"One of many, I'm guessing."

He started to open the refrigerator, but Jordan said, "I wouldn't do that if I were you."

"Nothing?"

"Oh, there's something in there, all right. You just can't eat it. Well, you could if you wanted to, but I wouldn't recommend it."

He gave up on the refrigerator and walked back to her. "Nothing at all? Not even a nibble?"

"Not even rat droppings. You'd think there would be rat droppings, right? Are there even any animals left on the island?"

"The birds."

"Land animals, I mean."

"Probably not. Once they turned the population, they'd have to resort to other things for blood."

"And here we are..."

"And here we are. Did Dave find anything on the second floor?"

"If he did, he didn't say anything. Maybe he's hoarding the food all for himself." She laid her forehead against the counter and sighed. "We should have gone to Galveston Island, Keo. There are more houses there, more supplies..."

"We'll go there tomorrow. Find some gas, load up on some food, and get the hell away from here for good."

She gave him a wry smile. "When did you become such an optimist?"

"Why shouldn't I be?"

"For one, you lost the woman you love to some guy. To add insult to injury, she's carrying his child."

"Yeah, but other than that, things have been going pretty swell." He sat down on a stool. "You know what the funny thing is?"

"You mean there's something funny about all this? Please enlighten me, because I can use a good laugh right about now."

"Back at the marina—at T18—I saw something that I'm still not entirely sure I actually saw."

"That sounds overly complicated."

"You don't know the half of it."

He ran the memories back in his head. Keo had lost count of the number of times he had relived last night. And like all the other times, nothing he saw—or *thought* he saw—still made any sense.

"What happened?" Jordan asked, looking at him curiously with her good eye.

"I don't think you'd believe me if I told you."

"Even after everything that's happened?"

"Even after everything that's happened," he nodded.

"Wow."

"Yeah."

"Well, feel free to tell me about it later. Right now, there's a very good chance I'm too tired to care anyway."

They heard footsteps behind them as Dave came back down the stairs.

"Anything?" Keo asked him.

Dave shook his head. "Nothing that you didn't already find earlier. You?"

"Nope."

"Figures."

Keo got up and turned toward the window facing the backyard. It had gotten noticeably darker since the last time he looked.

"Let's get ready for tonight," he said.

───────────

Silver bullets. That's what he needed right now, even more than food.

Christ, he wished he had silver bullets.

It didn't take very long before they came out. He saw just one at first, darting across the street in front of the house. It had come out of the ugly blue building next door and made a beeline straight for the western marina.

Then another, and another...

"One fifty, give or take a few dozen here and there. Could be

less. Could be more. I'm just spitballing numbers, though," he had told Gene when they were trying to guess how many ghouls were still on the island.

As he watched them coming out of the homes around him, their strained dark flesh reflecting back the bright moonlight, he probably hadn't been too far from the truth. He had stopped counting around fifty, and there were definitely more than that.

Maybe a hundred. Maybe almost 200.

"Could be less. Could be more."

What mattered was that there were too many. There were always too many, but even more so now because he didn't have a single silver bullet to go around. Hell, he would have made do with a silver butter knife. Or a fork. Anything, as long as it was silver. Was it possible the entire island was barren of the precious metal? One of the houses around him had to have what he needed—a candleholder, a picture frame, or maybe if he was really lucky, a sword made entirely of silver. Oh, the things he could have done with that...

Except there hadn't been time to do a thorough search of every single house, because they had wasted most of the day waiting for Steve to finally charge across the waters. Which meant he had screwed up. Maybe he had even overestimated Steve's determination to avenge his brother's death.

Or maybe, just maybe, Steve really was dead. Maybe the man really had been one of those soldiers either he or Dave had shot back at Marina 1.

Was that possible? Yes. Likely? Maybe...

Daebak. My entire life is a series of maybes these days.

He focused on the western marina from the sanctuary of the master bedroom, keeping out of view behind the back window. Somewhere outside the room on the second floor, Dave was keeping watch out the front window at the eastern marina on the other side of the island. An approaching vehicle, even one that was powered by trolling motors, would be noticeable against the glistening dark ocean.

He could easily make out the docks under the generous pool of moonlight, along with the creatures crawling all over them at the moment. The white twenty-footer they had arrived in remained tied in its slip, looking incredibly lonely against the blanket of night. Not surprisingly, the ghouls were drawn to it like a beacon. Maybe it hadn't been such a good idea to keep the boat there. Should they have dragged it out of the water and hid it? Too late for that now.

His stomach growled, a low rumble that gradually increased in volume.

"I heard that," Jordan said from across the room. She was sitting against the wall next to the open door.

"Heard what?" he said.

"Uh huh. So what are they doing out there?"

"They're at the marina. I guess they found the boat."

"Not exactly hard to find. Maybe we should have hid it."

Definitely should have hid it, he thought. "Yeah, probably."

"So what are they doing, exactly?"

"Nothing."

"Nothing?"

"You expect them to jump into the boat and drive it back to the mainland?"

"Given everything I've seen so far, would that really be all that crazy?"

Keo thought about T18, about the blue-eyed ghoul that had saved his life... "Not that crazy, I guess."

"Keo," Jordan said.

"What?"

"I'm sorry about Gillian."

"Are we doing this again?"

"There's a bright side..."

"Yeah?"

"I've always had a bit of a crush on you. So if you're looking for some rebound sex, I'm available."

"*Shit,*" Keo said.

"Ugh, never mind, then. I was just trying to be friendly—"

"No, not that. Something's approaching the island."

He saw it again—*a single orb of light* bouncing against the water's surface, followed quickly by the familiar and slowly growing whine of motors.

"What is it?" Jordan asked.

He looked across the semidarkness of the master bedroom at her, clutching the AR-15. "They're here."

"How many?"

"Just one."

"Just one?"

"I only see one."

Jordan gave him a confused look. "That doesn't make any sense—"

BOOM!

The entire house shook, as if it had been hit by a meteorite, and every inch of the wall and floor and ceiling seemed to tremble and threaten to come unglued at the seams. The shock of the explosion tossed Jordan forward, the rifle spilling from her grip. A cloud of debris and smoke flooded through the open doorway and splashed into the master bedroom, swallowing up Jordan in its path.

Keo ducked instinctively, even though he didn't have to. Jordan was somewhere on the floor in front of him, trying to get up; he only knew she was there because he could hear her coughing.

Dave!

He staggered to his feet and rushed through the billowing smoke—*crunching* chunks of the wall and ceiling that had fallen free under his boots—over to Jordan's struggling form. He pulled her up, and when she was steady on her feet again, he continued on toward the door. He slipped through it, stumbling over more debris.

Once outside, he froze in his tracks.

Half of the second floor ceiling was gone, exposing the open, dark skies above. A cold chill swamped the remains of the room, and there were no signs of Dave. In the spot where Keo had last seen the other man, there were only shreds of clothing buried underneath fallen rubble and pieces of what looked like an assault rifle sprinkled across the floor.

Keo zeroed in on the gaping hole in the front wall, the same one that faced the eastern marina. The almost perfect half-circle opening in the floor looked down at a bathroom and parts of another bedroom. It looked like the explosion had torn out a huge chunk of the house, as if some giant monster had gobbled it up, leaving behind a jagged crater in the shape of its mouth.

He hadn't gotten more than a few steps toward what remained of the front wall when—

Pop-pop-pop!

He dropped to the floor—

Pop-pop-pop!

Bullets *zipped* past his head and slammed into parts of the ceiling that were still above him. Keo rolled away from the opening, ignoring the stabbing pains; it seemed like every sharp edge along the Mossberg shotgun slung over his back was digging into his body.

Whoever was shooting at him must have anticipated that he would be scampering away from the opening, because they started shooting through the wall in front of him. Pieces of the house splintered, and a window that had escaped the blast unscathed shattered and rained glass around him.

He kept moving—kept rolling—because he didn't know what else to do.

He didn't stop until he bumped into a wall and scrambled up and ran back toward the master bedroom. Jordan was at the door, clinging to a nearby bureau to keep herself upright, and she almost shot him with her reacquired rifle when he darted back inside.

"Jesus, Keo!" she shouted. "Where's Dave?"

He shook his head. Dave was probably dead. Or injured. Or somewhere buried on the first floor. Bottom line: Dave was out of action, and there was no telling how many men were coming into the house at this very moment.

Not just men, either, but *them*, too.

He ran past Jordan and to the window. He kept away from the glass and peered out and was immediately drawn back to the western marina where the boat he had seen earlier had docked in the slip next to the one holding the white shape of their twenty-footer.

What the hell is happening?

None of this made any sense. If Steve's people—and there was no doubt that was them out there right now—had success-fully sneaked unnoticed onto the island from somewhere else, then who was the lone dark figure walking calmly up the dock?

Keo might have been seeing things (*again?*), but he swore the throng of ghouls gathering inside the marina were separating, scrambling to get out of the figure's way, like Moses parting the Red Sea...

TWENTY-SEVEN

"Hey, Keo, you in there?"

Steve.

Of course it was Steve, shouting like an idiot from somewhere outside the house, though where, exactly, Keo couldn't quite pinpoint. Who else would it be? He hadn't for a single second (okay, maybe for a few very optimistic seconds) thought the man was dead. It was too good to be true, and if everything he had gone through since the world ended had taught him anything, it was that when things were too good to be true they usually were —especially when he was involved.

If it wasn't for shitty luck...

"One down, two to go!"

The man sounded like he was having fun, which was more than Keo could say for him and Jordan as he scrambled out of the main bedroom while keeping as far away from the cratered wall as possible. A cold gust of wind made him shiver involuntarily, and the scar along the left side of his face tingled, the first time in a long time.

"I could be wrong, of course. It's kind of dark out here. Hard to see."

His one big advantage was the stairs. There were plenty of ways to get into the house—the back door, the front door, the windows—but there was only one path up to the second floor. He moved in a crouch toward it now and leaned against the wall, listening for sounds and vibrations that would signal entry.

Now this is familiar, he thought, remembering the last time he was pinned on the second floor of a house.

"But it's going to get even darker real soon, buddy." The voice was clearly on the move, from the back of the house toward the front.

Earlier, Keo had locked the doors and windows on the first floor, but there were no additional (and obvious) barricades over the other entrances, just in case the creatures decided to look inside. It was a risk, considering everything Gene had preached about not messing with a house's status quo, but Keo had to risk it. The idea of hiding inside a place that wasn't locked *on purpose* made his skin crawl. And besides, Gene's way of doing things hadn't exactly worked out the last time he was on the island...

"You still alive in there, Keo? Don't be shy! I thought we were friends?"

Think again, Keo wanted to shout back down, but held his tongue.

"Gillian's still waiting for you back in town. You'll be happy to know I've decided not to punish her. Or Doc Jay. They're not responsible for your bad decisions, after all."

Right. Steve hadn't hurt Gillian because he was feeling generous. More likely it was because he needed her to keep Jay in line. Jay might not have the makings of a rebel, but every man had his limits. Harming a woman like Gillian, along with her unborn baby, was a good way to piss off one of the only two doctors in town.

Steve's words made Keo feel a lot better about leaving Gillian behind in T18. Of course, that probably wasn't Steve's intent.

"Man up, Keo!" the man shouted now. "Don't make me go up there! It's not gonna be pretty if I have to do that!"

A brief silence. Maybe Steve expected him to respond. If so, he was going to have a long wait. Keo was too busy listening for the telltale signs of an impending assault, because he knew damn well one was coming. And soon.

"All right, have it your way!" Steve shouted.

Thanks for the warning, asshole, Keo thought, just as he heard the first *bang!* against the front door downstairs. That was followed by the *crash!* of glass panes as they began breaking their way through the windows at the same time.

He glanced behind him at Jordan, crouched near the open master bathroom door with the Remington in her hands, the AR-15 slung over her back. Her right eye had gotten much better in the last few hours, though at the moment he could really only see her left even with the thick pool of moonlight splashing inside through the gaping hole to their right—the result of some kind of grenade launcher, most likely.

He nodded at her and could just barely make her out giving him a crooked, almost wistful half-smile back, as if to say, *This is it. We're both going to die.*

He couldn't disagree, so he smiled back and turned around, then swapped the M4 for the Mossberg with the pistol grip. The 12-gauge pump-action shotgun was thirty-one inches long and held six shells. He had the rest stuffed into his pockets, but what he wouldn't give for a shell carrier. Of course, what he wouldn't give for a whole lot of things, including his MP5SD with the built-in suppressor. There were a lot of weapons still waiting inside the master bedroom's tub, but one non-MP5SD was the same as another.

If wishes were assholes...

He faced the stairs again and pressed his left ear against the wall.

They were coming. The banging against the door had ceased, probably because they realized coming through the windows was easier. Right now, he could hear the *crunch* of glass under heavy combat boots. Then, in no time at all, those same sounds approaching the bottom of the stairs.

Definitely more than one. How many would Steve bring with him? That would depend on how many boats he had managed to land on Santa Marie Island without them noticing. He couldn't have achieved that using the eastern marina. Dave would have seen them. And Keo had the western side scoped out, but by the time he had seen the lone boat, it was too late; they were already on the island.

Christ, how did they get on the island so fast?

Things weren't adding up. If Steve had made it onto the island unnoticed, who was piloting the lone boat that landed at the western marina? Was that some kind of diversion? Draw his attention as they moved on the house?

Maybe. Steve was clever enough to do something like that. The guy had sent him out of T18 to be shot at, only to swoop in and decimate Tobias's people. Many of the opponents Keo had met in the last few months had been devoid of tactical ability, but Steve wasn't one of them. Far from it.

And Dave. Shit. He was either dead or lying somewhere on the first floor under some rubble. Either way, Dave wasn't going to be much help right now. Keo just hoped it was at least a fast trip to the afterlife for the poor guy. He hadn't really gotten to know Dave all that well, but he'd liked the man nonetheless.

Focus.

He didn't have very long to wait for Steve to show his hand. Keo didn't so much as see the man's head as he spotted the protruding lens of the night-vision goggles peeking around the corner before turning up the stairs.

Keo fired, buckshot tearing into the NVG and shattering the lens, slamming into flesh and bone on the other side.

Even as the body collapsed, a second man appeared, jumping over his fallen comrade. The man landed on the second step and was lifting a laser-equipped M4 when Keo racked the Mossberg and put the contents of the second shell into the man's chest. The black-clad figure was flung back by the blast, tripped over the body behind him, and did an almost impressive backward flip onto the living room floor.

They took the hint after that and he heard heavy footsteps, this time moving away from the staircase.

Keo took advantage of the momentary retreat and grabbed two shells from his pocket and fed them into the shotgun. Behind him, he heard Jordan crouch-walking over to his position, her labored breathing doing more to alert him than the *crunch* of her boots over debris strewn across the floor.

"You okay?" she whispered.

He nodded. "Anything going on back there?"

She shook her head. "I don't see anything. They're either all inside the house already, or they're sticking to places I can't see from the back window."

"What about the rest of the island?" He thought about adding, *"What about* them," but Jordan already knew what he meant.

"I don't know where they went," she said. "It's like they just disappeared. But it's so dark out there, they could be right under the window and I might still not have seen them."

That's encouraging, he thought, smiling slightly to himself.

He focused back on the stairs.

"Do you really think they're holding back?" Jordan asked.

SAM SISAVATH

Like him the last time, she didn't have to elaborate on who "they" were.

"I don't know," he said. "They did exactly just that a few nights ago when I was here with Gene. They were attacking when Steve showed up, then they retreated to let him finish the job."

"That's...freaky."

"You haven't seen freaky yet," he said, memories of the blue-eyed creature at the T18 marina flashing back across his mind.

"What now?"

"Wait them out, if we can."

"That's a big if."

So what else is new?

"Keo!" a voice shouted from below, very close to the stairs. Steve again. Who else would it be? "Nice shooting."

"Thanks!" Keo shouted down. "Close quarters! That's kind of my specialty, didn't I tell you?"

"Yes, you did. It must have slipped my mind."

"Consider those two bodies a reminder."

"I was right about you. You're just too dangerous to ever be fully trusted. I should have trusted my instincts and taken you out of the equation when you showed up at the bridge."

"Shoulda, woulda, coulda, pal."

Steve chuckled. "Who's still up there with you? Tobias's girl? I know Dave's dead. That's his name, right?"

"How'd you know?"

"One of the cafeteria cooks didn't show up for work this morning. Wasn't hard to put two and two together."

"And here I thought you were dumb as a rock, Steve."

Another forced chuckle. "Bye-bye, Dave, it was nice not knowing ya. I put a grenade round into the window where he was standing myself. I know, I know, big time movie cliché, right? Kill the black guy first? But I guess you wouldn't know anything about that; not being a movie guy and all. Anyway, what's that's saying? Payback's a real bitch."

Keo exchanged a look with Jordan, and she looked back at the crater behind them, the pieces of clothing (*Dave's*) still stuck among the debris.

"How'd you sneak onto the island without us seeing you?" Keo shouted down.

"That's your problem, Keo," Steve said. "You think you have everything figured out. But it never occurred to you that my guys have been keeping an eye on Santa Marie Island for months now. Those marinas aren't the only way onto the island, sport. Dave learned that lesson the hard way."

Keo cursed himself. He had chosen the two-story house on the hill because it gave them an expanded view of the island, along with both marinas. If he had known there were other ways onto the place, he would have opted for hiding instead, the way Gene had done the last few months when he continually evaded Steve's people.

Live and learn, pal.

"How many men you got left down there, Steve?" he called down.

"Don't you worry about me," Steve said. "I got plenty more where they came from."

"I'm sure the rest of your guys are glad to hear you say that."

"Don't you worry about my boys. Everyone knows where they stand. You have to, or you'll get stepped on."

"You come up with that yourself?"

"You like it?"

"Eh, could use some work."

"You wanna workshop it with me?"

"Sure, why not? Come on up and we can do that right now."

Steve let out a strained laugh. "You'd like that, wouldn't you?"

"I got a bottle of J&B up here. Let's have a drink."

"Nah, I'm going to have to pass."

"You're no fun."

Keo waited for a response, but he didn't get one. At least, not for a while.

He thought he might have heard some back and forth whispering below him, though. Some kind of argument that was getting more heated by the second.

"Sounds like the villagers are getting restless!" Keo shouted. "Maybe you shouldn't have let them know just how expendable they were in your eyes."

He waited for a comeback, but there was only silence.

"Steve? You still down there, ol' buddy? Talk to me."

"You know what?" Steve shouted up. His voice had changed, and whereas before he had been cavalier—even though Keo didn't believe it for a second—there was none of that pretense now. "I'm tired of this shit. I'm tired of *you*. I was going to drag you back to town and string you up in the fields like a scarecrow to make an example of you. Show your girlfriend and the Doc that I could be nice, but there was a limit to my generosity. But as far as I'm concerned, it's mission accomplished. I got what I needed—Jack's killer in pieces."

Keo looked back at Jordan and was about to tell her to get ready, but he didn't have to. She already knew, and she nodded back at him and clenched her teeth, mentally preparing herself for what was coming next.

"There's more than one way to skin a cat," Steve was shouting, his voice rising noticeably. "You want to stay on this island? You're going to have to fight its residents for it! You know who I'm talking about, Keo?"

Keo knew *exactly* who he was talking about.

"Here they come right now," Steve said. "Good luck—"

Someone screamed, cutting off whatever Steve was about to

say, followed by the sound of glass breaking. Then someone—no, more than one—opened fire, the *pop-pop-pop* of automatic rifles filling the first floor below them. The renewed burst of activity was sudden and ferocious, and for a few seconds Keo remained crouched and frozen. He listened, unable to pull away even if he had wanted to.

For a moment, just a moment, he thought it was a trick. Some elaborate game concocted by Steve to mess with their heads. But the more he heard, the more he realized it wasn't. Those were real screams down there. Real gunfire, and the very real sounds of men *dying*.

Steve's men.

Keo stood up, said, "Go!"

She was already up and moving, and he followed her straight into the master bedroom.

Frantic screaming continued from below them as he slammed the door shut and hurried over to help Jordan push and drag the wooden dresser over. The continuous gunfire rattled under his boots and Keo did his best to ignore them. He concentrated on getting the goddamn heavy furniture over to where he needed it, grunting through stabbing pains from his thigh and shoulder the entire time. He should have sutured both of the wounds earlier. Shit.

Shoulda, woulda, and totally screwed, pal.

Finally—*finally!*—they got the dresser all the way across the room and slammed it up against the door. It went up only half-way, leaving the top half vulnerable. Keo had seen what the ghouls could do when they were determined enough to get into a closed room, and he had a very bad feeling they were going to be very, very determined tonight.

They stumbled back, out of breath, listening to the gunfire rattling on and on below them, even though every gunshot sounded as if it were coming from right in front of them, on the other side of the door.

"It won't hold," Keo said. "It'll never keep them out. Not all night."

"I know," Jordan said.

They started looking around for more things to block the door with. There was a nightstand, but it was too slim and probably wasn't even worth carrying over. A large full-length mirror on a swivel in one corner had a sturdy look to it. And then there was the bed. A large king-size, worthy of being put into a master bedroom on a two-story house on an island hillside. It was going to be heavy, too. Really heavy. It was bad enough he was moving on a gimpy leg and a bum arm, and now he was going to have to carry that monster.

Shut up and do it!

Jordan saw where he was looking, and they both moved toward it simultaneously when—

Silence.

The shooting and screams from downstairs had stopped.

There was no prelude, no hints that it was winding down. It had simply just...*stopped.*

They stared at each other, and he guessed her confused face probably mirrored his own.

What the hell had Steve's people been shooting at? Was it the ghouls? But that didn't make any sense. If the creatures had let them onto the island and then ignored them, allowing them to assault the house, why would they attack now?

What was that Steve had said just before the gunfire started?

"Here they come right now. Good luck!"

Except Steve wasn't going to stop at "good luck." He was going to say something else, but never got the chance.

Why? What was out there? What did he think was "coming"?

Whatever it was, it wasn't anything Steve had expected. The screams and shooting were proof of that. So what—

Something flickered at the corner of Keo's eye and he spun around, unslinging the Mossberg at the same time. A black object was moving outside the back window just a split second before it smashed its way inside.

Jordan ducked her head against the flying glass, but Keo didn't have that luxury. He was too busy lining up a shot. Between raising the shotgun and pulling the trigger, he had just enough time to register that it was a man that had crashed its way through the window.

No, not a man. Not exactly.

It was a *ghoul* wearing a long trench coat, the flaps swirling around him (*it*) like some kind of cape. Its eyes glowed blue against the semidarkness of the room and it began standing up, lengthening its impossibly gaunt frame like some kind of contortionist.

It seemed to stretch and stretch, the coat fluttering around its painfully thin legs (*Like chopsticks, I can break those with my bare hands,* Keo thought), and although he was sure it was just the moonlight and shadows playing tricks with his mind, he swore the damn thing had to be well over seven feet tall.

He pulled the trigger, the loud *boom!* ear-splitting in the closed confines of the master bedroom.

He didn't know how the creature did it, but it twisted its body to avoid most of his shot. But it wasn't quite fast enough—it didn't help that it was partially still straightening up from the floor when Keo fired—and half of the buckshot tore into its left side and the rest slammed into the wall behind it. Keo had fired without aiming, because there hadn't been any time. He had simply pointed at the biggest part of the monster, even as Danny's words echoed inside his head:

"If you see them, run the other way, Obi-Wan Keobi. Or shoot them in the head. That seems to work pretty well."

The head.

Shoot them in the head!

He racked the shotgun and tilted the weapon up slightly, but before he could squeeze the trigger a second time, the thing moved.

No, that wasn't true, because to say it moved meant Keo could see its body in motion. Because he couldn't. Not really. Maybe it was the darkness and shadows and moonlight once again messing with his eyes, but Keo swore he only saw a black blur (*Like back at the T18 marina...*) just before the shotgun was jerked out of his hands.

It was so swift, so unmercifully forceful, that he hadn't quite come to grips with what had happened until the creature's pruned black flesh filled his vision, because it was now standing in front of him. Tightened black skin seemed to be vibrating in the dark room and suffocating heat emanated from its eyes, even as an icy coldness radiated from every pore of its flesh. Those things shouldn't have been possible, the incongruent nature of hot and cold warring inside Keo's head.

He struggled to understand what he was seeing and feeling, but all he could focus on was the thin trickles of coagulated black blood dripping out of holes in the creature's trench coat. Except Keo couldn't see gaping wounds through the openings—if they were there, they had somehow healed themselves. He wished his own injuries were that efficient.

Why was it even wearing clothes at all, he wondered. The sight of the fabric wrapped around its elongated frame was almost absurd, and for a moment Keo wanted to ask the creature if it *knew* what it was.

Then, unfathomably, the creature spoke.

"Keo," it hissed. "I've been looking for you."

TWENTY-EIGHT

Daebak. It knows my name, too.

The sight of the creature standing in front of him, its blue eyes like twin otherworldly orbs, made Keo hesitate. He wasn't sure for how long, though; it could have been just a second, or two, or possibly a minute.

He didn't know how long he stood there staring back at the creature, replaying the sound of his own name coming out of its impossibly thin and blackened lips. But when he finally did manage to gain some semblance of control, the first thing he did was shout, "Jordan!"

But the ghoul reacted before Jordan could, and it pointed the Mossberg at Keo—no, not at him, but *past* him, and at Jordan standing over his shoulder. The fact that it even knew how to use a shotgun surprised him for some reason. And the way it held the weapon—as if it had been doing it all its life—made Keo more curious than scared, and he was pretty goddamn scared to begin with.

For the next few seconds, Keo didn't know what Jordan was doing behind him. Maybe like him, she had frozen in place and was unsure how to respond to the sight of this thing in the room with them. Maybe like him, she couldn't understand how it could radiate heat and icy coldness at the same time.

However long the next few seconds passed for the three of them, the monster must have no longer thought she was a threat because its eyes (*Christ, they're blue*) shifted back to him, and Keo saw it clear as day and without a shred of doubt:

The creature was intelligent.

He was so focused on that (*impossible*) sudden realization that he forgot to reach down for his sidearm. Not that he would have had much of a chance, anyway. This *thing* had crossed the room in less time than it had taken him to rack the shotgun. Did he really think he could draw the Glock before it fired, taking both him and Jordan out in a hail of buckshot?

No way in hell. Not even close.

"If I'd wanted to kill you," it hissed, "you wouldn't have escaped T18."

T18.

Back at the marina...

"You," Keo whispered.

He didn't know exactly why he was whispering. Maybe it was the sound of the creature's voice—it was so low, as if just talking (hissing) was painful somehow, and he wanted to...do what? Match its pitch?

Crazy talk.

"You saved my life," Keo managed to get out. Then, because he couldn't think of anything else to say or do, "Why?"

"You'll find out soon enough," it said, and cocked its head slightly to one side. "They're coming."

"Who?"

"The others."

Others? What others—

Oh, right. The others.

"The door won't hold forever," it hissed. "There's too many of them."

"Keo?" Jordan said behind him. She sounded breathless, which made him wonder how *he* was sounding at the moment. "What's happening?"

"I..." *Have no fucking idea,* he wanted to say, but finished instead with, "It saved my life. Our lives. Back at T18. We wouldn't have made it out of there if it hadn't shown up. I've been, uh, meaning to tell you."

"And...now?"

It looked past him—at Jordan, or the door, or both—before settling on him again. "You'll never survive the night. Not alone."

Keo nodded. He didn't know why he was so calm all of a sudden. Maybe it was the way the creature talked, or possibly it was the lack of animal urges behind its cool blue eyes. He had faced enough of the black-eyed ghouls up close and personal to recognize the absence of a soul behind the hollowed holes that used to be their eyes. This thing standing in front of him was so far removed from those frenzied monsters that Keo wondered if he was dreaming, if this was all just one long (albeit very vivid) nightmare.

Wake up! Wake up, you idiot!

But he didn't wake up, because he wasn't asleep. This was real. Jesus, this was real.

"I agree," he said. "We can't survive alone."

It pulled back the Mossberg, then held it, stock-first, to him.

Keo stared at the shotgun, then at its unmoving face, those pulsating blue eyes. He didn't react for a long time.

Five seconds...then ten...

He reached forward and took the Mossberg back from the ghoul.

It lowered its hand, bony fingers unfurling at its side.

Behind him, Jordan might have shuffled her feet nervously,

though it was hard to tell because he was so glued to the creature, on its every movement, waiting—*waiting*—for the first hint that it would prove him right, that it was, after all, just another undead thing waiting to end his existence.

"Now what?" Keo asked.

"You can't climb," it said.

"Is that how you got up here? You climbed?"

It nodded.

"Damn," Keo said.

"Keo," Jordan said, and he could almost hear her doing everything humanly possible not to scream out his name.

He turned around and saw her looking back at the door.

"They're inside the house," the creature hissed behind him.

Keo moved across the bedroom and pressed his ear against the wall. He didn't have to wait very long. They were out there, on what was left of the second-floor living room. The unmistakable sounds of shuffling bare feet, the growing smell of their numbers swelling on the other side of the thick slab of wood.

Behind him, Jordan was staring at the creature in the trench coat, her shotgun pointed at the floor. She was gripping the Remington so tightly that her fingers looked ghost-white against the darkness. For its part, the thing looked unbothered by Jordan's unwavering stare or the weapon in her hand.

"*What are you?*" Jordan finally asked.

It opened its mouth, as if to answer, but then it stopped and seemed to pause for a moment.

It doesn't know, Keo thought. *Or it's not sure.*

Instead of answering her, the creature hissed, "The marina. Get to it."

"Easier said than done," Keo said, walking back. "How many are out there?"

"Hundreds."

"You attacked them," Jordan said. "The soldiers on the first floor. That was you."

It nodded.

"Why?" she asked.

Its eyes shifted to Keo. "I need him alive."

Keo didn't know if that was supposed to make him feel better or worse. He just hoped the creature and Jordan didn't notice when he trembled involuntarily for about half a second before he could force himself to stop.

He looked back at the door instead. "Why haven't they attacked yet?"

"They're confused," it said.

"Confused? By what?"

"Me."

Well, at least I have that in common with them, Keo thought, and said, "So what now? What are they doing out there?"

"They're waiting."

"For what?"

"Orders."

"Whose orders? Yours?"

It shook its head. "Someone else's."

*Some*thing *else's, you mean,* Keo wanted to say, but bit his tongue.

"You're not like them," Jordan said. She hadn't looked away from the blue-eyed ghoul...or lessened her grip on the shotgun.

"No," it said, resting its blue eyes on her. Keo swore the damn things seemed to be glowing—*pulsating.* "I'm...more."

"Can we wait them out?" Keo asked. "Until sunrise?"

"No," it said. "The orders will come, and when they do, they'll attack. You won't survive to see morning. The marina is your only chance."

"We'd never make it. It's a long island and you said it your-self, there's too many—"

It turned and began walking back to the window.

"Where are you going?" Jordan asked, and Keo thought she actually sounded terrified to see it leaving.

"Stay here," it said, and before he or Jordan could respond, the creature leaped through the broken window and disappeared into the dark void beyond.

Keo ran over and looked out just in time to see it bounding across the backyard, then catapult over the iron fence as if it were a foot high instead of ten-feet-tall. The flaps of its trench coat fluttered in its wake before vanishing into the night.

Now I've seen everything, Keo thought, except even when the words popped into his head, he didn't think it was true. He had a very strong feeling that tonight was just the beginning, that things were about to get...stranger.

Jordan appeared next to him. "Keo..."

"Yeah?"

"That just happened, didn't it?"

"I think so, yeah."

"I just wanted to make sure." She paused, then, "It knew your name."

"I noticed that."

"Keo, it *knew your name.*"

He sighed. "Yeah, I know."

"And it could talk."

"I heard."

"I didn't know they could talk. Did you?"

"I...yes."

"You knew?"

"I heard stories."

"What kind—"

Thoom-thoom-thoom!

They spun around simultaneously as the dresser shook against the door.

"I guess they finally got those orders they were waiting for," Jordan said breathlessly.

Thoom-thoom-thoom!

"The bed!" Keo shouted.

He started moving toward the king-size bed when a long, thin shadow fell across the floorboards in front of him. At first he thought it was just him or Jordan, but that didn't make sense because he knew exactly where his shadow was, and Jordan was to his right, but this one was coming from his left and over his shoulder—

Keo turned around just as the ghoul flung itself from the top frame of the window and landed on the windowsill, impaling its bare feet on shards of jutting glass. For a split second, Keo thought it was the blue-eyed ghoul returning to finish him and Jordan off, having decided they weren't worth the effort to save.

But no, because the eyes glaring at him were solid black and not ethereal blue.

The creature lunged into the room and Keo lifted the Mossberg and fired, punching a hole through the creature's chest, flesh and muscle splattering the wall behind it, while the blast itself had enough force to throw the ghoul backward and to the floor.

"Keo!" Jordan shouted.

"The bed!" he shouted back, and racked the shotgun.

The ghoul was picking itself up from the floor when Keo shot it again, this time taking its entire right arm off at the shoulder joint. When that didn't stop it, he racked and fired a third time, chopping one of its legs out from under it.

The creature toppled to one side, landing in a *splash* of its own thick pool of blood. Instead of trying to get back up on its remaining leg, the ghoul started crawling toward him, using its one arm to grab, fingernails digging into the floorboards, and pull itself forward. Then it repeated the process.

Keo stared at the absurd sight for a moment before taking a

quick step toward the creature. It raised its head to look up inquisitively at him just before Keo fired, shattering its skull and splattering flesh and blood across the floor.

It didn't have a head anymore, but the damn thing was *still* dragging itself toward him...

Keo's stomach lurched and he took a step back before starting to reload the shotgun. He didn't have to go very far, because even though it wouldn't die, the ghoul had been reduced to a tortoise's speed, sliding across the floor in almost slow motion.

"Keo!" Jordan shouted. "I could really use a hand here!"

She had cleared the pillows and blankets off the bed and was trying in vain to drag it by one bedpost toward the door. Looking at her straining, Keo wondered amusingly if Jordan would get to the door before the ghoul got to him—

"Keo!"

He slung the shotgun and hurried across the room, giving the back window one last look just in case another one of the creatures had managed to climb up the wall outside. When he didn't see any further threats, he grabbed his end of the bed and pushed.

His left shoulder screamed and his right thigh throbbed against their bandages. Ripples of pain sliced up and down his body and he was probably bleeding again, and he was thankful he didn't have time to stop and make sure—

Clack.

Keo spun back toward the window just in time to see the blue-eyed ghoul pick up the now-headless black-eyed one from the floor by its remaining leg and casually toss it through the window.

THOOM!

Splintered wood flew across the room and almost impaled itself in Keo's face. He ducked just in time and watched as a pair of dark eyes peered into the master bedroom through the slit in the door.

THOOM!

Another piece slid across the floor, the slit on the door widening both horizontally and vertically. As if they knew exactly where the weak spot was, the creatures began slamming into the opening until it was big enough that one of the ghouls could begin to squeeze itself through, slashing its flesh against the edges.

Black blood arced through the moonlit room.

"The marina," the blue-eyed creature hissed. *"Now."*

The creature had gone to get an extension ladder, the same one Keo had used earlier to retrieve Gene's water bottles. It was leaning outside the back window of the master bedroom and Keo climbed down first, doing his very best not to think about what awaited him below, but only knowing he had to get away from the room above him and the creatures amassed outside its door at this very moment.

THOOM-THOOM-THOOM!

He could *feel* the relentless pounding in his bones as he climbed.

The night air swirled around him, threatening to grab and toss him off the ladder. He spent almost as much time looking down, waiting for the inevitable black-eyed ghouls to appear out of nowhere, as he did looking up at Jordan as she maneuvered herself to follow him down.

He hopped the last few meters and landed in a crouch, quickly unslinging the Mossberg. Out here, in the middle of the night, the spreading power of the shotgun was preferable to the M4. Not that he expected them to do the job completely, but placed at the right spots, maybe he could slow them down just enough to outrun them.

THOOM-THOOM-THOOM!

The door had to have been weakened drastically by now, and when it could no longer be called a door, there would be nothing to stand in their way except Ol' Blue Eyes, as Keo had come to call his savior. It was better than just referring to it as, well, *it* all the time. Given what the creature had done for him at T18 and now, on Santa Marie Island, Keo felt almost obligated to give it a name, and with it, some measure of respect.

Just don't fall in love with it, pal. It is a monster, after all.

His heart was racing even as he swept the backyard with the shotgun and continued to wait for the first ghoul to pop out of the bushes like in the movies. It was pitch-dark back here, and what he wouldn't give for one of those night-vision goggles Steve's people had been wearing. Of course, those were inside the house behind him at the moment, likely drowned in a sea of undead.

Even now, with his back to the two-story building, Keo could smell them, so many that he imagined the walls of the house bulging with their numbers. He was very aware that all it would take was for one ghoul to stray from the task at hand, from their deadly single-minded determination once they set their sights on a goal, and check the backyard and it was over. Jesus Christ, he was a sitting duck out here.

Jordan jumped the last few feet and landed with an *oomph!* next to him. She quickly sprang back up and gathered herself and unslung her Remington, even as—

THOOM!

The crash was so loud that Keo felt the door finally, mercifully crumbling all the way down here.

"Go!" he whispered sharply to Jordan, and the two of them began running across the moonlit backyard and through knee-high grass, toward the fence on the other side.

The very loud explosion of chaos, of flesh smashing into walls and floor and ceiling, thundered from the second floor master bedroom behind them, the *bang-bang-bang!* like machine-gun fire.

Keo didn't look back and kept running. Ol' Blue Eyes had been strict about that.

"Run to the docks," it had said, in that unnatural hiss that gave Keo goose bumps every time. *"Take my boat. It has every-thing you'll need. Don't stop. Don't look back. Just run."*

A shrieking sound, unlike anything Keo had ever heard before, made him break his promise and he glanced back while still moving at full stride.

He glimpsed a flurry of clothing—a trench coat—flashing across the window just before a ghoul trying to climb out was grabbed from behind and jerked back inside.

Bang-bang-bang!

Jesus, it's doing it. It's actually stopping them.

But it wouldn't last. It couldn't. Sooner or later, the flood would drown even Ol' Blue Eyes. It didn't matter how fast you were; you couldn't outswim the ocean. Like most of the lessons he had learned in his life, Keo had accepted that one the hard way, too. It didn't matter how strong or fast (or unnatural) you were.

Jordan had outdistanced him and reached the gate first. Of course she did. She wasn't limping on one bad leg. He watched her sling her shotgun, then jump and grab the top of the spikes and scamper up and over. He smiled to himself, remembering how she had told him she had gone to Tulane University on a softball scholarship. He didn't even know schools had competi-tive softball.

Keo mimicked her movements and pulled himself up and over the fence. He didn't land on the other side quite as grace-fully as her, spilling on the tall grass with one of the M4's parts jamming into his side. He grimaced, hoped it didn't puncture skin, and scrambled back up.

"I didn't know you were so clumsy, Keo," Jordan said next to him.

He grinned. "Shut up and run."

Jordan jogged across the weeds until they finally felt hard pavement under their feet. He couldn't see the marina from here, but there was no doubt about the direction: South.

"Take my boat," Ol' Blue Eyes had said. *"It has everything you'll need."*

Everything? What's everything? Keo wanted to ask, but by then the door was already bursting at the seams.

He glanced back toward the house one last time.

The tall, white two-story structure stood out even in the darkness, its size dwarfing the other houses around it. The building was so big he had no trouble believing that a hundred, maybe more, of the ghouls had managed to squeeze themselves inside its wide two floors. They would be assaulting the master bedroom right now, waiting their turn to enter, only to find Ol' Blue Eyes standing in their way.

How long before they overcame him? (*Him? Did I just refer to the ghoul as a* him?) Or how long before they realized he and Jordan were no longer inside—

"Oh, shit!" Jordan shouted in front of him.

Keo turned around and lifted the Mossberg just as two skeletal forms bounded across one of the unkempt lawns to the left of them.

"Run to the docks," Ol' Blue Eyes had said to them. *"Take my boat. It has everything you'll need. Don't stop. Don't look back. Just run."*

Like I said, pal, easier said than done, Keo thought, and pulled the trigger.

TWENTY-NINE

"Run! Don't look back! Just run!"

She was glancing back at him while still in mid-stride, her face covered in sheets of sweat despite the chilly night air, the gust of wind coming from the ocean and over the ridgeline and between the houses before finally pouring into the street around the both of them.

"I said, don't look back!" he shouted, just before he spun around and fired, the flame from the shotgun stabbing forward and lighting up two ghouls as they were shredded by buckshot.

He racked the Mossberg and fired again even before they had a chance to pick themselves up from the pavement. His second shot obliterated the legs out of one of the creatures, and his third blew the right arm off the other one.

Behind him, Jordan's own shotgun roared once, twice, three times.

It wasn't going to be enough. He knew that without having to think too hard about it. It wasn't even close to being enough. Sooner or later, they were going to run out of steam, or run out of bullets, or just plain run out of space.

Should have hid. Should have found a basement and sealed it tight.

Shoulda, woulda, coulda, but didn'ta, pal.

They hadn't gone more than twenty meters down the sloping hill when the first creatures appeared. His first shot was like thunderclaps across the island, and he might as well have lit a torch and carried it down the street with him because after that they came out of everywhere.

Then they were running and shooting, and they were still too far from the marina. Much, much too far.

Both his legs were already burning, not just the one with the bullet hole. And he had only been running for about three minutes. What would happen at the five-minute mark? The ten?

Curiously enough, he barely felt any pain in his left shoulder. Either the entire arm had numbed over, or he was doing a very good job of ignoring it. Of course it didn't help that he hadn't eaten anything in...how long had it been? Too long, which explained why he was already sapped of energy. Normally, he could run for much longer than this.

Excuses, excuses.

The only positive that he could come up with was that so many of the ghouls had gone into the two-story house that the ones left behind were sporadic in number. Instead of hordes coming out of the homes around them, there were pockets of one and two, but mostly one at a time. That, more than anything, allowed them to make steady progress down the street toward the marina, shooting the entire way.

Jordan was in front of him, firing and racking and reloading as she ran. He was doing the same thing while keeping the creatures from overtaking them. As they got closer and closer to the marina (he could smell the ocean, and God, was the scent intoxicating, calling to him), there seemed to be less and less of them, allowing him more time to reload.

They had to keep moving. Always moving. They couldn't stop. Not for a second. Not even to breathe.

Shooting them didn't kill them. No surprise there. But it did slow them down. The buckshot was effective, the concussive force like a sledgehammer. It was even better when he aimed for the legs. It was hard to run without legs, though that didn't seem to stop them from crawling after him anyway.

It was difficult to see exactly how far the marina was with just the moonlight to guide him. Fortunately, the street and sidewalks stood out from the lawns, giving him a visible clue of where to go. All he had to do was keep south—

Oh, shit.

He made the mistake of throwing a quick glance over his shoulder, because that's when he saw them—*all* of them. It looked like every single ghoul on the island, which meant they were now coming from the two-story house. Which in turn meant Ol' Blue Eyes was either dead (if it could even still die—*again?*) or out of commission.

The sight of them pouring down the street, racing around homes and catapulting over fences, took his breath away. He might have kept on staring like an idiot if a shotgun blast didn't roar behind him and pull him back.

He spun around just as Jordan was leaping over a ghoul whose legs she had cut out from underneath it. Keo mirrored her movements even as the creature groped for him, fingers clawing at empty air.

"Faster!" Keo shouted. "Faster, Jordan!"

She looked back, then past him, and saw for herself. Her right eye had improved, but it was still too bruised to fully open.

"Don't look!" he shouted. "Run! Just keep running, whatever you do!"

She might have nodded, or just turned around. He couldn't be certain.

Keo was too busy reaching into his pocket for another shell anyway when his fingers found nothing but empty spaces.

Empty!

He threw the shotgun to the street and unslung the M4.

The ghouls had stopped coming out of the houses around them. Instead, the entire nightcrawler population of Santa Marie Island was behind him at the moment, an unrelenting tide of black flesh and *clacking* bones, the *tap-tap-tap* of bare feet against the cold, hard road filling like mini explosions around him. If that wasn't bad enough, their foul stench traveled downwind, the result of so many of them packed into so limited an area, and threatened to make him heave his stomach's empty contents. Thank God he hadn't eaten a single damn thing all day.

He hadn't looked forward again for more than half a second before he spotted it: the entrance into the marina. It was coming up in *forty meters—*

Thirty-five—

"Faster!" he shouted. "Faster, Jordan!"

She didn't look back this time. Instead, she actually started moving even faster, and it suddenly occurred to him that she had been running at a slower pace for his benefit. Because for all her wounds and bruises, Jordan was still more athletic than him before the world ended, and even more so now that he had two bullet holes in him.

Thirty meters—

She made a sharp right turn and disappeared behind a dirt and rock wall. From there, she would have to run down the incline parking lot, which would help her pick up even more speed on her way to the docks on the other end. Then Ol' Blue Eyes' boat would be waiting for them, next to the twenty-footer that was out of gas.

"Take my boat," it had said. *"It has everything you'll need."*

Everything they would need? Besides gas, what else did they "need"? Silver bullets? Was it talking about silver bullets?

Two days ago that would have been ludicrous, but after everything he had seen, that word itself was absurd. Anything was possible, including a blue-eyed ghoul that had gone to great lengths to save his life not once, but twice now.

"I need him alive," it had said.

Him. Keo. It needed *him* alive.

Ludicrous? There was no such thing anymore.

He spun around until he was backpedaling at full speed, or at least as fast as he could manage while moving backward. He should have been surprised by what he saw, but he wasn't—*they were almost on top of him.*

He squeezed the trigger and swept the M4 from left to right and watched pruned flesh writhing as bullets punched through them, the only sound the occasional *ping!* of his rounds ricocheting off bones. The ones up front stumbled from the impact and fell and were immediately swallowed up by the stampeding herd.

Two shotgun blasts roared behind him, one right after another. Jordan, inside the marina. Apparently the docks weren't as empty as they had been hoping—

Click!

He tossed the M4 and spun around and picked up more speed. Or tried to. At this point he wasn't entirely certain if he had any more speed to draw on. If his tank wasn't already empty, it was pretty damn close. He could practically envision the needle scraping against the *E* and an alarm going off to remind him of that fact.

Faster. Faster!

He drew the Glock with one hand and unclasped the gun belt with the other. He still had spare magazines in the ammo pouches, and when it slipped off his waist and clattered to the ground, he was instantly lighter and faster. He might not actually be moving any swifter than seconds ago, but it sure as hell felt like he was.

The entrance!

He was making the turn into the marina when he was greeted by the ferocious roar of boat motors powering up from the other side of the wide parking lot. A spotlight had snapped on, and a thick beam of light was cutting across the slanted concrete floor.

He completed the turn and glimpsed a figure (*Jordan!*) on Ol Blue Eyes' boat, though at this distance Keo couldn't tell what kind of vessel it was. Not that it mattered. Right now, it was the one with gas (*"It has everything you'll need."*), and Jordan was revving the motor, maybe trying to direct him over to her, not that he needed the extra attention or the encouragement.

Keo ran right for her—or really, for the light—while dodging a ghoul as it attempted to grab at him. Its legs looked like broken wooden baseball bats, and he expected to see a second one (hadn't Jordan fired twice?), but there were no signs of it, if it ever existed.

The smell hit him, and Keo couldn't help himself and he looked back—

A wave of black flesh and rotting teeth was collapsing on top of him.

Jesus Christ! When had they gotten so close?

He stuck out the Glock behind him and squeezed off a couple of shots. Even the handgun began feeling too heavy, and after six shots, Keo threw it away and picked up even more speed as a result.

Or, at least, that's what he told himself.

Faster!

He was halfway through the parking lot now, his breath crashing out of his lungs, every part of him burning from inside out.

Faster! Faster!

The *clacking* of bones, the *tap-tap-tap* of bare feet, and that foul pervading stench pressing up against the back of his neck like a living physical thing, unlike anything he had ever experienced before and never wanted to again—

Faster! Faster! Faster!

Jordan, standing tall in the middle of the boat, behind the steering wheel, was backing the vessel away from the slip. Smart girl. He would have told her to do exactly that if he thought he could shout loud enough to be heard over the roar of the motors.

And there, the edge of the marina, coming up fast. Almost there.

The water glistened under the moonlight, waves *sloshing* back and forth against the docks. Calm, welcoming, calling to him. He imagined he could hear it moving despite the roar in front of him, the noises of the creatures stampeding behind him, getting closer and closer, louder and louder...

Almost there.

The stench of the creatures continued to fill his nostrils, the manic *tap-tap-tap* of their bare feet invading his space even further.

He wasn't going to be able to run fast enough. He knew that now. He would never reach the water before they got to him. Unlike at Song Island, when he could just leap for it, here he was still too far away from the water.

So close, and yet so, so far.

"Half-dolphin, this guy," Danny had once said about him.

Too bad dolphins can't fly.

Then he saw it out of the corner of his right eye, the thing he had been waiting for. It was just a single, long bony finger, but it was a harbinger of what he knew was coming. The black-fleshed digit brushed against his shirt, sending an electric sensation through his entire body. It started to curve, to grab onto him, when—

Something sailed over his head.

Keo didn't hear it coming (the boat's motor was too powerful, the relentless pounding in his chest, the patter of death behind him), but he actually felt it rippling through the air.

He tried to turn his head, to follow its trajectory, but he might as well be moving on quicksand compared to its speed. A heartbeat later there was a loud *BOOM!* and the ground shook. The wall of ghouls behind him let out one long singular shriek, the sound of things dying (*again*). Keo had seen shrapnel rip into flesh before, but he'd never seen what they could do to an entire wall of them.

The concussive force slammed into him from behind like a sledgehammer and Keo was picked up and launched through the air as if he were little more than a rag doll. He was trying to orient himself, make sense of what had just happened, when a second *BOOM!* shattered the night. His eardrums rang and the metallic taste of blood filled his mouth. His bones shook from the vibrations, but his ears were still ringing from the first impact, so this second one was more of a dull *THOOM* instead of the familiar blast of a grenade impacting.

The screams behind him, like the wails of dying animals, somehow managed to pierce through the internal thrumming slashing up and down his body. Then he shut everything down and missed the wooden bulkhead that separated the marina from the ocean by barely a foot and hit the water headfirst and went under like a stone.

Maybe it was all those days and nights and months on the San Diego beaches, but he had enough awareness and ability to fight through the pain and spin around even while he was crashing through the water until he was looking up again. The moonlit night sky stared back at him on the other side of the surface, just before the air began filling with a red and orange glow. It was beautiful and inspiring, and he found himself gazing up at the spreading color and smiling, or thought he was, anyway.

He wanted to look at it forever, but for some reason he was still free-falling, going deeper and deeper into the Gulf of Mexico.

Keo was a strong swimmer. He'd always been, and those skills had come in handy the last few months. But for some reason, he couldn't call on them at the moment. His legs didn't move, and neither did his arms. There was a continuous throbbing pain from behind him, as if someone (or a hundred someones) were repeatedly stabbing him in the back, over and over and over again.

He didn't want to go anywhere, anyway. He found himself incredibly content to stare at the blooming spectrum of colors beyond the surface and wondered if this was what it was like to witness the birth of the universe.

Daebak, he thought, and smiled up at the sight of the night sky burning. It was glorious.

THIRTY

"I thought you were dead," Jordan said. "Again. Though I guess I can't be that mad at you this time; it was kind of my fault."

He smiled up at her. Or thought he did. He might have just spat out some of the water he had taken in while he was drowning.

So how did he get up here?

"I didn't know it would do that," she said. "I thought it was a riot gun or something. You know, the kind that shoots smoke? Shit, I almost killed you."

"What was it?" he asked. Or tried to. It sounded suspiciously like a loud croak.

"It's uh...this."

She held up an M32 grenade launcher. The last time someone had fired one of those at him—it might have even been the same one, for all he knew—they were using tear gas. This time it was 40mm grenade rounds. He had seen what one of those could do to an area and had launched a couple himself back at Beaufont Lake not all that long ago. But he had been firing a single-shot weapon back then, whereas the one she was showing him could launch six in a few seconds.

"M32," he said.

"What?"

"It's an M32 grenade launcher."

"Oh. I didn't know that. Sorry."

"'s okay. What happened?"

"I, uh, hit one of the trucks in the parking lot with the first round by accident. I don't know what happened after that, it was dark and it looked like the entire marina was exploding. Then I saw you flying through the air. It was kind of cool, actually. That is, until I realized I might have killed you in the process of trying to save you." She frowned. "They were almost on top of you and I didn't want to lose you, too. If I didn't do something, you'd never have made it into the water."

"You saved my life."

"I almost blew you up. That blast should have killed you."

"Shrapnel?"

He remembered the ghouls shrieking behind him, the sounds of flesh rendering, metal bouncing off bones...

"I didn't find any on you," Jordan said. "But your entire back is black and purple, kinda like my face the last few days. I guess we have that in common now. When you didn't swim back up to the surface, I thought your back might have also been broken."

"Is it?"

"Can you feel your legs?"

He tried. "Yes."

"Then it's not. Thank God." She gave him a pursed smile. "You've got to be the luckiest man I know, Keo."

"Yeah, that's me, lucky."

He found it incredibly difficult to focus on her face with all the darkness around her. He would have been immediately alarmed, except he could feel the gentle ocean's surface under him. Under the boat. They were out at sea, safe from land. Or, at least, safe from the black-eyed ones.

It came to Santa Marie Island on a boat. Ol' Blue Eyes. It actually came on a boat...and left a lot behind, apparently.

"Take my boat," it had said. *"It has everything you'll need."*

"Everything" included an M32 grenade launcher, apparently. Keo had to admit, whether the creature was still alive back on the island or not, it had come through for them. Three times now.

The question was: *Why?*

Under the soothing morning brightness, Keo sat on a bench at the stern of Ol' Blue Eyes' boat and tried to remember how to breathe again. The vessel was at least a twenty-eight-footer, with a canvas T-top to keep out the harsh sun, though at the moment he didn't want to be separated from the warmth.

The M32 grenade launcher rested on top of a small armory at his feet. Three M4 rifles, gun belts, handguns, and a pair of knives. He idly wondered if one of those knives was made of silver, like Danny's cross-knife. Was his luck really that good?

Of course not, so he didn't even bother to check.

Jordan was leaning against the center console, looking back at the marina about sixty, maybe seventy meters across the ocean. The impact of six 40mm grenade rounds had left craters in the parking lot and caused half of the docks to catch fire. Their boat was gone, sunk to the bottom in the aftermath, where he would have also gone if Jordan hadn't jumped in after him.

The weapons weren't the only things Ol' Blue Eyes had left behind for them. Jordan had found two tactical packs with bags of MREs and nonperishable canned goods, along with two bottles of water. She had eaten her fill even before he woke up.

She changed his bandages (he was much too weak to protest) then opened a can of beans for him, and Keo attacked it with gusto, momentarily forgetting that every part of him was throbbing. Just breathing hurt, and swallowing wasn't any better, but an entire day without food and a night where he almost died had left him too starved to care.

"It must have killed them," Jordan was saying, "so it could take their boat."

"The soldiers?"

"Uh huh. Where else would the guns and packs come from?"

He nodded, remembering how Ol' Blue Eyes had waded into Steve's soldiers back at T18. It had demolished almost a dozen men on horseback as if they were children, effortlessly. So what were a few soldiers that had something it needed, like a boat to cross Galveston Bay with?

"What do you think happened to him?" she asked.

Keo didn't answer right away. Instead, he spooned beans into his mouth and looked toward the island.

It was still back there, somewhere. Was it even still alive? They couldn't see anyone (*anything*) along the ridgelines, but of course it wouldn't be there anyway, even if it had survived last night. Blue eyes or not—smarter than the average ghoul or not—it still had to avoid the sunlight like the rest.

"I don't know," he said.

"Well, we have a quarter tank of gas left." She tapped the console with her spork. "Where should we go?"

"Back there."

"Where?"

He nodded at the island.

Jordan stared at him with her good eye. "No way. We barely survived last time, remember?"

"It's still there."

"Keo..."

"It knew my name."

"I know, but..." She shook her head. "We should just go. Let's just go."

"I can't," he said. "I need to know, Jordan."

Jordan sighed and sat down and stared in the opposite direction of the island. She didn't say anything for a long time. Then, finally, "What if you don't like the answers?"

"I have to find out either way."

Half of the docks had sunk into the ocean from the fire, and the still-standing parts that they sidled alongside of and climbed up were slightly charred and blackened. They were armed again, even if they couldn't find any more 40mm rounds for the M32. Too bad, because Keo would have loved to carry that thing back onto the island. Instead, he had to make do with a fresh M4 and a gun belt with a Beretta 9mm in the holster.

Jordan followed him up the pockmarked parking lot with another rifle. Like him last night, she had ditched all of her weapons and ammo in order to lighten her load in her dash to the boat. It still amazed him how fast she had been.

Competitive softball. Damn.

Keo walked across the parking lot wearing his damp clothes, thankful he could still move his legs at all after getting broadsided by the exploding truck last night. That was the kind of "accident" that could have just as easily snapped his spine and paralyzed him—or sliced him in half with shrapnel—instead of just leaving his entire back and the upper parts of his thighs bruised and battered.

Maybe my luck's finally turning around after all...

Captain Optimism, as Danny would say.

The place was a surreal sight, with multiple craters scattered from one end to the other. Jordan told him that once she saw him flying through the air, she had kept firing until the M32 was empty, after which she jumped into the water after him.

Most of the vehicles that had been calling the marina home for the last year were now charred, scattered husks, which seemed appropriate given the piles of skeletal remains. The explosions hadn't killed them, though they had severed arms and legs and detached heads from shoulders. The number of limbs spread around the area—represented this morning by the familiar sight of bleached white bones—were too many to count. And these, he reminded himself, were just the ones that hadn't managed to crawl away before sunrise.

The lingering acidic smell of dead ghouls filled Keo's nostrils as he walked through the cemetery of bones.

He was glad he was walking in front of Jordan so she couldn't see him grimacing with every step. Despite taking two more of Jay's painkillers (he had already taken two last night), he wasn't sure how long he was going to last on his feet. His back was intact (*Thank you, God*), but it was constantly letting him know it was far from okay. He wanted badly to sit down and rest but forced himself to keep moving anyway.

He must not have hid the pain well enough, because Jordan asked, "Are you okay?" from behind him.

"Fine."

"Then why are you walking so slow?"

"I'm just taking my time. It's a nice, sunny day. Perfect for a stroll."

"Right," she said, but thankfully didn't press the issue.

There were more bleached bones and partial skeletal remains in the streets beyond the marina. These were spread out, as some of the creatures attempted to crawl toward the houses for salvation, and some had made it onto the lawns before the sun caught them. There was more of the sharp, acidic smell in the air, and

Keo picked up his pace—or as much as he could, anyway—to get through it faster.

The two-story white house was exactly where they had left it last night, but being able to see it from afar and getting to it were two different things. During the long walk up the slanted road, he finally surrendered to the pain and stopped to gather his breath.

Jordan, meanwhile, stood guard. "No rush. We got all day."

Unlike him, the morning had been a good one for Jordan, and the swelling around her right eye had gone down noticeably so that when she looked at him, it was now with both eyes.

"How's the back?" she asked.

"Throbbing."

"How's everything else?"

"Throbbing."

"Lots of throbbing."

"Yup."

"Here," she said, handing him one of the water bottles from her pack.

"Save it for later," he said, and stood up with a flinch and walked on before she could argue.

***

There were no signs of Steve or his men on the first floor of the house on the hill. They had left their weapons behind (including an M4 with an attached grenade launcher, probably the same one that had killed Dave), but the bodies were gone. Dead men still bled, especially the freshly dead ones. Keo imagined a feeding frenzy as the ghouls, having been locked on the island for a year, got their first taste of fresh (or, well, mostly fresh) blood.

Sucks to be you, Steve.

They kicked stray bullet casings on their way through the house. Holes dotted the walls, and any furniture that wasn't nailed down was scattered in pieces. Large patches of blood covered the floor and walls in spots where the sun couldn't reach.

The staircase was battered and broken, with the kind of damage that could only be caused by repeatedly ramming someone's skull into the frame. Or a lot of someones' skulls.

Mister Blue Eyes. Did you do this?

They found more evidence of last night's fight on what was left of the second-floor living room. Sunlight highlighted white bones along the floor, including evidence of incomplete ghouls that had been unable to crawl away as the morning stalked them. All Keo had to do was follow the trail of bones to the master bedroom, which he did while holding his shirt over his nose to keep out the stinging smell that had become nauseating after breathing it for the last hour or so.

They went in cautiously, guns at the ready in case there was a ghoul or two (or a dozen) still hiding in the shadows. He could see the broken back window from the open door, but there were no guarantees the place was empty even if the stench attacking his nostrils was more of the acidic odor of vaporized flesh than the rotting garbage of living (*hah*) ghouls.

The master bedroom looked as if a tornado had hit it. The bed, dresser, and door had been reduced to unrecognizable splinters. Sunlight poured in through the lone window—the opening had widened, the wall surrounding it gashed, as if someone had hit it with a wrecking ball—and illuminated the evidence of a massive fight that had taken place here last night. The walls were heavily cratered, and the parts of it and the floor that avoided coming into contact with the sun were awash in thick coats of black blood.

"Must have been some fight," Jordan said next to him.

"Yeah."

"Wonder if your friend survived."

Keo smiled. His "friend."

He looked around the room, hoping to find signs of Ol' Blue Eyes. Would the black-eyed ones take him (*It, it's an* it) with them if it were dead? The way they had absconded with Steve and his men?

He had no idea. All of this was new territory for him.

"There," he said, pointing the barrel of his rifle at the bathroom doors.

They were closed but were also the only doors in the entire room—maybe even the entire house—that were still intact. Or, well, mostly, despite the generous layer of black blood spread across them.

"Be careful," Jordan said when he started moving toward the doors.

He wiped a thick layer of dark liquid off one of the doorknobs with a shirt from the floor, then used the same fabric to turn it. Jordan moved over and they counted down to *five* before he pulled open one of the doors and they both took a step back.

A large trail of plasma, jagged and thick, led from the doors to the remains of a badly destroyed trench coat lying in a crumpled heap near the bathtub. The guns, ammo, and supplies Keo expected to find in the tub were tossed to the floor, some resting in enough blood for two people, maybe even three.

Having made room for itself, it now sat inside the tub, facing him. There were no windows inside the bathroom, so the creature hadn't needed to risk the sun in here.

Ol' Blue Eyes.

It looked asleep, and when he opened the doors, it slowly, almost lazily, lifted its head. The blue eyes that looked across the mostly darkened room at him weren't quite as pulsating (*alive*) as they had been last night.

"You came back," it said. Even its hiss seemed weaker. Much, much weaker.

He could tell it was badly hurt, even if Keo couldn't see its wounds from the open door. He wanted to get closer but was unwilling to abandon the comforting warmth of the sunlight at his back. After all, he had seen just how fast the thing could move. Even if it was injured, Keo didn't want to take the chance.

"I had to know," he said.

It looked at him but didn't say a word.

Next to him, Jordan's breathing had accelerated noticeably.

"Last night," Keo continued, "you said you were looking for me."

"Yes," it said, with that same soft, labored hiss that wasn't quite human, but wasn't quite inhuman, either. "I've been searching for you."

"How did you find me?"

"I saw you through one of them. At the cabin, when it attacked you. I saw your face and heard your name."

"The cabin," Jordan said. "Outside of T18?"

It nodded.

"So you...saw me through their eyes?" Keo asked.

"I can see what they see, hear what they hear, even feel what they feel," it said. "We're linked, because we share the same blood. All of us. Like veins in a river. Tens of thousands. Millions. You have no idea the full extent of their number. What you've seen so far is only a raindrop in the ocean."

Keo exchanged a glance with Jordan. If she understood any of this, he didn't see it on her face. He wondered if he looked as perplexed, or even more so.

He turned back to the creature. "What do you want from me?"

"To find someone," it said.

"Who?"

"Lara."

The name caught him by surprise, and it took Keo a few

seconds to respond. Finally, he said, "What do you want with her?"

"To help her."

"Help her do what?"

"To save everyone," the blue-eyed ghoul said. "There is a way to end this nightmare. Lara needs to know. She needs to know…"

Printed in Great Britain
by Amazon

61286315R00234